FIVE YEARS FROM NOW

ALSO BY PAIGE TOON

Only Love Can Hurt Like This
Someone I Used to Know
The Minute I Saw You
If You Could Go Anywhere
The Last Piece of My Heart
The One We Fell in Love With
The Sun in Her Eyes
Thirteen Weddings
The Longest Holiday
One Perfect Summer
Baby Be Mine
Pictures of Lily
Chasing Daisy
Johnny Be Good
Lucy in the Sky

SHORT STORIES

One Perfect Christmas and Other Stories
A Christmas Wedding (eBook short story)
Johnny's Girl (eBook short story)
One Perfect Christmas (eBook short story)

YOUNG ADULT

All About the Hype
I Knew You Were Trouble
The Accidental Life of Jessie Jefferson

FIVE YEARS FROM NOW

Paige Toon

G. P. PUTNAM'S SONS

New York

PUTNAM
— EST. 1838 —

G. P. PUTNAM'S SONS
Publishers Since 1838
An imprint of Penguin Random House LLC

Originally published in slightly different form in the United
Kingdom in 2018 by Simon and Schuster UK and self-published
in the United States in a digital edition by the author in 2019.
Copyright © 2018, 2023 by Paige Toon
Seven Summers excerpt copyright © 2023 by Paige Toon
Penguin Random House supports copyright. Copyright fuels creativity,
encourages diverse voices, promotes free speech, and creates a vibrant culture.
Thank you for buying an authorized edition of this book and for complying
with copyright laws by not reproducing, scanning, or distributing any part of
it in any form without permission. You are supporting writers and allowing
Penguin Random House to continue to publish books for every reader.

Printed in the United States of America

Book design by Ashley Tucker

This is a work of fiction. Names, characters, places, and incidents
either are the product of the author's imagination or are used
fictitiously, and any resemblance to actual persons, living or dead,
businesses, companies, events, or locales is entirely coincidental.

ISBN 978-1-63910-950-0

In memory of Pascale Honore

FORTY

"OH, BABY," I MURMUR, BRUSHING LUKE'S HAIR away from his forehead as he fights back tears.

He's still my "baby," even if he is almost fifteen years old.

"I can't believe I'm going to be holed up for the rest of the summer," he says in a choked voice. "*And* I'm going to miss Angie's party," he realizes.

I suspect this fact hurts him even more than his broken ankle.

"She'll probably get off with Jake and that'll be that, then," he adds bitterly.

I lean in and squeeze his shoulder. "Angela Rakesmith looks at you like the light shines out of your backside," I say pointedly. "You have nothing to worry about there."

Despite himself, my son grins, but it's quickly followed by a grimace.

"Do you need more painkillers?" I ask with concern, my hand halfway toward the button to call the nurse.

He shakes his head. "They make me feel sick."

"I'm sorry you'll miss the party." I am genuinely sympathetic. Luke has been looking forward to it so much. "That sucks. But think of all of the attention you'll get when you go back to school. The girls will be clambering over themselves to sign your cast. Angie will be jealous as hell."

His bottom lip wobbles and he swallows rapidly, but there's no holding back his tears of misery and frustration.

"I had so many plans for this summer! How did I do this *surfing*?" He slaps his hand on the bed.

"It could've been worse." I shudder at the thought.

He rolls his eyes, putting a halt to the direction my thoughts were taking. "It could *always* be worse. That doesn't make me feel better, Mum."

"I know it might not make a lot of sense right now, but one day . . ." A shiver goes down my spine as I hear myself saying the words, ". . . maybe five years from now, you'll look back and understand why this happened."

"No, I won't," he retorts grumpily. "I'll just think I was a stupid dick for inviting Jensen to come surfing with us."

I cast my eyes heavenward.

That's how it happened. Luke's friend Jensen got caught up in the rip current and Luke went after him. They hit the rocks on their way back in. Jensen face-planted on the reef and had to have three stitches on his eyebrow, but was otherwise unharmed. My son was less fortunate.

"You're right. You *shouldn't* have invited him," I say. "*None* of you should have been surfing at Porthleven in those conditions, *especially* Jensen, who is *way* too inexperienced."

Unlike Luke, who has been surfing almost every day since he was ten years old.

He bites his lip, knowing that he hasn't heard the last of this.

"But," I persist with making my point, despite his earlier dismissal, "maybe some good *will* come of this. Maybe, one day in the future, Jensen will think twice about surfing in similar conditions. Or *you* will. Or one of your friends will, and it might save their lives. Or perhaps there's something else you'll do this summer, someone you'll meet who you wouldn't have met otherwise, who'll have an impact on your life. This may strengthen Angie's feelings for you, or it may not—but at least you'll know and won't waste your time on her. All I'm saying is, although this feels like the worst thing ever right now, something positive might come out of it. My dad once gave me that 'five years from now' advice and I've never forgotten it."

Luke takes a deep breath, his face creasing with pain.

"Are you sure you don't need more medication?" I ask worriedly.

He shakes his head. "I'm fine. Just . . . take my mind off it. *Please*," he adds in a strained voice.

"You want me to tell you a story?" I flash him a hopeful smile.

"As long as it's not about Fudge and Smudge," he replies, chuckling and wincing in quick succession.

"How *dare* you?" I ask mockingly. "Fudge and Smudge are my greatest creations!"

Not strictly true and he knows it.

He grins at me. "You know I love them, really. So when did Grandad say that 'five years' stuff to you?"

"When I was your age, funnily enough. But I overheard someone say a similar thing a whole decade before that."

"And you *remember*?"

I nod. "Ruth was a hard person to forget."

"Who was she?"

"The love of your grandad's life," I explain. "And she *wasn't* Grandma," I add with a significant look.

"What happened to her?"

"Well, that's a whole other story . . ."

He gives me a rueful look. "I'm not going anywhere."

"All right, then," I say with a small smile. "I guess I'll start at the beginning."

Which, for me, was when I was five years old . . .

FIVE

THERE WAS A BOY ON NELL'S BED.

Nell's grip on Rabbit tightened as she stared down at him. He stared back sullenly.

"Nell, this is Vian," Daddy said in his trying-to-be-jolly-nothing-wrong-here voice.

"Vian, come off the bed," Ruth urged gently.

Nell had already met Ruth downstairs. Ruth had a nice smile and red curls that bounced when she walked. Nell instinctively liked Ruth. But if Ruth was the reason Nell had a boy on her bed, Nell might have to rethink her affections.

"Vian," Ruth urged again.

Nell dragged her eyes away from the boy with his dark, unfathomable eyes and looked up at her father. "Why is he on my bed?"

Daddy seemed momentarily uncomfortable, but quickly put his jolly voice back on. "We thought you'd like to sleep in the top bunk, now that you're a big girl."

Nell shook her head. "I want *my* bed."

Her father exchanged an awkward glance with Ruth.

Ruth knelt down. "Can you get up, please, Vian?"

"No," Vian muttered, edging back until his entire body was flush against the wall. His dark hair looked stark against the white paint.

Nell's eyes roved around the room, taking in the unfamiliar teddies on the duvet and the toy cars lined up on the narrow shelf behind the pillow. Something told her that Vian had been sleeping in her bed for some time.

And it *was* *her* bed. It had always been *her* bed and *her* bedroom. She even had glow-in-the-dark stars stuck to the wooden slats holding up the top mattress. Nell had a quick look to see if they were still there. They were.

"It's fine," Nell's father brushed Ruth off, touching his hand to her arm. "Why don't we all go and have a nice hot chocolate and a cookie?"

Hot chocolate and cookies *before* dinner? Nell loved the idea of this, but Vian continued to scowl. It was as though he thought *she* was the intruder.

"Daddy, I don't want to sleep in the top bunk," she whispered anxiously as she followed her father out of her bedroom, not understanding the reason for the upheaval. "What about my glow-in-the-dark stars?"

"We can get you some more to put on the wall," Daddy promised, turning around to scoop Nell up into his arms as he reached the bottom of the stairs.

"But I like looking *up* at them," she said, her eyes pricking with tears as her father carried her the rest of the way into the kitchen.

"Then we'll get you some stars for the ceiling," Daddy replied.

"But I *like my* bed."

"Nell, *please*." Her father's forehead creased with impatience as he set Nell back on her feet. "Be a good girl, OK?"

Nell was stung. She *was* a good girl. She loved coming to stay with her daddy in Cornwall. This was *their* time. Why did things have to change? Why did these people have to be here too?

Mummy had explained, of course. Daddy had a new girlfriend who had moved in *"faster than the speed of light"* . . .

"Very unlike your father. Completely uncharacteristic. I did wonder if he'd been brainwashed, but we've spoken and she seems nice enough. Probably do him good—stop him from being such a hermit. Plus you'll have company because her son's the same age as you, born literally two days before you. Your dad thinks it's fate, that you're going to be like Topsy and Tim twins or something."

Nell's head had spun with all this information, but she had lapped it up because Mummy was usually too busy to talk and now she was actually laughing.

The only person who had made Mummy laugh lately was Conan, Mummy's tennis coach.

Not that Mummy had played tennis with Conan in a while.

"Ruth? Are you coming?" Daddy called loudly.

"Be there in a minute," she called back.

Daddy smiled at Nell. "Vian is a bit shy, but he's really nice. You'll like him, I promise."

He had claimed as much on the phone.

"Now, which cookies shall we have?" Daddy asked. "Chocolate chip or custard creams?"

"Chocolate chip," Nell replied with a smile. Her father beamed at her as he tore the packet open and upended its entire contents onto a plate. "Here they are," he said merrily, as Ruth appeared hand-in-hand with Vian.

The boy was about Nell's height, possibly a couple of centimeters taller. Nell could see now in the light of the kitchen that his eyes were blue. Dark blue. He still looked very grumpy.

Nell cuddled Rabbit to her chest and stepped behind her father's legs.

"All sorted," Ruth said jovially. "Vian will sleep in the top bunk from now on."

"But—" Nell's dad started.

"Shh," Ruth cut him off. "It's fine. He'll be fine. Won't you, darling?"

Vian glared at his mother and pulled a chair out from the table, the sound of the wood screeching across the floor tiles making everyone except the perpetrator flinch. He slumped down on the chair in a sulk, his bottom lip jutting out and his arms folded across his chest as he stared straight ahead.

Vian did not look fine.

Nell tried not to care. She only had restored what was rightfully hers, after all. And she really did like her bed.

LATER THAT NIGHT, after what had been an uncomfortable dinnertime—Nell's father had talked *way* more than usual, while Vian hadn't said a word—Nell sat on the floor, fidgeting, in the dark outside the bathroom. Ruth was helping her son to get ready for bed while Nell's father cleaned up the kitchen. Nell was waiting to brush her teeth and go to the toilet, like Mummy always made her do on her own, but Vian and Ruth seemed to be taking ages. The door was open a crack and

Nell could see Vian standing next to the bath, his head hanging down.

"I don't want to wear it," he mumbled and Nell mused that his face looked pink.

"It's only until you get used to the ladder," Ruth said in a low voice.

"But nappies are for babies."

Nell listened with interest. *Did Vian wet the bed?*

Vian sniffed.

Was he crying?

Ruth crouched down beside him. "It'll be OK, Vian, I promise. Everything will be better tomorrow, after you and Nell have had time to play together."

"She doesn't like me."

"She doesn't *know* you. This is very new to her too, remember. She's used to having her daddy all to herself when she comes here. It's the only time she sees him."

"Why don't I see *my* daddy?"

Ruth sighed heavily and straightened back up. "Come on, honey," she chided.

Nell's mind ticked over. Who *was* Vian's daddy? *Where* was he?

"Put this on for tonight, to be on the safe side. You don't want to have an accident when Nell is beneath you."

Nell's eyebrows jumped up.

When they were both in their PJs, Daddy read Nell and Vian a story on the downstairs couch, not up on Nell's bed as he usually did. Nell looked across at Vian, who was sitting totally still, listening intently. He had curls like his mummy, but they were shorter and came around his face, partly falling into his eyes. His hair was very dark brown, almost black.

Vian hadn't spoken to Nell directly since she'd arrived. She couldn't imagine how he could possibly become a *playmate*, someone she *wanted* to spend time with.

"Right, that's it. Bedtime," Nell's dad said, patting both children on their bare knees.

Nell jumped up and kissed her father on the lips.

"Night night, love you," she said.

Her father looked taken aback as she turned away and hurried up the stairs.

Nell had dragged bedtimes out as long as possible in the past, begging for just one more story, just one more kiss, maybe even a song . . .

But tonight, determination carried Nell to her bedroom.

She threw Rabbit onto the top bunk and climbed up the ladder. By the time Vian appeared in the doorway, she was already snuggled under her duvet. He looked up at her with surprise.

"You can have the bottom bunk," Nell said graciously. "I don't mind."

Vian tore out of the room, shouting: "Mummy! Nell says I can sleep at the bottom!"

"Oh, what a kind, considerate girl!" Nell heard Ruth gush from the living room.

Nell felt her insides expand with happy bubbles as she listened to her father's footsteps on the stairs. He appeared in her room, his chocolate-brown eyes glowing with pride.

"Thank you," he murmured, stepping onto the middle rung and planting a big kiss on his daughter's cheek. "This means a lot to me. I really appreciate it. You did the right thing."

Yes, Nell had.

And it honestly had had very little to do with the fact that she didn't want Vian to wee on her head.

NELL'S FATHER, GEOFFREY Forrester, had lived in the same two-bedroom cottage on the Helford River his entire life. It had been passed down to him by his mother after her untimely death, and Geoff reckoned that he too would be carried out of it in a coffin.

Set at the top of a steep hill, with far-reaching views right down the river, Geoff liked nothing more than to sit on the bench seat in his garden, in front of the large purple hydrangea bush, peacefully watching the tide roll up and down the river from the nearby sea.

Today, however, he had company, and peaceful was not a word that could be used to describe the experience.

"Ready, steady, go!" Ruth called.

Nell concentrated on making her body as pinlike as possible before setting it in motion. She squealed as she rolled down the steep incline, hoping Ruth would indeed catch her, as promised, before she tumbled over the edge onto the riverbank. The tide was out, but the mud *oozed*, Nell remembered, having lost a rain boot to it the year before.

Ruth caught the giddy girl and swung her back onto her feet, but the sound of her laughter was drowned out by Vian's war cry as he took his turn.

"You rascal!" Ruth exclaimed, catching her son at the bottom. "I wasn't ready!"

Vian clambered to his feet, yelling, "Again! Again!"

He caught Nell's eye and she knew that the competition

was on, so she ran, ran, ran, up the hill as fast as she could, before launching herself, panting, to the ground.

Ruth squealed. "Oh no, *Geoff*! HELP!"

Ruth reached Nell just in time, while Geoff caught Vian, but he spilled hot tea on his hand in his haste to get to him.

Nell and Vian did feel bad when Geoff cursed out loud, but then Ruth threw her head back and laughed and everyone else joined in.

"YOU'VE GOT GRASS in your hair," Ruth said later, picking recently mown lawn out of the children's hair as they ate cheese sandwiches, made with crusty bread from the village shop. They were sitting at the kitchen table, which had a picture-window view of the wide river stretching out before them. The steep banks on either side were wooded with mature oak trees and the green tops looked soft, like cotton wool.

"Yes, your mother told me I'd better do a better job of brushing it this year or she'd lop it all off," Geoff said wryly, patting Nell on her shoulder.

Nell was nonplussed. She knew the threat was an empty one. She'd already asked if she could have hair like Isabel's from school, but Mummy had replied that Isabel looked like a boy and, from her tone, Nell had gathered that this wasn't a good thing.

"I'll brush it for you," Ruth said kindly. "It's such a beautiful color. It's like the wheat growing in the fields across the river."

"Do you want to go over there again this evening and paint?" Geoff asked casually, and Nell remembered Mummy saying that Ruth was a painter. "I can look after the children," he offered.

"No, I want to go too!" Vian said with excitement. "Can I?"

Ruth smiled at her son. "Of course you can."

"Yay!" He shot a look at Nell. "I'm building a den," he confided.

"Can I go?" Nell asked her father hopefully.

"Well, I suppose we could *all* go and take a picnic," he replied. "I could help with your den while Mummy works."

"WHERE'S *LOULOU*?" NELL asked later of the rowing boat that had been named after her mother.

Her mother's actual name was Louise. Nell had never heard anyone called her LouLou, but apparently her daddy had, once upon a time.

"She was a bit too small for all of us so I bought a new one," her father replied.

Nell looked down at the bright-orange rowing boat rocking gently on the murky green, slightly spongy water.

"What do you think about *Platypus* as a name?" her father asked. "It's Ruth's suggestion."

"Platypuses are from Australia," Vian chipped in seriously. "My daddy is Australian."

Nell knew the first part already—her teacher was Australian and often brought in books about native animals to read at storytime—but the second part was new information.

Nell took in the expectant expressions of the people around her, her gaze finally resting on Vian. "I like it," she decided.

The sight of Vian's smile filled Nell with warmth.

The tide came in and went out twice a day, but the tidal times differed daily. Today, and for the next couple of days, it was possible to traverse the river in the late afternoon and return home shortly after sunset, without the fear of getting banked.

Ruth took to the front of the boat, while the children sat at the rear, their bodies double their usual width due to the thick yellow lifejackets they were wearing. Nell's father was in the captain's seat, but halfway into their journey, Nell asked to have a turn, prompting Vian to demand one too. The boat wobbled precariously as Geoff exchanged places with the children, but after ten minutes of going around in circles, they swapped back so Ruth could get on with her work.

Once the boat was safely tied to the low-hanging branches of a tree, the new family of four made their way beneath the oak trees growing by the bank to the grassy slopes at the edge of the farmers' field.

Nell watched as Ruth trudged on up the hill alone, a folded wooden easel tucked under her arm and a bag swung over her shoulder. Her curly red hair glinted in the afternoon sun.

Later, when the den-building lost her interest, Nell climbed up after Ruth, curious to see what she was up to.

"Hello there," Ruth said with a kind smile. She stood among the biscuit-colored wheat fronds, holding an orange-tipped brush in her left hand. "Does your daddy know you're here?"

"Yes, he said I could come," Nell replied, breathless from climbing the hill. "What are you painting?"

"That," Ruth said, nodding at the view.

Nell looked over her shoulder. The clear blue sky arced above her head, caressing the tops of the fluffy-looking tree-tops on the other side. The river below was so still that it created a mirror image and, off to her right, their cottage and the annex stood at the top of a green hill, shining brilliant white in the sun.

"Do you want to have a look?" Ruth asked, indicating for Nell to come around to her side of the easel.

Nell did. She was surprised by what she saw. The canvas burst with color: vibrant blues and greens, vivid yellows and oranges, and shimmering reds and purples. It was pretty, but it didn't look at all realistic.

"Do you like it?" Ruth asked.

"Yes," Nell replied honestly.

"I don't always paint what I see," Ruth explained. "Sometimes I paint what I feel."

Nell thought about this. She glanced at Vian's mummy. "Are you happy?"

Ruth laughed, her freckled nose creasing and her blue eyes dancing. "Yes, sweetie. Yes, I am." She smiled at Nell. "Do you like art?"

Nell nodded seriously. "I do it at school." But her pictures never looked as bright or as beautiful as this.

"Well, sometime you can have a turn with my watercolors. Would you like that?"

Nell wasn't sure what watercolors were, but she grinned from ear to ear.

"You are so sweet," Ruth mused, her lips pursed. "One day, maybe I can paint you?"

She said it like a question so Nell nodded.

"Look," Ruth said, snapping off a golden ear of wheat and holding it against Nell's hair. "I wasn't far off. See?" She gathered a lock of Nell's hair and twisted it around to the front of Nell's face so she could compare the color. "But your eyes," Ruth said, with a frown of concentration. "Your eyes are more difficult . . . They're like . . . Like the color of runny honey. In sunshine," she added, thinking aloud as she scrutinized the small girl. "Very, very beautiful."

Nell liked this description a lot.

At that moment, her father called out to her from the riverbank below, his brown hair lifting from his forehead in the breeze as he beckoned for her to return. Nell saw that he had laid out a red-and-black-checkered rug, upon which Vian was sprawled, already tucking into the picnic. Nell smiled at Ruth one last time and then set off at a run, her blond hair streaming behind her as her feet carried her downhill.

"WHAT'S YOUR FAVORITE color?" Vian asked Nell later as they lay in their bunk beds.

"Green," Nell replied without a moment's hesitation. It had always been green, ever since she could remember. "What's yours?"

"Red," he replied. "But it used to be blue."

"Why does your daddy live in Australia?" Nell asked, jumping miles ahead in small-talk terms.

No reply came from the bottom bunk. "I don't know," Vian said eventually.

Nell heard a rustling sound and, a moment later, Vian's face appeared at the top of the ladder. "He sends me postcards," he mumbled, passing her a cardboard rectangle.

Nell sat up and looked at the picture in the fading light, the yellow fabric of the curtains being too thin to snuff it out, even at this hour of the evening.

The scene was of a boat on a vast blue ocean.

"He's a fisherman," Vian said, hooking his skinny arm around the bunk's wooden safety railing.

"Do you miss him?" Nell asked, because she missed her daddy a lot when she was in London. Cornwall was too far away to come for weekends, and in the last year she had only been able to see him during the school holidays.

Vian shrugged. "I don't know."

Nell thought this reply seemed strange. "Do you like him?" she asked.

"I don't know," Vian said again, startling Nell further. "Mummy says she'll take me to Australia one day to meet him."

"You haven't *met* him?" She wasn't sure she had understood that correctly.

Vian shook his head and took back the postcard, ducking underneath Nell's mattress to his own.

"Are you sad?" Nell asked.

"No," Vian replied.

But Nell wasn't so sure.

AFTER THAT FIRST week of Nell's month-long stay in Cornwall, Geoff had to return to his day job. He was a gardener at Glendurgan, a National Trust property across the river from Helford, and Nell often accompanied him to work. She preferred it to staying with the moody teenage girl up in the village who had babysat her in the past, but even though Geoff kept her busy with small tasks like deadheading flowers and weeding, the days felt long to a girl of her age.

So when Ruth said that Nell could stay at home with her and Vian, Nell seriously considered the offer. In the end, she chose to stick with what she knew, but as she meandered alone through the maze while her father trimmed the hedges, she found herself missing her new playmate.

In the last week, they had built dens on riverbanks and sandcastles on the beach. They had flown kites on blowy hill-tops and run headfirst down steep dunes. When Vian had dropped his ice cream on the sand, Nell had shared hers. And when Nell had admitted to missing the stars that her father hadn't got around to replacing, Vian had peeled off her old ones and attached them to Nell's ceiling with glue.

Reaching the tiny thatched hut in the middle of the maze, Nell sat down on the wooden seat and allowed her mind to wander back to last night. She and Vian had once again kept each other awake with their whisperings, telling stories and talking about their mutual longing for a puppy. Nell had re-membered that she'd left her cuddly dog, Barky, outside in the garden, but as she'd left her room to retrieve it, she'd overheard Ruth talking to her father in the living room. At the mention of her own name, Nell had paused.

"The look on Nell's face today was priceless," Ruth had said, and Nell had guessed that she'd been smiling even though she hadn't been able to see Ruth's face. "That little laugh of hers when she ran down the sand dune after Vian . . . She's *adorable*, Geoff. Already I love her to bits."

Nell's heart had warmed and her Daddy had responded with a gentle, "Aah."

Hearing a noise, Nell had shot her head around to see Vian creeping out of their bedroom. She'd pressed her finger to her lips and pointed to the top stair, then they'd settled down, pre-paring to eavesdrop.

"When I found out I was having Vian, I thought my life was

over," Ruth had said, and Vian's grin had frozen on his face, causing Nell to tense up at the sudden, strange turn in the conversation. She had hooked Vian's little finger with hers.

"I had to go back and live with Mum and I was so scared. But if I had known then where I'd be in five years' time," Ruth had continued, "I never would have worried. I love you, Geoff. Vian does too, and we are so very happy here with you and Nell. Thank you for everything you have done for us."

"No, thank *you*, my darling," Nell had heard her daddy reply and she'd noted that his voice sounded gruffer than normal. "You've brought light back into my life. I feel incredibly lucky to have you all here with me."

Nell had breathed a sigh of relief before meeting Vian's eyes. He'd sweetly returned her smile and then they'd both crept back to bed, Nell deciding that Barky could survive outside for one night.

Now, as she sat in the middle of the maze, a thought came to her. She jumped to her feet and went to find her father.

"Daddy," she said, tugging on his green shirt and gazing up at him hopefully.

"Almost time for a tea break and a cookie," he promised, figuring that was his daughter's reason for seeking him out.

She shook her head. "Vian and I have been talking."

"Oh?"

"Can we have a puppy, Daddy?" she asked, watching as her father's bushy eyebrows pulled together. Before he could say a word against the idea, she pressed on. "Please, Daddy? We would really, *really* love a puppy! We'd take it for walks and feed it and we'd play with it all the time. Vian and I both *really* want a dog and we *promise* you that we'll look after it!"

Nell had begged her father for a dog before, but he had

always said no—he worked too much and Nell was hardly ever in Cornwall. But now, for the first time ever, he actually seemed to be considering it.

By the weekend, Geoff had crumbled under the pressure and, with the cottage puppy-proofed in anticipation, he drove Ruth and two extremely excited children to a village a few miles away where the owners of the local pub had a litter of mongrels ready for rehoming. They chose a black-and-white fur ball and named him Scampi.

It was the greatest summer of Nell's life, and as August rolled to a close, she didn't want to go home. She cried when Vian tried on his new uniform, all set to begin Year One at the small school up in the village, and Nell begged and pleaded to be able to stay in Cornwall so she could attend with him, rather than return to her strict private school in London.

But alas, it was not to be. At least, not for another two years, when it suited Louise to pack up and move to the French Riviera in pursuit of a man. Then Nell got her wish, and when she next made the long journey to Cornwall, she was finally going to stay.

TEN

N ELL!" VIAN SHOUTED, BURSTING THROUGH THE front door. "Where are you?"

"Here." She was at the kitchen table, making a start on her half-term homework. She'd only arrived home from school half an hour ago.

Vian, typically, had declined to join her.

Energy radiated from him as he beckoned at her wildly. "There's a duckling! It's lost its mother! Quick!"

Nell immediately jumped up and tore after him.

They had often talked about how much fun it would be to raise a duckling but, so far, no duckling had been unlucky enough to make itself available.

Scampi was caught up in the children's excitement as they ran down to the water's edge, but even over the noise of his barking, Nell could hear cheeping. She caught a glimpse of fuzzy brown and yellow in among the weeping willow branches.

"Put Scampi back inside and grab the life jackets," Vian commanded. "I'll get the boat ready."

"But your mum said not to disturb her," Nell argued.

Nell's dad was still at work and Ruth was in the studio— the small, separate annex building set five meters away from the main body of the cottage. It used to house an entire family centuries before, but had been renovated and turned into a playroom for her father when he was a boy.

"We're not going to disturb her," Vian replied with a cheeky grin. "Now hurry, before we lose sight of it."

From the ripples on the water, Nell guessed that the tide was on its way out, and she knew that when the water drained, it happened remarkably quickly. She had never yet been banked, but there was always a first time, so she had the good sense to bring rain boots for the journey, as well as the fishing net that they used when they went crabbing.

Although anxious about getting told off for taking the boat out on their own, Nell was buoyed by her sense of righteousness. She had seen ducklings being plucked out of the water by huge herons so she knew there wasn't a moment to lose. She sat at the stern, her body twisted to face the water and her net at the ready. Listening intently, she soon heard the tiny bird's cries.

"There!" She pointed. The duckling was darting in and out of the tree branches that were caressing the water. It was headed in the direction of the bridge and after that it would reach the creek, where no boat could follow.

Vian rowed with increased determination. Nell stretched out with her net, hoping to scoop up her prize like hook-a-duck at the funfair, but the duckling scooted away with agile speed. Once more, Vian set off after it, but again Nell's net came back empty. A car motored by over the bridge and Nell looked up in time to see the pale face of a brown-haired boy peering down at them. When she returned her gaze to the river, the duckling was nowhere to be seen.

"Uh-oh."

Nell heard the panic in Vian's voice and saw mud banks protruding from the middle of the river, like slippery wet whales' backs.

"We'd better go back," Vian said miserably.

"No way," Nell replied with nerves of steel. "If we have to, we'll get out and walk." She scanned the water. "Where are you, little one?" she asked aloud. "We're trying to save you."

"There!" Vian shouted, pointing toward the bridge. He rowed hard, grimacing when his oar hit the muddy riverbed. Sensing this was their last chance, Nell held onto the edge and leaned out as far as she could, almost toppling over as the boat jolted to a stop. It had run aground and would stay that way for the next six hours or so, but the children didn't care. As Nell's net revealed, they had caught the duckling, and they were absolutely delighted.

RUTH WAS STANDING outside the cottage with a couple and a child when the children arrived back.

As well as selling her artwork, Ruth worked as a caretaker for the owner of a row of holiday homes up in the village. This family were likely here to collect the keys.

"What on earth?" Ruth exclaimed at the sight of Nell and Vian.

They had had to abandon both pairs of boots and walk the rest of the way barefoot. Their legs were coated practically to their knees with thick, squelchy mud.

Nell held up their find, beaming. But her expression slipped at Ruth's horrified face.

"Oh, no!" she cried. "Put it back!"

"We can't, Mum," Vian interjected. "It'll die!"

"Its mother must be around here somewhere," Ruth lamented.

"It isn't," Vian insisted fervently. "It was all alone. We *had* to save it."

Ruth sighed and when she spoke, she sounded weary. "Kate, Simon, this is Nell and Vian."

Nell smiled at the grown-ups. She liked Kate's dress—it was pale blue and fluttered around her ankles.

"And this is Edward," Kate introduced her son, ushering him forward.

He was around the same height as Nell and had light-brown hair that framed an open, friendly face. His eyes were big and dark and reminded Nell of Bastian's from *The Never-Ending Story* which they had seen at the cinema the month before.

She had *really* liked that film.

"Why are you so muddy?" Ruth asked tersely.

Nell stared at the ground.

"We got stuck when the tide went out," Vian mumbled.

"Did you go out in the boat? Alone? Where is it?" Ruth's voice was going up in pitch with every question.

Vian pointed down the backwater. "We tied it to a branch so it wouldn't drift out to sea."

"Goodness me," Ruth said, shaking her head. She turned to Kate and Simon. "I'm sorry about this."

"It's no problem," Kate replied with a smile. "We appreciate you letting us come a day early." Saturday was technically changeover day. "We could go for a drive and come back?"

"Or you could stay for a cup of tea?" Ruth suggested. "The cleaners are thorough but prompt. Half an hour and you'll certainly be able to go in."

"A cup of tea would be lovely," Kate accepted. "It's been a long journey. But no rush. When you're ready."

Everyone looked at Nell's cupped hands. The duckling's eyes were opening and closing, sleepily. It seemed surprisingly content.

"I suppose you'd better put it in the bathtub for now." Ruth sounded resigned. "I'll set it running. You two go and get cleaned off under the outdoor tap. You're not bringing that mud inside."

The adults and children parted ways, the latter heading around the side of the cottage.

"I can hold it for you," Edward offered to Nell when they reached the tap.

"No, *I* will," Vian cut in sharply. "Hang on." He set about cleaning himself with the icy water. To his irritation, Edward loitered.

"It's so small," Edward said to Nell, who had opened her hands to show him the downy bundle. The duckling craned its neck and tried to stand, letting out several shrill cheeps.

"She's probably only a couple of days' old," Nell replied, closing her hands and prompting the duckling to settle back down. She liked the feeling of its clammy, webbed feet on her palms.

Frankly, she still couldn't believe their luck.

"How far away is the beach?" Edward asked.

"There are lots of them," Nell replied. "We're learning to surf at one really close by, aren't we, Vian?"

Vian grunted.

"Wish I could surf," Edward said.

"You should come with us!" Nell offered instantly.

"Could I?" Edward replied, as Vian shot Nell a look of outrage.

"Definitely! Ask your mum and dad." She ignored Vian. She was good at making friends, and Vian got used to new people eventually, even if he did initially struggle with change.

"OK, I will," Edward said.

"How old are you?" Nell asked, making conversation while she waited for the tap to become free. Vian was taking ages and didn't seem to have made much progress. The mud was like glue.

"Ten, almost eleven. What about you?"

"Ten," Nell replied. She nodded at Vian. "Vian's ten too. Our birthdays are two days apart."

Edward looked confused. "Are you twins?"

"How can we be twins if we're not born on the same day?" Vian asked crossly.

"We're not really brother and sister," Nell explained, unfazed by Vian's tone. "My dad loves his mum, but my real mum lives in France and Vian's real dad is in Australia. Where do you live?" she asked.

"London," Edward replied.

"Me too!" she exclaimed. "Well, I did, until my mum moved away. I'm going to France in the summer holidays."

Vian looked utterly miserable at the reminder and Nell felt a pang of empathy. She herself had been desperately lonely the year before when Ruth had taken him to Australia. It was the second time he'd gone—the first was when he'd met his father, aged seven. She knew she'd miss him while she was in France, but it was always harder on those who stayed behind.

"That'll do," Vian said, wiping his wet palms on his red T-shirt and holding them out to Nell. She carefully transferred the duckling into his cold grasp and went over to the tap, glancing round in time to see Vian walking away.

"Wait!" she called out with dismay as he disappeared from

view. Was he going to put the duckling in the bathtub without her? "He's so annoying!" she erupted.

Edward kicked his foot awkwardly against the paving stones.

"You're lucky *you* don't have a brother," Nell sniped crossly, scrubbing vigorously at the slimy muck coating her legs.

"I did have a brother once," Edward replied offhandedly. "But he died."

Nell was shocked. "What happened to him?"

"He got sick. I was a baby so I don't remember him. He was two years older than me."

Nell didn't know what to say, but she was full of compassion.

"My mum's going to have a baby," Edward revealed. "We don't know if it will be a boy or a girl, though. I'm going to be a *very* big brother," he said proudly, folding his arms across his chest. "New babies cry a lot, but I'll help."

Nell smiled at him. She could tell that he was kind. She liked him.

"CAN I GET you a drink, Edward?" Ruth called from the kitchen when they returned indoors.

"No thanks," Edward responded, kicking off his trainers in the hall.

The bathroom was straight ahead and Nell looked in to see the duckling swimming around quite happily in the bathtub. Vian was dangling his hand over the side, his fingernails still rimmed with river mud.

"Why didn't you wait?" Nell hissed.

Vian acted like he hadn't heard her. She huffed and followed Edward into the kitchen.

The adults were sitting at the table and the fabric of Edward's mother's dress was pulled tight across her tummy so Nell could see her bump. It hadn't been at all obvious when she had been standing in the garden.

"When are you due?" Ruth was asking.

"The end of August," Kate replied. "It'll be a bit strange going back to dirty nappies and sleepless nights after all this time."

"I bet," Ruth said.

"Mum and Dad, can I learn to surf?" Edward interrupted. "Nell and Vian are going to do lessons."

"Yes, at Poldhu Beach," Ruth chipped in. "It's a ten-, fifteen-minute drive from here. They start in the morning."

"Can I?" Edward looked hopeful as his parents glanced at each other.

Simon turned back to Ruth. "Do we need to book?"

"You could probably just turn up," she replied, "but I'll find you the number, to be on the safe side."

Kate pulled her son onto her lap. "I told you you'd make friends," she said in a teasing voice.

Edward blushed and stood up again, flashing Nell a shy smile.

"WHY DID YOU have to go and invite him?" Vian griped that night, startling Nell back to full consciousness. They were in their bunk beds and she had been nodding off.

"He's nice," Nell replied sleepily. "I think he looks like the boy from *The NeverEnding Story*."

"I thought you said that *I* looked like him," Vian muttered after a moment's silence.

"You remind me more of Atreyu, even though you've got short hair now." Atreyu's hair came almost to his shoulders.

Nell peeked over the railings from the top bunk—they never had swapped back. "Edward is more like Bastian," she said.

Vian still looked grumpy, but Nell knew he'd be happier about that comparison. Atreyu was brave and heroic: a horse-riding, monster-hunting saver of the universe. Bastian only read about the action in a book, although he *had* got to ride the Luck Dragon at the end.

"I feel sorry for him," she said. "He's all on his own. His brother died," she added gravely.

Vian looked stunned.

"It was when he was a baby, but it's still awful, don't you think?"

Vian nodded. He stared up at Nell and his eyes filled with tears.

"What's wrong?" she whispered.

"I wish you didn't have to go away this summer," he replied in a choked voice.

Nell threw back her duvet and climbed down the ladder. Scampi was lying on the floor beside Vian and his tail thumped halfheartedly as she stepped over his solid, furry body to get to the bed. Vian edged over for her and she hopped in, slipping her arm behind his shoulders. He did the same to her and they held each other tightly.

"I wish you could come with me," she whispered. "I'm going to be so bored."

"At least your mum has a swimming pool."

"That *is* brilliant," Nell conceded. "But I'd still rather be swimming in the sea with you."

"Even though it's freezing cold?"

"Yes, even though it's freezing cold."

They usually wore wetsuits, but they were such a pain to put on that sometimes they braved the water without them.

"I hope the duckling's OK," Vian said.

"Me too," Nell replied. "I can't believe we've got her!" she said excitedly.

It was currently in a box in the kitchen with the door closed, much to Scampi's dismay, but tomorrow they were going to fill up their old shell-shaped wading pool with water and make a pen for it.

Nell's dad had been surprisingly blasé and even quite accommodating when he'd come home and found out what had happened. Not only had he arranged to borrow some chicken feed from Steven and Linzie, the farmers who lived up the road, but he'd also convinced Ruth that the children were old enough and capable enough to take the boat out alone again in the future, as long as they checked with an adult first and made sure the tide was working in their favor.

"What do you think to calling him Webster?" Vian asked.

Nell frowned. Him? She wanted a girl, and Webster *definitely* sounded like a boys' name.

Ultimately, though, Nell wanted to make Vian happy and if that meant their duckling had to be a boy, then a boy it would be. "Yes, I like Webster," Nell said. "Let's call him that."

Vian grinned.

They had been so deep in conversation that they hadn't heard the footsteps on the stairs. The door creaked open and Vian whipped the bedcovers up and over their heads, staring at Nell with alarm.

Two heavy footsteps later and the covers were flipped back. "Get to bed!" Geoff shouted, prompting Scampi to scarper.

Nell scooted out of Vian's bed and hurriedly climbed back up into her own before daring to meet her father's eyes.

"Sorry, Daddy," she mumbled. He looked very cross.

"Sorry," Vian echoed.

"No more talking!" Geoff commanded, stalking out the door.

LATER THAT NIGHT, Nell was again jolted from sleep. She cocked her ear to the wall and heard her father and Ruth speaking in raised voices downstairs.

"They're arguing," Vian murmured from the bottom bunk, sensing her wakefulness.

"What are they arguing about?" Nell asked apprehensively.

Vian slid out of bed.

"Vian!" she hissed. "Don't!" But he was already at the door, opening it.

She crept down the ladder and tiptoed over to where he was standing, eavesdropping.

"I don't want to move," they heard Ruth say.

"Do you think I do?" Geoff replied. "This is the house I grew up in! But they should be in their own rooms—and beds— by now."

"They're only ten! You say it like they're doing something wrong."

"I know it's only innocent, but children grow up so fast. It's only a matter of time before—"

"Oh, stop!" Ruth cut him off. She sounded disgusted.

Vian and Nell glanced at each other with confusion.

"We need to think about these things," Geoff said wearily. "Maybe we could turn the studio into a bedroom," he suggested.

"Where would I work?" Ruth asked. "And who would want to sleep out there, anyway?"

"Vian might like his own space."

Vian jolted and Nell felt physical pain. Without another word, she pushed past him and ran down the stairs.

"You can't make him sleep outside!" she yelled from the halfway point.

Ruth and Geoff stared up at her in shock, but a moment later her dad's shoulders slumped. "We're only talking, Nelly. This is a grown-up conversation—"

"I don't care!" she yelled. "You can't make him! I'll sleep outside if someone has to, but not Vian!" She stamped her foot.

A pale-faced Vian stumbled down the steps behind her. "No! Don't make her! Why can't we share? We want to be together!"

"You're growing up now, kids. You should have your own rooms," Geoff stated firmly.

"Why?" Vian asked.

"It's just . . ." Ruth shifted from foot to foot, uncomfortably. "It's not appropriate, kids. Boys and girls are not supposed to sleep together."

Vian and Nell were stumped. Why on earth not?

"*You* sleep together," Vian pointed out.

"That's different," Ruth replied with frustration. "We're adults and we're . . . Well, we're *not* married," she acknowledged, "but we almost are."

"Nell and I are going to get married too," Vian told them.

Nell nodded. They had agreed to this when they were six years old. It was an accepted fact.

Ruth threw Geoff a glance.

"You're far too young to be talking about that sort of thing," Geoff snapped, pressing on before they could argue. "Nothing is certain. We were discussing the possibility of moving to a bigger house and you two should not have been listening. You *should* have been fast asleep. Now, go back to bed."

"I don't want to move!" Nell cried.

"Perhaps Ruth and *I* will end up in the studio," Geoff said to appease her. "It's not something we need to worry about right this minute. But," and for this next part, his voice got increasingly louder, "if you two don't go to sleep *immediately* and stop climbing into each other's beds and keeping each other awake, then you *will* be separated, and it *will* happen *sooner rather than later*!"

The threat worked. Nell and Vian ran back upstairs and not another peep was heard from them for the rest of the night.

THERE WAS A loaded atmosphere in the cottage the next morning, but no one broached the subject of the night before. Even little Webster didn't do much to lift the heaviness that hung around Nell's heart.

They got ready for the beach straight after breakfast and although Nell had encouraged Edward to join them at surf school, she was now hoping he wouldn't. She didn't want anything else to cause Vian distress.

However, Edward was already waiting in line to register

beside his parents when they arrived. He looked over his shoulder, his face breaking into a grin. Nell reached for Vian's hand and squeezed it, but he squirmed out of her grasp. She managed only a small smile at Edward in return.

"Are you OK?" he asked later as they struggled into their wetsuits. Edward's borrowed gear was still sandy and wet from its last use and looked especially awkward to pull on, but Nell and Vian had brought their own.

"Yeah," Nell replied, bumping her elbow against one of the other kid's dads. There were a dozen or so people of all ages in the class. "Are you?"

"A bit nervous," he admitted. "Aren't you?"

"Not really." Nell wasn't at all. She had been excited for the last two weeks, but not nervous. She and Vian had been wanting to learn to surf for ages.

They carried their surfboards in pairs—one under each arm—down to the shore and lined up in a semicircle opposite the instructor. Vian positioned himself right at the end beside Nell and ignored Edward on the other side of her.

Nell hated that Vian was being standoffish—not only with Edward, but with her too. He got so jealous. He wasn't really like this at school. At school they had their own friends and rarely played together at break. But holidays were their time and Vian was making it clear that Edward was encroaching.

Nell felt caught in the middle. She tried to put all of her focus into the lesson, which was a lot easier once they were in the sea and doing their own thing. When Vian stood up on only his second attempt and rode the wave almost to the shore, she cheered as loudly as she could. Vian looked over his shoulder and gave her the thumbs up. It brightened him up immensely to see Edward fall off.

THAT AFTERNOON IT poured down, so Ruth invited the children into the studio to paint with her. Nell was more of a writer than an artist, but she enjoyed using Ruth's watercolors and she quite liked the smell in the studio, although she couldn't ever imagine sleeping in it. The room had four big windows with vistas straight down the river, but otherwise it was a mess, with color splatters all over the wooden floorboards and rows of canvases propped up against the walls.

Nell didn't use Ruth's expensive oils or acrylics, but Vian did. He had inherited Ruth's artistic talent and had even had his artwork displayed in a gallery in Truro after entering a children's art competition. The gallery owner had been impressed by his abstract sailing boats, but Nell loved his piskie drawings more than anything else.

A couple of years earlier, Ruth had taken them to a storytelling session at the library that had described different types of fairies. Nell had been motivated to come up with her own stories about Cornish pixies—or piskies, as they were called here. So she had conceived Fudge and Smudge, two cheeky piskies who lived on the Helford River and whose homes were under constant threat from the naughty Spriggens up the creek.

On Nell's request, Vian had brought the characters from her stories to life, painting tiny scenes onto smooth pebbles that they'd found at the beach. Nell had a whole series of these pebbles lined up on the windowsill in their bedroom and she counted them among her favorite possessions.

Nell loved watching Vian paint. She was fascinated by the look on his face, the way his dark brows pulled together and his eyes narrowed in concentration. He focused on painting like no other task. It was the only time he appeared to be truly absorbed. She never got very far with her own work because she was usually too preoccupied with his. Even now, she kept looking over.

"What are you painting?" she asked eventually.

"Don't you recognize it?" He didn't take his eyes from his canvas as he spoke.

"It looks like an upside-down *Platypus*." She meant their boat, not the animal.

"It *is* an upside-down *Platypus*," he replied, adding a touch of orange to the greenish appearance.

Nell frowned. "Er, why?" she asked.

He glanced at her and grinned. "You know how you told me that Fudge and Smudge were homeless after the Spriggens attacked their crab-apple tree?"

Fudge and Smudge had lived in the tree since the spring when they had given gifts of apple blossom to the Hedgerow Fairies in return for some of their magic flying dust. With help from the nature-loving Brownie fairies, they had cared for and cultivated the tiny apples for months. Then the bad Spriggens raided the tree, taking the shiny, ruby-red fruit for themselves. The Spriggens were obsessed with treasure and to them, the apples looked like jewels. They had no interest in eating them—they only liked to munch on snails and slugs and leeches from the creek. All they wanted was to display them like ornaments until they turned bad, whereupon they'd wastefully cast them down the river.

As the Spriggens had stripped the crab-apple tree of both fruit and leaves—the latter purely to cause mischief—Fudge and Smudge were currently homeless. They were living in the leafless branches, shivering with cold and completely unprotected from passersby. Fudge had almost been spotted by a human and that would have been catastrophic.

Nell stared at the picture in front of her, while Vian patiently waited for her to join the dots.

"They live under the boat for the winter!" she cried at last.

Vian laughed and nodded. "Look, I've even made them a little door. What do you think?"

She shook her head with amazement. "I love it." Already, her mind was ticking over, creating jeopardy in the form of the tide rolling in and a storyline that involved a flippy-flapping fish getting trapped and needing to be rescued.

Ruth came over, her curiosity piqued by the children's conversation. She had her red hair loosely tied back with a green ribbon and she looked especially beautiful today, Nell thought.

"The algae is *incredible*, Vian!" Ruth exclaimed.

Vian blushed, proud as punch.

"Honestly, I think you two could publish these stories. I bet there are plenty of people out there who would buy them. I could type them up for you," Ruth said, addressing Nell. "And perhaps I could help you choose some key scenes for Vian to illustrate. We could photocopy and bind them up and maybe even send some off to the people who make books to see what they say."

Nell gawked and then jumped up and down with excitement. Ruth kissed the top of her head, but as she straightened up, her green satin ribbon slipped from her hair and fell onto the floor. Nell, who had been coveting it, swooped it up with a giggle and attempted to fasten her own hair with it. But she had recently had it cut to chin-length so the ribbon tied itself to thin air.

Ruth laughed and gave one of Nell's locks a gentle tug. "You'll have to grow it back if you want to wear it like that."

Ruth had tried in earnest to keep Nell's hair tangle free over the years, beginning with that first summer that they'd all spent together. She hadn't been entirely successful—Nell's mother had still claimed it looked "like straw" by the time Nell had returned to London. Eventually, Nell had won her battle to cut it shorter, but now, for the first time, she found herself regretting it.

"I know what we'll do," Ruth said, and she fashioned the ribbon into a hairband and fastened it around Nell's head.

"What color do you want the door?" Vian asked, bringing a delighted Nell's attention back to his picture.

"Green," Nell replied without a beat.

Vian and Ruth looked at each other and smiled. Nell was so predictable.

"Which is your favorite green, Nell?" Ruth asked, plucking tubes of acrylic out of a box as she spoke. "Ever since you were a little girl, you've said green is your favorite color, but which green do you like the best? There's lime-green, grass-green, pine-green, sage, olive, mint . . . Do you like jade? Or teal? Or the color of the ribbon? I'd call that emerald."

Nell studied the colors before her. She liked lots of them, but she was mostly drawn to mint and teal.

"Interesting," Ruth said. "They're not what I'd call the greenest greens. This is more of a bluey green," she said of the teal. "What if you look out the window?" Ruth asked, guiding her away from the box. "Do you like the color of the leaves on the trees? The oak leaves are darker than the sycamore ones down by the deck. What about the color of the grass? Or the river water?"

Nell screwed up her nose at that last one and Ruth smiled.

Nell had never questioned why green was her favorite color. She didn't own any green clothes, but if they played a game that had colored counters, it was always a given that she would have the green one. Her toothbrush had always been green and when they had got Scampi, she had begged for him to have a green collar. In the end, Vian had won the coin toss and Scampi had ended up with a red one. Not that Vian's favorite color had remained the same. Right now, it was yellow.

"How about the wheat in the farmer's field?" Ruth asked, pointing across the river. It wouldn't turn golden for another month or so.

Nell went closer to the window and looked out. "Yes, I like that color," she said decisively.

"Again, I would call that an almost bluey-green," Ruth commented. "I'd say it even has a hint of gray. It's certainly not as bright green as the barley that grew there last year. That was lime colored."

Vian sighed.

"Am I boring you, son?" Ruth teased.

"Can I go and watch *Inspector Gadget* now?" he asked, his shoulders slumping.

Ruth smiled and cast her eyes to the heavens. "Go on, then. Leave your brushes, I'll do them with mine."

"Thanks, Mum," Vian said with a grin, giving her a quick hug before running out of the door. Nell copied his actions to the letter.

THERE WAS NO surf lesson the next day as it was Sunday so Nell and Vian decided to kill time by taking *Platypus* across the river for a picnic. They also planned to go fishing for minnows. Webster was still being fed a diet of chicken feed and the children thought a few tasty fish morsels might make a nice change. The duckling had really taken to the paddling pool, and Scampi had really taken to the duckling. Fortunately, Webster didn't appear too fazed by the excited dog's barking.

Today they took Scampi with them to give Webster some peace and quiet and, as usual, he leaped out of the boat before it had reached the shore and waited for the children to join him before shaking his wet fur in a frenzy all over them.

While on the other side of the river, Nell took a closer look at the wheat.

It still just looked green to her, but she could see what Ruth meant about the stalks having a slightly blue hue.

"I *really* like this color," she said to Vian, who was already tucking into the cookies that were supposed to be for dessert. "I think it is my favorite green. Can you do the door like this?"

He shrugged. "Pick some so we can take it back with us. I'll see if I can match it."

WHEN THE CHILDREN returned home, they were taken aback to see Edward sitting inside the duckling pen, cradling Webster in his hands.

"Hi!" he exclaimed.

"What are you doing here?" Vian asked rudely, as Scampi set about, barking his head off.

"Your dad said I could come and see her. He saw us walking down the creek."

Nell forced a smile, trying to buffer Vian's impoliteness. "He's cute, isn't he?"

Vian climbed into the pen and upended the contents of their bucket into the paddling pool. Tiny fish zipped in every direction.

"Give him to me," he snapped.

Edward hastily handed Webster over and Vian put him in the pool. Almost immediately, the duckling bobbed underwater and zoomed, stealth-like, in search of food.

The children looked on with glee, the tension between them momentarily forgotten.

"Have you been out in your boat?" Edward asked Nell, crouching down to pat Scampi. Scampi immediately rolled over to give Edward access to his belly.

"Yes, we went to the other side for a picnic."

"That sounds like brilliant fun."

Before Nell could even think about inviting him along the next time they went out, Vian gave her finger a pinch.

"I'll see you in the studio," he said meaningfully. "I'll get the key."

Embarrassed by Vian's behavior, Nell remained where she was.

"Your brother doesn't like me," Edward said.

"He gets jealous," Nell admitted, kneeling beside him and patting Scampi too.

Edward pulled a face. "Why?"

"I don't know," Nell replied. It's not as if she was going anywhere.

But she felt protective of Vian. That was the way it was. He seemed to feel things more deeply—things that, to her, were like water off a duck's back.

She still remembered those early days of them all living together and how much he'd struggled when Ruth gave her attention. But he'd soon got used to it, because Nell became family too, and family, to Vian, was of the utmost importance.

It hurt Nell's heart when his father sent him postcards from Australia. Vian would be on cloud nine when one came through the letterbox, but later he'd withdraw into himself and nothing Nell said could bring him out of his black mood. She had learned to simply give him a hug when that happened. They had fallen asleep together on his bottom bunk on countless occasions.

Nell felt a pang at the reminder that their parents wanted to separate them. It still didn't make sense to her.

Vian appeared from the cottage. He stood for a moment and glared at Nell and Edward before going over to the studio to unlock it.

Ruth had taken some of her artwork to Padstow to meet with a gallery owner so she was out for most of the day. Hopefully she wouldn't mind Vian going into the studio alone—they weren't actually supposed to.

"Surfing again tomorrow?" Edward asked casually.

"Yeah," Nell replied, downcast. "I'd better go and give this to Vian." She scooped up the bundle of wheat.

"What's it for?"

"He's going to paint it for me."

"Why?"

"Because I like the color. I'm writing a book," she explained, feeling proud as she said the words. "Vian is doing the pictures."

"What's it about?" Edward asked with interest before remembering Nell had been about to leave.

"Sorry," Nell mumbled, feeling bad as she walked away.

Vian was rooting around in a box in the studio, pulling out various shades of green and blue.

"Why are you so mean to him?" she asked him crossly.

"I'm not."

"Yes, you are, you're rude!"

"Why do you like him so much?"

"He's kind and he doesn't have anyone to play with. I feel sorry for him."

"So go and play with him."

Nell glared. Vian ignored her, continuing to rummage around in the box. She was infuriated.

"Maybe I will," she said. "It's not like you need me here."

"Nope," Vian replied.

"Fine, then."

He didn't say another word as she left the studio.

Edward was still sitting on the grass, patting Scampi. He looked up as she approached.

"Would you like to hear about my stories?" she asked.

"Yes," Edward replied with a smile.

It wasn't long before Edward's dad came to find him and said they needed to go home for tea, so Nell went to check on Vian's progress.

"Are you all right?" she asked, poking her head around the studio door.

"Yep," Vian replied.

She caught sight of the sheet of paper taped down on Vian's easel—it was almost entirely covered in bluey green paint.

"Do you think it's right?" he asked her, holding up the bunch of wheat.

The color started out bluey green with a hint of gray at the bottom, and gradually became more of a pale-green toward the top.

"It's perfect!" she said. "I want to stick that on my wall!"

"You can, if you like." He looked pleased. "Hopefully I'll be able to remember which ones I mixed together so I can do Fudge and Smudge's door."

She was relieved that he wasn't still put out about Edward.

"Can you write your name on it?" she asked.

He rolled his brush in the last dregs of bright blue paint and Nell watched as the words appeared on the paper in cursive writing: *Vian Stanley Stirling.*

Ruth's surname was Stanley. Vian's father's surname was Stirling. At some point during the last five years, Ruth had decided that Vian should have both.

"What are you two up to in here?" her dad interrupted from the door. "Gosh," he said as he spied Vian's picture. "That's a whole lot of green."

"It's the color of wheat," Nell told him.

Geoff frowned. "Wheat is yellow."

"No." Nell shook her head and gathered up the bundle she'd picked earlier. "Not at this time of year. Can we trim the edges so it's all completely green?" she asked Vian.

He nodded.

Geoff ruffled Vian's hair fondly. "Want me to do that with a Stanley knife so it's dead straight?"

"OK," Vian agreed. "Can you do it now?"

Ruth came home as they were finishing up.

"Vian's painted the color of wheat!" Nell parroted.

But Ruth did not look at all happy.

"Oh, Vian, you've used up all my cerulean!" she exclaimed

with dismay, coming forward to inspect the paint tubes. "I needed that to finish my piece."

Vian's face fell.

"We can get more," Geoff butted in softly.

"How? When?" Ruth demanded to know. "You're out at work tomorrow and we're at the beach—when am I going to get to Falmouth to buy more paint?" They had only the one car between them. "*And* you've used up all the milk so I can't make macaroni and cheese."

"I'll go to the shop right now," Geoff said calmly, trying to appease her.

"It's Sunday! The shop is closed!" she snapped. "Forget it. I'll walk up the road and ask Linzie if I can borrow some."

"*I'll* go."

"No, I need the fresh air and exercise. I've been stuck in a car for over two hours. The traffic has been hell." She stormed out the door in a huff.

Geoff gave the children a small smile, but Vian still looked upset as he tidied up.

"It's all right, son," Geoff said kindly. "I don't think Mum's meeting went well, judging by her mood. We'll cheer her up at dinner."

RUTH WAS AGES getting milk and Nell's tummy started to rumble. Vian was upstairs, sulking, but she hung around the kitchen, picking at the grated cheese that her father had prepared in anticipation of dinner. Geoff's glances at the clock were becoming more and more frequent.

"Where is she?" he muttered eventually. "I know Linzie can talk, but this is ridiculous! Maybe I should call her," he decided out loud, heading into the hall to look up the number for the farm.

"Oh, hello, Steven, it's Geoff," Nell heard him say. "Yes, very well, thank you. Yourself?" There was a pause. "I'm after Ruth, actually. The children are getting a bit peckish so I thought I'd better give her a nudge." Another pause. "Oh. She was coming up your way to ask if she could borrow some milk." He sounded confused. "Oh," he said again. "Yes, if you could. That's a little worrying. Actually, I might get in the car and—"

The sound of a siren wailing stopped Geoff short. Nell peeked into the hall in time to see her father yank open the front door and run out. The phone, still hanging from its cord, bashed against the wall and she could hear a tinny voice coming from the receiver.

"Geoff? Geoff?"

Nell joined her dad in time to see the blue-and-red flashing lights of an ambulance coming down the hill from the direction of the village. The sirens screamed and she pressed her hands to her ears as the vehicle passed right by the cottage and headed up the road, toward the farm. Geoff stared after it and Nell felt her stomach go cold.

"Stay indoors," her dad told her in a shaky voice, and he hurried past her to retrieve the car keys from the hall. His face was pale. "Stay with Vian. I'll be back soon."

Nell watched with fear as he ran to the car and got in, tearing off after the ambulance.

The phone was still hanging off its hook when she returned inside, and she could hear a long, dull beep coming from the receiver. In a daze, she picked it up and put it back in its cradle, then walked through to the living room. She looked at the stairs, but didn't want to climb them.

A moment later, their bedroom door opened and Vian's footsteps could be heard.

"Where's my mum?" he asked when he saw Nell.

Nell looked up at him and shook her head. "I don't know."

He sighed. "I'm starving."

"I'm sure she'll be back soon," Nell said, but her voice sounded funny.

Vian jumped down the last three steps, landing with a thud at the bottom. He wandered through to the kitchen. Nell followed, her insides prickly with dread.

"Where's your dad?" he asked, looking around with a frown.

"He heard an ambulance," Nell whispered.

Vian shot her a sharp look. Then all at once it dawned on him.

"Vian, wait!" Nell cried. "Dad said to stay here!"

But Vian was already pulling on his trainers.

"Please," Nell begged. "Don't leave me here alone." It was the only thing she could think to say to stop him.

"Come with me," he urged, passing over her shoes.

She could tell by the look of determination on his face that she wouldn't be able to stop him.

But she would soon wish with all of her heart that she had tried harder.

FORTY

LUKE IS ASLEEP. I THINK HE NODDED OFF WHEN I started talking about shades of green, but I've continued telling my story in a whisper. It's been a good distraction.

I stand up and stretch my arms over my head, yawning. I'm exhausted. I should go for a walk or get some food from the hospital cafeteria to keep me going, but I don't even have the energy to do that. I lift the chair to move it closer to the bed and then sit back down again, hunching forward to rest my cheek on my arms. I close my eyes, wondering if I'll be able to drift off in this position.

But my mind ticks over, and it's not long before I'm back in the past . . .

FIFTEEN

THE FIRST THING I SEE WHEN I WAKE UP IS THE COLOR of wheat.

The first thing I think is *Vian*.

I sleep in his bed now and still call it his bed, even though it was mine for the years before he came and has been mine for the years since he left. I sleep here to feel closer to him but, geographically, we could hardly be farther apart.

My eyes drift to the postcards Blu-Tacked to the wall around the painting: surfers riding waves, rugged Australian coastlines, backwater towns with tin roofs, and fishing boats, big and small . . .

My friends have posters—everything from Bros and Milli Vanilli to Guns N' Roses and George Michael—but I have only postcards and they are all from Vian.

He doesn't write as much as he used to. He's been busy with school and surfing and work. I can't imagine being at sea for days on end, but he often goes out on the prawn boats with his father. It all seems very alien to me.

My alarm jolts me from my daze. I roll over and turn it off before getting out of bed, shivering on my way to the window. The tide is in and the water is as still as glass, reflecting the trees that are staggered down the banks. Only a few weeks ago they were topped with red, orange and yellow, but now the branches are brown and leafless and will stay that way for months. I lean in closer to the glass to check the lawn. It's still shaded by the cottage and looks as if it's been frosted with white icing. The glass fogs up with my breath and I retreat.

Definitely a tights day. Rummaging around in my drawers, I pull out what I need and head downstairs to get ready.

Dad is cutting a lonely figure at the kitchen table, sitting there in his baggy brown cardigan with a mug of tea nursed between his hands. I remember when that old cardy was the same color as his hair, but he's almost entirely gray now. Losing Ruth so suddenly aged him.

"Hi," I say in a sleep-groggy voice.

"Morning," he replies, his smile catching me before I head into the bathroom.

He has a cup of tea ready for me by the time I reemerge, dressed in my school uniform.

"Scrambled eggs?" I ask, planting a kiss on his cheek.

"That would be lovely," he says gratefully, squeezing my shoulder.

I always make my own breakfast and, if he hasn't already left for work when I come downstairs, his too.

He lost a lot of weight after Ruth died, and hasn't put anywhere near enough back on. I try to help where I can.

After the accident, Mum wanted me to move to France. She didn't think Dad would be able to cope with me, not when we were both so thick in the midst of grief. But I fought tooth and nail to stay. I couldn't think of anything worse than leaving him on his own.

It has been hard, though. And that is one hell of an understatement.

Losing Ruth broke us all, but losing Vian too . . . Well, that was just . . . Words cannot describe how I felt—how I *still feel*.

Vian's father wanted him to go and live with him in Australia, and my dad told me that we had to let him go. Dad and Ruth weren't married, and Vian wasn't Dad's adopted son, so he said we had no choice.

But deep down, I believe Dad could have tried harder to keep Vian. He was like a brother to me, my metaphorical twin, my fellow pea in a pod. Ruth's death shelled us and spat us in opposite directions, far, far away from each other.

Sometimes, at night, I lie in bed, unable to sleep, and I am filled with bitterness and rage and even hatred toward my own father for letting Vian go.

So I try not to think about it.

And we rarely speak about Vian at all.

DAD AND MY friend Ellie's mum do a carpool share—Ellie's mum takes us to school on her way to work and Dad brings us home. Dad still works at Glendurgan Garden and starts early, at seven thirty, but he finishes in time to collect us. However, today Ellie's mum had a meeting so Dad is going in later.

Ellie—Eloïse Culshaw—is my best friend and lives up the hill in Mawgan, but we don't hang out as much as you'd think, considering our close proximity to each other. Dad still won't let me walk to or from her house—not after what happened to

Ruth. The country roads are winding and narrow and there are too many dangerous drivers around. They never did find the driver of the car that killed her.

Dad pulls into the cul-de-sac where Ellie lives. I need to drop off my stuff for later—I'm sleeping over tonight—so I get out of the car and run up to her front door.

I squeal when it swings open.

Yesterday afternoon, Ellie's chestnut hair came to her shoulders, but after an evening trip to the hairdresser, it is now several inches shorter, thanks to the curls. She's been wanting a perm for ages.

"What do you think?" she asks with a grin, turning this way and that.

"You look like a brunette Baby from *Dirty Dancing*!"

It is the biggest compliment I could bestow. It's our favorite film—we've watched it on video a thousand times.

"Here, let me take that." Ellie grabs my bag and dumps it in the hall before pulling the door shut behind her.

We climb side by side into the back of the car. I gave up riding shotgun after I did my neck in swiveling round to talk to her.

"Your hair looks cool," she notes. "Did you scrunch it?"

"Yep." My hair has a slight kink to it anyway, but with mousse and a diffuser, I can get it to go curly.

"For the party?" She gives me a conspiratorial nudge.

Dad's ears prick up. "What party?" he asks from the front.

"Brad Milton's sixteenth," I reply, giving Ellie a look that says, *Here we go . . .*

Brad is our classmate Brooke's older brother—they're only a year apart in age and it's largely down to the two of them that our year groups socialize so much.

"When did you tell me about it?" Dad asks.

"Last week," I state firmly. "It's why I'm staying at Ellie's tonight, remember? Her parents are giving us a lift."

"Where's the party?"

"At Brooke and Brad's house in Helford."

"And what time will Ellie's parents be collecting you?"

"I don't know, eleven-ish?" I roll my eyes for Ellie's benefit.

In actual fact, Ellie's older brother Graham has offered to bring us home—he has his driving license and is going to an eighteenth-birthday bash at the nearby sailing club tonight.

But Dad'll only stress out if I tell him that.

"WHAT IF HE speaks to my mum?" Ellie asks that evening when we're tottering down the steep, narrow road into Helford in our high heels. Her mum dropped us off in the car park at the top because it's hard to turn around at the bottom and if the tide is in, it's practically impossible because the road is cut off by water.

"He won't," I brush her off, trailing my fingertips over the cobbled stones jutting out of the wall to my right. Ferns sprout from between the cracks and the air is filled with the smell of damp, peaty earth and saltwater.

"He's so protective of you," Ellie says.

"*Over*protective," I correct. "But he can't wrap me up in cotton wool forever." I trip over a bump in the road and stumble, grabbing Ellie's arm to steady myself and almost pulling her down in the process. We both crack up laughing.

"You been drinking, Forrester?" comes a cheeky voice from behind us.

A glance over my shoulder reveals Drew Castor walking a

few meters behind us, grinning. He's wearing jeans with a black blazer and looks even hotter than usual.

"It's these stupid heels," I reply, facing forward again before he sees me blushing.

I have a bit of a crush on Drew. He's a friend of Brad's and has gorgeous toffee-brown hair that is too long to be called short, but too short to be considered long. I don't know what product he uses, but when he rakes it one way, it stays there, slightly sticking up, and if he shoves it in the other direction, it does the same. Sometimes it falls forward into his green eyes and I've lost minutes of my life daydreaming about being the one to push it back again. His last girlfriend had the honor, but they broke up a couple of months ago.

Can't say I cried about it.

We hear footsteps as Drew treads the asphalt to catch us up. "Are you on your way to Brad's?" he asks, falling into step beside me and taking my arm. "Keeping you upright," he jokes.

I laugh and elbow him away. "Yep. You?"

"Yep."

"Shouldn't you be coming from the other direction?" Ellie asks.

Drew's parents own the village pub a few minutes' walk farther on from here—his family lives in the cottage opposite.

"Dad wanted me to run an errand," he explains.

Drew and his older brother, Nicholas, work for their parents part-time. Nick serves behind the bar and Drew helps out in the kitchen—I've spotted him when Dad and I have been in there to eat, which sadly isn't often.

Madonna's "Like a Prayer" is blaring out of the speakers as we approach the Miltons'—a chocolate-box cottage that is hemmed in between the road on one side and the Helford

River on the other. We enter the garden via the outdoor gate to see trees rigged up with fairy lights and loads of our school friends milling around. It's far too cold to take off our coats, but we do so anyway, our arms instantly breaking out in goose bumps. I'm wearing a black, off-the-shoulder dress that comes to just above knee-length, and my thick gray school tights have been replaced by sheer black ones. It's freezing, but we stand there, teeth chattering, until everyone moves indoors.

Later, we have the opposite problem when the living room turns into a furnace. We're all crammed into the small space like sardines, with sweat coating our skin and condensation running down the windows as we dance. I glance over at Drew and not for the first time that evening, catch him already looking at me. A moment later, he heads into the kitchen.

I wait for B52s' "Love Shack" to come to an end before turning to Ellie and Brooke. "Drink?"

They nod and follow me.

Drew is at the fridge, getting out a two-liter bottle of Coke while Brad and a couple of mates tuck into a bowl of crisps.

Brad and Brooke look so alike. They're both tall with identical long, straight, blond hair. Some of the girls at school think Brad looks like Scott from *Neighbours*, but I'd say that's a little optimistic.

"Can you pour us some of those?" Brooke asks Drew.

"Sure."

I feel Drew watching me as I separate disposable cups from a tall stack and line them up on the counter.

"You look hot," he says.

Our friends fall about, sniggering.

"I meant *warm*," Drew mutters with a smirk, pouring fizzing liquid into the cups. "Not that she doesn't look hot in the other sense too," he murmurs flippantly, his dimple making an appearance as he gives me a cheeky grin.

My heart skips at the compliment and I can't help blushing. Again.

Brooke picks up a paper plate to fan my face.

I laugh and shove her arm. "Right, that's it. I'm going outside to cool down."

We all go, and the December air is blissful on our hot, clammy skin as we wander down to the bank. Drew's parents' pub is directly across the creek from here, and the reflection of the outdoor lights strung up around the deck sparkles in the dark water.

"Do you still have that Saturday job at the café?" Drew asks me.

"No, annoyingly." I used to work up near the sailing club. "They don't get enough customers over the winter, but said to come back in the summer. What about you—you didn't have to work tonight?" I have to look up at him—I'm only five foot four and he's getting on for six foot.

"No. I'm doing tomorrow night and all day Sunday instead."

"Do you like it in the kitchen?"

He shrugs. "It's all right. I'd prefer to be behind the bar."

"You'll have to wait a couple of years, though, I guess?" That's when he'll turn eighteen.

He gives me a wry smile and shakes his head, his eyes glinting in the fairy lights hanging from the trees. "I doubt Nick will ever let me muscle in on his turf—he likes pulling the girls too much."

I roll my eyes and sip my drink. I'm aware of his brother's reputation.

"What are you up to this weekend, then?" Drew asks, raking his hair to the right.

"I'm hanging out with Ellie. I'm staying at hers tonight. You?"

"Surfing with my brother and some mates."

"I can't believe you go out in winter."

"It's the best time!" His perfect white teeth gleam as he smiles. "The waves are bigger and better and there are way less tourists."

"I can't surf," I say. "I started a course once when I was ten, but . . ." My voice trails off.

"You didn't like it?"

"No, I did." I hesitate before explaining, but I've started now so I decide to continue. "We'd only done one lesson when my dad's girlfriend died—I don't know if you remember that."

"Yeah, of course I do. I'm sorry. Didn't your . . . Well, he wasn't your real brother, but what was his name?"

"Vian."

"Didn't he have to go and live in Australia?"

"Yeah. Now *he* can surf," I say proudly. "He's actually won a couple of competitions."

Drew looks impressed. "Well, if you're not working tomorrow, you're welcome to come with us. There's room in Nick's car."

"Oh! Thanks." I'm thrown by his easy invite.

"Oi, Nell, is that your dad?" Brad interrupts.

I shoot my head around to see an all-too-familiar figure hovering by the garden gate.

"Hang on," I mutter, hurrying away. "Dad! What is it? What's wrong?"

He shakes his head at me and I'm filled with dread. *Vian?*

"You said Ellie's parents would be taking you home." My father's voice is laden with accusation. "Why didn't you tell me it was her brother? He's only just got his license."

I stare at him, gobsmacked. Is that why he's here? To pick me up and drive me home rather than let Graham take us?

"But I'm staying at Ellie's!"

"I'm here to give you *both* a lift. I've spoken to her parents. Come on, get your coat," he urges. "What are you doing outside without one?"

"But . . . But . . . it's only ten thirty," I stutter. How could he do this to me?

Out of the corner of my eye, I see Ellie approaching.

"Is everything OK?"

"Dad's here to give us a lift home." My eyes convey my absolute mortification at the situation.

"Oh," she says. "But—"

"We'll go via the sailing club to let Graham know," Dad says. "I'm parked up the hill."

"We'll meet you there," I tell him through gritted teeth. "We need to say goodbye to our friends."

Thankfully, he concedes.

I make my way back to Drew and the others.

"We've got to go," I tell Drew miserably. "I'll have to ask my dad about tomorrow. He's a bit funny about other people driving me places."

"Oh, right." He looks bemused. "Call the pub and let me know. Ellie too, if she likes."

"What's this?" Ellie asks.

"I'll tell you on the walk to the car," I interrupt, mumbling my goodbyes to everyone and giving Brooke a hug.

On the way home, my disappointment and embarrassment give way to anger. I sit there, seething, while Ellie makes awkward small talk with Dad.

I know he only came to get me because he's worried about me, but he can't keep treating me like a child—I'm fifteen!

"Ellie and I want to go to the beach tomorrow with Andrew and Nicholas Castor," I state as he pulls up outside Ellie's house.

It's the first thing I've said since we set off.

"Nicholas is giving us a lift," I add.

Dad shakes his head. "I don't trust Nicholas Castor."

"Dad, this is ridiculous!" I shout, making poor Ellie flinch.

"I'll just . . ." she starts to say quietly, opening the door and getting out.

I wait for her to shut the door before continuing. "Tonight was so humiliating! What was wrong with Graham bringing us home? He was right there in Helford!"

"You should have told me," he says crossly.

"I didn't because I knew you'd freak out about it! I want to go to the beach tomorrow and I want you to let Drew's older brother take me."

"Absolutely not."

I shake my head, tears of frustration filling my eyes. "Dad, I can't bear this. What happened was . . . *awful* . . ." I shudder. "But I'm not Ruth! I need space and independence! I bet Vian gets lifts from friends all the time. In fact," I say, as the rage that I sometimes feel at night begins to swallow me up, "I bet, if he was still here, you'd let him get into a car with just about anyone. You didn't give enough of a shit about him to keep him, so why would you care who he hangs out with?"

"How could you say that?" Dad looks stunned. "I didn't have a choice—"

"Ruth would be so disappointed if she knew what had happened to him—what *you'd* let happen."

Even in the darkness of the car, I can see that his face has drained of color.

"Oh, Nell," he murmurs, and a wave of guilt swiftly snuffs out my anger. "I miss Vian as much as you do."

"How can you say that?" I'm agog at his claim. "That is such a *lie*! I think *Scampi* missed him more than you did when he left! You never talk about him—"

"I don't talk about him because I know it hurts you to be reminded of him!" he cuts me off. "And the reason I know that is because *it hurts me too*! But that doesn't mean I don't miss him, and despite what you say, Ruth *would* have wanted him to be with his biological father. She felt guilty that John and Vian didn't have a proper relationship."

His eyes are glistening as he reaches into his back pocket for his wallet, pulling out a folded scrap of paper. "I think about him all the time," he says as he hands the paper to me. I open it up and stare down in a daze. "I've carried this with me ever since he left."

It's one of the edges from Vian's green painting that Dad trimmed off almost five years ago.

The lump in my throat trebles in size.

"I still miss him so much!" I burst into tears. "I don't feel like I know him anymore, who he is now. He sounds so different on the phone. I'd give anything to see him again."

"Maybe he could come and visit," Dad suggests gently. "Perhaps I could offer to buy his ticket. I've been putting some money aside," he divulges as my insides fill with hope. "It was supposed to be for a car for you, but . . ." His voice trails off.

"I can't imagine you ever letting me get behind the wheel myself," I mumble.

"No, maybe not." He purses his lips.

"Could he come for Christmas?" I ask.

"We could call and see?"

"Now?"

"What about Ellie?"

"I'm not in the mood for a sleepover," I reply. "She'll understand. I'll grab my stuff and let her know."

IT'S AFTER ELEVEN by the time we get home, which means it's Saturday morning in Australia. As I stand in the hall with the phone pressed to my ear, feeling flatter with every second that passes without Vian answering, I think back to one of the last times I saw him. He was stoically fighting back tears as his dad knelt in front of him, saying that he couldn't wait to take him home.

John scared me, the first time I saw him. He was so tall, much taller than my dad, and he had to bend right down to pass through the rooms of our cottage. I remember that his clothes seemed dark and foreboding, and he had a bushy, black beard. I couldn't believe we were letting this giant of a man take our beloved Vian away.

But when he knelt down, I was glad to see that his face was kind.

I shake my head quickly—I can't bear to think about those hellish days. I've tried to block most of them out. But sometimes, I can't escape the nightmares, where I'll be running, running, running up the road, trying to prevent Vian from reaching his mother's broken, lifeless body and my father screaming with agony at her side.

I fail to stop him in my dreams, just as I did in reality.

There's a click at the other end of the line.

"Hello?"

"It's me, Nell!"

A beat passes. "Hi."

He has an Australian accent now—and a deep voice. I still remember when it broke: in the months between us speaking, Vian turned into a stranger.

"I thought you must be out surfing," I say.

"No, the phone ringing woke me up."

"Oh, sorry." He does sound sleepy, I realize.

"S'OK."

We don't speak often and not simply because it's expensive. It's actually kind of awkward. Vian isn't much of a talker—he never was.

"Are you all right?" he asks.

"Yes." I glance at Dad. "I have something to ask you. Dad and I have been talking and we wanted to know if we could persuade you to come here for Christmas. Dad wants to pay for your ticket."

There's no answer from the other end of the line.

"This Christmas?" he asks after what feels like forever.

"Yes, as in, a few weeks' away."

There's another long pause. "I'm not sure," he replies eventually. "I'd have to ask my dad."

"Why, because you're working? Can't you get out of it? Your dad wouldn't mind, would he? We miss you!" I ramble. "Hang on, Dad wants to talk to you."

I place the phone in Dad's waiting hands and pace the

floor, crossing my fingers while I listen to my father offer to speak to John on Vian's behalf. Eventually they say their good-byes and Dad hangs up.

"He says he'll ask," Dad repeats what Vian told me. "He'll call us back."

"When?"

"I don't know, but it won't be in the next few hours so we may as well get some sleep."

It belatedly occurs to me how tired he looks—the bags under his eyes are protruding almost as far out from his face as his bushy eyebrows do.

I feel a rush of affection and step forward to give him a hug. "I love you. Thank you."

He kisses the top of my head. "I love you too," he says. "I'm sorry if I embarrassed you tonight. It's only because I care."

"I know," I mumble. "But *please*, Dad, you're going to have to lay off a bit."

"I'll try," he promises gruffly.

THE NEXT MORNING, Vian calls with news—his dad has said yes! He breaks up from school at around the same time as me, but has the whole of January off, so we get straight onto booking his tickets.

"Where will he sleep?" I ask Dad, wondering if he'd still fit in my bunk.

"I was thinking we could clear out the annex and turn it into a guest room."

I'm hit with a memory of Vian and me standing on the stairs, shouting at our parents.

They wanted us to have separate rooms.

At the time, of course, we didn't understand why boys and girls shouldn't sleep together, but now . . .

Dad is still waiting for my response.

"That sounds great." I try to sound bright and breezy. "Shall we get started on it today?"

ON MONDAY, I bump into Drew coming out of the dining hall.

"How was the surfing?" I ask.

"Good," he replies coolly.

Uh-oh. I've messed up. I've been so sidetracked by Vian that it didn't even occur to me to call the pub and let him know I couldn't go to the beach.

"Sorry I couldn't come," I say quickly, going on to elaborate more than I would've under different circumstances. "I had a huge falling-out with my dad. It was awful, but it ended up with him asking Vian to come and stay for Christmas!"

"That's great!"

"Maybe we could take him surfing when he comes?" I go on to ask, hopefully.

"Absolutely." He flashes me his dimple. "Keep me posted."

I definitely, definitely will . . .

TWO WEEKS LATER, Dad and I go to collect Vian from the airport. I'm buzzing with nervous excitement as we stand in the Arrivals hall, waiting for him to come through. Will we even recognize him? I haven't seen a photo of him in years. His dad sent us a picture of him in his school uniform when he was about twelve, but that's the last one I remember.

"There he is!" Dad cries, waving madly.

I follow the line of his sight and my jaw hits the floor.

If I thought Vian *sounded* like a stranger, it's nothing compared to how he *looks*.

My eyes travel up . . .

. . . and up . . .

. . . and up . . .

. . . until he's standing in front of us and I'm cricking my neck, staring up at the human version of the Eiffel Tower.

Dad throws his arms around this . . . this . . . *alien* . . . while I stand there, completely lost for words.

He must be six foot three or four—taller than Dad by at least half a foot—and very slim, as if his body has been stretched and he hasn't had a chance to fill it out yet. His sleek head of dark, slightly wavy hair comes to well past his chin, and he's wearing black jeans and a denim jacket over a gray hoodie.

The two of them break apart and then Vian's arms are around me and he's hugging me hard. My heart is going haywire—can he hear it? Can he feel it pounding against his ribcage?

Who are you?

He withdraws and looks down at me, his smile reaching his dark-blue eyes.

I blush and avert my gaze, but as Dad starts to natter on, asking about the flight and whether he managed to get any sleep, my attention is drawn back to Vian's face, taking in his long, dark lashes, his striking, angular brows, his sharp, high cheekbones and his dead-straight nose.

I try to focus on what's being said and realize that he even *sounds* different than he did on the phone.

Man, this is freaking me out.

"Come on, let's get to the car," Dad says in a no-nonsense tone, taking Vian's suitcase.

Vian slings a battered army-green canvas rucksack over his shoulder. I give him a shy sideways glance as we walk and he catches my eye.

"You look so different," he says.

I can't help it. I burst out laughing.

"What?" he asks with a frown.

"*You're* unrecognizable!" I exclaim.

His face breaks into a wide grin, making the angles of his face look even more pronounced.

"It's been a while," he says, but the humor I heard in his voice vanishes from his expression.

THE CLOSER WE get to home, the more on edge Vian becomes. I've been sitting in the back, watching him, and I've noticed the tension creeping into the set of his shoulders and the butterflying of his jaw as he grinds his teeth.

The conversation dried up a while ago—he always was quiet in the car, preferring to sit and stare out of the window than chat incessantly like Ellie and me. He and Dad have that in common, at least, so the silence has been relatively comfortable.

"I recognize this village," Vian murmurs.

"Yes, we're not far from home," Dad replies.

When we pull up outside our cottage, nobody gets out of the car. It's a bright, crisp winter's day and the silvery slate tiles are glinting in the sunlight. Between the crack in the buildings, green grass rolls down to the river, and beyond that, the tide is out, and small rivers from the creek carve through the thick mud on their way out to sea.

Dad turns to look at Vian, and from his side profile, I can see my father's unkempt eyebrows pulling together with concern. "How about a cup of tea and a cookie?" he asks.

In his mind, those two things could solve quite a lot.

The air is punctuated by the sound of car doors clunking shut, Dad's keys jangling, and the scuffling of Vian's suitcase on the narrow garden path, but Vian's pain resonates through all of that and hits me square in the gut. As Dad passes through the gate and opens the front door, Vian hangs back, staring at the annex—once his mother's studio.

Scampi squeezes out past Dad, instantly diverting Vian's attention.

"Scampi!" He laughs and sinks to his knees as Scampi's tail waggles excitedly from side to side. Vian cups the dog's head, chuckling as Scampi licks his cheeks. Scampi breaks away to greet me in the same manner, but Vian stays kneeling on the freezing paving stones, his eyes glistening with tears as he watches his old friend scamper back inside.

"How do you like your tea, Vian?" Dad sounds jovial, but Vian jolts visibly.

"Milk, one sugar, please," he replies in a strained voice, getting to his feet. His narrow shoulders hunch upward and inward as he follows Dad into the kitchen.

"Are you OK?" I whisper when we're sitting at the table and Dad is at the sink, filling the kettle.

Vian nods, but his attention is fixed on the dog rather than me.

"Do you want to have a look around first?" I ask.

He hesitates, then nods again.

"I'm going to show Vian the cottage," I tell Dad, getting to my feet.

Vian's chair legs screech on the tiles as he pushes out from the table, making Dad and me cringe.

He only ever used to do that when he was angry or upset . . .

"Everything seems so small," he comments, when I lead him through to the living room. He takes in the cozy space with its low ceiling and tiny windows. This is the original part of the four-hundred-year-old cottage, and it still has traditional cob walls, made from mud, straw, and stone. The bathroom, hall and kitchen were a later extension.

"Careful on the stairs," I warn, nodding at his head as we walk up. He has to duck under the beams and beneath the doorframe when we go into my room.

His eyes rove from the window to the chest of drawers to the bunk bed.

"You wouldn't fit in it now." I state the obvious.

"No," he agrees, bending down to look at the wall and freezing.

"I still have your picture," I say. "And all of your postcards."

His dark hair has swung forward to obstruct his face, but I have a clear view of his Adam's apple bobbing up and down, once, twice, three times.

"And if you look under . . ." I point at the wooden slats holding the top mattress, "you'll see I still have all of your stars too."

He says nothing, so I fill the silence.

"We've turned the studio—I mean, the *annex*—into a guest room."

My correction was fast but not effective, judging by the mask of agony he's wearing when he straightens back up.

Before I can say anything, Dad calls up the stairs.

"Kids! Tea's ready!"

"We're not kids anymore," Vian mumbles, more to himself than me, I think.

He's agitated as we sit at the table. He keeps glancing toward the door and I know that he's impatient to get the rest of his walk down memory lane over.

Dad is eager to show off what we've done to the annex, but the invisible thread that tied me to Vian—though pulled thin and tight—still connects us and I can feel his grief as his eyes rake over the pale-blue, freshly painted walls, the double bed with its red-and-navy-striped bedspread, and the new rugs on the polished floorboards. The old built-in wardrobes still line one wall, but Dad points out a chest of drawers for him to put his things in instead. Vian wears a polite smile throughout all of this, but his eyes are flat and dead.

"It's great," he says blandly.

"You could have my room if you prefer," I offer hastily. "He might prefer to be in the house," I say to Dad, who is clearly wondering what on earth has got into me. *After all our work!* "I'd be more than happy out here," I persist.

"But—" Dad starts to say, flummoxed.

"No, this is amazing," Vian cuts him off. "Really." He almost sounds sincere, and then he smiles at me—properly. "Still the same," he mouths, prompting a bubble of happiness to burst inside me.

"Right then," Dad interrupts awkwardly. "Vian, would you like to freshen up? I could run you a bath?"

Vian nods, but when he speaks again, the strain is back in his voice. "That'd be great."

"Want to have a quick look down on the deck first?" I ask.

"OK."

"Don't slip," I caution as we make our way down the hill.

"I can't believe how steep it is!"

"We used to roll down. Do you remember?"

"Yeah." His expression is tainted by sadness and I realize then that every memory of ours is contaminated. I try not to dwell on that thought, concentrating on navigating the slick, slimy deck instead.

"Wow," he says drily, staring at our small, grubby rowing boat, resting, lopsided, on the muddy riverbed.

"Want to go out in it?" I joke.

He wrinkles his nose. "Maybe another day. You know, when the tide is actually in. Hey, what happened to Webster?"

"She grew up and we let her go."

He raises one eyebrow. "She?"

I smile and nod. "She came back a few times after we set her free, but after that, she disappeared, until . . ." I pause for dramatic effect, "the following spring she appeared with ten ducklings!"

"No way!" He's delighted.

"Yep, she wandered straight into the house with them—I couldn't believe it! I'm sure it was her."

"It *must've* been! Did she keep coming?"

"Only for a few weeks." I purse my lips. "I'm afraid she was a terrible mother. Her ducklings kept dwindling until she only had about three left."

"Vian!" Dad calls from up at the house, and I'm not sure if it's his voice or the news about the ducklings that makes Vian grimace. "Bath's ready!"

Vian closes his eyes and hooks his hands behind his neck, not making any move to leave.

"What is it?" I ask him.

He sighs heavily, and when he speaks, he sounds resigned. "It's the way you guys say my name."

"What do you mean?"

"Dad, my friends, *everyone*—they call me Van."

I pull a face. "Van? But your name's Vian."

Again, he winces. "No," he says. "Now, it's Van."

"But . . . *why*?" I don't understand. "Since when?"

"*Years*," he replies, and my mind presents me with a mental image of the "V" that he signs his postcards with. When did that start? "Dad called me Van when I first went over there. It stuck."

"But . . . But . . ." I splutter again. "That's . . . *No!* Your name is *Vian*, not *Van*!" I screw up my nose.

"I *like* Van." He's not only defensive, he's angry.

I take a step backward, part of me afraid of the hostility radiating from him, and another part feeling a thrill at the force of his glare. *Now* he's familiar to me.

I shake my head, unwilling to give up on this. "Can't you be Vian to us?"

"No," he replies firmly. "My name is *Van*. Are you going to break it to your dad, or am I? Because it will really piss me off if you don't call me that."

My insides blaze with unexpected fury. I stalk past him and up to the cottage.

WHY DIDN'T HE correct his dad? How could he let it slide? Isn't it bad enough that so much changed after he left? Why would he want to lose his name too? He's already like a stranger to me—this makes it even worse.

"Vian is a beautiful old English name," Dad laments with a frown. "It's very unusual."

Vian rhymes with *Ian*. Van rhymes with, well, *van*. I know there's only one letter in it, one syllable, but they feel completely different to me.

Dad and I are sitting in the living room, quietly talking while Vian—*Van*—is in the bathroom.

"Vian, Van," I say out loud, trying on the accent that I've picked up from religiously watching Aussie soaps. "Don't chuck a mental, *Van*. I suppose they do sound more similar with the Australian accent."

Dad pats my knee benevolently. "Well, it *is his* name."

The bathroom door clicks open and Vian emerges in a cloud of steam. His dark hair is dripping water onto his orange T-shirt, making it look as red as blood.

"Do you want a hair dryer?" I ask.

"No, it's all right."

"Don't catch a cold," Dad chides with a frown.

"I'll be fine, thanks."

"How about I make a fire, then?" Dad suggests. "We could have a mince pie, Nell?"

"OK." I take my cue to leave, not meeting Vian's eyes on my way out. I'm surprised when he joins me in the kitchen a moment later.

He leans back against the counter, his knuckles white as he grips the countertop on either side of his hips. I don't know what to say so I choose silence as I switch on the oven to heat the mince pies and set about making more tea. He's so quiet as I wait for the kettle to boil that I wonder if he's still there. Curiosity gets the better of me and I shoot a look at him. He's staring at the floor and he seems so exhausted and full of misery that I'm hit with remorse.

He glances up and meets my eyes.

I open my mouth to say I'm sorry, but he speaks first.

"It reminds me of her," he explains. "Mum. Every time you or your dad say my name, I think of her. You three were the last people to call me Vian." He hangs his head.

I try to swallow the lump in my throat, but I can't. Instinctively, I walk over and stand, flush to his side with my back against the counter.

"Vian died with her," he whispers as my eyes fill with tears.

"I'll try to remember to call you Van," I mumble, resting my cheek against his shoulder and adding more splashes of blood-red to his shirt.

I feel as though I've lost my childhood friend all over again. I'm grieving him.

THE NEXT DAY is Tuesday, four days before Christmas. I come downstairs at seven o'clock—the crack of dawn for me when it's not a school day—to find Vian lounging on the couch, his long legs dangling over the end and his bare feet tangled up in Scampi's black and white fur. He has a book in his hands and a CD Walkman resting on his stomach, the tinny strains of INXS's "Kick" playing out of his headphones.

Scampi's bushy tail thuds on the carpet at the sight of me.

"You're awake!"

"I've been awake for hours," he replies with a wry smile, putting his stuff on the floor and propping himself up on his elbows.

I feel slightly self-conscious in my pink-and-white polka-dot PJs and fluffy slippers, especially when I see that he's already dressed. I'm sure my hair looks like a yellow bird's nest.

"Have you had any breakfast?"

"Your dad got me some cereal."

"Are you still hungry? I'm a whiz at omelets."

"Sounds great." He sits up properly and swings his legs around to the floor, reaching for his discarded socks and pulling them on.

The shower is running. I knock as we walk past the bathroom, calling to ask if Dad wants to join us.

"Yes, please, I'll be out in a minute," he calls back.

We only have the one bathroom—the bane of my life—so we've both learned to be quick.

Scampi follows us through to the kitchen, his nails clip-clipping on the floor tiles.

"Do you think he remembers me?" Vian asks, kneeling and rigorously scratching behind the dog's ears. Scampi pants with happy contentment and then flops on the floor, upturning his belly.

"Looks like it," I say to be kind, although in truth I'm doubtful. If I think that Vian looks and sounds like a stranger, I can't imagine how Scampi might know who he is after almost five years. He'd be friendly like this with anyone.

"We thought we'd go and get a Christmas tree today," I tell Vian, cracking an egg into a bowl and reaching for another. Usually we'd have the house Christmassified at least a week before now, but we held off for Vian because we thought it might be a nice thing to do together, to get us in the festive spirit.

"Dad and I never bother with trees and tinsel," he confides, sitting on the floor and drawing one very blissed-out dog onto his lap. "It's too much of a hassle to take it all down again. Plus we've been hectic at work."

"What's prawn fishing like?" I ask, because I really have no idea.

"Full on," he replies.

"I mean, how does it work? What do you actually do?"

"We shoot the nets out at sundown, and the second it's sun-up, we've got to get them up straight away. Then we separate the prawns from all the other rubbish, box them up, and snap-freeze them. I've sometimes gone eighteen hours without sitting down, and I might only get three hours' sleep before I'm back at it again the next day."

"Whoa!" I exclaim. "How long does that routine go on for?"

"We were away for seventeen nights on our last trip."

"*Seventeen nights?*" I'm astonished. I had no idea he was out at sea for that long.

"It takes a day to get out and a day to get back. But we get a lot of time off too. You can't trawl for prawns when there's a full moon, as they all disappear."

I've stopped making breakfast because I'm too absorbed in what he's saying.

"Is it ever scary?" I ask, settling myself on the floor opposite him.

He shrugs. "Can be, if one of your nets hooks up on a rock or whatever. The whole boat leans right over and you can capsize in bad weather. We've hooked up a car before." He grins. "A Volkswagen Beetle off the coast of Whyalla. Some fishermen had dumped it to create an artificial reef. They marked it on their GPS so they could find it again, but obviously we didn't have it on ours."

"That's nuts!"

"Yeah. The worst thing is the seasickness. We trawl in the Spencer Gulf and when there's a strong wind against the tide, you get really short, sharp waves. You're thrashed around more than you would be in the middle of the ocean. Then there's the crabs that pinch and the fish that sting—your whole arm will be throbbing, all the way up to your armpit. It's excruciating, but it doesn't matter if you're vomiting or have the shakes—you've got to keep on working through all of it."

"It sounds absolutely *horrible*!" I can't believe he's doing all this and he's only fifteen!

He chuckles. "Yeah, it's hard work."

Dad walks into the kitchen and starts with surprise at the sight of us both sitting on the floor.

"Everything OK?"

"Yep!" I jump to my feet. "Vian's been telling me—"

Vian's smile dies on his face.

"Sorry," I say contritely. "I'm not sure I'll ever get used to calling you Van."

"Try," he pleads.

"DON'T YOU HAVE a warmer coat?" Dad asks as we're leaving the house.

"Only this one," Vian replies. He's wearing the same outerwear as yesterday.

Dad frowns. "You'll be freezing. Let me see if I have something that'll fit."

Vian rocks on his heels as we wait outside the cottage. He's wearing scuffed black Chelsea boots.

"How was the annex?" I ask, making conversation as his attention drifts toward the door. "Was it warm enough?"

"Yeah, fine." He swallows. "When did you clear it out?"

"A couple of weeks ago."

He shoots me a sharp look. "Only a couple of weeks ago?"

I nod. "It's been locked up since . . ." My voice trails off. "We only did it up for you."

He's staggered.

Dad returns with a long, grass-green scarf and his old Barbour jacket, saying out loud that he hopes the extra layers will be enough. "Oh, gloves!" he exclaims, hurrying back into the house.

Vian wraps the scarf around his neck. "Is this yours?" he asks me.

"Because it's green?" I smile, feeling a little funny inside. I shake my head. "No, it's Dad's."

He nods and pulls the jacket on over his denim one. "I remember this," he says. "It looks too big for your dad now."

"He's shrinking in his old age," I whisper jokily, trying to ignore the pang of worry that follows. He's only fifty, but sometimes I think he looks closer in age to Ellie's grandfather than to her father.

THAT AFTERNOON, WE play festive music and decorate the house. The smell of fresh pine mingles with the scent of mince pies heating in the oven as we hang ornaments on the tree and drape garlands from the curtain rails. But all attempts by Dad and me at camaraderie are falling flat, and eventually Vian asks if we'd mind him going to his room for a rest.

"Do you think it's *just* jet-lag?" I ask Dad with concern as we sit at the kitchen table, our mince pies untouched.

"I don't know, Nell," he replies heavily. "I wonder if we should get it out of the way."

When we cleared out the studio, we kept all of Ruth's things that Vian might want—her paintings, her art materials, even her old smocks. It's all right there, under his nose in the annex, locked in the built-in wardrobes. We've been waiting for the right time to show him.

I drag myself into the hall and pull on my shoes. It's only a few meters to the annex, but I feel chilled to my bones as Dad knocks on the wooden door, neither of us saying a word.

"Come in," Vian calls.

He's lying on his bed, but sits up when we enter.

Dad takes the lead in explaining, and as he gets out a small key, Vian's eyes dart to the wardrobes. He's racked with tension and half covers his face with his hands as he hunches forward and stares, waiting for the contents to be revealed. And then I see his nostrils flare and his eyes widen as the astringent smell hits him full force. Previously muffled by the scent of freshly painted walls and new carpet rugs, now the aroma that was once so familiar to us as children is completely overwhelming. Vian's bottom lip begins to tremble and his eyes fill with tears as he stares at the stack of canvases propped against the wall. The one at the front is of us—him and me—building a sand-castle at the beach. It's more realistic than most of the pictures Ruth used to paint, but still has elements of her trademark abstract style in the bold streaks of rock, rich in grays and browns, and the graduated color of the water, beginning with brilliant aquamarine by the shore and ending in emerald green farther out.

We were about seven when Ruth painted it, and I still remember the yellow swimming costume that I wore, right down to its frills around my chest and legs. Vian is wearing pale-blue shorts and is bare-chested, his skin golden and his dark hair coming almost to his chin. It was the way he wore it then, before he had it all cut off the following year. It's not dissimilar to how it is now.

"Do you want us to leave you to it?" Dad asks.

This goes completely against my natural instincts, but before I can intervene, Vian nods, tearfully. I watch with a swollen throat as teardrops slip from his eyes and run down his nose. He doesn't look at us as we walk out the door, even when I hesitate. I want to go to him so badly, but Dad draws me away.

"He wouldn't want us to see him cry," he murmurs as he closes the door behind us.

How would he know?

As I lie in my own fog of misery on my bed, it occurs to me that maybe Dad's the one who can't handle seeing our grief. He has also retired to his bedroom and for once our tiny cottage feels like a mansion.

VIAN DOESN'T EMERGE for dinner and when Dad finally agrees to let me check on him, I find him curled up and fast asleep under the covers of his bed.

At some point in the night, I bolt awake to hear a door opening downstairs. Without another thought, I leap from my bed, hoping to catch Vian before he returns to the annex. I'm too late. The front door is closed, the bathroom empty and the cistern filling.

My eyes are stinging and my body feels weighted with

exhaustion, but I don't even stop to put shoes on before running out the front door and rapping on the door to the annex.

Vian opens it a moment later, wearing jeans and a gray T-shirt with a neon graphic on the front.

"Hi!" He's taken aback.

"Can I come in?" I hop from foot to foot on the freezing paving stones.

He looks down at my bare feet with alarm and opens the door wide.

"You're dressed." I shiver as I pass into his room. It's lit only by his bedside lamp.

"I wasn't going back to sleep," he replies.

"What time is it?"

"Three thirty."

"Shit! Really?" I hug myself to keep warm, but my teeth are chattering.

"Get under the covers," he instructs with a frown, flipping them back for me.

I don't need to be told twice. I snuggle under the warmth of his duvet, pulling it up to my chin. A glance to my right reveals that the wardrobe doors are closed again.

Vian sits on the end of the bed, bringing my attention back to him. "What are you doing up?"

"I heard you in the bathroom. I was worried about you."

"I'm OK," he says simply.

My eyes drift again to the wardrobes. "Are you sure?"

"No," he whispers and I sharply meet his gaze. "But people don't tend to want to hear that."

"I do," I say quickly. "You can talk to me about anything."

"Still?" The look in his eyes is heart-rending and suddenly

I see in him the boy that I grew up with, the boy who used to be able to confide in me, and vice versa.

"Definitely." My nose prickles. "I haven't changed."

"We all change," he says wearily.

"At our cores, we're the same."

He bites his bottom lip and looks down. "Maybe."

There you are, Vian . . .

"Do you still paint?" I find myself asking.

He shakes his head. "Not since Mum died."

"But you were so good at it!"

"I was *ten*," he states.

"Yes, but even your mum said you were talented."

"She was my mother, she had to say that."

"No, that's not true," I insist fervently. "Dad thought you were talented too. I still have your Fudge and Smudge stones— do you remember?"

"I noticed they're not on your windowsill anymore."

I cringe. "I put them away a couple of years ago. All of my friends were doing up their rooms and, I don't know, they seemed a bit . . . immature."

He grins at my discomfort. "Don't worry, I get it. Do you still write?"

"Not about Fudge and Smudge."

He frowns. "Why not?"

"That was our story," I say. "It reminded me too much of you."

He reaches over and squeezes my hand.

"Your fingers are ice-cold!" It detracts from the unfamiliarity of his hand in mine. "Get into bed too."

He hesitates, but does as I suggest. We lie side by side, our heads on our pillows, facing each other. We probably lay like this a thousand times as children, and I keep that fact in mind as I try to get accustomed to this new "Van," hoping he'll fill the place in my heart that Vian did.

"What's your dad like?" I want to know more about his life now. Postcards and rare phone chats don't cut it.

He takes a deep breath and pauses for thought. "He's cool. He's a lot younger than your dad, did you know that?"

I shake my head.

"Mum was only twenty when she had me. She and Dad were the same age. I didn't realize Mum and Geoff had an age gap of fifteen years."

"Neither did I." I'm startled, to be honest.

"Mum was in Australia on a gap year when she met my dad," Vian continues. "He was doing a stint up the coast, taking tourists out on a sailing boat, and she was a stewardess. They had a holiday fling. She didn't know she was pregnant until after she'd returned to the UK. Her mum convinced her that she should raise me on her own—I don't know why—but after my grandma died, Mum changed her mind. She and Dad hadn't stayed in touch, but Mum hunted him down by ringing the pubs in Port Lincoln, where Dad grew up, asking if anyone knew him. Apparently, she only remembered the name of the place after studying the seaside towns in South Australia on a map and trying to jog her memory."

"When was this?" I ask.

"Not long before we came to live with you."

I'm lapping up these new facts that put things into perspective, things that I probably wouldn't have understood when I was younger.

"Had you always lived in Cornwall?" I ask.

"No, we were with my grandma in Somerset, but Mum used to visit Cornwall as a child and after my grandma died, she rented a room in a B&B for the summer so she could paint. She met your dad at the gardens where he works."

"Glendurgan," I remind him.

"That's right. Mum used to paint there and I was *so bored*," he groans. "Your dad would chat to us and try to entertain me. He used to show me butterflies and bugs and stuff while Mum was working."

"They got serious so quickly. I wonder how that happened," I muse. "I mean, I love my dad, but he's not what I'd call a catch. Mum always used to say he was a bit of a hermit. How did he pull your mum? She was so young and attractive."

He smiles. "I think he used to make her laugh."

I wrinkle my nose. "I wouldn't exactly describe him as funny."

"I don't know how he did it, but she was very fond of him. He was kind to her—and me—and he loved her, he really did. I don't remember Mum having a boyfriend or anyone when we lived with Grandma. I don't remember much of those days at all, apart from Grandma always telling me off," he says with a rueful smile.

"Dad still works at those gardens," I tell him.

"Does he? I'd like to go back. That maze! You were so annoyed the first time we did it together and I beat you to the middle."

I crack up laughing, clapping my hand over my mouth to hold in the sound. "That's right!" I whisper loudly. "I was so pissed off! I was *intent* on beating you—I'd been in that maze more times than I could count and I thought I was such an expert, but you *still* managed to get to the middle before me!"

We were only five at the time.

He laughs. "I can't even recall how many times I'd done it before you came to Cornwall that summer. Mum was at those gardens every freaking day for what felt like weeks. I could've done that maze blindfolded."

"Dad'll be at work again after Christmas," I say. "We could go then."

"Yeah, I'd like that." He stares at me, thoughtfully. "I'm sad you don't write about Fudge and Smudge anymore."

"They were just silly stories."

"No, they weren't. They were good."

"Like your artwork was good," I reply pointedly.

He rolls his eyes and looks up at the ceiling. "Where was that place that had the Fudge and Smudge tree?"

"I'm not sure where you mean."

"It was on a cliff by the ocean, and you could see the river mouth. There was this old gnarled tree that had been split apart by lightning and you said it would make a perfect home for Fudge and Smudge, but then you set it by the river and made it a crab-apple tree so the Spriggens would have something to steal."

"You've got a good memory!" I exclaim.

He turns his face toward me. "There was this cliff track—we'd gone to have a picnic and our parents stayed on the rug while we went off and explored."

"By a cliff edge?" I ask with alarm. You wouldn't catch Dad doing that now.

"You couldn't get to the edge because it was so dense with blackberry bushes," he tells me. "I scratched my arm on one and you licked off the blood."

"Did I?"

He laughs at the disgusted look on my face. "You were only trying to stop it from hurting, trying to make me feel better. You did that sort of thing a lot." His eyes are shining. "You still do," he adds with a sweet smile.

My heart expands inside my chest and I reach across and take both of his hands in mine, squeezing them hard. "I love you," I whisper.

"I love you too," he whispers back, and then he slides one arm behind my shoulders and I go to him, sensing that he desires as much as me to feel the kind of closeness we used to have as children.

But as I rest my hand on his chest and feel his heart beating strong and hard against my palm, a surreal feeling settles over me. Out of the blue, I feel wildly uncomfortable.

I hope he doesn't pick up on my unease as I withdraw and sit up, pretending to yawn. "I should probably go back to bed. Do you think you'll fall asleep again?" I try to feign normality.

He shrugs. "I doubt it. Will you pass me my book? I'll probably read for a bit."

I reach for the novel on his bedside table. "*The Power of One*," I read aloud. It's by Bryce Courtenay.

"My aunt gave it to me before I left. She thought I'd like it."

"I forgot you have an aunt."

"I have two."

I shake my head. "I can't believe I didn't know that."

"Lots to catch up on," he says.

Indeed.

I DON'T KNOW why, but the next morning I feel shy at the prospect of seeing Vian again. There was something about the dark and quietness of the night that had us opening up to each other. Now it's broad daylight and, with Dad around, I've retreated back into my shell. Perhaps it's the same for Vian, because he doesn't make eye contact when we meet in the kitchen at breakfast time.

"What would you like to do today, kids?" Dad asks.

"Do you want to go and find that track?" I glance at Vian before turning to Dad. "It's where the Helford River spills out to the sea," I explain. "I thought we could go for a walk and then maybe a pub lunch."

"What a wonderful idea," Dad says with a smile.

THAT NIGHT I bolt awake again. Once more, I get out of bed and creep downstairs, peering out of the hall window. I feel a rush of joy at the sight of light spilling from beneath Vian's curtains. I hurry across and rap softly on his door and this time he opens it with a wide grin—the best smile I've seen on his face all day.

"Again?" he asks.

"Couldn't sleep," I lie, pushing past him and climbing into his bed.

I belatedly realize that he's only wearing boxer shorts and a T-shirt, so I avert my gaze until he's lying beside me in the same position as last night.

"What are your friends like?" I ask, blinking back tiredness. I went to bed early, but *still* . . . Dad said the sea breeze and cliff walk must've worn me out. I don't have the excuse of jet-lag.

We found the track and it was exactly as Vian had described. My memory came flooding back as soon as I saw the Fudge and Smudge tree.

"What do you want to know?" Vian replies.

"How many do you have?" I'll start with that.

"There are about ten of us in our group."

"Boys or girls?"

"Both."

"Who's your best friend?"

He thinks for a moment. "Probably Dave, but I go surfing a lot with Sebastian too."

"Do you have any pictures of them?"

"Yeah, I brought some with me."

"Can I see?"

He climbs out of bed and goes over to his suitcase, rummaging around inside and returning with an envelope of photos. He props up his pillow against the wall and edges closer to me. I do the same, jerking when his bare knee knocks against mine.

He shows me pictures of Port Lincoln, where his dad grew up and where they still live together in a two-bedroom house with a tin roof and a small front garden peppered with dry, scraggly-looking weeds. His dad has a black beard and dark-blue eyes and is wearing a brown beanie hat in most of his shots. I recognize him from when he came to take Vian home, five years ago.

I like the look of one of his aunts more than the other, telling Vian that I think Aunty Pam seems a bit stern compared to smiley Aunt Nora. He agrees that she's not the most fun. They alternated looking after him when he was younger and his dad was out on fishing trips. Since he turned thirteen, he's been allowed to stay in the house by himself—a fact I find hard to believe, considering how protective Dad is of me.

He even has a grandad, although he's a bit of a recluse, allegedly, and they only see him once in a blue moon.

"That's Herbert," Vian says when we come to a photo of the prawn trawler boat and crew. "He's the skipper and he owns the boat. That's Connor, my fellow deckie. Deckhand," he reveals when I glance at him for an explanation. "Dad's the deck boss. There are four of us in total." The next two pictures are of him holding up huge fish. "That's a snapper," he says. "And that's a flathead." The first is red in color and the second looks a bit like a crocodile. "Sometimes we hook up fish and if they don't look too happy, we'll hang onto them and eat them for breakfast or dinner or whatever. They don't go to waste."

I come to a shot of a dark-haired boy riding a curling, blue wave. "Is this you?"

"Yeah."

"What are *they*?" I ask with alarm, spying dark shapes in the water.

"Dolphins."

"Oh, *wow*," I breathe. "Have you ever seen a shark?" I'm still staring at the picture. His hair is black and wet and flying out from behind him as his board cuts down through the face of a wave.

"A fair few Bronzies."

I shoot my head around to look at him. "Bronzies?"

"Bronze whalers. It's rare to be attacked by one. I've only seen one great white." He grins. "It was a few weeks ago. We'd come in from a surf and this enormous—and I mean *enormous*—black shadow went by. I don't know how big it was, but it was *gigantic*. It probably swam past us while we were in the water."

"I don't want you to go surfing anymore," I state as cold fingers of fear clutch at my chest.

"It's fine," he replies dismissively. "Sharks are always on

your mind, but you just have to keep an eye out and hope one never comes your way hungry."

The next photo is of a whole group of teenagers sitting on white sand with streaks of green brush and blue sky behind them.

"That's at Sheringa Beach," he says, "one of my favorite places to surf. It's almost a two-hour drive toward Elliston so sometimes we'll go and camp out for a few days. That's Dave," he points out. He's tanned and good-looking with blow-away light-brown hair. "And that's Sebastian." He's broader and darker with a warm, friendly smile. The girls are all, without exception, long limbed and gorgeous—everyone looks like they could have stepped off the set of *Home and Away* or *Neighbours*.

"Do the girls surf too?" I ask.

"Some of them."

I feel a pang of envy and try not to stare at them for too long.

"Do you still surf?" he asks.

"Not since our one lesson."

He falls quiet. Presumably he remembers that his mother died the day after we started.

"Where did we do that lesson?" he asks, as I realize I've come full circle.

"Poldhu Beach," I reply, putting the photos on the bedside table. "We used to go boogie boarding there a bit. Do you remember? It's not far from here—maybe we could go tomorrow."

"Sure. What are *your* friends like?" he asks. "Is Ellie still your best friend?"

"Yeah." I smile at him. I've told him about her in my letters.

He rolls on his side to face me. "She lives up in the village, right?"

"Yes." Boy, I go into a lot of detail. "Do I bore the brains out of you?"

"No, I like hearing about your life," he tells me with a smile.

"It doesn't make you sad?"

"Sometimes." Pain washes across his features and he swallows. "Which beach did we build the sandcastle on?"

"Dad and I think it was Kynance," I tell him softly, knowing he means the one in his mum's painting. It was the only piece of him and me, aside from notebooks full of sketches. The other pictures were sold in Ruth's last exhibition.

"The beach is practically nonexistent when the tide is in," I remind him, "but when it goes out, you can get around to another whole section of hidden beach. It's magical. We could go there too, one day?"

Vian nods and swallows again.

I reach over and hook my little finger through his. This is something else we used to do. Right on cue, he squeezes.

He's becoming more and more familiar to me with every minute we spend together.

I don't know how long we lie like that, but when the gray light of dawn creeps into the room from behind the curtains, I decide I'd better get back to my own bed.

"HAVE I MET your mum?" Vian asks me on our third night together. We're in his bed again and it's almost five in the morning. I might have to set my alarm tomorrow as I'm waking up later and later.

"I don't think so, no," I reply. "She never comes to Cornwall."

"How did you used to get here, then, when you'd come for the school holidays?"

"My nanny brought me—whichever one I had at the time. I went through quite a few."

He recoils. "That's so weird."

"Yeah, I guess my mum was tricky to work for."

"Does she still live in France?"

"No, New York now, with her new husband, Robert. He's American, but they met in France. Things weren't working out with her last boyfriend and they fell head over heels in love, apparently. He's a boat salesman and was there on business."

"What sort of boats?"

"Wouldn't have a clue. Big expensive ones, I think."

"Yachts?"

"Probably. They travel together a fair bit. Mostly around Canada and the US, but sometimes to Europe."

His expression merges into one of concern. "That must make it harder for you to see her, with her being that much farther away."

"I prefer being here with Dad, anyway."

"How did she and your dad meet?" he asks, seeming to sense that I don't want to dwell on my relationship with my mother.

"Dad was doing a stint in London as a landscape designer."

"Your dad worked in London?" He seems surprised.

I understand. It's kind of hard to imagine my dad being anywhere other than Cornwall.

"Only for a year or so. A mutual friend introduced them and, when Dad's mother died, they moved back here to live. I think Mum thought the idea of living in a cottage on the river sounded romantic, but she missed city life. They broke up the year after I was born."

"What does she look like? Your mum?"

"She's about my height, blonde, slim, beautiful."

"Like you, then."

I laugh. "The beautiful part too?"

"Yeah, of course you're beautiful."

I snort, trying to cover up my self-consciousness.

"What color eyes does she have?" He chooses to ignore the fact that I'm blushing like crazy.

"They're similar to mine. Sort of a pale brown, I guess."

"My mum used to describe them differently." He inches forward. "She said they were like honey. In sunshine!" he remembers. "She was right," he adds thoughtfully. "They're *exactly* the color of runny honey in sunshine."

"Are they?" My voice wavers. I'm not used to being under such close scrutiny. "Do you have your dad's eyes?"

"Mm. Everyone reckons I look like him."

"You have your mum's smile, though, and the shape of her face." I reach out and trace my finger along his jaw. He inhales sharply and my eyes cut to his lips. A second later they fly up to meet his gaze and suddenly my stomach is awash with butterflies. His stare is intense and the urge to look away is overwhelming, but I can't seem to break eye contact. My heart is pounding ten to the dozen and then his gaze drops to *my* lips and I completely freak, scrambling out from under the covers.

Vian sits bolt upright and looks at me with alarm, shaking his head quickly as if to bring himself to his senses. "You going back to bed?" he asks, and his words sound weird, like he's got a chest full of water.

"Yes," I reply hurriedly. "It'll be light soon."

"OK! See you in the morning."

"Night night!" I hurry out the door, pulling it shut behind me.

"EVERYONE SEEMS VERY tired today," Dad comments aloud the following morning when we're in the car on our way to Bodmin Jail. The weather is atrocious so we've decided to save the beaches for another day.

"Yeah, I didn't sleep very well," I disclose over the sound of the pounding rain and the windshield wipers on high speed.

Dad looks across at Vian. "Not over your jet-lag yet, Van?"

I frown at the sound of his new name.

"Not yet," he replies.

Once more, I'm finding it hard to meet his eyes, but from here, I can bore a hole into the back of his head.

THE NEXT MORNING, I wake at six a.m., but I don't get out of bed. There was an odd tension between Vian and me yesterday. Luckily, as Dad was with us, we didn't have any one-on-one time, but if we had, I'm sure it would have been awkward.

I haven't told Dad about our nightly meetings. I suppose I wanted Vian and me to have a secret, like we used to have as children. But I do wonder what Dad would say if he caught me coming out of the annex in the early hours of the morning.

Down the corridor, I hear Dad's bedroom door open.

Well, that's that, then, I think with relief. I can't go to the annex if he's already awake.

Then I remember that it's Christmas Day! I manage to catch my father before he reaches the stairs.

"Merry Christmas!" he says as we embrace. "It's been a few years since you've woken up at the crack of dawn for Santa," he teases. "I thought it'd only be Van and me for a bit."

"Is he awake?" I whisper with a nervous flutter inside my chest.

"I presume so. He's been down in the living room, using Scampi as a hot-water bottle, every morning this week."

I've always returned to bed after our middle-of-the-night catch-up sessions, so I wouldn't know.

I throw on some clothes before venturing downstairs. Vian, as Dad predicted, is already awake, and he and Dad are at the kitchen table with mugs of tea.

"Merry Christmas!" I say with forced cheer.

"You too," Vian says, standing up to give me a hug.

I'm alarmed to feel my face heating up, so I pull away and hurry over to the cupboard to get out a mug.

"I'll make you a cuppa, Nelly. Sit down."

"No, no, I'm fine," I brush Dad off, wanting to have something to do.

The phone rings. "That might be my dad," Vian says.

"Well, it won't be my mum—it's the middle of the night in New York." She'll expect me to call her later.

It *is* Vian's dad, and it's hard not to eavesdrop on the conversation that carries through from the hall. It's reassuring to hear that Vian sounds stilted on the phone to his dad too, and is not only awkward with us.

"I guess we should take these through to the living room and open our presents in front of the tree," Dad says when he reappears.

"I'll go grab mine," Vian says.

As soon as he's out of the room, I turn to Dad. "Do you think he'll be OK with his present?" I ask worriedly.

"Why wouldn't he be?"

"He doesn't paint anymore. He told me."

"Maybe this will give him the impetus to start back up again," Dad replies, set on the decision we made before Vian flew out here.

Although most of Ruth's paints were still in a usable state, we decided to buy him a new set, one that he could call his own. Now I have a horrible feeling that we've misjudged the situation.

It warms my heart to watch Vian opening the presents from his family in Australia, knowing that he has people on the other side of the world who care about him. One of his aunts knitted him a navy jumper, and she even knitted me a scarf and Dad some socks.

"Sorry, it's a bit childish," Vian says to me with a self-conscious smile when I open his present—a cuddly koala toy.

"No, it's not. I love it," I reply with a grin.

Finally, only one present remains, and I feel slightly sick as Vian opens it.

He stares down at the paint set in his hands, his shoulders pulled together with tension.

I know at that moment that we have completely messed up.

"Nell said you don't really paint anymore," Dad blunders forth with no notion of the pain that his one-time sort-of son is in.

"No," Vian replies shortly.

"We thought this might get you back into it."

"But only if you want to," I say quickly, moving to sit beside him on the couch. "Otherwise we could return this and buy something else."

"Yeah. Thanks," Vian says quietly, closing the wrapping back around the set and putting it down on the floor beside the Christmas tree.

Dad goes off to take a shower and, as soon as the bathroom door closes, Vian makes an attempt to stand up. I put my hand on his arm to stop him and he stays where he is.

"I'm sorry," I whisper as he stares at the floor. "I can see that we made a mistake."

He doesn't reply.

I edge closer to him, leaning my knees against his lap, all thoughts of awkwardness gone from my mind as I attempt to comfort him.

"Is it because painting reminds you of her?" I ask gently.

"It's because painting *killed* her." He turns to look at me, his expression tortured. "And it was *my fault*!"

"What are you talking about?" I'm aghast.

"That picture," he says. "The green one on your wall." His eyes are wide with horror at the recollection of a memory I don't share. "I used up all of her cerulean to finish it. She was upset. She went out to buy some more and that was when the car hit her."

"No! No, that's not it at all! Vian—"

"My name is VAN!" he yells in my face.

"Van! Stop!" I say, panicking. "You've got it wrong! She didn't go out to buy paint, she went out to get milk!"

He stares at me.

"She needed milk for dinner!"

"No." He shakes his head. "It was paint. She said she had to finish her picture. She was angry."

"She was disappointed because her meeting with the gallery owner hadn't gone well!" I've raised my voice. "And she was annoyed because she'd had a long car journey! It wasn't because you'd used up all of her cerulean." I stumble over my pronunciation of the word.

He shakes his head again, disbelieving. In his mind, he knows what happened and I'm only trying to make him feel better.

"I promise you," I say. "It wasn't your fault."

"You *would* say that!"

"What's going on?" Dad demands to know from the doorway. He's still hurriedly tying up his dressing gown, the hairs on his legs stuck flat to his skin with shower water.

I stare up at Dad, desperate for help. "Vian—"

"VAN!" he bellows.

I jolt, my eyes pricking with tears. I *must* call him Van from now on—I *have* to, even in my head. "*Van* thinks it's his fault that Ruth went out that day, the day that she was—"

Dad looks appalled. "No, that's not right at all. Why would you think that?"

"He says that he used up all her cerulean," I explain. "That she went out to buy more."

"No, she went out to borrow some milk from Steven and Linzie, the farmers who live up the road." Dad kneels on the floor in front of Van, who stares at him, helplessly, tears streaming down his face. I know he wants to believe it wasn't his fault, but he's going to take some convincing.

"It was Sunday. *Sunday*," Dad repeats. "None of the shops were open. There's *no way* she could have gone out to buy more blue paint that day. She couldn't even buy *milk*! She had to borrow some. I offered to go, but she said she wanted fresh air after being stuck in traffic for two hours. If it's anyone's fault, it's mine, because we'd used up all the milk. Believe me, I've tormented myself thinking about it, but she didn't *have* to make macaroni and cheese," Dad says tearfully, placing his hand on Van's knee. "There was plenty of other food in the fridge."

Van shudders. "I always thought it was my fault," he says in a pained voice.

"No. *No*," Dad says firmly. "The only person to blame is that goddamn driver who took her off the road!"

Van crumples over and the most heart-wrenching sound comes from deep within him. I throw my arms around him and hug him hard, and he buries his face against my neck and sobs, his whole body heaving violently as his arms come around my waist.

There's no way we're leaving him alone to deal with his grief this time, Dad. No way.

WE VISIT THE cemetery that morning to place flowers on Ruth's grave—a red rose and holly berry bouquet that Dad made. I style my light-blond hair in a topknot that Mum taught me how to do in one of her rare motherly moments and wear my red velvet fitted dress—the most festive-looking thing in my wardrobe.

Dad looks handsome in a smart gray suit, but when I come downstairs, it's Van who draws my attention. He's wearing a white, slightly crumpled shirt—this is not a guy who owns an iron—which fits his long, lean frame to perfection. The top button is undone, revealing the smooth, golden skin on his chest. He grabs his denim jacket on the way out.

We're going to Drew's family pub for Christmas lunch. I was elated when Dad made the suggestion, but now I can't think past my concern for Van.

He's held onto that guilt for years, believing he was some-how responsible for his mother's death. It's devastating.

I glue myself to his side as we walk down the road from the car park, needing to keep him close. He's very quiet, but I hope he knows that I'm here for him.

The Boatman is an old thatched pub, right on the river, and as we approach we can hear Christmas music playing. The outdoor festoon lights are on and they cheer up the gray day, as does the crackling fire in the hearth when we enter.

Drew's mum, Theresa, welcomes us, handing Van and me glasses of sparkling cranberry and lemonade and Dad a glass of champagne.

"One won't hurt," I tell him when he dithers—he never drinks and drives. "I suppose we'll be here for a couple of hours," he accepts, chinking our glasses.

At the bar, Drew's older brother, Nick, is serving a couple of women. He's a bit taller and broader than Drew, with curly blond hair. There are always an array of admirers hanging around the bar area—I'm glad that Drew works in the kitchen.

At that moment, Drew appears, wearing a black suit and a crisp white shirt, his hair styled back off his face.

"Hey!" He comes straight over.

I return his smile, recalling how pleased he was when I told him we were coming here for Christmas. "Do you remember Van?" I introduce them. "And you know my dad."

They greet each other and then Drew leads us into the restaurant, grabbing three menus on his way out of the door. He gestures to a great table, right in front of the floor-to-ceiling glass doors. We can see straight down the river from here.

Drew pulls out my chair for me and I sit down, smiling up at him.

"I thought you'd be in the kitchen."

"One of our waitresses called in sick so I was needed out here," he reveals.

I'm diverted by Van, who looks to be about to take the chair next to Dad. "Sit next to me," I urge, patting the chair to my right.

"We won't give you too much trouble," Dad says as Van obliges me.

"Glad to hear it," Drew replies. "I'll leave you to look over your menus."

"Thanks," I say distractedly, helping Van to get settled. He picks up his menu and studies it intently.

About halfway through our meal, I excuse myself to go to the bathroom. Drew catches me on my way out.

"Enjoying your lunch so far?" he asks.

"Mmm, it's lovely." It's hard to go wrong with a turkey roast.

He frowns and jerks his chin in the direction of our table. "Is Vian all right?"

"Yes, why?"

"He seems a bit moody."

"No, he's fine." I don't want to share the details of how hard the last few days have been. "And actually, it's Van now," I think to point out.

He smirks. "Like Van Morrison?"

I bristle, not appreciating his mocking tone. "I think it suits him."

"Yeah, it does! It's cool." He quickly backtracks. "Hey, do you still want to take him surfing?"

I instantly perk up again. "Yes, definitely! Do you know when you're next going?"

"Possibly tomorrow. I'll check with my bro."

As I walk back to the table, it dawns on me that Van *does* suit him, because he *is* cool. I think of the boy in the photograph, riding that wave. I remember his friends and those girls, all tall and tanned with long, sexy legs, and I can picture *Van* hanging out with them, being a part of their gang.

Has he dated any of those girls? Is one of them his girlfriend?

Jealousy shreds my insides.

I don't understand. He was always the jealous, possessive one, not me.

"YOU'RE COMING TO our New Year's Eve party, right?" Drew asks later. I'm hovering in the bar area, waiting for Van to return from the bathroom. Dad is chatting to Drew's dad, Christopher.

"Nah, we're going to the one at the sailing club."

His face falls and I laugh.

"Yeah, of course we're coming here."

Loads of people from school are, including Ellie and her parents, who are giving us a lift. Dad intends to have an early night.

Drew tuts and elbows me, making me laugh again. Van chooses that moment to return, looking grumpier than ever.

"Oh, I spoke to my bro," Drew says, shoving his hair off to one side. "We're going to Porthleven the day after tomorrow if you're up for it?"

"Ace!" I turn to Van. "You want to go surfing?"

"Yeah!" His face lights up. "You know where I can hire gear?" he asks Drew.

"My brother has a 3:5 wetsuit you can borrow and a seven-two pin-tail, big wave gun," Drew replies. "Don't worry, we won't make you go out on an eight-foot floatie."

I have absolutely no idea what they're talking about, but Van grins.

"You'll love Porthleven. It's like the Holy Grail of British surfing," Drew tells him. "You get some really serious waves, man—proper barrels."

"Sounds awesome."

My attention darts between them. I'm reeling at the change in Van.

"You're experienced, though, right?" Drew asks. "'Cos it's a reef break and the waves unload *really* heavy, so you do *not* want to wipe out."

I detect a warning in his tone. *What does that mean? Is it dangerous?*

Van shrugs, unfazed. "It's pretty much all reef breaks where I come from."

And because I'd give anything to keep him smiling like this, I try to ignore my pang of worry.

Damp earth and sheep shorn grass . . . Glossy, ripe blackberries among sharp thorns and feathery ferns . . . I try to keep up with Vian as he leaps over patches of thick, squelchy mud on the winding track. Every time I jump, I can see the line where the sea meets the sky.

We come to a stop on a steep hill, high above a glittering cove. The air is heavy with the scent of sun-warmed grass and cowpats. I don't know where our parents are—somewhere on the other side of the hedge. The sound reaches us of distant waves crashing onto the rocks far below. We won't be rolling down this hill.

Vian pulls some flaky gray moss from a tree branch and I notice tiny droplets of blood beading out of a scratch on his arm.

"You've hurt yourself." I take his hand. "Does it sting?"

"It does now you've pointed it out," he mutters.

I pull him closer and press my lips to his wound, my tongue tasting the metallic tang of his blood.

"What are you doing?" His nostrils flare as he asks the question.

"Kissing it better," I reply.

"You just sucked my blood." He's alarmed. "Like a vampire."

I giggle at the look on his face. But my laughter dies as the years catapult us forward. Standing in front of me now is not ten-year-old Vian, but fifteen-year-old Van. The look in his eyes is intense as he stares down at me. He steps closer. I step back. He keeps coming and I trip and lose my footing, landing on the soft grass. He falls to his knees and drops forward, his hands trapping me on either side of my shoulders. My heart races as his lips come down to meet mine.

I jolt awake, and then shame engulfs me.

VAN FINDS ME down by the water. I'm cleaning out *Platypus* after the recent rainfall.

"Shall we go out in it?" he asks as I scoop up another bucket of water and dump it into the river.

"It's very early," I mumble. Not to mention cold.

"So?"

"OK," I reluctantly agree, blowing a strand of hair out of my face. I've tied it up into a messy ponytail today and I'm wearing my old Levi 501s. "Can you ask Dad for a towel to wipe down the seats?"

I watch his departing back and feel something akin to seasickness.

He was like a brother to me for almost five years. So why am I dreaming about kissing him?

"Can I row?" he asks when he comes back, clutching the lead of an excited-looking Scampi.

Van always used to insist on taking the dog out with us, even though we hated cleaning his paws afterward—he has a habit of leaping out of the boat before we've come to a stop.

"If you want."

He throws me the towel.

I busy myself wiping down the seats, then turn around to help Scampi aboard. Van passes me the oars and I slot them into place, then he climbs on, the boat wobbling precariously. Our ensuing laughter breaks the ice, but I still feel on edge as I sit at the back and he settles himself opposite me, his long legs knocking against my knees. Scampi is at the other end, his claws skittering around on the slippery surface as he tries to make himself comfortable.

Van uses one of the oars to push us away from the bank and then he rows properly, propelling us slowly through the water.

"It's been ages since I've been out in this," I confide. "Even longer since anyone else rowed me."

"Who rows you?" he asks.

"Ellie has a few times," I reply. "We went for a picnic on the other side in the summer. I don't go out much by myself. Only when I want the peace and quiet."

"Because your dad's so noisy," he teases.

I smile. "You know what I mean. It's so still out here and lonely—in a good way. It gives me time to think . . . and write."

"So you *do* still write."

"Only poetry—nothing I'd ever show anyone."

"Not even me?"

"No one," I state firmly.

Especially not you.

"What are your poems about?"

"I don't know." I shrug. "Stuff."

"Drew?"

I jolt and quickly shake my head. "No. Of course not."

"Why 'of course not'? You do like him, don't you?" His stare is piercing.

I pull a face and avert my gaze, but he knocks his leg against mine to bring my attention back to him.

"Don't you?" He's not letting it lie.

I shrug. "I don't know."

He pulls on the oars with more force.

"Do you have a girlfriend?" I ask as we glide through the water.

He shakes his head. "Nope."

"Have you ever?"

"Have you? Had a boyfriend?" he replies.

"No."

He seems surprised.

"So?" I persist.

He shrugs. "Sort of."

My stomach folds over. "One of the girls in your photos?"

He nods. "Jenna."

"Which one was she?"

"She's tall, with long, brown hair."

I know exactly which girl he means and I'm breathless with a hurt that I don't understand. Why should I feel betrayed?

"How long did you go out?"

"On and off for a few months. We never had sex, or anything."

I blush violently at his casual admission. "I can't believe you never told me about her," I mutter when I've recovered.

"You never told me about Drew," he bats back, clenching his jaw.

"Why would I?" I pull a face. "Nothing's happened—at all! I've never even kissed a boy!"

"Haven't you?" He cocks his head to one side and grins.

My burning cheeks tell him all he needs to know.

Still grinning, Van nods ahead to the bank that we're about to collide with. "Shall we get out and go for a walk?"

I turn around and make a grab for a branch.

Scampi scrambles out as soon as the boat hits the bank, his legs sinking about ten centimeters into the mud.

I sigh and watch as he climbs up onto the grass and shakes himself, panting happily. Van catches my eye and laughs.

"You're cleaning the mud off," I warn.

"Yeah, yeah." He waves me away dismissively.

AFTER OUR ARGUMENT of a couple of weeks ago, Dad promised to lay off a bit and try to give me some more space and independence. But I'm still astonished when he agrees to us hitching a lift with Drew and Nick to Porthleven.

"Take care of her," Dad urges Van as we leave. "Find a pay phone and call me if he drives too fast or in any way dangerously. I'll come and collect you."

Van agrees to Dad's request, taking his responsibility seriously. I bite my tongue.

"The great thing about Cornwall," Nick explains on the way, "is you have about forty different beaches that all face in slightly different directions, so there's nearly always some-where with a decent, surfable wave. Even in huge storms, you can find a nice, sheltered spot."

I'm sitting in the backseat of the car, feeling kind of un-settled. It's not only that I have Drew on one side of me and Van on the other; it's also that I've never been anywhere on my own with four boys before—it's a little intimidating.

Nick's friend Max is at the front and he swivels around to talk to Van. "Drew says you compete." He means surfing competitions.

"Sometimes," Van replies offhandedly. His arms are folded across his chest and his bicep is pressing into mine.

"Looking forward to seeing what you can do."

I hear the challenge in Max's voice and my unease grows, but Van just smirks and leans his head back on the headrest.

There is *way* too much testosterone in this car. I wish Ellie were here.

Eventually we pull up on the side of the road. We're parked parallel to the coastline, some fifty feet above the sea, and through the foggy windows, we can see the steely blue-gray of the ocean.

Van rubs a hole in the condensation on his glass and peers out.

"Whoa." He sounds reverent.

Nick leans past Max to look out of the passenger-side win-dow. "*Shiiiit.*" He draws the word out.

Max glances at him and they laugh, their eyes wide. "Shall we go to Praa Sands instead?" Nick suggests. "It should be a bit more manageable there."

"No way." Van is already reaching for the door handle.

Nick and Max grin, shrug, and get out of the car.

"Wait—" I say, as Van slams the door. I slide over to his window and peer out. What I see scares the life out of me.

I clamber out of the car as an absolutely *enormous* wave explodes onto the rocks. I kid you not, I can feel the ground rumbling from up here.

"No." I shake my head, catching Drew's look of apprehension over the roof of the car. His usual cheeky grin is very much absent. "No." I storm around to the back and jolt to a stop when I see that Van is naked from the waist down. Luckily his hoodie is long enough to cover his front bits, but I blush madly as I turn away. "Don't do this," I plead.

"Nell, it's fine," he replies flippantly, zipping up his wetsuit while Nick and Max get his board down. I jump as another wave detonates on the reef.

To my right is the end of a row of fishermen's cottages and to my left are a couple of modern houses, but ahead is a lawned garden, and beyond it, the ocean.

There's a group of guys standing farther along the road. I think they're locals. A couple are wearing wetsuits, but the others are in jeans and hoodies. One of them glances over and turns back to his friends, saying something that prompts them all to look our way. There are a few raised eyebrows.

"Please," I whisper to Van. "You're not under any pressure."

He scoffs and pulls on his boots.

I don't want to embarrass him, but this is crazy! Those waves are bone-crushers!

"You going out, mate?" one of the surfers from farther along comes over to ask.

"Yep."

"You sure?" Nick checks with a grin, propping Van's board up against the car.

"You're going to get hammered," Max adds teasingly.

I want to wipe the smile from both of their faces, but Van grins, not looking the least bit fazed as he grabs wax from the trunk and rubs it onto his board.

I'm guessing that Nick, Max, and Drew have zero intention of joining him, but I can't even get angry because if anyone's to blame here, it's me.

Van keeps staring at the ocean, a look of intense concentration on his face. The sky is overcast and huge, gray waves are marching in, breaking from right to left and crashing like thunder onto the rocky shore a hundred meters away. There are a few other surfers in the water, sitting toward the channel on the left-hand side. I swear they look nervous.

Van's brow furrows as he shuts the trunk and scans the beach. Is he having second thoughts?

"Where do I get in?" he asks the surfer who came over.

Oh no, he's not . . .

The guy points to a cream stone building, right by the water. "Down there by the old lifeboat house. Jump off the rock, on the left, into the channel, then paddle round to the right into the take-off zone."

"Got it."

Before I know it, Van is walking away from us, his board under his arm.

Drew materializes by my side, but I can't look at him and I think he senses that I'm incapable of casual conversation. I chew the inside of my cheek, watching anxiously as Van launches himself into the water and begins to paddle out.

"He's paddling right past the other surfers," Max comments, as though this is somehow frowned upon. "I hope he knows what he's doing."

"They're not taking off on anything anyway," Nick replies.

The minutes tick by. The other guys farther along have somehow integrated into our group, but I try not to listen to their banter as I stand and stare at Van, way out in the vast ocean, all alone.

He's waiting . . .

And then the horizon turns black.

"That is a *massive* set!" Max exclaims.

"He's going to get smashed!" someone else shouts.

I feel sick to my stomach as a huge, dark wave rolls toward Van.

"Here we go," Drew says.

As it starts to feather, Van swings around toward the shore and paddles hard.

"He's going!" Nick shouts.

Even in my overwrought state, I can feel the tension from those around me.

"He's going to get sucked over the falls." Max sounds uncharacteristically worried, but then Van gives two more powerful strokes and jumps to his feet.

"He's got it!" Nick yells as Van knifes the rail of his board into the face of the wave. *My heart soars* . . .

. . . And then the lip of the wave curls over into a tube. Van stands tall and drags his hand in the water to slow himself down, before *disappearing from view* . . .

One . . .

Two . . .

"He's gonna wipe out!" I hear someone say.

Three *torturous* seconds . . .

Four . . .

"*Fuuuuuck!*"

Five, and suddenly, Van is spat out of the wave into the channel, looking like he's been ejected from a giant fire hose. And he's still standing!

The cheers from around me are mental. I clutch my hands to my face, holding back tears, as Nick claps me on the back, laughing.

"I thought he was a goner!" he cries. "That was the biggest barrel I have *ever* seen!"

Van flicks his wet hair out of his face and glances our way. I can see his grin from here.

I FEEL LIKE I need time to myself when we get home. The atmosphere was buzzing in the car, the boys plying one another with horror stories about surfers they knew who'd broken bones or had to have stitches, and one guy who'd literally been scalped.

I still feel shaken now, even as I lie here on my bed. They're all a bunch of freaking nutters, the lot of them.

There's a knock on my door.

"Yes?"

The door cracks open to reveal Van. He regards me with amusement and I narrow my eyes at him in return. He bobs under the doorframe and nods at the bed. "Budge up."

"Where's Dad?" I ask warily.

"Asleep on the couch," he replies.

I edge over and he lies down, resting his head on my pillow. He still smells of the ocean: cold, wild, and free.

"Sorry for scaring you," he whispers, folding his arms across his chest. His little finger snags mine and my heart contracts.

He turns his face toward me and I tense, but when I look at him, his eyes are staring past me to the wall.

"The color of wheat," I murmur, reaching out to run my fingers over his name, written in cursive in what I only now realize is cerulean: *Vian Stanley Stirling*. "It's my favorite green. Do you remember?"

I glance back at him and his eyes meet mine. He nods seriously and turns on his side, propping his head up with one hand.

"Will you ever paint again?" I ask.

He hesitantly lifts his shoulders in a small shrug.

"What would you paint," I ask, "if you had to paint one thing?"

He doesn't answer me, but his stare is prompting butterflies to crowd my already jittery stomach.

"Van?" I prompt.

His lips tilt up at the corners. "You're calling me Van, at last," he notes.

"I guess it does suit you," I admit reluctantly. "So what would you want to paint?"

"I know what I'd *want* to paint, but I wouldn't attempt it."

"What's that?"

"Your eyes," he says.

Goose bumps spring up all over my body.

"Why wouldn't you attempt it?" My voice breaks on the question.

"I'd never be able to pull it off."

We both start as we hear movement downstairs. Van slowly

gets down from the bed, stretching his bent arms over his head as he walks over to the window and looks out. I sit up, feeling edgy as hell.

IT'S THE FOLLOWING day and we're at Kynance Cove. Van is staring into the sun, which is low in the clear blue sky. There's only a light breeze, but it's very, very cold. The cove we're in is only accessible when the tide is out. A towering rock almost as tall as the nearby cliffs sits alone on the beach to our left and aquamarine waves crash at its base—the water is so clear that you can see through it as it curls.

The grass-topped cliffs are sliced through with colored layers: brown, orange, purple, silver, and charcoal. The base of the cliffs looks sandy, but it's an illusion created by millions of beige barnacles clinging to the rock surface.

"I think that's where we built our sandcastle." Van's voice cuts through the silence, currently punctuated only by the cries of gulls. "I recognize the shape of the cove."

We're alone—Dad stayed up at the café with Scampi. We had to wait until the tide went out a bit before we could get round here, and even then, we had to take off our shoes and socks and wade through the freezing water obstructing our path. My feet still feel numb, but it was worth it.

"The rock surfaces are so varied," Van says as we wander. "Those look like they're part of a game of Tetris, all chunky and solid, and those slick black ones are like melted wax. And check out those! They're green and red!" he exclaims.

They look like snakeskin, polished by thousands of years of crashing waves.

"I think that's called serpentinite," I tell him, smiling at his enthusiasm. "Does this place inspire you? Could you imagine painting here?"

Instead of answering, he climbs up onto a rock, turning around to hold his hand down to me. I stretch up and take it, allowing him to hoist me up to his level.

"I can see how it inspired Mum," he says eventually.

"It's very different in the summer." I try to avoid standing on the beds of mussels clinging to the surface in clusters like shiny blue-black beetles. "You can barely move."

At the moment, ours are the only footprints on the sand.

Van cups his hands and blows on them.

"They're blue!" I observe with dismay. He left his borrowed gloves at home.

I pull off my own and shove them into my pockets before taking his hands in mine and rubbing vigorously. He stares down at me and I return his smile. His face is drenched in sunlight and at that moment, I realize something. His eyes are not simply dark blue. Shards of green and gold are spliced through the navy, like a firework exploding in a night sky. I haven't noticed before. But then, I haven't really been looking.

"Why have you stopped?" he murmurs.

I wasn't aware that my hands had stilled.

"Better?" I ask quickly.

"Not really," he replies, opening his mouth to show me that his teeth are chattering.

"Do you want to go back to the café?"

"No." He grins and places his hands on my waist. I'm thrown for a second, but then his freezing fingers find my bare skin and I scream.

He bursts out laughing as I jerk away from him. But a

split-second later his face falls and he grabs me before I stagger off the edge.

"Whoa!" He tugs me forward and we collide. "Sorry, that was close!"

I laugh, feeling skittish. "Funny, though."

"Yeah." He bends his head and blows hot air down my collar.

"What are you doing?" I ask warily, shivering.

"Warming you up. You're shivering."

"I shivered because you blew on my neck," I point out.

He responds by blowing on my neck again. This time the tremor ricochets through my body.

"That tickles." I tense as his hands land back on my hips. "Don't you dare put them up my jumper again . . ."

"I won't," he promises and although I could step away from him, I stay where I am.

He bows his head again, but this time his lips touch my neck and all of my nerve endings stand to attention. What is he doing? I don't ask. I'm completely frozen in place. His lips trail up my neck and brush against my ear. My heart is pounding against my ribcage, threatening to break out. Then he rests his cheek against mine. Despite the cold, his skin is warm. Is he simply seeking closeness? Because what I'm feeling right now is very confusing.

I do not feel sisterly. Not one bit.

He pulls back and stares at me.

"Van?" I ask uncertainly, edging away, but he closes up the distance between us again and his pupils dilate, flooding out the fireworks with black.

An electric shock sparks and fizzes against my lips and I dazedly realize it's because he's kissing me.

I gasp with shock and his tongue slips through my parted lips to brush against mine.

"What—" I say, but his tongue cuts me off and a frisson spirals all the way down my body, starting at the top of my head and bursting out through the tips of my toes.

His lips are soft and his hands hold me steady, which is just as well because I'm dizzy from the short, sharp breaths I'm barely managing to take. And then he abruptly breaks away from me. My eyes come into focus in time to see a look of panic cross his features as he stares over the top of my head.

I hear Scampi bark.

Van forces a grin and waves, jumping down to the sand with a soft thud.

I cast a look over my shoulder to see Dad, in his green trousers and brown cardy, trudging across the sand toward us.

"Didn't even have to take off my shoes!" he shouts with a smile, acknowledging the retreating tide. "What a beautiful day it is!"

At least I can be sure of one thing: he didn't see us kissing.

WHEN WE GET home, I go straight to bed, telling Dad I don't feel well. It's not even a lie.

If Dad had seen us . . . I can't bear to imagine how shocked he would've been . . . How disappointed . . . How *disgusted* . . . He thinks of Van as a son, as my *brother*, and the thought makes me feel sick with shame. It's as though the explosion in Van's eyes has detonated in my stomach and all of the sparks have subsided, leaving behind only ash and rubble. Why did Van do that? I can't even look at him so how am I going to be able to ask?

THE NEXT DAY, Dad has to return to work so we've got two choices: stay together alone at the house, or go with Dad.

"I've been wanting to see the maze again," Van says at breakfast.

He's acting like nothing happened. Maybe I can too

But I doubt it.

WE'RE WANDERING ALONG a damp cobblestoned path, underneath feathery palm fronds that umbrella out over our heads. Van runs his hands over the leaves of an evergreen bush and they spring back up after him, flicking drops of rainwater onto his coat.

His hands are going to be turning blue in a minute. I won't be warming them up this time.

"I can't believe you left your gloves at home again," I mutter.

"At last! She speaks!" he says sardonically. "I thought we were going to walk around here all day in silence."

I sigh heavily and fold my arms across my chest.

"We used to hide under these." Van crouches down beside a giant gunnera plant—the leaves are absolutely enormous. "You used to imagine fairies throwing parties here." He smiles at me and stands back up.

I'm not really in the mood for casual reminiscing. "There's the maze," I point out as we continue walking.

It looks like a brain, all wiggly lines and organic curves planted into the hill.

"It's tiny!" Van exclaims.

He means the height of the cherry laurel hedges. "They only used to come up to our heads," I remind him.

His brow furrows, but he's grinning. "Yeah, I suppose they did. I wonder if I still know how to find my way."

He sets off at a jog, cutting across the grass instead of following the path as you're supposed to.

Then again, we never did follow the paths. Dad used to tell us off for it.

By the time I reach the bottom, he's already well into the maze. The hedges only come to his chest height and I can't help but smile at the look on his face as he jumps over the muddy patches on the path. It reminds me of running along the coastal track with him, that time he scratched his arm on the blackberry bush.

Of course, I dreamed about that very same day, but when I think about how my dream unfolded, heat collects on my face. I imagined kissing him well before it became a reality.

A loud whistle brings my attention back to him. Van is already at the thatched hut in the center, looking pleased with himself. I bite my lip and wait for him to find his way back to me.

"Isn't there a beach?" he calls on his approach.

"Yes, at the bottom."

"Can we go and see?"

"We've got all day."

Dad is looking after the volunteers today, so he'll be occupied, but we can retire to the crib hut—staff room—when we get fed up with aimlessly wandering. There are lots of books and magazines to read there, plus tea and coffee, not to mention cookies.

The lush green gardens are planted across steeply sloping land, and there's a stream that cuts through the middle, spilling out at the bottom.

We push through a wooden gate and come out in the tiny hamlet of Durgan. The stone cottages have slate roofs and red-brick chimneys and, in the summer, their gardens are over-flowing with flowers. But now everything is green and brown with the only bright colors coming from the red and blue boats upended on the side of the track.

Crunching across the gray rocks on the beach, we come to a stop on the claggy sand by the shore. The river mouth is in the distance on our left and, beyond that, the wide blue Atlantic Ocean. Sailing boats are moored to buoys in the water in front of us and vibrant green seaweed has washed up onto the shore, along with the occasional jellyfish. Van prods one with his boot.

"I remember these jellyfish," he says. It's clear with a brown star on its back. "We used to come here and skim stones." He reaches down and picks up a flat pebble, walking toward the water. I watch as he cocks his long, lean body to one side and sends a stone skipping across the surface.

"Why did you do it?"

Van's eyebrows knot together as he glances over his shoulder at me. A few seconds tick by before he answers. "I wanted to be your first."

I pull a face. "*Why?*"

He picks up another stone. "Because you never forget your first," he mumbles, launching the stone at the water. It skips seven times before sinking.

"I was never going to forget that, anyway," I mutter. "The image is burned onto my retinas every time I close my eyes."

His lips quirk up into a smile.

"I still don't understand why you did it."

"I wanted to," he replies in a low voice.

"But *why* did you want to? I'm like your *sister*," I hiss, my insides flooding with shame once more.

He recoils and then shakes his head. "No, you're not," he states firmly.

"What if Dad had seen us?"

"He didn't."

"You wouldn't have wanted him to, though, right?"

He looks away, then kicks at the stones at his feet, bending down to pick up another. I can tell he's uncomfortable.

"If it was really OK for you to kiss me, why should you care who sees us?" I persevere.

"He's your *dad*," he says pointedly, cutting his eyes to mine. "I wouldn't have been comfortable kissing Jenna in front of her dad, either."

"Was she *your* first kiss?" I ask miserably.

"No." His reply is short.

"How many girls have you kissed?"

"Before yesterday? Three." He pauses, while I stand there feeling inexplicably ill. "My first was my friend's older sister, Kerry-Ann. I was thirteen and she was fifteen."

"Spare me the details!"

"OK." He's nonplussed. "You asked."

"Who was your second?"

He raises his eyebrows. "I thought you didn't want to know."

"Just tell me."

"A British girl who was in Australia on holiday. Her name was Nicola."

"I don't want her name," I snap.

"You sound like you're jealous."

"I'm not," I reply through gritted teeth.

"Because if you really *do* think of me as a brother, it's kind of weird that you feel jealous."

"*You* used to get jealous of other kids!" I accuse with embarrassment. "What about poor Edward?"

"Who?"

"That boy! Edward! The one who was here on holiday when we caught Webster!"

"Oh. Him." Van grins and skims another stone. "That was different. We were ten. I only wanted your attention."

I sigh. "I still don't understand why you wanted to be my first."

He regards me for a long moment before answering. "I figured it was me or Drew."

So he kissed me because he was being his usual possessive self? That was his way of dealing with an outside threat? I don't know whether to feel relieved or disappointed.

"Well, don't let it happen again, OK?" I say under my breath.

He shrugs. "OK."

Definitely disappointed.

THAT EVENING WE arrive home to two messages on the answer machine. The first is from Ellie and I smile as I stand in the hall, listening to her rambling on about being bored out of her brains. She begs for us to do something tomorrow because she can't wait even one more day for New Year's Eve. I giggle when her voice cuts out because the time limit on her message has expired.

"Sounds like she's missing you," Van comments with amusement.

"Yeah." I feel bad that Ellie and I haven't had a chance to

catch up, but she knew how much I needed to spend some one-on-one time with Van.

I start with surprise as the next message begins to play.

"Hi, it's Drew. I wanted to let Nell know that a few of us are going to Chapel Porth tomorrow. Thought she and Van might like to come."

Van presses his palms together in a prayer and gives me a beseeching look.

My shoulders slump. I'm not sure I can handle the stress of watching him surf again. "I'll see if Ellie wants to come too," I say resignedly.

AS IT TURNS out, quite a few of our friends are up for a day trip, and the next day I find myself sitting between Van and Ellie in the backseat of her brother Graham's car, while Graham's girl-friend rides shotgun.

While I'm loving my newfound freedom, being able to go out with people my own age instead of having to ask Dad to drive me places, I'm not exactly relaxed being this close to Van. He's staring out of the window in silence as Ellie chats ten to the dozen about what she's been up to over the holidays. I ask lots of questions to keep her talking, but I'm uncomfortable knowing how much lies unsaid between the two of us. I wonder if I'll ever confess to Van kissing me.

We pull up in the car park and see that Drew, Nick, Max, Brooke, and Brad have just arrived. Ellie and I clamber out to greet Brooke, leaving the boys to get ready while we go to the coffee shop. This place is famous for its "Hedgehog" ice-cream cones—Cornish vanilla rolled in caramelized hazelnuts—but today we're stocking up only on hot drinks.

The café is nestled in the crevice of two, big grassy hills. From back here the hills climb skywards toward the ocean until they become high cliffs, dropping straight down onto the white beach or crystalline green water, depending on whether the tide is in or out. Sitting on the cliffs to the right are the old Wheal Coates tin mine ruins that Dad and I sometimes walk Scampi around.

There's a queue, and by the time we've been served, the others are ready to go.

"We were here yesterday and there were these really glassy sets coming through," Nick tells Van as they walk on the sand in front of us. "Perfect A-frames, not a drop of water out of place."

"His tail-end was shredding," Max says gleefully.

Ellie nudges me and rolls her eyes at all of their surf speak, but I like listening to the way they talk. I look past her to Brooke, but her attention is fixed on Van. Ellie notices and nudges me again.

Brooke glances at us. "What?"

Ellie nods at the back of Van's head and grins.

Brooke shrugs. "Your brother is *hot*," she mouths at me.

I shake my head. "He's not my brother," I whisper.

She doesn't care about the technicalities.

Her fixation with Van does *not* improve when she sees him surf. I struggle to take my eyes away from him too. Even Ellie seems impressed.

"Whoa," she says, as Van makes a rapid change of direction, sending spray into the air. He gathers speed as he surfs down the face of a clean, green wave and boosts his board off the lip before coming back down to continue riding.

I'm having a much better time than the other day. Not only

do I have my friends with me, these waves are a lot friendlier than the huge ones at Porthleven. It's kind of hard to talk, but we try, falling silent every so often to watch.

"Who was *that*?" I ask with amazement as one surfer's tail fins disengage the wave and the guy rides backward for a couple of seconds. "Was that Brad?"

"I think it was Nick," Brooke replies. They have the same color hair.

I have to admit, I'm in awe of these guys.

Suddenly Van flies off the lip of the wave and does an actual 360 in the air before coming back down again and continuing to ride.

"Oh my God!" Ellie gasps, her jaw hitting the sand.

"Holy shit!" Brooke erupts, leaping to her feet.

Wow.

That was *beautiful*.

ALL ANYONE CAN talk about when we arrive at The Boatman for New Year's Eve is Van's 360 maneuver. Half of our friends saw it, but *everyone* heard about it.

"I've never seen *anyone* do an air reverse," Brad raves.

"No, not aside from professional surfers," Max says.

"Would you like to surf professionally?" Brooke asks Van, her face alight with interest.

He shrugs, embarrassed by the attention, and Brooke's is *avid*.

I decide to leave them to it and go to find Ellie. She's on the deck, under the festoon lights. We perch together on a bench seat, facing outward. A bunch of other friends are out here too, so we kill time chatting.

"She wanted to know what was happening in *Neighbors*," Van mutters in my ear about ten minutes later. I stiffen at his close proximity.

"*I* want to know what's happening in *Neighbors*." I look up at him. "Jason Donovan hasn't even left here yet." Australia is eighteen months ahead of us in terms of episodes.

"I don't watch it." He nods at the bench. "As you well know."

I scoot over, but he still ends up pressed against my side. The warmth from his body seeps right into my skin and I have to admit, it feels nice. I was a bit cold, even with all the people teeming out here.

"Brooke likes you," I say. Ellie is talking to another friend from school and isn't paying us any attention. "You know she lives right over there." I feign nonchalance as I nod across the creek at Brooke's chocolate-box cottage. It seems like way more than three weeks ago that I was there for her brother's birthday.

"Yeah, she invited me to go and see her place later."

"Did she?" I glance at him. "So you're up for a fifth?"

"Fifth?" From his side profile, I can see his confusion, but then understanding dawns on his face. *Fifth kiss.*

"I wasn't intending to go." He glances at me out of the corner of his eye. "What about you? Going for a second?" He nods straight ahead and I follow the line of his sight to see Drew weaving through the crowd with a tray of canapés. He catches my eye and comes over, saving me from having to answer Van's question.

"Please take some of these off my hands." He presents his tray to us.

"Thanks." Van grabs a mini Yorkshire pudding and gets to his feet, leaving us to it.

Where is he going?

"That's it, I'm taking a break," Drew decides, making space for the tray on the table among the empty glasses. He sits down in Van's vacated spot on the bench.

Is Van going to Brooke's?

I try to concentrate. "Did you cook these?" I'm sure they're delicious, but to my anxious taste buds, they have the flavor and consistency of cardboard.

"Not those ones. My biggest contribution to tonight is the playlist," Drew replies. "The best the eighties has to offer."

I can't believe that tomorrow is a new decade, 1990.

"I love this song," I say.

It's "Don't You Forget About Me" by Simple Minds, which is on the soundtrack for *The Breakfast Club*, another of my favorite films.

"Me too."

"You do like cooking, though, right?"

He shrugs. "I don't mind it, but it's not what I want to do with my life."

"What do you want to do?"

"I don't know. I'm thinking about studying philosophy at university, hoping it'll inspire me a bit. What about you?"

"English, I think." I glance over my shoulder. *Is Van at the bar?*

"No, I mean, what do you want to do as a career?"

"Oh! Maybe something to do with publishing—books or magazines." I know I sound vague, but I'm distracted. *Maybe he went to the bathroom . . .*

I take another canapé and at the same time do a sweep of the room. I'm looking for Brooke now, as well as Van. I feel ill when I spy neither.

"Guess I'd better get this back to the kitchen." Drew stands up and grabs the tray. "See you later."

I feel bad as he walks off—was I rude? At Brad's birthday party, he had my undivided attention and my stomach was full of butterflies.

Where are my butterflies now?

Almost as if in answer, my mind recalls Van's kiss and my stomach is rapidly alive with the winged, fluttery creatures.

Oh my God.

Has Van ruined Drew for me?

Van reappears and settles himself back on the bench. Confusingly, my butterflies multiply, vanquishing my worries of only moments before as to his whereabouts.

"I thought you'd gone to Brooke's." I feel breathless as he passes me a nonalcoholic cocktail.

"No." He frowns. "Bar." He chinks my glass. "I can't believe I gave up an Australian summer for a British winter," he adds wryly.

"I'll try not to take that personally." I take a sip of my drink.

He smiles while staring into the crowd.

"Seriously, though, are you glad you came?" I ask.

He hesitates before nodding. "I'm a bit homesick," he admits.

"Are you?" His comment not only surprises me, it hurts.

He shrugs. "I miss my friends. And Dad."

The hurt deepens. I don't know why. I suppose I want us to be enough for him, but why *should* we be enough for him? I should be glad we're not all he's got. I *am* glad. So why do I feel injured?

His little finger hooks mine and I try to swallow my hurt, but then he presses a tender kiss to my shoulder and I instantly tense up, scanning the people around us to see if anyone noticed.

"Chill out," Van says, wearily.

"My friends think of you as my brother," I reply darkly, extricating my finger.

"Jeez, Nell," he mutters, shoving his hair from his face. He turns to look at me and his hair falls forward again as he leans in close. "I am *not your brother*." He stresses the last three words. "And you want the truth?" His eyes flash. "It actually kind of kills me that you hated it because all I've thought about since I fucking did it is doing it again."

I'm stunned, and then the most overwhelming urge comes out of nowhere and slams into my back, trying to propel me forward.

He withdraws slightly and I drag my focus away from his lips to meet his eyes.

"There," he murmurs, as though he's just received the answer to a question he's been asking himself.

"Nell, you've got to come and dance with me to this song!" Ellie practically shouts in my face.

I can barely gather together my thoughts. What does she want?

"Come on!" she urges as I stare at her blankly. "Dance!" She throws her hands up with frustration before reaching down with a laugh and pulling me to my feet.

She drags me inside to the dance floor, where the tables have been moved out of the restaurant area and disco lights are bouncing balls of sparkling color off the walls. I belatedly notice that the song playing is Kim Wilde's "Kids in America"—one of our favorites—but I'm too dazed to have fun.

I don't go back and join Van for the rest of the evening, but

I'm always aware of where he is and I know he's never on his own, mostly talking surf with the other guys.

As the minutes count down to midnight, I'm surrounded by my friends on the dance floor. Drew is close by, as are Ellie and Brooke, but Van is on the other side of the room with Nick and Max.

"Ten, nine, eight . . ." The crowd begins to chant. "Seven, six, five . . ." Van and I lock eyes with each other across the jam-packed space. "Four, three, two, one . . ." Everyone erupts with cheers and I'm engulfed by Ellie, followed by Brooke, and then Drew is in front of me, smiling and flashing his dimple.

I'm immune to it. He cups my face with his hands and bends down to kiss me, but at the last second, I turn my face away so his lips land on my cheek. When he withdraws, I'm staring at Van.

"DO YOU WANT to use the bathroom first?" I whisper when we arrive home, kicking off my shoes in the hall and attempting to act normally.

"No, go for it," Van replies, also in a whisper so we don't disturb Dad.

I walk straight ahead, pulling on the light switch and closing the bathroom door behind me. I take off my makeup and brush my teeth as quickly as I can, knowing that he's out in the hall, waiting his turn.

My heart stutters when I open the door to find him right there. His night-sky eyes penetrate mine as the moment draws out. And then my heart does an about turn and speeds up. He takes a step toward me and I slowly back into the bathroom. Without breaking eye contact, he closes the door behind him and locks it, his hand reaching for the light switch. There's a click and the room falls into darkness.

I am intensely aware of the sound of our breathing. He edges closer so we're hip to hip, my lower back pressed against the cold, hard edge of the basin. My eyes adjust enough to see the shape of him, so I know that when he bows his head he's going to kiss me, but it still comes as a shock to feel his lips on mine.

I'm effervescent as I kiss him back, my hands twisting in the fabric of his shirt as my knees turn to jelly. He clasps my face and deepens our kiss, and my head spins as our tongues entangle. Out of the blue, Ellie's and Brooke's shocked faces assault my mind and I slide my mouth away, panting. But Van is still there, pressed up against me, and the pull is too strong. I shut out Ellie and Brooke and Dad and everyone else, and return my lips to his.

A WEEK AND a half later, I lie in bed, experiencing the strangest, most confusing mix of emotions. Tomorrow morning, Van flies home to Australia and I am devastatingly, *crushingly* sad at the thought of him leaving. As soon as Dad is asleep, I'm going to him.

Over the last ten days, our relationship has fast-forwarded at a whiplashing speed. It's been near impossible to keep our hands off each other when Dad has been in the room, and we've stolen kisses and caresses at every opportunity—behind doors, down on the deck, even on the couch when Dad has been in the bathroom. But in the two hours between Dad leaving for work and Ellie's mum picking me up for school, we haven't had to hide.

At first, we stayed in the house, kissing and cuddling in the living room, but the last few days have seen things getting increasingly heated, and as soon as Dad's car has pulled away from the drive, we've retreated to Van's bedroom, where we've been getting to know each other on a much more intimate level.

Yesterday, we came scarily close to going the whole way. The same thing happened this morning, with us *only just* managing to stop. We haven't had any protection and it has been agonizing, but we couldn't buy condoms from the village shop without fear of Dad finding out, and although Van has been surfing with Nick and Max on a few occasions, he hasn't found any on his ventures.

Then, this evening, he discovered that the sailing club has machines in the men's bathrooms . . .

We are taking that final step tonight.

I always thought that I'd have a boyfriend for months, maybe a year, before I'd consider going the whole way, and I certainly didn't think I'd lose my virginity at the age of fifteen.

But I desperately want Van to be my first—in every way— and he wants *me* to be *his*.

I'm excited, apprehensive, miserable about him leaving, and I still have lingering feelings of guilt and shame. Van and I may not technically be siblings, but we lived like brother and sister for five years and I hate to think of people judging us. Dad, without a doubt, would be horrified at how our feelings have developed.

I'm also sad that I'm about to jump over this huge milestone and I can't even tell my best friend. Ellie already feels snubbed because I haven't invited her to hang out with us after school.

I crane my neck and listen. Dad must be asleep by now. It's not the first time we've taken a risk, but there is a very big difference between those early days when I lay in Van's bed and we innocently talked to what we're doing now.

We both feel terrible about deceiving Dad and going behind his back, but tonight we'd do just about anything to deaden the pain of Van's impending departure.

I slip out of bed and creep over the floorboards, carefully avoiding those that creak and softly open my door. Moments later I'm in the hall, slipping on my shoes and hurrying through the freezing night air to the annex. I tap lightly on the door and it opens.

All the emotions I've been experiencing intensify when I stare into Van's eyes. He tugs me into the room and closes the door before pressing my back up against the wall. His jeans are rough against the soft material of my PJs and when he breaks our kiss to stare at me, his eyes are black with desire.

Past his shoulder, I catch sight of his packed bags and tears spring up in my eyes. His expression becomes tormented as he rests his forehead against mine. I blink back tears, not wanting to waste precious moments by crying.

We undress each other and move to the bed, kissing and caressing and getting closer and closer to the point of no retreat. I feel crazily on edge—like something inside me will snap if it doesn't happen soon.

"Are you ready?" he whispers, his breath hot in my ear.

I nod and he sits up, the duvet falling from his back and leaving me completely exposed.

"You're so beautiful," he murmurs, running his hand along the curve of my waist.

I shiver with the cold, but reach up to touch him too, tracing my fingers over the contours of his chest.

"*You* are," I reply and he smiles such a sweet smile at me before reaching for the condom on his bedside table.

My eyes are as round as saucers as he rolls it on, nerves ricocheting around my stomach.

And then I blink and wake up in a nightmare.

The door has flown open, the lights have gone on, and Dad is standing in the middle of the room. He shakes his head quickly, as though he can't believe his eyes.

Van jolts backward, accidentally leaving me uncovered. He realizes his mistake and hastily tries to repair it, but in doing so, Dad catches sight of Van's own exposed frame and I swear, I never again want to see that look on my father's face.

"*What the HELL is going on?*" he shouts, his eyebrows practically hitting his hairline as Van wilts in front of him. "*What are you DOING?*"

It's a rhetorical question. There is absolutely no doubt about what we're doing.

"*She's like your SISTER!*" he yells, shock and horror streaking across his features.

I realize with a pang that his fury is, at this moment, entirely directed at Van.

Dad's eyes are wide as he advances, Van hastily reaching for his hoodie and pulling it on. "I *brought* you here!" Dad yells in Van's face. "I *paid* for your ticket! You were—you *are!*—like a *son* to me! And you're doing this *here*," he looks around the room, "with *my daughter* . . . under *my nose* . . . in your *mother's studio*?"

My heart splits in two as Van jolts viciously.

"Dad, please!" I interject, knowing that the damage my father is doing to him is irreparable. I grab Van's hand. "Don't blame him!"

Dad looks at me as though he can't believe I'm actually here, but he breaks eye contact almost immediately.

"Put some clothes on," he spits in my general direction, gathering up my pajamas from the floor and hurling them at the bed. "How *could* you?" He sounds so hurt that I burst into tears, weighed down with regret and remorse.

"I'm sorry!" I blub as I slide my arms into my pajama top. Van comes out of his daze and pulls on his jeans.

"He's like a *brother* to you!" He can't even look at me. It's all of my worst fears realized.

"We are *not* brother and sister!" Van raises his voice angrily. "I *love* her!" He shakes his head rapidly and points at me. "I've *always* loved her, but what I feel for her now is *not the same* as when we were ten. I am *in love* with her."

Dad's eyes rest on me and I nod, my heart squeezing excruciatingly.

"We love each other," I whisper, willing him to understand, to accept this for what it is. "I'm in love with him."

He stares at me for a long moment, but then his confused expression clouds over with dismay and disappointment.

"Go back to bed," he tells me in a choked voice before looking at Van. "If you weren't already leaving in the morning, I'd be booking you on the next flight home."

Van slumps on the bed and buries his head in his hands as Dad waits for me to leave the room.

I DIDN'T KNOW it was possible to feel this bad. Obviously, we all went through worse five years ago, but this is a different kind of agony. This humiliation, this level of remorse . . . I don't know how I'll ever recover.

Two weeks have passed since Van left and I'm still not sure how I'm getting up and functioning each day. Ellie thinks I'm heartbroken over my "brother" leaving, and the thought of her finding out what actually happened fills me with dread. I come home from school each day and retreat to my room. I can barely eat, I barely sleep, and on top of all that, I feel absolutely heartbroken—because I've lost Van too.

"Nell." Dad is outside my bedroom door.

I don't reply, but he comes in anyway. It's Saturday so I don't have to drag my bones from bed, and I don't intend to.

"I thought we might take Scampi for a walk on the beach," he says quietly.

I shake my head.

"Nell, we can't keep living like this."

I roll away to face the wall, pulling the cuddly koala Van gave me for Christmas against my chest.

Dad sighs heavily and the end of my mattress compresses as he sits down on my bed.

"It's time to move on," he tells me in a husky voice. "What's done is done."

My chest heaves as I begin to shake with silent sobs.

"*Nell,*" Dad murmurs.

"I miss him!" I cry.

This time he doesn't say anything, but after a minute I feel his hand on my shoulder. He gently but firmly turns me to face him.

"I love you, darling," he says in a voice racked with emotion, his eyes brimming with tears as he brushes hair away from my face.

I feel like it's the first time he's looked at me properly since he found us together.

"This is for the best. You're too young to be doing that sort of thing. You're only fifteen!" he says imploringly, squeezing my shoulder. "I know it might not seem like it right now, but one day, maybe five years from now, you'll understand why this happened."

A feeling of déjà vu overcomes me and I flashback to Van and me, aged five, at the top of the stairs. We were eavesdropping on our parents and Ruth said something similar.

But no. I'll never understand this, not in five years, not in twenty, not when I'm an old lady, shriveled and gray.

The only boy I've ever loved is halfway round the other side of the world. And God only knows when I'll see him again.

TWENTY

T"HANKS FOR DRIVING." I REACH ACROSS AND RUN my fingers through the short dark-brown hair at Joel's temple. He yawns and gives me a sleepy smile.

"Yeah, it's a long one, isn't it?"

"Now you understand why I don't do it very often."

He rubs at his right eye with his knuckle. "Do you reckon your dad is still up?"

He sounds shattered. I doubt he's in the mood for meeting my father for the first time.

I glance at the whitewashed cottage ahead and shrug. Light glints through cracks in the living room curtains, but that could be the lamp that's left on at night.

"Let's find out." I open the car door and step out into the cold air, stretching my arms over my head to release some of the tension after the long car journey. Eight hours, door to door—but we did travel through rush hour.

We're in Cornwall for the Easter holidays. Joel and I go to university together in Liverpool where we're both doing media studies. I wasn't sure about him at first. He was always cracking jokes and making quips during lectures and I thought he was a bit too cocky and over-confident, but then he helped me out with some coursework and I found that he had a sweet side. Sparks flew one night at the student union and we ended up back at his place. We've been together for about seven months.

His parents live in Stoke-on-Trent, which is only about an hour away from our campus, so I've met them a couple of times. I feel bad that Joel still hasn't met Dad. I haven't been home since Christmas and it felt too soon to be bringing my boyfriend back then.

I was supposed to be going to New York to see Mum, but she and her husband, Robert, decided to go on a cruise at the last minute. She only ever puts pressure on me to visit when it suits her. I hate leaving Dad alone at Christmas, anyway, so I was relieved when she made other arrangements.

"You can leave your bag here," I say to Joel, dumping my own on the annex doorstep.

"Are you sure your dad is OK with us sleeping together?" he asks.

"I think so. He said he was." It was an uncomfortable conversation, to be honest, but it seemed strange to make us sleep in separate rooms when we've been practically living together for the last few months.

I unlock the front door and lead the way. The hall and living room lights are on, but the TV is off and the cottage is silent. I poke my head around the door of the living room and grin. Dad is fast asleep on the couch.

"Dad!" I whisper loudly.

He stirs, blearily opening his eyes and gasping at the sight of me. "Nell!" he exclaims in a croaky voice, slowly removing his tired limbs from the cushions.

Smiling, I go and help him to his feet. Joel hovers by the door as we embrace.

"Dad, this is Joel."

Dad steps forward to shake his hand. "Hello, Joel. Sorry I'm not more awake to welcome you." Has my father shrunk since I last saw him? Joel is five foot ten, but he seems quite a bit taller than Dad. "What time is it?" Dad asks me.

"Eleven," I reply.

"Would you like a cup of tea?" Dad's eyes dart between us.

"Joel?" I ask.

He nods. "Sure."

I have a feeling that my boyfriend would rather go straight to bed, but he's being polite. I squeeze his jumper-clad forearm as we follow Dad through to the kitchen.

"I'll give you a tour in the morning," I tell him.

"It won't take long," Dad pipes up.

"Nell told me you've lived here all your life." Joel tries to make conversation as we sit down at the table.

"Fifty-five years," Dad confirms.

"He's always said he'll be leaving in a coffin," I state wryly.

"I don't blame you." Joel grins. "I've seen pictures of the view."

This is the right thing to say to my father.

We retire to the annex after not too long. Dad looks absolutely exhausted—we all are.

"I'll see you in the morning." I press my lips to my father's warm, gravelly cheek and he kisses my forehead in turn.

"It's good to have you home, darling."

Joel uses the bathroom while I grab the keys and let myself into the annex. My heart always speeds up a little when I come in here—it's almost as though the place is haunted, squashed so full of memories that it overwhelms me. I've never slept in here before, but friends have when they've come to stay. I'm hoping it'll help, being here with Joel.

Joel falls asleep almost as soon as his head hits the pillow, but I lie there for a while, staring over at the wardrobes.

Ruth's work still lies within, along with Van's paint set. He didn't take anything with him five years ago, but he left a letter on his bed for Dad. Dad disclosed that he'd asked if we could keep his mother's artwork safe for him until he was in a position to take it home, but that was all he revealed about the letter's contents. I searched for it on and off for a few months, but never found it.

I squeeze my eyes shut, trying to block out the past. It still hurts when I think about it. Luckily I've learned not to do it very often.

THE NEXT MORNING, I awake to see Joel over by the window, in his boxer shorts, peeking out of the curtains.

"Morning," I say groggily.

"Hi." He casts a smile at me over his shoulder.

"Some view, huh?"

"Incredible." He kneels on the bed and leans forward to plant a kiss on my lips. "I was about to nip to the bathroom." He stands up and grabs his clothes from the chair he threw them on last night. "You could do with an en suite in here."

"Tell me about it." Dad and I always made do.

"Do you reckon your dad's up?" Joel asks, buttoning his jeans.

"Probably. He wakes at the crack of dawn."

He looks nervous and I smile. "Do you want me to come with you?"

He nods, so I get out of bed and dress quickly.

Dad is at the kitchen table with his usual cup of tea when we enter the cottage. Joel says good morning, then goes to take a shower.

"Have you any plans for today?" Dad asks when we're alone.

"Not today—we're all yours. Tonight, though, Ellie and some of the others are going to The Boatman for a few drinks. Do you mind if we join them?"

"Of course not. You know me, I'll be quite happy to have an early one."

"Sorry we kept you waiting so long last night."

"I wanted to see your face before I went to bed," he replies, pressing my hand.

"It feels like ages since I saw you at Christmas."

"One day I'll drag myself to Liverpool," he promises.

"Hopefully we'll have more room next year."

Right now, I live in a house with three other girls and, more often than not, their boyfriends too, but in our third year, Joel and I might get something together. We'll probably share with another couple.

"Joel seems nice." Dad nods toward the bathroom.

"Yeah, he's great."

He hesitates, then takes a sip of his tea, but I sense he has something to say.

"Everything OK?" I prompt.

He sighs. "I heard from Van a few days ago."

My heart lurches.

"He's here, in the UK."

In my head, I'm scraping the chair across the tiles in my hurry to get out of here, but I force myself to stay seated.

"He asked if he could come to visit."

I know Dad has stayed in touch with Van, but sporadically—they send Christmas and birthday cards, but probably only speak once a year.

"What did you say?" My voice sounds like it's coming from someone else.

"I told him you'd be here with your boyfriend . . ."

My heart clenches.

". . . so we wouldn't have a lot of space," Dad finishes.

"He could stay in my room," I find myself offering.

"He's traveling with a friend, anyway."

"Which friend?" I ask. *A girlfriend?*

"Dave, I think he said."

I'm unsettled by the pang of relief I feel.

"They plan to spend a few weeks surfing the coast before heading to Europe, so they've invested in a camper van. I said I'd check with you, but thought they could park on the drive."

My head spins as I nod.

Dad covers my hand with his, patting it lightly before getting up to stack the dishwasher. I help him.

I HAVEN'T SEEN Van since he left under those horrific circumstances five years ago. Dad banned me from ringing Australia, but eventually I defied him, willing to suffer the consequences. I must've called a dozen times before Van finally answered, revealing that he'd been away on a fishing trip. He sounded like a different person. Our conversation was strained and tense—much, much worse than any of the stilted exchanges we'd had in the past. My dad had spoken to Van's dad and had landed him in a lot of trouble. I knew Van felt deeply ashamed about what had happened. The aftermath hit him hard.

I wrote him letters—dozens of them. But it was months before I received a reply. I'd even accused Dad of keeping them from me. I became paranoid and bitter—I was *horrible* that year.

But when Van's letter finally arrived, I wished Dad *had* been hiding others, because what I imagined receiving was very different to what actually came.

Van told me that he felt sick about what we'd done and that he wished he'd never crossed that line with me. He would always care for me, he said, but there was no point in me pining for him because we could never be together. He admitted he'd dropped out of school months earlier and had been too embarrassed to tell me at Christmas. Now he was working with his dad full time and just wanted to be happy, surfing and hanging out with his mates. He thought we'd both feel better if we gave each other some time and space to recover, and he hoped we could be friends again one day.

That was the gist of it. I tore it up and burned the pieces.

"WHO'S VAN?" JOEL asks when I tell him about our forthcoming visitor.

"He was sort of like a stepbrother to me between the ages of five and ten," I explain, having so far managed to avoid the subject, which will probably always be sore to me. "My dad and his mum got together and they moved in with us."

I tell him about Ruth's death and how Van had to go and live with his real father in Australia.

"He came over here when he was fifteen, but that's the last time I saw him."

"How long ago was that?" Joel asks, and I realize I haven't explained that we're the same age.

"Five years ago—our birthdays are two days apart."

"You're practically twins!"

"Our parents used to joke about it. We had to share birthdays and everything."

"Ooh, I wouldn't have liked that."

Joel has an older brother and a younger sister. They get on OK, but there's always been a bit of competition between them—they're not super-close.

"To be honest, by the time I moved to Cornwall from London, I was so happy to be here that I would have shared pretty much anything."

"And you were in the same bedroom?"

"Yep." I smile. "The titchy one at the top of the stairs."

"Huh."

"Bit different to your house, eh?"

His home is a veritable mansion compared to mine.

"Still, what a place to grow up," he says, holding back a tree branch for me.

We're in the wooded area, to the left of the deck and down by the water. The cottage may be small, but it's built on an acre of land. I'm showing Joel around. I step onto a dead tree trunk on the path, feeling the rotten wood give a little beneath my feet.

Spriggens . . . I think to myself, as a memory floats back to me of the naughty fairies who I once imagined jumping out from behind this very tree trunk, frightening Fudge and Smudge so much that they tumbled down the bank and splashed into the river.

I open my mouth to tell Joel about it, but change my mind and snap it shut again.

"NELL!" ELLIE PRACTICALLY catapults herself into my arms from across the other side of the bar area.

I haven't seen her since Christmas. She goes to Newcastle University and has a boyfriend there too, so our trips to visit each other have been few and far between since the first year, when we caught up every couple of months.

She and Joel hug. They met in October when she came to Liverpool for my birthday weekend. He and I had only recently got together.

"Brooke!" I squeal, looking past Ellie to our friend, who's just walked in the door. Her brother, Brad, is close behind her.

"I called out to you, but you didn't hear me," Brooke chides, as we repeat the same process of hellos.

She's at university in Glasgow, so she's even farther afield than Ellie.

"Aah, together again," Nick teases from behind the bar. He still has longish light-blond hair and curls that Ellie would've killed for when we were younger. Her beloved perm dropped out after only a few weeks. Now she wears her chestnut hair straight. It comes to past her shoulders, but mine is even longer. Not that you'd be able to tell—I'm wearing it in a braid tonight.

I go to the bar, taking Joel with me. "Where's Drew?" I ask, after I've made the introductions.

"He's 'oop north' with his girlfriend for Easter," Nick replies, affecting a terrible northern accent. Drew's girlfriend, Charli, is from Yorkshire.

"That's a bummer. I haven't seen him in ages."

Drew and I ended up becoming friends, once he'd got over my New Year's Eve snub. He knew after that night that I wasn't interested, and soon moved on to date a girl from another school. They were together for about a year, but he's never flown solo for long.

Unlike his brother, who is perpetually single.

"Guess who's coming to stay for Easter?" I say as Nick sorts us out for drinks. I'm amazed at how I've managed to sound casual, considering I feel anything but.

"Who?"

"Van."

"Cool! Is he here to surf?"

"Yeah, I think. He and a mate are traveling around Europe in a camper van."

"A camper van! That sounds fun. Make sure you get him to give me a call. Does he still compete?"

I shrug. "I'm not sure."

I'm embarrassed to admit that I never speak to Van at all. The last time I heard from him was when he sent me a card for my eighteenth birthday. That was over two years ago and made me feel very strange indeed. He sends Christmas cards, but they're also addressed to Dad, so they don't count.

We don't stay too long as Joel is driving and can't drink, but we all make a plan to go to the beach in the next few days. Everyone's around for a good couple of weeks so there'll be plenty of time to catch up.

"I've always wanted to be able to surf," Joel says on the journey home.

"You could learn. Why don't you do a couple of lessons while you're here? There's an amazing surf school at Poldhu Beach, not far from us."

"Bit old, aren't I? And isn't the water freezing?"

"Yeah, but you wear a wetsuit, and you're never too old. Take a right here."

He flicks on his indicator. "Maybe I'll look into it."

I'm tense as he drives past Steven and Linzie's farm. Around the bend is where the driver took Ruth off the road.

"Careful on this stretch," I warn. "It's tight."

"It's fine," he scoffs, and my insides draw tight with anxiety. Another car zooms around the corner toward us, making Joel swerve. "Shit!" he erupts. "He was right over on my side of the road!"

"I told you," I say through gritted teeth. I'm clutching the armrests with white knuckles.

"Yeah, all right, Nell, I didn't realize the drivers around here were freaking crazy."

I don't bother to tell him that the people on holiday are the worst.

It's because I'm so stressed that I don't notice the camper van until we're almost upon it.

"Is he here already?" Joel asks with a frown, pulling up on the drive.

My entire body is racked full of tension.

"Bit small, isn't it?" He peers out of the front window. It's a VW Syncro, not one of the vintage VW split-screen campers, but more of a modern eighties one. The bottom half is black, the top half is cream and there are two surfboards strapped to the roof. "How do two blokes fit in that for months on end?" Joel glances across at me. "Are they gay? I wouldn't care if they were," he continues nonchalantly, getting out of the car.

I'm glad he doesn't really require an answer, because I can't give him one. I'm struggling simply to breathe. An electric eel has slithered into my gut and has coiled around my insides, pulsating and squeezing and filling me with nervous energy.

The camper van is dead silent, so they're either out cold or they're inside the cottage. As it's only ten o'clock, I predict the latter.

My hand is shaking as I retrieve my keys from my purse. I manage to unlock the door, hearing deep voices spilling through from the kitchen.

"Here they are," Dad says as I put one foot in front of the other.

I'm vaguely aware of there being three people at the table, but my vision tunnels toward Van. He's at the end, sitting in a laidback pose with one long leg crossed over the other, his ankle resting on his opposite knee. An empty beer bottle sits in front of him and another is in his hand, his elbow propped on the table. His hair is a little longer than it was, coming to below his chin. It falls like a dark slash across his forehead, but I have a clear view of his eyes resting on mine. His lips very slowly tilt up at the corners.

I feel as though my heart has been sucked over the falls of a wave and has wiped out at his feet.

Joel grabs my shoulders and cheerfully propels me into the room. Dave jumps up to shake his hand and Van unfurls his lean body from his relaxed position and languidly gets to his feet to do the same. In a daze, I watch him step forward to greet my boyfriend. He seems even taller than he was when I last saw him, and broader too, like he's filled out some of his skin. He's wearing ripped denim jeans and a faded black T-shirt with a graphic print that has partially rubbed off in the wash. He's unbearably attractive.

Dave appears in front of me, breaking me out of my stupor. "It's really good to meet you," he says in a warm, Aussie accent, shaking my hand. I try to smile at him, but I'm shaken. He's tall too, with bronzed skin and light-brown hair that has been so highlighted by the sun that it's almost blond.

"Did you have a good night?" Dad asks us perkily, and I imagine he's trying to keep the atmosphere light. He must know that this is difficult for me.

I'm grateful when Joel answers on my behalf. "Yeah, it's a great pub, isn't it? Right on the river," he tells Van and Dave.

"You guys want a beer?" Dave asks, indicating a bucket on the floor that's full of bottles on ice.

"You came prepared!" Joel exclaims.

"I know," Dad says. "I feel like a bad host."

"Don't be silly," Dave reproaches. "We didn't want to impose. We're happy you're letting us park up on your drive."

"I'll grab a beer," Joel accepts Dave's earlier offer. "I couldn't drink at the pub as I was driving."

"Nell?" Dave asks.

"Sure." My voice breaks, but I nod. I'll have the whole bucket, please.

"Jeez, you're tall," Joel erupts with a laugh. He's looking at Van, but Dave is almost the same height. "How do you guys fit in that thing out there?"

Dave casually throws his arm around Van's shoulders.

"With difficulty," he says easily. "We need to get a tent, don't we, mate?" He shakes Van's shoulder.

"We do," Van answers slowly and he sounds sleepy or drunk, I can't tell.

Once more his eyes return to mine.

It hits me then that we haven't even said hello. We haven't touched, we haven't hugged, we haven't so much as shaken hands. And I get the feeling we're not going to. He's standing only three feet away from me, but he may as well still be on the other side of the world.

An icy-cold beer finds its way into my hand. I put it straight to my lips and drink.

"Come and sit down," Dad urges us.

I go around to the other side of the table and pull up a chair next to Dave, opposite Dad, leaving a space for Joel to sit between Van and me.

Dad meets my eyes across the table—his are full of concern. I take another swig of my beer, finding it hard to concentrate as Joel asks about their trip so far. He's good at making small talk.

Dave does most of the answering, but Van says very little unless prompted.

"We met a couple of surfers at the pub earlier, didn't we, Nell?" Joel says. "Nick and . . ."

"Max," I tell him, glancing in Van's general direction. "You remember them?"

He nods. "Of course."

"They said they'd like to catch up with you while you're here."

"That'd be cool."

A shiver goes down my spine every time I hear his voice.

"I was wondering about doing a few lessons," Joel says as I turn back to him and smile. "I can't surf. Not that I've ever tried, but it'd be cool if I could. Do you surf, Mr. Forrester?" he asks Dad.

"Call me Geoff, please," Dad bats back. "And no, I do *not* surf. You'll find me in the garden, but not the sea."

"Dad works at Trelissick, a National Trust property about forty minutes from here."

"I thought you worked at Glendurgan Garden," Van interrupts with a frown.

"Not anymore," Dad replies.

"But he's going for the head gardener job, so if he gets it, he'll be working across Trelissick *and* Glendurgan." I say this with pride.

Dad wriggles self-consciously, but he returns my smile.

"I'd like to go to a few National Trust places while I'm here," Joel says.

His parents got him membership as part of his Christmas present.

"There are loads around here." I smile at him and he reaches out to tuck a loose tendril of hair behind my ear. I shake it free again and he laughs softly.

I've been steadfastly avoiding looking at Van, but my eyes slide past his as I return my stare to Dad and I feel like I've been punched in the stomach.

As soon as I've recovered, I affect a yawn. "Time for bed."

"Yep, sounds good," Joel agrees, draining the dregs of his beer.

"Do you want to use the bathroom first?" I ask him.

"No, you go for it."

I push my chair out from the table and go round to give Dad a kiss on his cheek.

"Night, darling," he says fondly, patting my hand.

I say good night to the room in general and then head into the bathroom and close the door, my heart racing so fast that I feel like I could pass out. I grab my toothbrush and brush my teeth with the fervor of a crazy person, blood mingling with my tears as I spit foamy toothpaste into the basin. Then I straighten up and stare at myself in the mirror.

"*The color of runny honey in sunshine . . .*"

"*We are* not *brother and sister!*"

"*I am* in love *with her.*"

And let's not forget: "*I wish I'd never crossed that line and I hope we can be friends one day,*" I remember bitterly.

I take a deep breath and inhale slowly.

I love Joel, I remind myself. I've moved on. I'm twenty now, not some stupid teenager who believes everything a good-looking boy tells her. I've grown up. I'm in an *adult* relationship.

My heart feels marginally lighter after the pep talk and I leave the bathroom, heading straight for the annex without looking toward the kitchen as I go.

A moment later, there's a light rat-a-tat-tat on my door.

I open it a crack, my breathing quickening at the sight of Van on the doorstep.

"We're calling it a night too," he says. "But at some point I'd love to get into the wardrobes." He nods toward them. "Not now, obviously, but maybe tomorrow."

"Sure." I clear my throat. "Sure," I repeat and sound comes out this time.

"Thanks." He smiles a small smile, his eyes dark and impenetrable. I want to tear my gaze away, but find that I can't. My fingers are numb as they clutch the doorframe.

Joel must be in the bathroom. I wish he'd hurry up.

I wish he'd take his time.

"It's strange being here without Scampi," Van says despondently.

I nod, finally managing to break eye contact. "He died about three years ago."

"What happened to him?"

"He had leukemia." I swallow, but he stays silent, and I feel compelled to go into more detail because I think that he wants me to. He was his dog too, after all. "He'd lost a lot of weight, but we thought it was old age. The vet said the kindest thing to do would be to put him down. Dad and I were with him at the time." We held his furry body and tried not to cry until after he'd slipped away. It all happened so fast.

"I'm sorry," Van says softly as my eyes prick with tears. It still feels raw.

"Thanks." I finally look at his face and feel oddly thankful that he wasn't with us to suffer through what happened in person.

The front door opens behind him and Joel comes out. Van takes a couple of steps backward and forces a smile at him. "See you guys in the morning."

"Sleep well," Joel replies, while I stay silent.

"I doubt I'll be sleeping as well as you," Van says drily and Joel chuckles, moving past me, into the room.

"What did he want?" he whispers, closing the door.

"His mother's paintings are in the wardrobes," I explain. "He asked if he could have access to them tomorrow."

"Oh, right! I wouldn't mind seeing them too."

The thought of Joel being in here when Van opens those wardrobes makes me feel deeply uncomfortable.

He undresses down to his boxers, while I spend ages merely trying to undo the buttons on my jeans. He's already snuggled under the covers by the time I'm putting on the pastel-pink and white shorts and vest PJs set that his parents got me for Christmas. I climb into bed and Joel spoons me from behind, drawing me close. I'm rigid as his hand slides up my waist, his thumb brushing against the curve of my breast. He presses a kiss to my neck.

"I'm sorry, I'm too tired," I tell him in a clipped voice.

"Really?" Surprise tinges his disappointment. We have sex most nights, but it's been three days.

"Tomorrow," I promise and after a moment he lets me go and rolls over.

I lie there in the darkness, staring at the wardrobes. Out of the blue, I'm struck with the most breathtaking stab of fury. Waves of anger roll over me, chased by bitterness.

I will not let him get to me like this. I will not. He made his bed five years ago. Now he can sleep in it.

On impulse, I turn toward Joel and slide my hands around his waist. He comes to pretty quickly.

THE NEXT MORNING, I walk into the kitchen to find Dave crouching down in front of the washing machine with a perplexed look on his face.

"You want some help?" I ask.

"Yes, please," he replies gratefully.

He moves aside for me and I set the machine going before reaching for the kettle. "Cuppa?"

"I'd love one."

"How long are you guys planning on sticking around?" I ask.

"Not sure. We don't want to outstay our welcome."

"It's hardly a problem, is it, you being parked out on the drive."

He shrugs and grins at me. He has an open, friendly face with a likable, approachable demeanor. I was too distracted last night to appreciate him.

"Is Van up?" I ask offhandedly, getting four mugs out of the cupboard and hesitating.

"He's down on the deck with your dad."

"Oh, right." I reach for a fifth mug as Joel comes into the kitchen.

"Have you got the number for that surf school you were talking about?" he asks me.

"Are you going to do it? Lessons?"

"I figured we're here for long enough."

"I could give you a few tips, mate, if you want to save your pennies," Dave offers amiably.

"No, it's all right," Joel says. "It'll be more fun if I'm in a group with others who can't do it. Like Nell, for example."

I shoot him a look. "What?"

He comes forward slowly, an impish grin on his face. "You're doing the course with me."

"What? No, I'm not." I shake my head.

"Oh, yes, you are." He stops in front of me and tucks my hair behind my ears. I slept in my braid last night and only brushed my hair out ten minutes ago, so now it's falling down my back and is riddled with kinks.

Van walks into the room, closely followed by Dad.

"Good morning," Joel says brightly.

I stiffen, but don't step away.

"Morning," Dad replies. "Aah, lovely, Nell, I was about to put the kettle on."

Joel smiles at me, pinching my chin between his fingers.

"I'm not." I shake my head, looking up at him.

"You are." He nods determinedly.

"I'm not." Out of the corner of my eye, I see Van watching us.

"What's this?" Dad asks.

"Nell and Joel are going to surf school," Dave explains with amusement. "I offered to give them a few pointers, but they declined."

"I didn't know you wanted to learn to surf, Nell," Van says and his low, deep voice makes my insides tremor.

"I don't," I reply flatly.

How can he sound so casual and easy when I'm breaking apart inside?

Out of nowhere, the fury I felt last night returns and slams into me.

That's better . . .

For a few glorious seconds, I revel in it. Then I turn to my boyfriend and smile. "But if that's what you want to do, then I'm up for it."

"Yes!" He punches the air in a ludicrously over-the-top manner, prompting us both to laugh at each other.

My anger is swept away, but it collects in a calm red pool, lying flat at the bottom of my psyche.

"I'll go hunt out the number." I cast my eyes heavenward

and walk out of the room, throwing a smile back over my shoulder at Joel.

VAN AND DAVE head out soon afterward, and I feel much more relaxed when it's only Dad, Joel, and me in the house. We go to a pub a couple of villages away for a Sunday lunch and have a perfectly pleasant day, taking a walk along the cliffs near Poldhu, where we end up dropping in to sign up for our course in person. That night, we sit in front of the TV, watching a video. When Joel gets up to go to the bathroom, I check my watch and turn to Dad.

"It's a bit off, isn't it?" I complain. "What if we'd been waiting for them to come back for dinner?"

"They told me they'd be out all day," Dad replies.

"Oh. Did they?"

"Yes, Van said so when we went for a wander this morning." He hesitates. "He wanted to give you space." He reveals this in an awkward whisper, not wanting Joel to hear. "He asked if I thought they should go, as in, not stick around for Easter."

I'm shocked.

"I said I'd speak to you," Dad finishes, glancing my way. His eyes are full of pity. I can't actually bear to look at him.

"That's ridiculous," I snap, also in a whisper. "He doesn't have to leave. I'll be fine. It's a bit weird, that's all. But I'll get used to it. It'll probably be good for me."

The toilet flushes.

"It's been years," I continue. "But I'm with Joel now, so that makes it easier."

"That's what I thought," Dad whispers, taking the video off pause as Joel comes out of the bathroom.

DAD STILL HAS a few more days of work before the Easter break, so the next morning he heads off early while Joel and I take our time. Our first surf lesson kicks off at 10 a.m. and we have to be there only half an hour before to get kitted out.

I'm standing in the bathroom braiding my hair so it's out of my way, when Van appears in the reflection of the mirror. I freeze.

"Your hair has grown," he says.

"Hair tends to do that," I reply sarcastically, recovering.

A moment passes. "Do you mind if we join you at Poldhu today?" he asks.

"You've got to be kidding, right?" I frown at him in the mirror. "You, surfing on beginners' waves?"

"You'll be on the white water closer to the beach." He leans against the doorframe and folds his arms. "We'll paddle out back, past the breakers. There should be some nice peelers out there."

"Can't you go somewhere else?" I hope no one is in earshot to hear how rude I'm being. It's the only way I can think of to cope with the constant onslaught of up-and-down emotions.

"Aw, look at his little face," Dave says, materializing with a grin.

Shit.

"He hasn't seen you in five years," Dave adds, ruffling Van's hair.

Van bats him away, smirking.

My heart sinks. I turn around and purse my lips at Dave, jokily. "Fine. As long as neither of you takes the piss."

I nod at the doorway and they both step aside to make way

for me. Dave is entertained, but I get the feeling Van is decidedly less so.

JOEL JUMPS AT the offer to all travel together. He and I sit on the camper's bench seat while Dave and Van ride up front.

"I can't believe you're making me do this," I mutter at him over the sound of Oasis blaring from the car's stereo.

"It'll be fun," he replies, squeezing my hand.

And it *is*, once I've got the climbing-into-a-soggy-sandy-wetsuit part out of the way. We warm up and practice on the beach before taking to the waves. I actually manage to stand up on my third try and before the end of the lesson, I'm surfing almost the whole way to the shore.

Joel holds his hands aloft and claps and cheers for me. I think it helps that I'm so small. I remember Van surfing to the shore on only about his second or third try when we were ten.

"I SAW YOU stand up," Van comments casually later. We're at the café, seated at a table on the dunes among big tufts of marram grass. Joel and Dave have gone up to order. "That was good."

"Thanks," I mutter, tapping my fingers on the table.

He sighs quietly. "Are we going to be OK?"

"I don't know, are we?" I sound totally narky.

He doesn't speak for a few seconds. "Should Dave and I just leave?"

I shake my head, begrudgingly, but don't say anything.

"This is hard for me too, you know." His tone is beseeching, but I can't take it.

"Could've fooled me," I snap, digging my toes into the soft white sand beneath my feet.

An expression of deep sadness comes over his features. After a moment, he reaches across the table and hooks my little finger with his.

I snatch my hand away like I've been burned.

At the edge of my vision, I see Joel and Dave returning and plaster a fake smile on my face.

Luckily, they're both talkers, because Van and I say next to nothing. As we're getting back in the car, Van turns to Dave. "Let's go to Porthleven."

"Now?" Dave asks him.

"Yeah, I'm not done yet. Are you? We'll drop these guys home first."

"Thanks," Joel butts in. "I'm keen to take a shower."

For the rest of the afternoon, I can't shake the feeling that I'm never going to see Van again. When their camper van pulls up at four thirty, I almost cry with relief. This is my chance to make amends and I'm taking it.

"Dinner's on us!" Dave calls, coming around the corner with supermarket shopping bags in his hands. Van follows with a couple more.

"Thought we'd have a barbecue," Dave adds.

"What a great idea!" I say with enthusiasm. Joel and I are sitting at the table on the patio outside the annex. "What can I do?"

"Nothing. Stay there and chill out. You, on the other hand," he points at Joel, "can go and get four of our beers from the fridge."

Joel grins and gets up. I project a friendly smile at Van, but he's wearing a hardened expression. He juts his chin in the direction of the annex. "Can I get into the wardrobes?"

"Sure." I jump to my feet and lead the way, my pulse jumping unpleasantly as I get the key from a hook by the door and unlock the wardrobes. Opening the doors, I step back and we stand and stare at the sandcastle painting before us.

"We'll be out of your hair in the morning," Van says in a low, tense voice.

"Don't go," I blurt. "I don't want you to go."

"I can't bear it, Nell," he whispers, and my heart wrenches from my chest at the sound of my name on his tongue.

"It'll be OK," I say. "Don't leave. Please."

He's staring straight ahead, but I take a step closer and get a hit of the ocean—cold, wild, and free.

"Everything all right?" Joel asks loudly from the door, making us both jump.

"Fine," I reply sharply. "Can you give us a minute?"

He loiters.

"We'll see you outside in a bit." My tone is firm.

He stalks out of the room.

Van's eyebrows pull together as he turns to look at me.

"You don't need to go," I stress, earnestly. "I want you to stay. I'll try harder. Maybe we can be friends like you said. Maybe we can put things behind us. I'll try, OK?"

He nods slowly. "OK."

A FEW DAYS later, I answer the phone and hear Van on the end of the line. He's been out surfing with Nick and Max and they're now at The Boatman.

"Brooke and Brad are here," he tells me, and from his loose, easy-going tone, I'm guessing he's not on his first drink. "Brooke's calling Ellie to get her to come down. Can you guys make it? Nick's promising a lock-in," he whispers loudly.

Things have been much more relaxed between us. It's been a blessing having Dave around, who is so laid-back, sweet, and funny that I actually look forward to our evenings together.

"I'll have to pass it by Dad and Joel."

"Get Joel to drive and leave the car here," Van urges. "We'll catch a cab back and pick it up in the morning." They got a lift with Nick and Max today so the camper van is still on the drive.

"I'll see what I can do."

As soon as I hang up, the phone rings. It's Ellie, offering to drive. "I can't drink, anyway, I'm seeing my grandparents first thing," she says.

I commit to the plan then and there, filling Joel in afterward. Dad won't mind—he never needs an incentive to have an early night.

I get ready quickly, choosing wedge heels, jeans, and a soft, black jumper that falls loose off my shoulder, revealing the hot-pink bra strap underneath. I washed my hair after our lesson today and didn't bother to dry it, so it's falling down my back in loose waves. Spritzing some perfume on my wrists, I'm ready.

EVERYONE IS OUTSIDE around a bench table when we arrive. The sun has set and the black river glints with the reflection of the festoon lights. Van is sitting sideways on the bench seat, looking relaxed in his ripped jeans and a blue-and-black tartan checked shirt. Brooke throws her head back and laughs at something Dave has said and Van glances our way, his attention fixing on my face.

"Nell! Damn, you're a babe, tonight!" Nick exclaims with a grin, jumping to his feet.

Joel recoils with alarm.

"Nick, you remember my *boyfriend*, Joel," I say significantly as Nick wraps one arm around my shoulder and plants a kiss on my cheek. He's clearly drunk.

"All right, mate," Nick says to Joel with a grin, offering his free hand.

Joel shakes it with a frown.

"Looks like you guys have got some catching up to do." Nick flashes me a mischievous grin as he sets me free. "I'll go to the bar. What are you having?"

"Are you working?" I ask with surprise.

"Hell no, I'm wasted, but I can still get you a drink. Or ten," he adds, grinning at Joel.

"Ignore him," I say to Joel when we've sat down. "Nick's a flirt, but he knows he'd never get anywhere with me."

"Nor me," Ellie says.

Brooke's cheeks turn pink. Ellie and I notice and burst out laughing.

"Shuddup," she mutters. "It was once."

"It only ever *is* once," Max interjects with a chuckle.

It's a known fact that Nick doesn't do commitment— holiday flings are about all he manages these days, partly because he's exhausted the local girls.

By the time Nick comes back with a tray full of shot glasses, we've moved on to another topic of conversation. "These are for you," he says meaningfully, placing four shots in front of Joel and me.

"No way!" Ellie states firmly when he places another two in front of her. "I'm driving."

"Don't be boring," Nick says. "Catch a cab back."

"Nope. Can't. Not doing it." She pushes them away.

"Fine. In that case . . ." Nick slides them over to Joel and me.

"Are you joking?" I ask. "I'll be legless."

"Excellent." He rubs his hands together with glee. "I've never seen Nell legless."

He distributes the remaining shot glasses to the rest of the table, picking one up for himself. Everyone except Ellie follows suit, our mass of tiny glasses coming together with a series of *chink-chink-chinks*. Van knocks his back without hesitation, dragging his hand across his mouth and placing his empty glass down on the table. I swallow mine more slowly, wincing and pulling a face the entire time.

"Next," Nick prompts, chuckling as he nods at Joel's and my line of glasses.

Joel shrugs and accepts the challenge, knocking his second one back. I can feel Van's dark eyes on me as I pick up mine. What the hell, I don't get drunk often. This shot goes down easier than the first, and I feel light-headed as the warmth rises up from my belly.

Joel takes on his third with a grin. I groan and copy him, knocking it back in one.

"OK, now we've caught up," I say with a saccharine smile at Nick.

"Awesome." He grabs a second tray of drinks from behind him and hands me the cider that I'd originally ordered.

Brooke nudges me. "He's even better-looking than he was at fifteen."

"He is *right there*," I say with a laugh, indicating Van, who totally heard what she said.

He smirks at her, and suddenly I'm glad that she has a boyfriend back at university.

"What do you do these days, Van?" Ellie asks. "Do you still work on the prawn boats?"

I told her all about his job when he was last here—she was fascinated too.

"No, tuna fishing before I left," he replies.

"What does that involve?"

"Sitting on a boat for two months, watching movies in his cabin," Dave interjects with a grin. "The boat goes this slowly." Dave holds his hand up, moving it from left to right at a snail's pace. "They drag a huge cage—net—full of thousands of live tuna back to Port Lincoln from way out in the open ocean. Van has to scuba dive down into the cage every day and get rid of any dead fish, but the rest of the time he sits around, reading and playing video games."

"And I cook," Van chips in. "I do a lot of cooking."

"Yeah, yeah," Dave replies, waving him away.

"Do you ever see any sharks?" Ellie asks curiously.

"Lots. Mostly bronze whalers," Van says.

"They chomp through the net with their razor-sharp teeth," Dave interjects. "Van has to help them get back out again."

"How do you do that?" Brooke's eyes have gone round.

"You grab them by their gills and—"

"You *touch* them?" Brooke asks with a gulp.

Van shrugs. "They're kind of mellow. Once they're in the cage, they just want to get out again. But they're not always friendly. If they turn around and come toward you, you put your foot up and they tend to go round."

"Have you ever seen a great white?" Nick asks with interest.

"Yeah," Van replies. "Had a bit of a close shave with one, recently, actually."

Everyone around the table leans in, listening with rapt attention.

"Out in the open ocean, the water is crystal-clear," he explains. "But the closer you get to Port Lincoln, the worse the visibility becomes. You might only be able to see one or two meters in front of you. A few weeks before I came out here, I was at the bottom of the cage when this white pointer came up from the murky water beneath me. His mouth was wide open and he was ready to bite. It scared the shit out of me—it could've easily torn through the net. I swam out of the way pretty fast."

"Oh my God!" Brooke and Ellie squeal in unison.

I feel sick to my stomach. "*Van!*"

"No one's ever been hurt," he says with a small smile. But his eyes find their way back to me and stay there, locking us in a stare for several torturous seconds.

"Tell them about the killer whales," Dave encourages.

"Ah, that was one of the best experiences of my life." Van shakes his head, awed, before catching my eye again. "There was a pod of them, swimming under the cage, eighty feet deep." I feel like he's talking only to me. "I was with my mate, pushing a dead fish out through a hole in the net and this huge killer whale came up and very, *very* gently took the fish from out of my hands. It gave this little kick of its tail and went straight up to the surface, then this baby whale followed it up and started playing with the fish. But the way that big whale took it from my hands . . . *Man* . . . It was *so* gentle. It didn't want to hurt us at all. It was like a big puppy dog."

I am totally and utterly captivated.

Beside me, Joel coughs. It takes me a moment to realize that he just did the "bullshit" cough. I stare at him, my mouth agape. He grins, but I can't *believe* his rudeness. I'm disgusted.

"I'm joking," he mutters with a roll of his eyes.

I turn back to Van, feeling shaken.

Closing time is upon us before we know it, but with Nick promising a lock-in, we all move inside. I grab as many empties as I can carry, taking them through to the kitchen.

"Where do you want these?" I ask Nick from the doorway.

He's stacking glasses into the dishwasher.

"Aw, thanks, Nell. Do you want a job here?"

I grin and stick around to help.

"How long have you been seeing Joel, then?" Nick asks casually, raking his golden curls away from his eyeline.

"Seven months," I reply.

"He seems fun."

I don't know if he's being sarcastic.

"He is," I reply and he grins at me, his bottle-green eyes sparkling.

"Come on, let's get some more drinks in." He pings my bra strap on the way out.

Joel frowns at us as we appear in the bar area, Nick sniggering like a naughty child and me rolling my eyes.

"What?" I reply to the question—or accusation, I'm not sure—on Joel's face. "I was helping with the empties. You *really* don't have to worry about Nick. I wouldn't touch him with a bargepole."

Joel tugs me into his arms, bending his head to press an

amorous kiss to my neck. I giggle and squirm because it tickles, prompting him to chuckle and do it again. I look up to
catch Van watching, his jaw twitching and his eyes slightly un-
focused. *How much has he had to drink?*

I try to detach myself from Joel, but he's stuck to me like
glue. I'm too drunk to do anything about it, so I point at a
stool in a last-ditch attempt to free myself. He lets me go so I
can sit down.

"I'm off, love," Ellie says to me. "Do you want a lift?"

"No, I'm fine."

"Are you sure?" She seems concerned.

"Yes, really." *Am I slurring?*

Van is leaning right over the bar, his body twisted in such a
way that his shirt has ridden up to expose a stretch of smooth,
honey-colored skin on his waist. I have an immediate, overwhelming desire to bend down and kiss him there. I'm literally
aching to touch him. Aside from him hooking my little finger at
Poldhu, we've had zero contact.

Ellie pats Van on his back. "Look after her," she warns as he
glances over his shoulder at her.

"That's what I'm doing," he replies, turning back to take
the pint of tap water Nick is handing him. Van must've asked
for it.

"What am I, chopped liver?" Joel asks with mild outrage as
I accept the glass and down a third of it.

"He's practically her brother," Ellie brushes him off with a
grin. "That's what brothers do."

I almost choke on my drink. As soon as my friend has left
the premises, I hop down from the stool and make a beeline for
the bathroom.

"You OK?" Joel's voice comes from the door.

His is not the voice my heart was hoping to hear, but my head is thankful.

"You're not chucking up, are you?"

"No!" I exclaim.

"Oh good. Nick's ordering us a cab. So much for the lock-in."

"Joel, can you leave me to it? I'm doing a wee."

"Oh, right."

The room falls silent. I take a deep breath and exhale slowly, trying to quell the nausea that I suspect has very little to do with the amount of alcohol I've consumed.

VAN TAKES THE front seat in the cab home and I'm relieved. Joel is asleep before we even arrive and Dave helps him stumble to the annex, dumping him onto the bed, fully clothed.

"You gonna be all right with him?" he asks circumspectly.

"Fine," I reply, wrestling with Joel's boots. He's out cold.

"I'll leave you to it," he says with a chuckle.

"Thanks."

I don't know where Van disappeared off to—presumably bed.

Once I've dealt with Joel, I go to the bathroom. On my way back to the annex, a dark figure appears from out of nowhere and marches me around the side of the cottage.

"What are you doing?" I gasp as Van presses my back against the cold wall.

My skin is alive with shocks and tremors at the contact.

His hands are on my wrists, burning, scorching. He steps forward, his hips pinning me in place.

I draw a sharp intake of breath, and then his mouth is on mine. I wrestle my hands free and clutch his waist. In my drunken state, I register that he's more muscled than he was at fifteen. And then he's kissing my neck, pulling down the top of my jumper to expose my collarbone, and my head is *spinning, spinning, spinning*, and my hands are up inside his shirt, fondling the skin that I was so desperate to touch earlier. His fingers fly to the buttons of my jeans and—

What is he doing? We're just going to have sex, right here, right now?

I shove his chest, hard, and he stumbles backward, looking dazed.

"What the *hell*?" I hiss. "My boyfriend is *right there*!" I point with disbelief toward the annex.

"I'm sorry," he whispers, contritely.

"Don't touch me again!" I warn, hot tears springing up in my eyes as I hurry back to the annex, my head reeling.

The full extent of what happened doesn't sink in until the morning, when I come to, my head pounding. Joel is still snoring lightly beside me and I am so full of horror and remorse that I can barely look at him.

I can't believe I kissed Van last night. I know he started it, but I kissed him back.

I don't understand. If Van regretted what happened between us so much when we were fifteen, how could he do that with me now? Is it simply his jealousy taking over again?

He doesn't appear for breakfast, but Dave does, looking worse for wear. Joel is in the bathroom throwing up. I'm surprised I'm not, to be honest. I'm glad Dad's not around to see what a wreck we all are. It's his last day at work today before the Easter break.

"Is Van all right?" I ask Dave eventually, curiosity getting the better of me.

"I presume so," he replies. "He crashed in your room last night."

"My room?"

"Your old one, upstairs. Your dad said he could a couple of days ago."

"Oh."

The pull to check on him is too strong. I leave Dave at the kitchen table and go upstairs, knocking on my bedroom door. When there's no answer, I push it open.

The room is filled with a fug of stale booze. Van is in the single bed that replaced my bunk a few years ago, turned toward the wall. The duvet is tangled up in his legs and his muscular back is bared to me.

My eyes drift to the bedside table where a roll of familiar-looking paper lies there. It's his painting, the color of wheat. I took it down from the wall years ago, along with his postcards, and rolled it up, hiding it at the back of a drawer so I didn't have to look at it and be reminded of him.

He's found it.

"Van," I say, and he stirs. I say his name again and he rolls over, looking bleary-eyed. We stare at each other for a long moment.

He's the first to speak. "We'll go," he whispers.

My heart cries out with anguish, but my head nods, knowing it's for the best.

I feel desperately sad when he follows through on his promise later that same day, but it gives me some comfort to know that he's left his mother's paintings behind.

At least I know he'll be back for them.

TWENTY-FIVE

THINK THAT'S CLASSED AS SEXUAL HARASSMENT IN THE workplace, Nicholas Castor," I warn as he grabs me on my way past.

"You're killing me, Bella Nella," he says in my ear.

"And that is a *shit* nickname," I say over my shoulder, firmly removing his hands from my waist. "You're not Italian and neither am I."

"Suits you, though," he says with a cheeky grin, his green eyes twinkling as he hooks his forefinger through one of the belt loops on my jeans and stops me in my tracks.

This is my fault. I should never have slept with him.

I thought I'd just get it over and done with and he'd leave me alone, but to my near-constant surprise, it's had the opposite effect.

God knows how he found it so memorable—I barely recall the details, I was so drunk at the time.

"You've got customers." I nod at a couple of attractive young women who have walked in.

He sighs and lets me go.

I've been working at The Boatman for fifteen months now and it still seems unreal. After graduating from university with a 2:1, I moved to London, getting a night job at a bar so I could afford to do unpaid work experience at magazines during the day. I hoped that the contacts I was making would one day result in a job offer being made, but my whole world came crashing down when Dad got cancer. I put all of my plans on hold and moved straight back home to look after him. It's been two horribly hard years, but he's in remission now and for that I am immensely grateful.

At some point, I'll get my ass into gear and go back to London, but right now, I can't imagine leaving him. He's still so frail. Anyway, the pub is a friendly, sociable place and Nick's parents, Christopher and Theresa, are lovely and easy to please. Nick less so. He's stepped up into more of a managerial role and is a bit of a taskmaster.

"Oi, Nell," he calls from farther down the bar, delving into his pocket. "Can you go upstairs and get the indie mix-tape by my stereo?" He throws me his keys.

"Can't you get it yourself?" I ask with a frown, catching them.

"I'm busy." He slams the till shut and gives me a pointed look.

"Dad's going to be here any minute," I complain.

It's my birthday and we're going out to dinner.

"You'd better be quick, then," he replies firmly.

I huff as I stalk out from behind the bar—see what I mean? Taskmaster.

Nick and Drew grew up in the cottage across the road, but now Nick lives by himself in the apartment above the pub. It's a right shag-pad—God knows how many women have been up there. I can't believe I can now count myself among them.

I don't know how it happened. I'd stuck around after

closing time last Saturday to have a few drinks. I guess I was bored, lonely, and horny, and Nick had been flirting with me for ages. I'll admit, I kind of liked the attention. Plus, it's not as if I was in love with him, so I knew I'd be able to handle it when he moved on to the next girl—as much a certainty as the sun rising each morning. Still, I'm a little surprised at myself.

My walk up the stairs triggers a flashback. We were kissing, right here. I was lying down and Nick was on top of me, and he pulled my jeans off, and then my panties, and then he . . . *Oh my God*. My face is burning as I hurry to the top and unlock his door.

Inside his apartment, the flashbacks are even stronger. The door to his bedroom is open and, as I glance in at his unmade double bed, I'm struck with another memory of him hovering over me, staring straight into my eyes, his face framed by his glorious golden curls.

His body was ripped—like, *seriously*. Lean and sexy and muscled—a real surfer's body.

And, oh *shit*. I scratched my nails down his back as I came.

And I did come. Twice. Once on the stairs and—no, hang on, it was *three* times, total.

I press my palms to my burning cheeks to try to cool them down.

Nick Castor was good in bed.

Well, he's had enough practice, I think to myself wryly. Now where the hell is that mix-tape?

As I lock up again and walk downstairs, absentmindedly tapping the cassette against my palm, something seems off. I poke my head around the corner with a frown and almost jump out of my skin. All of the staff from the kitchen, bar and restaurant, plus a few regular customers, and even my dad, are standing in the middle of the room. They collectively launch into a rendition of "Happy Birthday to You," and then Nick comes out of the kitchen carrying a huge, chocolate-frosted birthday cake, topped with lit candles.

I beam from ear to ear as he comes to a stop in front of me, his eyes glinting in the candlelight. The singing comes to an end and everyone claps and cheers. I blow out the candles, then Nick holds the cake to one side and leans in to kiss me—right on the lips.

I'm used to him being tactile, but when he withdraws, I find it hard to meet his eyes.

Nick's mum, Theresa, interrupts our "moment."

"Happy birthday, Nell, sweetie," she says, giving me a hug.

"Thank you." I'm so touched.

"Nick's idea." She fondly nods at her son, who's plucking the candles out of the cake at a nearby table. Dad comes over and Theresa greets him warmly too. "Now, I know you two are heading straight out for dinner, but can you squeeze in a tiny piece of cake before you go?"

"I think we can manage that, don't you, Nell?" Dad asks with a smile.

"Absolutely," I agree.

Aimee, one of the waitresses, appears with a stack of plates, and Tristan, the chef, comes out of the kitchen with a knife. He hands it to Nick, but Nick passes it straight to me. "Make a wish," he says with a smile.

I take the knife and slice into the cake, closing my eyes briefly to silently ask that Dad's cancer never comes back.

When I open them again, Nick is still smiling at me.

DAD AND I catch the ferry to the pub on the other side of the river. It's more of a boat taxi, really, holding only a few passengers at any one time. But it's a lovely crossing and when the sun is setting, like now, it's absolutely gorgeous. It feels a bit strange to be going from one pub to another—especially when the second is a competitor—but they both do exceptional food and it's nice to have a change of scenery.

It's chilly out on the deck so we go straight to the table that we'd reserved by the window. Dad orders a bottle of champagne.

"It's not every day your daughter turns twenty-five," he says.

I laugh and he smiles at me.

"How was your day?" I ask.

"How was yours?"

"I asked you first."

He shrugs. "I finally got around to planting that crab-apple tree for you."

"Aw, thanks, Dad. I hope you didn't wear yourself out."

"I feel fit as a fiddle," he insists.

Dad never went back to work after his illness, but I know he misses the gardens. Sometimes we'll go and hang out at Glendurgan or Trelissick so he can catch up with his old friends and colleagues. He's also taken to going to flower shows—we went to London together for the RHS Hampton Court Palace one back in July and came back with a tray full of brightly colored begonias. The cottage garden has never looked prettier.

Dad waits until the waitress has poured our champagne before passing me an envelope. "Another birthday present for you," he says. "Oh, and it's also an early Christmas one for me," he adds cryptically.

Intrigued, I carefully open the envelope and pull out several pieces of white card. I turn them over and freeze at the sight of the red QANTAS logo in the corner. Tickets. To Australia.

"What are these?" I'm still not really sure what I'm seeing.

"I've never been to Australia," he says. "I've always wanted to go. If the last few years have taught me anything, it's that life is too short. I'd like to do these things while I'm young enough to enjoy them and there's no one I would rather go with than my beloved daughter." His eyes are shining as he covers my hand with his, prompting my throat to swell.

I look down at the tickets again and notice the date. "Is that the first of *this* November?" I ask with alarm. "As in, a fortnight away?"

"Yes. I know you'll need to take time off work, but I did run it past Christopher and Theresa first. They said it won't be a problem—they're happy for you to go."

I wonder if Nick knows . . .

"I'm paying for *everything*," Dad states adamantly as I shake my head in protest. "No, Nelly, I *won't hear* of it," he cuts me off. "This is *my* treat. I've got it all planned. Van has helped me. We're going to fly into Sydney and spend a few days there . . ."

He continues to elaborate, but my head is stuck at *Van*.

". . . visit Van at Uluru . . ."

"Sorry?" I interrupt as I hear this last part. "What did you say?"

"I said we'll go and visit Van at Uluru. You know, Ayers Rock, where he's working now. Then he'll come with us to Adelaide and on to Port Lincoln, where we'll spend some time with his dad. It'll be good to get to know John properly," Dad says. "I wasn't really with it when he came over fifteen years ago."

That was the last—and only—time we met Van's dad, when he flew over after Ruth's death to take Van home with him.

"So what do you think?" he asks. "Will you come?"

This is clearly something he's wanted to do for a long time.

I place my hands on his shoulders. "Are you kidding, Dad? Of course I'll come. I can't wait." I lean in to give him a hug, hoping that some of the peace and happiness emanating from him will rub off on me.

"WHAT *IS* VAN up to these days?" Nick asks the next day at work. He did know about the trip, as it turns out. He struggled to keep quiet about it.

"He works at a resort in Uluru. He's just a bartender—"

"*Just* a bartender?" Nick interrupts. "Is there anything wrong with *just* being a bartender?" He waves his hands to denote the area he's standing behind. I'm perched on a stool in front of him. It's too early for the lunch crowd so we've got time for a chat.

"You know what I mean. Anyway, you're not *just* a bartender. You practically run this place."

"I won't tell my parents you said that."

My eyebrows jump up. "No, don't."

He smirks at me and turns on the coffee machine. "You want one?"

"Yes, please."

"Yeah, so Van . . ." he prompts.

"He's a *bartender*—no 'justs' about it," I chirp. "His girlfriend,

Sam, works at the rock's cultural center with the aboriginal artists. She's an artist herself."

Van and I e-mail each other occasionally. I sent him one a couple of days ago to wish him a happy birthday.

Nick places a latte in front of me.

"Thanks." My favorite. "It was Sam's idea to go," I say with a shrug. "I get the feeling Van is smitten with this one. I think he'd follow her pretty much anywhere."

I might sound indifferent, but it's only because I've learned to ignore the sting. And I've come to accept that it will probably always sting. I doubt I'll ever stop feeling a bit sore where Van's concerned, but the pain is manageable.

It was Dad's illness that brought Van and me back together. I had to call Van to tell him that Dad had cancer and I think it put things into perspective for both of us. We never talked about what happened—neither when we were fifteen nor twenty—but we both seemed to make a decision to put the past behind us and move on. As Dad said, life is too short. It was time to try to be friends, like we'd said we would. We've been OK ever since.

"You wanna come and see *Fight Club* tonight at the cinema?" Nick asks casually. It's Friday night and by a rare miracle, neither of us is working.

"Brad Pitt?" I grin. "Hell, yeah! Wait. Is this a date?" I ask warily.

"Would it matter if it was?"

"I thought you didn't do dates, Nicholas Castor."

He clutches his chest and turns away, shaking his head. "It's the way you say my name," he mutters melodramatically.

I can't help but laugh and he flashes me a grin, turning back to lean over the counter, his elbows propped on top. "So? Wanna come?"

"Only because it's Brad," I state. "Not because it's you."

I call Dad to let him know I won't be needing a lift. Now that he's not working, he's sort of enlisted himself as my personal driver—we only have the one car between us and he seems to like ferrying me around. I already feel a bit weird, living with my dad at my age, so having him drive me too, makes me feel even more of a teenager. But, hey ho, it makes him happy.

"HOW MANY GIRLS do you reckon you've screwed?" I ask Nick when we're comfortably seated in the cinema.

"*What?*" He coughs up a kernel of popcorn.

"You heard."

"How many girls have I screwed?" He repeats my question with disbelief.

"Yeah. I don't care, I'm just interested." I cast him a sideways look and snigger at how uncomfortable he looks. "Are you blushing?" I ask with delight. "That's hilarious. Go on, have a guess. How many? Fifty, sixty, a hundred?"

"Jeez!" he erupts. "How much of a whore do you think I am?"

I'm taken aback. "What? Not that many?"

"Nowhere *near* that many!" he exclaims.

"But you're always on the pull!"

"I haven't pulled a girl in *weeks*! *Months!*"

"Haven't you?" I'm surprised.

"No! *Man*," he mutters.

The room goes dark and a hush falls over the audience.

I lean in closer, curious. "But all those girls on holiday?" I whisper.

He frowns. "What are you going on about?"

"Every summer, you used to have a different girl. Your relationships would never last longer than two or three weeks, depending on how long they were here for. Drew told me—"

"Drew?" he snorts. "Cheeky sod. What did he tell you?"

"About the holiday flings. About what a commitment-phobe you were when it came to anything lasting."

"He was only trying to put you off me."

"Eh?" I frown at him. "Why?"

"He had the major hots for you. You must've known that."

"Yeah, I did. Kind of." I shrug. "But he got over it long before he started going out with Deborah."

"That's right." He nods, remembering Drew's girlfriend from years past. He's still with Charli, the girl he met at university.

"What was the deal with you and Drew?" Nick sounds confused. "I thought you liked him too, at one point."

"I did," I reply carefully.

"He thought he'd messed up that time you and Van came surfing with us and you were worried about Van getting hurt. He was sure you blamed him for it."

I shake my head. "No, it wasn't that."

"Actually," he says with a grin, "that was the day he also started thinking that you might have a crush on *me*. He banned me from hitting on you after that."

"Did he?" I giggle. "That's so funny. Have you told him you've since dragged me up to your man-cave and had your wicked way with me?"

Nick cracks up laughing and the people in front of us turn around to glare.

"Sorry," I whisper an apology.

"It's only the trailers," he chides, but he does lower his voice when he answers me. "No, I haven't. He's back at Christmas. Maybe I'll break it to him, then."

"Why bother? It ain't happening again," I say facetiously.

That's the last thing that gets said before the film starts.

NICK IS NOT at work the next day—he's gone surfing with Max—and I find myself missing his banter. He was quiet when he dropped me home last night—like, weirdly quiet. Not on a Dad or Van level, but for Nick it was definitely out of the ordinary.

Theresa comes over for a chat after the lunchtime rush has passed, before the early birds appear for dinner.

"How was the film?" she asks with a smile.

She's lovely, Theresa. I've always liked her. We're about the same height—her boys tower over both of us—but she's quite voluptuous, with long, dark hair that she usually wears down. She's glamorous, but warm with it, not aloof or in any way full of herself. And she has her sons' eyes: Castor bottle-green.

"Brilliant," I answer her question. "Very entertaining. You can't really go wrong when it comes to Brad Pitt with his top off."

"Did Nick enjoy it?" she asks.

"I think so. Not for the same reasons as me, though."

She gives me an appraising look and I'm curious to know what she's thinking.

"I shouldn't interfere," she starts to say, and that little voice inside my head goes, *Uh-oh.* "But you do know that boy is smitten with you?" she finishes.

I stare at her, stunned.

"I haven't seen him like this before," she divulges, clearly in two minds about whether to say anything. "He's a different person on the days you're not working."

"In what way?" I'm taken aback.

"He's like a bear with a sore head," she reveals.

"You mean he's even worse when I'm *not* working?" I ask with alarm. The poor staff!

"Oh, sweetie," she says with an indulgent smile. "He only gives *you* a hard time because he's trying to get your attention. 'Bear with a sore head' is the wrong analogy. When you're *not* here, he's as meek as a mouse." She gives me a helpless shrug. "I know I'm his mum and I should stay out of it, but I've known you for a long time, Nell, and I love you to bits. You're such a good girl. He'd kill me if he knew we were having this conversation, but I hope you don't write him off. He's done a lot of silly things over the years, but if you could find it in your heart to give him a chance, I think he might surprise you."

I don't even know what to say once she's finished spilling her son's secrets.

She pats my shoulder and leaves me to ponder her words. And ponder them I do.

"WHAT HAPPENED?" I hear Theresa cry later that afternoon.

Nick has hobbled through the door on Max's arm.

"Wiped out on the reef at Porthleven," Nick mutters, looking utterly miserable as I hurry out from behind the bar.

"It was so fricking stupid. I wasn't concentrating."

His right foot is swollen and his face is very pale, his hair still damp from the ocean.

"Can you help him upstairs, Max?" I ask. "I'll go and ask Tristan for some frozen peas."

Nick is on the couch when I enter his apartment, his foot propped up on the coffee table in front of him. Max is hovering.

"It's all right, mate, you go," Nick urges.

"I'm late for work," Max tells me with regret. He's a fireman.

When Max has gone, I grab a cushion from the couch and carefully place it and a bag of frozen peas beneath Nick's foot. I lie another bag across his ankle.

His face creases with agony as he thanks me.

"Can I get you anything?" My tone is full of sympathy. "A cup of tea?"

"That would be great, actually."

I go into his kitchen. It's clean and tidy, save for a mug and a dirty bowl in the sink, with cereal bits glued to its side. There's a tiny window looking right out across the thatched rooftops of neighboring cottages to the river in the distance. The view from his living room is even lovelier, stretching past the moored sailing boats in the water to the bank on the other side.

"Have you eaten?" I call through to him.

"No, but don't trouble yourself."

"It'll take me two secs." I open his fridge and peer in, grabbing cheese, ham, butter, and pickle. I whip him up a quick toastie, then carry it through with his cup of tea.

His eyes are closed, but he opens them when he hears my footsteps. "Thanks, Nell," he murmurs as I pass him a couple of painkillers I found in his kitchen drawer.

"Is there anything else I can do?" I ask with concern.

"Can you call Jack and see if he can cover for me tonight and tomorrow?"

"I can cover for you," I say. "I need the extra spending money for Australia."

"Are you sure? You've been here all day."

"Yes, totally sure. Anything else?"

"Come check on me later?"

"That goes without saying."

I pop in a couple of times and at the end of the night, I find him fast asleep on the couch. He stirs and opens his eyes. "Hey."

"Want some help getting to bed?"

He smirks at me.

"I'm glad to see you've still got a sense of humor."

"Actually, I need the bathroom first." He holds his hand out to me and I help him to his feet. We start hobbling together toward the bathroom, but then he stops short, breathing in sharply and wincing, his hand clutching his side. I stare at him with alarm and then lift his T-shirt—his ribs are black and blue!

"Nick! What the hell?"

He ignores me, recommencing his journey.

"You should see a doctor."

"It's fine. I just need a couple of days to rest up."

"Damn surfers," I mutter. "I don't know why you take the risk."

"We're all a bunch of junkies."

"Yeah, I know it's addictive." I shake my head despairingly and leave him at the bathroom door. When he comes out, I help him to bed. Will he manage with his jeans?

He sees me dithering. "I'll be fine, Nell. Get home, you must be shattered."

"OK." I hesitate. "You sure you're going to be all right in the night?"

"Why, you offering to stay?"

His eyebrows lift with surprise when I don't immediately answer.

"Do you want me to? I could crash on the couch. I've got to be back here in the morning, anyway."

"Are you serious?"

I shrug, uncertainly. He stares at me for a long moment then jerks his chin toward the empty space beside him. "Sleep next to me."

I narrow my eyes at him.

"I promise I'll keep my hands off," he says. "Unless you don't want me to," he adds with a playful grin.

I roll my eyes and send Dad a text, explaining why I won't be home tonight.

SUNLIGHT IS STREAMING through the tiny picture window in the eaves of Nick's bedroom when I wake up. He's asleep beside me and I stare at him for a moment, studying the fan-shape made by his eyelashes. They're darker than the rest of his hair—more brown, less golden. The stubble coming through on his jaw is dark-blond, and I have a weird inclination to run my fingertips over it. He really is a very attractive guy.

I slept surprisingly well, considering I'm in a strange bed. I must've been exhausted after the double shift.

My phone buzzes on the bedside table. It's a text from Dad:

You be careful.

"What's so funny?" Nick murmurs from beside me.

I glance at him. "Dad, warning me to be wary of big, bad men."

"Does he place *me* in that class?" He sounds startled, his voice thick with sleep.

"He's always placed *you* in that class. Your reputation precedes you, Nicholas Castor."

I'm smiling, but he isn't.

"OK, I've changed my mind," he says. "I actually *don't* like it when you say my name like that." He turns his face toward the ceiling in a sulk.

"I'm kidding." I think I've hurt his feelings. "I'll make you some breakfast and then I'll go home for a quick shower." I swing my legs off his bed. "Don't want any of the staff to think I've been sleeping with you again."

"God forbid," he replies drily.

A COUPLE OF days later, I come into work early to find Nick sitting at a table by the window, paperwork surrounding him. He's staring at the view. He hasn't noticed me yet, and I'm stumped by the look on his face. He seems so desperately sad.

"Morning," I say at last, trying to inject some cheer.

He looks my way, his lips turning up at the corners, but the sadness lingers in his eyes.

"Are you OK?" I ask.

"Yep." He glances down at his paperwork. "Catching up on some stuff."

"You need anything?"

"No, I'm all right, thanks," he replies in a subdued tone.

My brow furrows as I leave him to it.

MAX COMES IN with his girlfriend, Dawn, on Friday night. We're busy, but they head to the bar area after their meal and, once things have calmed down, I go over to say hi.

I like Dawn—she has a heart of gold and the most raucous cackle of a laugh. She works at the pub across the river and Nick accuses her of being a spy every time she comes in here. It's all in jest—he adores her, really. His mate has been seeing her for about a year now and Nick is convinced she's the one.

"Is Nick all right?" I ask Max when Dawn has gone to the bathroom.

"In what way?" He's shorter and stockier than Nick, a bit more average-looking, but when he grins, his whole face transforms. He's not grinning now.

"He's seemed kind of down this week," I disclose. "Not only about his injuries."

He shifts uncomfortably.

"What?" I persist. "He's not properly ill or anything, is he?" Now I'm worried.

"No." He waves away my concern, then looks across the room to where Nick is collecting empties. Nick walks out of the room in the direction of the kitchen and Max turns back to me.

"He told me about your conversation at the movies," he reveals.

"Which part?" I'm confused.

"About all the girls you think he's slept with."

"Oh, that." I tut jokily.

"You know he mainly just fools around."

"I don't care."

"I bet you could count the girls he's actually slept with on two hands," he continues.

"That's still quite a lot of digits."

"I thought you didn't care."

"What about Brooke?" I ask. "He screwed her."

"He never screwed Brooke!" he scoffs. "They kissed!"

"I'm sure she said she slept with him. Why are you telling me all of this, in any case?"

"Because he's *heartbroken* over you, Nell! I've never seen him like this! *Shh*, he's coming back," he whispers.

"You guys coming up to mine for a few drinks in a bit?" Nick asks Max as I scrape my jaw off the floor.

"Yeah, for sure."

Nick glances at me. "Nell?"

"Um . . . OK."

Really? What am I doing?

His corresponding smile is the most genuine I've seen all week.

AN HOUR OR so later, I'm sitting beside Nick, my shoes off and my feet tucked up on the couch. Max is making us all laugh at an anecdote about a junior fireman at work, and the atmosphere is chilled and happy, with Blur playing on the stereo in the background.

But I feel strangely edgy. Nick's arm is stretched out behind me on the couch and he's been absentmindedly curling his finger around a lock of my hair for the last few minutes.

"Right," Dawn says, slapping Max's thigh. "You'd better take me home to bed before I conk out here."

They wearily drag themselves to their feet. This is my cue to leave too, but I hesitate. Max comes over and bends down to give me a kiss, but I get to my feet to hug Dawn.

Nick has to go downstairs to let them out of the pub. When he comes back after a couple of minutes, he seems slightly bewildered by the fact that I'm still on his couch.

"You want another drink?" he asks.

"Still got one." I raise my bottle of cider.

He returns to sit beside me again, twisting his body to face mine. Impulsively, he reaches out and twirls another lock of my hair around his finger. I lean into his touch and we stare at each other for a long moment.

My heart flips.

And then he very slowly leans forward and pauses. I don't make him wait before meeting him in the middle.

THE SAND IS pale orange, the color of the rising sun, and the desert is flecked with shrubs, as if a giant has shaken pepper all over it. Far away in the distance, the horizon fades in the heat haze. Then we see it—the rock—and all the passengers on our side of the plane start chattering excitedly.

Uluru looks very different from above to how I'd imagined it. The photos I've seen made me think it's narrow and elongated, but actually it's a squat bulk of sandstone.

There's nothing squat about it, however: it stands 348 meters above sea level at its tallest point—that's higher than the Eiffel Tower.

Van collects us from the tiny airport. I've spent almost five years—maybe even ten—hardening my heart toward him, but it squeezes at the sight of him now.

The first thing I notice is his hair—it's cropped short, which makes him appear more grown-up somehow. He's wearing a yellow T-shirt and dark-gray shorts and his arms are folded, the muscles on his biceps bulging. He comes forward with a grin, embracing Dad first. They hug tightly and his face is full of emotion when he pulls away and turns to me.

I'm not sure if we're going to do that awkward, not-touching thing again, but then I'm being crushed against his definitely-quite-a-bit broader chest and, before I can even gather my thoughts together, he's withdrawing.

"I am so happy to see you guys." He gives us a sentimental smile.

"We're happy to see you too," Dad says in turn, grasping Van's shoulder and shaking him affectionately.

On the car journey to the hotel, Van wants to know all about our trip so far, but more importantly, he wants to be sure Dad is on the mend.

"I've never felt better," Dad replies.

Van and I share a look in his rearview mirror.

He's driving a jeep and it suits him, the muscles on his toned, tanned arms flexing as he clutches the steering wheel and navigates us over the bumpy dirt track. He and Sam live in staff accommodations, a few minutes from the resort, but Van is taking us to our hotel so we can check in and freshen up. We're going to watch the sun set over Uluru later—Sam will meet us there, straight from work. Van has to work later so we'll no doubt be propping up the bar for a bit. At least we're over the worst of our jet-lag—I've never felt more out of it in my life and poor Dad was knocked for six. I don't think we saw the best of Sydney as a result, but luckily we're passing back through for a few days on our way home.

I DON'T *WANT* to make an effort with my appearance that evening, but in the end, I can't help myself. I'm about to meet Sam—the first girlfriend of Van's I have ever come face-to-face with. I don't know what she looks like, but I'm expecting her to be a stunner. I'm thinking: tall, slim and bronzed, like the girls in the photos from when he was fifteen. I feel as though I need war paint to give me confidence, so I take more care than usual with my makeup, dabbing golden brown onto my lids and sweeping a line of black kohl close to my eyelashes. With black mascara, peach blush, and sheer lip-gloss, I'm ready.

The heat from the day is fading, so I take a white cardigan to throw on over my navy sundress. I've fastened my still-damp hair into a loose bun on top of my head.

All of the above does nothing to combat my nerves.

Dad and Van are sitting on a couple of plastic chairs outside Dad's room when I emerge. Van's eyes graze over me before returning to my face.

"Ready?" he asks with a small smile.

HALF AN HOUR later, the sun has set over Uluru, casting not only the entire rock but the surrounding desert in the most spectacular orangey-red light.

"Here's Sam," Van says, nodding at a dark-blue Honda pulling into the car park. I've had a glass of bubbly—Van brought a bottle on ice—and it *was* giving me a lovely warm buzz, but now I feel sick to my stomach.

A hand on my arm prompts me to turn sharply toward Dad, who's gazing at me, his eyes filled with understanding. I step away from him, plastering a smile on my face as Van's girlfriend climbs out of the car.

"Hi!" she calls, grinning widely as she approaches us.

For a moment, I'm struck dumb, and then I come to life. "Hi!" I call back.

She is *nothing* like I imagined. Tall, yes, but far from skinny, with long, chunky auburn dreadlocks that tumble halfway down her back. Her skin is light-brown from exposure to the sun and her nose is pierced as well as her eyebrows, and who only knows how many rings are through her ears. She comes over and holds out her hand. I go to shake it and she laughs, pulling it away.

"I'm just fucking with ya, gimme a hug." She engulfs me in strong arms and then moves on to Dad.

Before I came out here, I wasn't sure what would be worse: hating her or liking her. I *think* I like her.

"Fuck me, you're pretty!" she exclaims, returning to gawk at me. "Shit, I really need to stop swearing. Sorry." She flashes Dad a repentant look, but he smiles, unfazed.

Van isn't fazed, either. I get the feeling he's quite used to his girlfriend's bad language.

There's something wild and untamed about Sam. It occurs to me that I once thought the same thing about Van, but right now, he seems almost conservative in comparison.

My mind is still ticking over with these thoughts when we're at the bar later, watching Van work. Sam went home to "crash out" and Dad and I retired here to keep Van company. We chat while he takes orders, but the rest of the time I'm distracted watching him. He's so attentive to the customers, totally focused on what they're ordering and then scarily speedy and proficient at delivering. I've never seen him in a professional capacity before and it's kind of strange.

Dad calls it a night after not too long.

"Do you want me to walk you to your room?" I offer.

"I'm not that old and doddery. I'll find my way." He bends down to kiss me on my forehead then says good night to Van.

I swivel back in time to see Van topping up my glass with more white wine.

"Thanks."

He nods seriously at Dad's departing back. "Is he OK?"

"I think so. Tired. He hasn't fully recovered from it all."

He nods, his lips pressed together in a thin, straight line as his eyes follow Dad out of the room. He grabs a cloth from behind the bar and proceeds to polish some wineglasses. There are no customers waiting.

"Sam seems nice," I say casually.

He raises one eyebrow at me, his expression mildly entertained.

"What? She does!" I exclaim. "Why? *Isn't* she nice?" I mock.

"It's not the first word I'd use to describe her," he replies with a smirk.

I'm intrigued. "How would you describe her, then?"

He shrugs. "I don't know. Difficult, probably." He grins, reaching for another glass. "We have a tumultuous relationship, to say the least. What about you? Anyone significant in your life?"

"Yeah, I kind of am seeing someone."

He glances at me, nodding for me to continue.

"You know him. Nick." I take a sip of my drink.

"Nick?" he asks with alarm. He's still clutching the cloth and a glass, but his hands have stilled. "Nick from the pub? Surfing Nick?"

"Yes. Nicholas Castor."

"Are you shitting me?"

"Nope."

He's reeling.

I can't say I blame him. Dad was horrified too, but he's come around to the idea now.

"How's *that* working out?" Van asks with a frown.

"All right so far."

"Is it serious?"

"Ask me again sometime." I shrug, but belatedly feel that I'm doing Nick—and possibly myself—a disservice. "I don't know, his mum and Max seem to think it's the real deal. They encouraged me to give him a go after getting sick of seeing him moping around." I'm aiming for flippancy and hope I haven't come across as conceited.

There's a woman waiting down the bar whom Van hasn't even looked at as he's been so focused on what I've been saying. I nod toward her pointedly.

Van comes out of his stupor and throws his cloth over his shoulder, going to attend to the customer. She's ordering cock-tails for a table of six, so while he gets to work mixing them, I take out my phone to reply to a message I saw earlier from El-lie. She still lives in Newcastle where she and her boyfriend, Liam, went to university. We stay in regular touch by e-mail and text—she wants to know how it's going in Australia.

As I'm typing out a message to her, another one comes through. It's from Nick. I finish replying to Ellie before read-ing it.

All it says is: Missing you.

Aw. I write back: You getting all sentimental on me, Nicholas Castor?

He replies: Might be. What you doing?

Sitting at the hotel bar, chatting to Van.

Say hi from me.

Will do.

Nell?

Yes? You do realize it costs money every time you send me a text? Make this one good . . . I tease.

I wait for his reply, but it doesn't come. I frown and put the phone down, looking up to see Van standing in front of me. He's polishing another glass, his expression blank. He nods at my phone. "Nick?"

"Yeah. He says to say hi."

My phone buzzes again. I pick it up and my eyes widen as I read what it says.

Feeling a lot of love for you right now.
Wanted to tell you that in person before you
left but didn't want to freak you out. Don't
suppose you can talk?

"What's he saying?" Van asks, curiosity getting the better of him.

I ignore him and type out a reply, trying to concentrate. He *has* caught me by surprise, but that's probably not helped by the company I'm in.

Can't at the mo but maybe later?

I have freaked you out, haven't I? Crap.

No, you haven't at all. It's a white lie, but I don't want to hurt him. I *do* care for him. Quite a lot, as it turns out. I still have my doubts, of course—a leopard can't change his spots overnight and all that. But I *do* like his company, he does make me laugh, and he *is* stupidly good in bed. That's three good reasons right there to give it a shot.

Van standing in front of me, I add.

Ask him what the hell he's doing living so far
from the surf?

I show Van the message and he grins. "Tell him I need to get my head read."

I sign off my reply with a kiss and a promise that I'll ring him later. God only knows how much that phone call will cost.

"So . . . Nick Castor, eh?" Van says drily, folding his arms across his chest. The action makes his biceps strain against the fabric of his long-sleeve white shirt uniform. "Who would've thought?"

"Stranger things have happened," I reply with a smile.

Closing time is upon us before we know it so I gather my things together and wait out by the swimming pool while Van finishes up and says goodnight to his boss.

"Will you come for a drive with me?" he asks when he appears.

"Um . . ."

"There's something I want to show you."

"OK." I nod. "Sure."

His jeep is parked at a place called Yulara, where the seven hundred and fifty staff members live, and as we walk there, he tells me about life at the "Gregory's"—the name for the dorm-room accommodation that he and Sam share with two other girls. They each only have a single bed with one tiny bathroom and kitchen between them, so things can be a bit fraught at times, especially between Sam and one of their roommates. The staff aren't allowed to hang out in the tourist areas, but they have their own swimming pools, plus the "ressies"—residents club—where a big chunk of their earnings are spent on booze. It doesn't sound like there's a lot to do out of hours, aside from playing pool and drinking, but his co-workers sound like a young, fun crowd and Van says he's made a few friends.

After about twenty minutes on the road, we pull off the asphalt onto a bumpy dirt track. Five minutes later, Van cuts the engine and hops out. "Come on," he says, getting something from the backseat.

I climb out of the jeep into pitch-blackness. "Van?"

"Up here."

It sounds like he's on the roof. He taps the side of the vehicle to orientate me and I follow the noise, coming to what feels like a ladder at the back. I climb up one rung and then a warm, strong hand fixes around my arm and helps me the rest of the way. He's brought cushions and blankets and we spend a short while getting comfortable, before . . .

"Look up," he says.

I tilt my face up to the sky and billions of stars blink back at me. It's the biggest, brightest night sky I have *ever* seen.

"Wow," I whisper reverently.

We lie down, so close that our arms are touching. "Are you warm enough?" he asks.

"Yes, fine." Forget the blankets, he's like a radiator, with the body heat coming off him.

"One thing I noticed after a few days of living here is how alive the desert is, despite seeming dormant at first," he tells me. "You won't notice it where you are at the resort because there's always someone to sweep the paths and stuff, but where we live, the sands are always there."

"Have you seen many spiders?"

"Oh, yeah. Mostly huntsmans."

I shudder and edge closer.

He chuckles. "They're huge, but harmless, apart from giving you a heart attack. The best thing I've seen has been a thorny devil."

"What's *that*?"

"A lizard. They have spines all over their bodies and they drink with their feet."

"What? *How*?"

"Apparently, they stand in a puddle and the water moves up by capillary action along grooves to the corner of their mouths. I saw this little guy on my way home from work one day and he looked up at me—he was so inquisitive, a real character. If you didn't need a license to own one, I would've been tempted to take him back to my dorm."

I smile. "So you like working here?"

"Yeah, it's all right. It's a change from tuna fishing. I'd been doing that for a few years so it was getting a bit tired."

"I still remember you telling us about it when we were at the pub that time. I was so angry with Joel that night."

"Yeah, he was a bit of a dick."

I snort with amusement.

"You guys broke up soon after, right?"

I tense, remembering the guilt I'd felt that contributed to me ending it. *If you really like someone, you don't kiss somebody else.* "Yeah."

"I'm sorry."

What for? For *causing* the guilt? I decide not to ask.

It's the last thing either of us says for a while.

"How's your mum these days?" His voice punctuates the darkness.

"Hmm." My response is dry. "I haven't seen her in a couple of years."

"Seriously?" He sounds surprised.

"We fell out when Dad was having his treatment," I reveal.

"I didn't know that." He sounds concerned.

"It's not like we were close before, but she was so unsupportive. She could've called to check on how Dad was doing, or how *I* was doing, but I was always the one to make contact. One day I stopped ringing her. I guess her selfishness finally got to me. We hardly ever speak now. I don't feel compelled to go and visit her in New York and she sure isn't bothered about coming to see me."

"That sucks," he murmurs.

"It's just the way it is."

"Is she still with the guy who sells yachts?"

"Robert. Yeah, they're still married, thankfully. At least I know she's being looked after."

The longer we stare at the sky, the more stars we see. Now it almost seems milky white with them, countless tiny galaxies bursting through the inky blackness.

"Do you want kids?" Van asks out of the blue.

"Um, yes. I mean, definitely, one day, with the right person.

I've always wanted a big family. I was kind of lonely until you came along so I'd prefer not to have an only child if I can help it. What about you?"

"Yeah. Same."

Before I can find out why he wanted to know, he asks another question. "Has your dad ever had another girlfriend?"

"No, he never moved on from your mum. At one stage, I tried to encourage him to get out more, but he wasn't having any of it. She was the one true love of his life and nobody could replace her. It's kind of tragic."

"What do they say?" he asks. "Better to have loved and lost than never to have loved at all?"

"Yeah."

I reflect on that statement. Would Dad have chosen a stable, uniform life rather than the five wonderful years he had with Ruth, followed by the crushing pain of losing her?

No.

He would have taken *one* year, if that's all he'd been offered. He probably would have settled for a month.

Sometimes I wonder, if Ruth hadn't died, if she and Dad had stayed together, if I didn't have to worry about his health—all of it resting on my shoulders—would I still be in London, working at a magazine and pursuing my dreams?

Would Van and I have ever felt an attraction if we'd grown up together from the ages of five to now?

You could do your head in, thinking about it.

I take a deep breath. "Dad once said to me, 'Five years from now, you'll look back and understand why this happened.'"

"When did he say that?"

"It doesn't matter. I'm telling you because it reminded me that we overheard your mum saying a similar thing."

I don't know if he recalls it himself or if he's waiting for me to fill in the gaps, but he listens as I continue.

"We were five years old and we were eavesdropping at the top of the stairs. Your mum was talking about how scared she was when she found out she was pregnant with you and had to go back and live with her mother. She said she thought her life was over." Van tenses and I instinctively reach for his little finger and hook it, protectively, just as I did all those years ago. My voice sounds choked as I continue. "But then she said, if she had known where she'd be in five years' time, she never would have worried. She was so happy with Dad, with us. She loved you to the stars and back."

He tightens his grip on my finger.

"You should call your mum," he whispers. "She might be crap, but she's still your mum."

VAN ISN'T WORKING the next day so he takes us on a tour of Uluru. The heat when we stepped off the plane came as a bit of a shock, and today it's the same when we climb out of his air-conditioned jeep.

I'll be honest, I was a bit underwhelmed at the thought of visiting a big rock in the middle of nowhere, but last night I was blown away by the sight of this huge mass drenched in light from the setting sun. Even more surprising is how breathtaking it is up close. You can't get a sense of the size and shape of it when it's towering above you—it's absolutely enormous.

Uluru is sacred to the Pitjantjatjara Anangu, the Aboriginal people of the area, and it's considered disrespectful to climb the rock. That doesn't mean people don't still do it, though—it's not illegal, unbelievably—and I'm disgusted at the sight of dozens of tourists trudging their grubby feet up the side. One heavily overweight man is practically on his knees as he hauls himself up by the rope and, astonishingly, there are children climbing it too. Dozens of people have died doing this trek since the 1950s.

"Are they completely stupid as well as ignorant and disrespectful?" I mutter.

Van clenches his jaw. "Yeah, it bothers me too. Don't get Sam started—you'll never hear the end of it."

We wander along a path, under the shade of a surprising number of trees. Elsewhere, everything seems so dry and arid, but here the grass is green rather than yellow.

"You should see it in a storm," Van says. "The water cascades down in dozens of waterfalls."

Dad is loitering by a cave, staring in at some Aboriginal paintings.

"It's so beautiful up close like this," I murmur, trying to take it all in. "The sandstone glitters under the sun." Shards of rock have slid off the surface, leaving behind speckled patches of gray-black that contrast with the orangey-red. "It's almost like a living, breathing thing, shedding scales," I say.

Van stares at me for a long moment, then he asks, "Do you still write?"

I shake my head and pull a face. "I haven't felt very inspired lately."

I try to ignore his look of disappointment and glance over my shoulder to check where Dad is. We're only walking slowly, but he doesn't seem to be in any hurry to catch up.

"Did you get hold of Nick last night?" Van asks.

"No." I remembered when Van dropped me back to the

hotel that I'd promised to call him. "He'd already gone down-stairs to work so I left a message. The mobile reception at the pub is terrible."

"I can't believe you work at The Boatman." His tone is as arid as the sand we're walking on.

"Why?" My hackles go up. "What's wrong with that?"

"Nothing, if you're me. Forget it," he says before I can get to the bottom of his comment. "I know you've had a lot of stuff to deal with. I'm sorry I wasn't there to help."

"It's all right. He's my dad."

"I care about him a lot too."

"I know you do."

We walk on in silence.

"I love this cave here," Van says, coming to a stop. "It re-minds me of a wave."

It's big—three times the height of Van—and it curves way up behind us and right over our heads as we walk inside. I can almost imagine Van surfing the face of it before he disappears from view into a barrel.

"I can't wait to go surfing again," he says.

"Not long now. Sam isn't coming with us, is she?" I double-check.

"Nah, she didn't want to take the time off work. We're go-ing home for a break at the end of January."

"Not for Christmas?"

"No. It's one of our busiest times of year."

I nod, turning to smile at Dad as he appears.

WE END UP back at the cultural center, where Sam works. It's interesting, reading about *Tjukurpa*, the traditional law that guides Anangu daily life, and I love the Dreamtime stories that claim to tell how Uluru came to be.

Sam is serving a customer when we go into the shop that sells Aboriginal arts and crafts. Two Anangu women are sitting on the floor, painting, and I stand nearby and watch, captivated, as they dab tiny, perfect dots onto a canvas to create a colorful picture. They don't so much as look at me as they continue to work, chatting to each other the entire time.

"How was the rock?" Sam asks when I go over to say hi.

"Incredible. So much prettier up close than I thought it'd be."

"Did you climb it?" From the judgmental look in her eyes, I'm very glad to be answering no to that question.

"So you're an artist too?" I glance over at the Aboriginal women again.

"I dabble," Sam replies.

"Have you ever tried to get Van back into painting?"

She frowns. "It was his mum who could paint, not him."

"No, he could paint too. He was really good when he was younger."

She gives me a funny look before coming out from behind the counter and going to the other side of the shop where Van is talking to Dad. "Oi," she says, whacking him on his arm.

He spins around. "What?" he snaps.

"Why didn't you tell me you could paint?" She sounds accusatory, but I'm not sure if she's being serious or jesting.

His eyes dart toward me and then he frowns at her, displeased. "I *can't* paint." He looks over at me again. "I was *ten*, Nell. I was only messing around."

"No, you were good," I hear Dad say. "You won a competition."

Van rolls his eyes and turns away. A moment later, he places his hand on Dad's shoulder and continues to chat as though they were never interrupted.

Sam returns to me with a shrug and a grin, totally unfazed. But I feel snubbed.

THAT NIGHT, DAD and I end up back at the bar while Van works. Once more, Sam declined to join us and I can't say that I'm not relieved. I'm not proud admitting it, but I'm glad she's not coming with us to Adelaide and Port Lincoln. I don't feel at all relaxed in her company.

I still feel stung about earlier, so when Dad starts making noises about going to bed, I force myself to leave too. Van seems surprised as I make my excuses and hop down from the stool.

"I haven't got hold of Nick yet," I tell him.

"What do you think about this, then?" Van asks Dad and although he nods at me affably, I detect an edge to his tone.

"Oh, Nick's OK," Dad replies glibly. "He makes her smile and that's all a father can ask. Anyway, innocent until proven guilty!" he jokes, nudging me.

"Tomorrow I'll take you guys to Kata Tjuta," Van says, moving on. "I think it's even nicer there than Uluru."

We've seen it from the car—it's a large group of domed rock foundations, the highest of which is nearly 200 meters taller than Uluru.

"Do you reckon you'll be up for a bit of a hike?" he asks Dad.

"Absolutely. But I'll also be happy sitting in the shade for a bit if you two want to go on."

"I'll bring a backpack with plenty of water," Van promises.

THE NEXT MORNING I wake up bright and early, keen to get going. My mood deflates when I see that Van has brought Sam with him.

I'm annoyed at myself. *She is his girlfriend*, the voice inside my head berates me. She's currently an important part of his life and I need to make an effort to get to know her. I resolve to spend the day stuck to her side.

At the end of a long, tiring hike, Sam gives Dad and me a hug. Van is working tonight at the hotel bar and tomorrow morning we all fly to Adelaide, so for Sam and us, this is good-bye.

"It was so good to meet Van's other family," she gushes. "Maybe one day we'll make it over to England. I hear it's stunning where you live."

"That would be great," I say with a smile that's as warm as I can make it.

Van seems more subdued at work that night. When Dad goes to the bathroom, he asks me if I'm up for another drive later.

I've been trying to ignore my craving to be alone with him, but now it's all-encompassing. I respond with a nod.

Once more, we head out to the middle of nowhere and climb up onto the roof of his jeep. We lie there in silence for a while, with only the stars as our witnesses.

"Have you ever told anyone about us?" Van asks.

"No!" Nervous jitters instantly start up inside my stomach. "Have you?"

"Dave guessed. After last time."

"Did he?! What did he say?"

"Not much. I didn't go into detail."

"Have you told Sam?"

"Hell, no."

My mind races as we fall silent.

"When are you planning on going back to London?" he asks eventually.

"I don't know," I reply. "I'm not ready to leave Dad, yet."

"Well, don't delay too long."

I frown into the darkness. "Why do you say that?" He's made me feel defensive again. "I like it at The Boatman." I know that's what his problem is. "*You* work at a bar . . ."

"Yeah. But I had higher expectations for you. You had plans. Hopes. Dreams."

"What about you? What about your hopes and dreams?"

"I don't have any."

"That's crap." I sit up, frustrated.

He sits up too. "Nell, I quit school when I was fifteen. This is my life. I'm not going to be a high achiever. But you . . . Why don't you write anymore?" he demands to know.

"What don't you paint?" I snap back, raising my voice.

"You didn't go to university to do a degree in waitressing," he says angrily.

"Well, you didn't go to university to do a degree in being an asshole, but you still are!"

"There. *There* you are," he states. "I thought I'd lost you today under all of the fucking pleasantries."

"Piss off, Van, I was trying to be nice to your *girlfriend*," I spit, getting up and making my way down the ladder. "Take me back to the hotel!" I climb into the jeep and slam the door.

Van joins me a minute later.

We drive in silence, both of us at simmering point. He pulls into the car park and cuts the ignition, but if I thought I was due an apology, I'm in for a blow.

"You're wasting your life," he states.

"I'm *not* wasting my life!" I scoff. "I'm *happy*. I'm having fun."

"With *Nick*? *Nick*, Nell? Seriously?" Van stabs the interior lights on with his finger and glares at me. "What the *fuck*? '*I wouldn't touch him with a bargepole* . . . ' *Your* words!"

He must've overheard me saying that to Joel years ago!

And he's not done. "That guy would screw anything on two legs. Why don't you have some fucking respect for yourself?"

The sound reverberates around the vehicle. I don't even know I've slapped him until a sharp sting registers on my palm.

I stare at him in shock. He's even more astonished than I am, a red welt mark springing to life on his cheek.

"I'm so sorry!" Tears of horror spring up into my eyes.

"It's all right," he mutters, averting his gaze. "I deserved it."

I cup my hands over my mouth, reeling. I've never hit anyone in my life.

"Fuck!" he erupts, slamming his hands on the steering wheel. His eyes are wide with misery as he stares out of the front windshield.

"I'm sorry," I whisper again.

He shakes his head. "No, *I'm* sorry. Nell, please just get out of the car." His voice sounds strained. "I'll see you tomorrow."

THE PLANE TO Adelaide is full so we don't end up sitting together. Dad is on the other side of the aisle and Van is asleep in the seat behind me. When he met us at the hotel to catch the airport transfer bus, he looked horrendous. His eyes were red and puffy, his skin looked clammy and pasty, and he stank of stale booze.

"Had a few too many drinks at the staff bar last night," he mumbled to Dad.

He and I have barely looked at each other. I'm glad I'm not sitting next to him.

I peer out of the window. The sun is low in the sky and it's reflected in the ocean, a ball of golden light rippling in the waves. The tidal water swirls around sandbanks and resembles clouds, and sunlight glints off the windows of the houses in the town far, far below, making me think of stars.

Sensing movement behind me, I glance down the side of my seat and come eye to eye with fireworks, exploding in a night sky.

"What are you thinking about?" Van asks. He's leaned in close, so he doesn't have to raise his voice.

I point out the scene below. "It looks like the sky is on the ground."

Seconds pass before I turn to look at him again.

"Sam is pregnant," he tells me in a monotone.

Everything inside me withers.

His eyes fill with tears. "I've asked her to marry me."

My heart crumples and folds in on itself, again and again, until it's a tiny, tough, origami heart. Once fragile, now it feels as hard as a stone and is impossible to shred.

Just like that, the book of my life slams shut on another chapter.

And a new one begins.

THIRTY

"ARE YOU LOOKING FORWARD TO DOING SOME gardening with Grandad?" I smile at Luke in the rearview mirror as we pull up on the drive.

"Yes." He nods, seriously, as he unclicks his seatbelt.

Too cute . . .

"Dad?" I call, entering the cottage via the hall. Luke diligently plonks himself down on the tiled floor and proceeds to yank off his navy blue Crocs. "Dad?" I call again. He's not in the kitchen or living room and he wasn't in the annex when we walked past, either—I peeked through the window.

"Maybe he's already in the garden," I murmur, more to myself than my son. I know he's here somewhere because his car is on the drive, but it's odd that he didn't appear when he heard us pull up.

I have a funny feeling in the pit of my stomach as I slip my feet back into my flip-flops. "Go play with your Legos, darling. Mummy will be back in a minute."

I hurry out onto the patio, but as I head around the corner of the cottage toward the flowerbeds I see him, down on the bench, overlooking the water. His body is mostly obscured by the hydrangea bush that's bursting with purple flowers.

"There you are!" I call.

He doesn't respond.

Is he asleep?

My heart begins to pound as I hurry down the steep hill, my feet slipping and sliding beneath me in my haste to get to him. He's crumpled over, his face gray and his eyes closed.

"*No, no, no . . . Dad!*" I cry, my hands on his arms.

He murmurs, stirring.

"Oh, thank God! Dad!" I exclaim. "Are you all right? Were you asleep?"

His eyes flutter open and he mumbles something.

"Dad?"

"Better call ambulance," he repeats.

Fear takes hold of my heart and crushes it to a pulp.

Because right then I know: the cancer is back.

NICK ARRIVES SOON after the ambulance leaves. He gathers me into a hug and I burst into tears, having somehow managed to hold it together until now. Luke is watching cartoons on the television in the living room.

"Aw, Nell," Nick whispers, cradling my head in his hands and pressing a kiss to my forehead. "I'm so sorry," he says in a gruff voice. "I'll go and grab Luke. You heading straight to the hospital?" He pulls away to stare at me.

I nod, brushing away a constant stream of tears.

He clasps my face once more and kisses my forehead again, squeezing my hand before letting me go.

My chest feels constricted as I watch Nick reappear with Luke in his arms. He's almost five and certainly doesn't need a carry from his daddy, but at times like these, a parent wants to keep their children close.

"Shoes on, buddy," Nick urges.

"But I was going to do some gardening with Grandad," Luke says, his little brow furrowing with confusion.

Nick pulls our son to his feet and ruffles his light-blond curls. "You're coming to the beach with me instead."

"YAY!"

"Are you sure?" I ask Nick. "I thought you had to work?"

"I can go in later. Mum said she'll have him this afternoon."

"Thank you," I mumble.

"Are you going to be OK?" he asks with concern. "Do you want me to drive you to the hospital?"

"No, it's better that I have the car. I'll be all right."

"OK. Big kiss for Mummy, buddy," Nick says merrily as I hurriedly dry my eyes and smile. He lifts Luke into his arms and dips him in my direction, making him giggle. He plants a sloppy, wet kiss on my cheek before Nick whisks him away, tickling his ribs as they head out the gate.

I listen to our son's raucous laughter with a smile, but as soon as the gate clinks shut again, I crumble.

I need to get a few of Dad's essentials together so I let myself into the annex. We finally put an en suite in here, after Dad relocated to this room. He was struggling with the stairs, anyway, and it made sense for me to sleep in the room next to Luke. We've been living with Dad ever since the split.

Nick and I had three incredible years together.

I don't mean the years themselves were incredible.

I mean it was incredible that we lasted three years.

Turns out that we are much better friends than lovers.

We tried to make it work, although the pregnancy came as a huge shock to both of us. It happened soon after I got back from Australia—a split condom that I didn't take seriously enough to bother going to the GP for the morning-after pill.

It's occurred to me that the same thing could have happened to Van and me when we were fifteen. If Dad hadn't interrupted us, would we have become parents before our sixteenth birthdays? It's a staggering thought.

Anyway, Nick asked me to marry him and everyone seemed so happy about it—his mum was beside herself! It really seemed to everyone that I was the one to tame Nicholas Castor.

We had a shotgun wedding followed by a brilliant reception at The Boatman. All our friends came and Theresa and Christopher did up the place beautifully, with triple the amount of festoon lights than normal, and pastel pink and white lanterns and tissue-paper pompoms hanging everywhere.

Even my mum and Robert joined us for the celebrations. I'd followed Van's advice and called her.

It was hard once the baby came, of course, but I thought we were managing quite well. Then, one day, I caught Nick flirting with our gorgeous new waitress. His mother got rid of her sharpish, but it was the start of something that wasn't going to be suppressed.

I really didn't want to end up hating him, but it was heading that way. We had countless arguments, followed by frank conversations, and we both shed a lot of tears. Eventually we decided that the best thing for Luke would be for us to part amicably and put all of our efforts into being good parents.

Having Luke meant that, once more, I had to put my life on hold. I never did make it back to London and I know I'm not going to, now. Nick and Luke have such a great relationship, and I would never try to take my son away from his father. So I'm settled in Cornwall and in Cornwall I will stay. I'm still at The Boatman, but it works well with shifts and childcare. Theresa and Christopher help out a lot—they're both retired now and are the best ex-parents-in-law I could wish for. I consider myself lucky.

Sometimes I feel a pang when I realize that I let a glamorous magazine career slip through my fingers, but Luke gives me more joy than a job ever could.

THE PHONE RINGS as I'm getting Dad's toiletries from his bathroom.

"Hello?" I sniff.

"Nell?" It's Van.

"How did you know?"

"Know what? I'm after your dad for a chat. What's wrong?"

"He's in the hospital. I think the cancer is back."

"Oh God, Nell . . ."

"I thought he was dead! I have a horrible, horrible feeling. I think this could be it." It's hard to speak for crying. "He didn't tell me he'd been suffering. I heard him say it to the ambulance men. He obviously didn't want me to worry, but he *knew*, Van, he *knew*!"

He listens in silence to me sobbing, and when he finally speaks, it's with a husky voice. "I'll talk to Sam. I want to be there this time."

"You can make a decision when we know more," I manage to say before ending the call and curling up into a ball on my father's bed. I give myself a couple of minutes to get it all out and then pull myself together and grab the rest of Dad's gear.

VAN FLIES TO the UK four days later. I go to collect him from the airport. I've been in and out of hospital nonstop. Dad's prostate cancer has spread to his liver and bones—he's *riddled* with it. There is nothing we can do this time; it's all about pain management. He may only have weeks—no one knows. But he won't be coming home.

I have a flashback as I stand in the Arrivals hall, waiting for Van to appear. I remember him walking through those very doors when we were fifteen. He seemed like a stranger to me then—an alien. I couldn't get my head around the fact that he had changed so much in five years.

Now it's been over five and a half since we saw each other and we've both gone through major upheavals during that time. We've both become parents. Van has a little girl, Libby, who was born four months before Luke. He sends us photos— she has blue eyes and auburn hair and the cheekiest smile. She's absolutely gorgeous and he dotes on her.

I didn't know when Van first broke his news to me that Sam was already almost three months pregnant when he'd asked her to marry him. He'd popped the question days before Dad and I had flown out.

She'd told him that she'd think about it while he was in Port Lincoln with us, but in the end she declined. They broke up before the baby was born—her doing, not Van's. He was devastated. Now they have a similar situation to Nick and me, although I have a feeling their relationship is a fair bit rockier.

Sam calls most of the shots where Van and Libby are concerned. She wanted to move back to Port Lincoln to be near her parents, so Van went too. He was always going to be a big part of Libby's life, wherever she ended up, but at least in Port Lincoln his family and friends are there too—not to mention the ocean—so I think he's happy. The last I heard, he was seeing someone called Cherie, but I don't know if it's serious.

Just then, the doors open and Van comes through. As his eyes scan the crowd, looking for me, I'm aware of my pulse speeding up. His hair is longer than it was, and he has dark stubble that's not quite a beard. His eyes lock with mine, darkening as I step out from behind the barrier and walk toward him.

He drops his bag and draws me into his arms, holding me close against his broad chest. Last time, he was a "guy." Now he feels like a man. My heart doesn't recognize him. It's beating wildly, slamming against my ribcage.

Or maybe my heart *does* recognize him. Maybe it recognizes him all too well.

I extricate myself before I'm ready to let go, turning away so he doesn't see my tears.

I don't ask him how his flight was—there will be time for small talk later. Right now, I need to get to the car without collapsing in a heap.

On the return journey, I fill him in on the latest news from the hospital. He wants to go straight there.

Dad is asleep when we arrive, so we sit quietly by his bed. When he rouses, the first thing he does is to look around for Van—I told him he was coming.

"Van," he says, reaching for his hand. Van's eyes fill as he clasps Dad's hand with both of his and hunches forward over the bed. I decide to give them some time alone and leave the room.

Van is shattered when we get back to the cottage—he barely slept on the plane.

"I've put you in the annex," I tell him. "I hope that's OK."

I know he may not feel that comfortable sleeping in Dad's bedroom, among Dad's things, but I've tidied everything away as well as I could.

"I might take a shower," he says.

"At least there's an en suite at last. I'll see you in the kitchen when you're ready. I'm going to sort dinner."

He joins me within fifteen minutes, his hair wet, but his stubble still very much in place.

"Is this your look, now?" I ask, boldly reaching up and brushing my fingers across his cheek.

"Yeah." He shrugs and gives me a small smile.

"What do you want to drink?" I ask. "We've got beer, wine, cider, soft drinks . . . I'm opening a bottle of red. I need a drink."

"I'm not surprised. I'll join you on the red. Where's the bottle? I'll sort it."

I choose one of the better bottles from the wine rack in the pantry and hand it to him. He still knows where to find an opener and wineglasses.

"That smells good," he comments, nodding at the oven as he makes short work of the cork. Sometimes I forget he worked as a bartender. He went back to tuna fishing when he returned to Port Lincoln, despite his earlier claim that he'd grown tired of it.

"Steak and ale pie. Nick brought it over from the pub earlier," I reveal. "All I had to do was heat it up."

"That was nice of him."

"He comes through when I need him."

I don't think Van knows what to say about that. I take the glass of wine he offers and sit down at the table, pressing my hand against my forehead. I have such a headache coming on. The wine probably won't help, but to hell with it.

"How's Sam?" I ask. "Was she OK in the end about you coming here?"

"Yeah, she was fine. Kicked up a bit of a stink about how

she'd manage with childcare, but Libby's at school and her mum will help."

It's August so Luke is on his summer holidays, but in Australia the big summer break doesn't occur until Christmas.

"What does she do these days?"

"This and that. She still paints. Murals and stuff. Mostly she's busy being Mum."

Sam also has a second child by a different guy—another daughter, Brittney, age two. She's not with Brittney's father, either.

"What about you?" I ask. "Were you all right with getting time off work?"

"Yeah, we'd finished harvesting so I was due a break."

"Is that different to what you used to do, bringing the nets full of tuna back in from the open ocean?"

"It's all part of the same job. Once we bring the fish in, they stay in holding cages to be fed up for four months. They're harvested after that."

I still don't know what harvesting entails, but Van changes the subject before I can ask.

"When am I going to meet Luke?"

"I need to pick him up tomorrow afternoon." I reach for my glass. "I can't believe I still haven't met your daughter."

"Yeah, it probably wasn't the time to drag her to the UK for a visit." His tone is flat, but then his expression crumples and he folds over, covering his face with his hands.

I put my glass down and go to him immediately, placing my hand on his back as he gulps back a sob.

"I'm sorry," he gasps, straightening up and vigorously rubbing at his eyes.

There's a lump in my throat the size of a golf ball, but I'm managing to hold it together.

"I've only just realized that Geoff will never meet my daughter," he says.

Nope. Now I'm a goner too.

The piecrust is burned by the time we get around to taking dinner out of the oven. I don't think either of us cares. We were going to struggle to eat, anyway.

After a while, we retire to the living room couch with refilled glasses of wine.

"How are you still awake?" I ask him, dragging my fingers under my eyes to collect stray teardrops. They're relentless. Van hasn't broken down again, thankfully. I never could handle seeing his pain.

"I don't think I could sleep if I tried. I'll probably conk out here after a couple more of these." He raises his glass.

"You can if you want, although you won't fit on the couch. You didn't when you were fifteen, either. I still remember Dad saying that he used to find you down here, using Scampi as a hot-water bottle."

"I miss that crazy pooch," he says nostalgically. "Libby is desperate for a dog, but it's too hard with my job."

"How is she these days?" I ask.

His smile lights up his face. "She's awesome. So funny and sweet. She was worried about me when Sam told her that 'Otherdad' was sick." He sees my quizzical expression and explains. "Sam once told her that I had family—another dad—over here in the UK. Libby got it into her head that his name was 'Otherdad' and it was too cute to correct."

"That's adorable," I say.

"Yeah, she's ridiculous."

His voice is full of love.

"How are things with Sam?"

He casts me a cynical look. "Same as always. Still unpredictable. She's seeing some new guy now. We'll see where that goes—probably nowhere. She's a good mum, though. That's all I care about."

"What about you? Are you still with Cherie?" The wine definitely helps me to ask that question.

He frowns. "We broke up ages ago. I'm not seeing anyone. You?"

I shake my head. "It's hard to meet people at the pub, which is ironic because enough men come through. But Nick and his parents are usually around so it wouldn't feel right."

We simultaneously raise our glasses to our lips. I don't know if it has occurred to him, as well as me, that for the first time since we were fifteen, we're both single at the same time.

I'm in no emotional state to dwell on that fact. I head upstairs to bed soon afterward.

THANKS TO VAN, and no doubt the wine, my fear about Dad wasn't all-consuming last night. But in the morning, it hits me again that I'm on the verge of losing him, and I'm a mess when I go downstairs to the bathroom and halt in my tracks at the sight of Van at the kitchen table, sitting where Dad normally sits, complete with a mug of tea. He looks over his shoulder at me.

"Hey," he says, scraping his chair out from the table with an almighty screech as he gets to his feet. I cover my ears, unable to help laughing, but then I'm in his arms and misery submerges my amusement.

"Shh," he murmurs into my hair as I clutch his waist, becoming aware once more of my heart skipping and skittering inside my chest.

I try to pull away from him, but he just holds me tighter and I give up, accepting the comfort for a bit longer. He seems reluctant to let me go when I finally extricate myself to go into the bathroom.

He's made me a cup of tea by the time I reemerge, my face freshly washed but still splotchy.

"What time do you want to go to the hospital?" he asks.

"As soon as we're ready," I reply. "I need to get back to pick up Luke this afternoon."

DAD IS ABOUT the same as yesterday—tired, but not in too much pain. He's glad to see us, but talking seems to exhaust him. Van shows him photos of Libby to pass the time, then after a while Dad nods off, so we sit with him in silence until the doctor comes in and starts talking about moving him to a hospice. It's very hard to get my head around that.

Dad wakes as we're preparing to leave.

"I've got to go and get Luke, Dad, OK? Shall I bring him to see you this evening?"

"No, love, please don't," he replies. "I don't want him to remember me like this."

How can I not cry when he says things like that?

"Oh, Nelly. It's OK. I'm not going anywhere, yet."

"I could stay?" Van offers.

"No, I should rest," Dad insists. "I'll see you tomorrow afternoon. Don't bring Luke," he repeats.

I'm still in tears as we walk to the car.

"Do you want me to drive?" Van offers.

"Could you?" I added him to my insurance before he came over.

"Of course. Put Nick's address in the GPS so you can chill out."

It takes about an hour to get to Helford, but Van keeps me preoccupied by talking about his life in Australia. Once again, I'm riveted by the details of his job, learning about how he hand-catches every fish, some weighing eighty kilos and almost two meters long. During harvesting season, he maneuvers *six hundred tuna a day* onto a conveyor belt that takes them up to a boat and, from there, they go to Japan. It's no wonder he's so fit.

In his time off, he works on an oyster farm in Coffin Bay, growing the oysters that we see in restaurants from tiny baby "spats." Every day he takes a twenty-minute boat ride out to where the baskets are clipped onto lines and posts and then he cares for the oysters, grading them and bringing the sellable ones back in.

I'm able to picture the places he talks about—the pubs and the beaches—because I've been to them, and I'm glad that I had the chance to visit Van's hometown with Dad, even if I did feel kind of numb at the time. But when I mention how happy I am that my father got to spend some quality time with John—something he had always wanted to do—we both struggle to contain our emotions.

We stop talking after that, and I reflect on how unusual it was for Van to be so chatty in the car. I appreciate his attempts to divert me more than he could know.

When we get to Helford, I direct him to Nick's parents' place, rather than the car park. The tide is out, so that means the road at the bottom is passable, although water from the creek still splashes up the sides of the car as we drive through.

"Here's fine," I say. Van pulls over in a parking bay and cuts the engine. "You coming?" I ask.

"Shall I?"

"Nick will want to say hi."

He hesitantly unclicks his seatbelt.

I haven't been paying much attention to the weather, but it's a gorgeous summer's day, and red fuchsias burst out from among the hedges lining the road, making it look like the hedges themselves are flowering.

Theresa and Christopher live in a chocolate-box thatched cottage opposite the pub. The scent of roses from their garden mingles with the smell of the tidal water as we enter through the white picket gate. I catch sight of Theresa at the kitchen window and she waves, making it to the door before we reach it.

"Hello, sweetie." She pulls me in for a comforting hug before greeting Van. "It's been a long time since we had you here for our New Year's Eve party," she says.

"Fifteen years, I reckon," he replies.

"Mummy!" Luke runs into the hall, the weight of his small body slamming into mine.

"*Oof*," I exclaim, grinning as I swing him up into my arms. He buries his face against my neck and I hold him close for several long seconds before turning him toward Van. "This is Van," I say. "Mummy's friend."

"Hello!" Van replies cheerfully.

Luke returns his smile.

We decline Theresa's offer of a cuppa and head across to the pub. I get the sense that Van is on edge, but Nick soon puts him at ease.

"Hello, mate!" he exclaims, coming straight out from the bar area and clasping Van's hand in a warm, easy shake. "It's good to see you! I'm sorry it's under such awful circumstances," he adds.

As they chat, Aimee, one of our longest-serving waitresses and also my friend, comes over to say hi. "You all right, hon?" she asks.

I nod, squeezing her arm. "How are things here? I'm sorry I haven't been around to help."

"We're fine," she insists. "We've taken on a couple of students for the rest of the summer hols. They're a bit hopeless, to be honest, but they'll pick up. You take all the time you need. Go see Tristan," she urges. "He's got some dinner packages for you."

When I come out of the kitchen again, complete with two bags laden down with the best ready meals imaginable, Nick and Van are talking about surfing.

"You reckon you'll be able to come out one day?" Nick asks.

"I'm not sure," Van replies, glancing at me.

"You should," I encourage. "You'll need a break. Maybe we could tag-team it—I'll go see Dad in the morning one day and you go in the afternoon."

"That would work," he agrees.

"Day after tomorrow?" Nick asks.

Once more Van looks to me for approval.

I nod.

"It'll be a bit more crowded than last time," Nick tells him with a grin.

That's an understatement—the beaches at this time of year are heaving.

"Eight to ten people is considered crowded where I come from," Van replies.

Nick laughs. "Well, we might not manage those numbers, but I do know a couple of more secluded spots." He wraps his arm around my shoulders and presses a kiss to my forehead. "You OK?" he asks softly.

I nod, fighting back tears. "Don't get me started again."

"I thought I'd pop into the hospital later."

"Really?" I ask with relief. "I've been feeling bad that I won't make it back until after I've dropped Luke off tomorrow afternoon."

"No problem." Nick kisses me again. "Love you. Go home, rest up. See you tomorrow."

He gives me one last squeeze before saying goodbye to our son.

"You guys get on well," Van says when we're back in the car. I've opted to drive the last leg home.

"Yeah, we do. It was a bit rough for a while, but we've made it work."

I say this in a whisper, glancing at Luke in the rearview mirror.

"Can we go out in the rowboat, Mummy?" Luke asks as soon as we're back at the cottage.

"Oh, darling, Mummy doesn't really feel up to that."

His face creases with disappointment.

"Go on," Van urges. "It'll do us good to get out for a bit."

It's the "us" bit that does it for me.

We have to clean out *Platypus* first, but the menial task takes my mind off Dad for a bit. I sit at the back, trying to balance my weight with Luke's so we're not all lopsided. Van rows while Luke leans out of the side with his net, trying to scoop up anything of interest. It's highly unlikely that will include fish.

"Shall we moor up on the other side?" Van asks, pointing us in that direction.

"Yeah!" Luke cries.

The fields have wheat this year, which is yet to be harvested. As we climb to the top of the hill, a memory comes back to me of being up here with Ruth, once, when she was painting. The wheat was creamy yellow in color and swaying in the wind, just as it is now. I remember Ruth pulling off an ear of wheat to show me how it matched the color of my hair. Van and Dad were building a den down by the water.

"That was right after you arrived from London," he says when I share the memory.

I push my fingers through my son's hair. "Luke's is even lighter than mine was at his age. He takes after his daddy, curls and all."

"He has your eyes, though," Van points out.

"Runny honey in sunshine," I say with a smile. "Your mum had such a way with words when it came to color, didn't she? Do you remember how persistent she was at getting me to choose my favorite green?"

He nods, his lips tilting up at the corners. "What's your favorite color?" Van asks Luke, crouching down so they're on the same level.

"Yellow," Luke replies solemnly.

"Ah, yellow's a great color," Van agrees. "The color of sunshine." He glances up at me. "Where *are* Mum's paintings these days?"

"They're still in the wardrobes in the annex. Did you sleep OK in there last night?"

He shakes his head and stands up. "I crashed out on the living room floor. It didn't feel right being in your dad's room."

"I'm sorry. You must be aching all over."

"I'm fine. I used the cushions. I've slept rougher. You should try being out on a boat for weeks on end." He ruffles Luke's hair. "You want to build a den, mate?"

"Yeah!" Luke yells.

"I'll race you to the bottom."

I laugh as they set off, Van pretending to catch my squealing son the whole way.

THAT EVENING, ONCE Luke is tucked up in bed and dinner is in the oven, we sit out on the patio with a couple of cold beers.

"He's awesome, Nell. You've done good," Van says.

"He's the best. I can't believe he'll be in his second year of school soon." Luke was born three weeks prematurely and is the youngest in his class. I was a wreck last year when he started pre-K.

"His birthday's next week, right?"

"Wednesday. I don't much feel like celebrating, to be honest, but we'll have to do something."

"Let me know how I can help."

"Thank you. Are you missing Libby?" I ask.

"Terribly." He checks his watch. "Do you mind if I call her from the landline later? I'll give you some money for the bill."

"Don't be silly. Of course you can."

"There's not a whole lot of time to be thinking about her when I'm out on a boat for weeks, but here, with him," he nods toward the top floor of the cottage, "it's harder."

"I understand."

Van puts the bottle to his lips and I watch his Adam's apple bobbing up and down as he drinks. He looks at me out of the corner of his eye, then swivels to face me, swinging one leg over the other side of the bench so he's straddling it.

"How are things with your mum these days?" he asks.

I shrug and reach up to tighten my ponytail. "Better than the last time we talked about her, when we were in Uluru. She and Robert came to my wedding."

"I'm sorry I couldn't make it."

"No, you're not."

"No, I'm not," he agrees with a smirk, taking another long draw of his beer.

I laugh lightly and shake my head at him, reaching for my own bottle of beer. "Guess you were right about Nick, after all."

His expression sobers.

"Why were you nervous when we went to the pub earlier?" I find myself asking.

He looks uncomfortable and I'm not sure he's going to answer me, but then he speaks. "The last time I saw Nick, he was just a regular guy. Now he's the man you chose to marry. That puts him on a whole other level."

A level that he can't compete with.

I get it.

"I am sorry it didn't work out," he says quietly.

"I don't regret it," I tell him.

"How could you?" Once more he nods toward the top floor of the cottage. "So your mum came to your wedding?" he asks, reverting to our earlier subject.

"Yep. First time in Cornwall since she lived here with my dad. She didn't approve of my choice of husband, either," I say wryly.

"Do you see much of her now?" he asks.

"Not a lot. She does send awesome Christmas and birthday presents for Luke, though. I need to call her, actually. I still haven't told her about Dad." I've been disinclined to after how unsupportive she was last time.

Van reaches over and brushes my jaw with his thumb. It's a casual, caring gesture, but it causes me to inhale sharply. He retreats and drains the dregs of his beer, nodding toward the annex. "Can I get into the wardrobes?"

IT'S ASTONISHING HOW strong the paint smell is, even after all these years.

"I thought you'd take them with you when you were twenty," I say as he brings out the piece of us on Kynance, building a sandcastle.

He shakes his head. "I didn't really have anywhere to put them, then. I thought they'd be safer here. But I'll take them home with me this time."

I feel like I've been kicked in the gut. Once they're gone, once *Dad's* gone, why would he ever come back?

"Hey, you OK?" he asks, noticing my expression.

I shake my head, pressing the heels of my palms to my eyes.

"I'm usually the one who loses it in here, not you," he says fondly, tugging me into his arms.

I have such a big lump in my throat, but I fight against sobbing, my pulse quickening as he holds me. The longer our embrace goes on, the more on edge I become. Perhaps he senses the shift in atmosphere because suddenly his hands are on my arms and he's separating us.

"I'll go check on dinner," I say shakily, leaving the annex.

LATER THAT NIGHT, Van goes into the hall to call Libby. I turn up the TV, trying not to eavesdrop, but it's impossible to miss how relaxed and happy he sounds—a far cry from the teenage boy who could barely string two sentences together when he was talking to us or his dad back home. Through a crack in the doorway, I see him sitting on the floor, his long legs stretched out in front of him and crossed at the ankles.

"I love you. I'll call you again in a couple of days, OK? Be a good girl for Mummy."

My insides are full of warmth, listening to him sign off the conversation.

"How was she?" I ask when he returns.

"Fine. She'd just woken up." It's Saturday morning in Australia.

He sits down beside me, but I don't mute the television and for a while we sit there and stare at the screen.

I'm not taking in a thing.

I'm too consumed with something else that's happening. The part of my heart that belonged to Van has been repressed for so long, but I can feel it unfolding and opening to let him in. It terrifies me—I don't want to get hurt again.

And how can I even be thinking about Van in this way when my dad is dying?

Once more I cut our evening short and head upstairs early.

THE NEXT MORNING, I wake up to sunlight streaming in through the cracks in my curtains. I almost jump out of my skin when I see that it's eight thirty. Luke never sleeps in this long! I feel more well-rested than I have in ages, but then it hits me again about Dad and I feel sick and sad to my core.

Desolately pulling on my dressing gown, I go to check on my son. To my surprise, his bed is empty, but I can hear voices downstairs.

Luke's high-pitched chitter chatter mingles with Van's deep rumble as I approach the kitchen. It would have surprised me to see them eating breakfast together, but what I actually see takes my breath away.

They're painting, using the Christmas set that we bought Van all those years ago. It's out on the table and they each have a piece of 11 x 17–sized paper in front of them. Luke is making a total mess and thoroughly enjoying himself.

"Look at my picture!" he exclaims in lieu of a greeting when he spies me at the doorway.

"That's amazing!" I go over and place my hand on his back.

"It's a flower garden," he tells me seriously. "I'm making it for Grandad."

"He's going to love it." I catch Van's eye and my heart unfolds a little more. "Good morning."

"Morning," he replies. "I heard him wake up and thought you could use the sleep."

"Thank you," I whisper. "And what are *you* doing?" I nod meaningfully at his picture.

"Only messing around," he replies self-consciously, dabbing brilliant orange onto a sunset.

"That's beautiful."

He hands me his phone. "You get the most incredible sunsets out on the boat."

I study the photograph he's copying. The deck of the boat is at the bottom of the picture, then there's a rough, gray ocean in the middle and, at the top, a sky bursting with color.

"I had no idea you've been painting again." I'm reeling. Delighted. "When did you start back up?"

"Just now," he replies, leaning in closer to see what Luke's doing. "That's awesome, mate. I like this color that you've mixed."

It's a sort of murky, green-brown-orange. I wrinkle my nose at the same time that Van looks up and grins at me.

"Did you sleep downstairs again?" I ask.

He nods. "I was awake when I heard him stirring."

"Have you eaten?"

"Yeah, we had some cereal an hour or so ago. Want me to get you anything?"

"No, I'm fine, thank you. You carry on."

Oh, Lord, I'm in trouble . . .

"DO YOU LIKE Van?" I ask Luke on my way to drop him back to his dad.

"Yes." He nods purposefully.

"Do you think he sounds like Tom from *Fireman Sam*?"

It's one of his favorite TV shows—Tom is the Aussie helicopter rescue pilot.

"Erm . . ." He pulls a face and shrugs. "Will you give Grandad my picture?"

"Of course I will."

"When can we do some gardening together?"

It's a while before I can answer. "Grandad is very ill, darling.

I don't think he's going to be up for much gardening. But you and I can plant some flowers together sometime, OK?"

I check the rearview mirror when he doesn't answer. He's staring out the window, lost in his thoughts.

"Is that OK, Luke?"

"I miss Grandad," he replies. "When can I see him?"

I draw a long, shaky breath. "I'm not sure, sweetie. Grandad is very sick. I don't think he's coming out of hospital."

"Can I go with you to see him?" he asks hopefully.

Oh God . . .

"He's not really himself at the moment." No. That won't make sense to a child. I rack my brain for how to explain. "Can you think about Grandad right now?"

His eyebrows pull together.

"What do you see, inside your head?" I ask. "How does Grandad look? What's he doing?"

"He's in the garden," he replies.

"That's it." Tears spring into my eyes and I flick on my indicator, pulling up at the curb. I can't talk like this when I'm driving. I swivel in my seat to look at my son. "What does he look like?"

"He's grumpy," Luke mutters, making me laugh. "And his hands are all dirty."

"Is he complaining about his knees?" I ask.

"Yes!" he exclaims.

"*That's* how he wants you to remember him."

HAVING LUKE WITH us helped, but now it's only Van and me again and we're quiet on the long car journey to the hospital. I tried to tell him about my conversation with Luke, but broke down so he had to take over driving again. I'm not sure what I'd do without him.

Dad's eyes shine with tears when he sees Luke's picture, but when I reveal that his grandson is desperate to see him, his face collapses.

"Not like this," he mumbles. "Not like this."

I try to cheer him up by telling him about how I came downstairs this morning and caught Van painting.

He reaches for Van's hand, grasping it. "Good!" he says. "Can I see what you've done?"

Van looks uncomfortable. "It's not finished yet. But I'll bring it tomorrow if it'll make you happy."

"Now we have to get her writing again," Dad says to Van, grabbing my hand with his free one. "Fudge and Smudge!"

"Oh, Dad," I reply dolefully. "Really?"

"*Yes*, really! Luke would love those stories! You should write them for him, not me."

"Yes, you should," Van says pointedly.

"Maybe I will, if you promise to do the pictures," I reply.

"Yes!" Dad urges and from the way Van jerks, I'm guessing he's squeezing our hands simultaneously.

"Sounds like we have a deal," Van says.

A shiver goes down my spine as he meets my eyes. Breaking the contact, I turn toward Dad, but I'm not comfortable with the look in his eyes, either.

IT HITS ME like a ton of bricks that night. We're going to lose Dad soon and I'm nowhere near ready.

"I wish I could take your pain away," Van murmurs as we sit together on the couch.

I'm inconsolable. I feel as though I've swallowed Sadness whole and it's sitting as heavy as concrete in my stomach.

"What can I do?" Tears glisten in his eyes.

"Hold me," I respond, knowing that, whatever Dad felt about our relationship in the past, he wouldn't deny me this small piece of comfort now.

Van gathers me in his arms and pulls me close, but it's not close enough and he seems to realize it too. He lifts me onto his lap and we hold each other tightly, and somehow we just *fit*.

I don't know how long we stay like that, but when my tears dry up, neither of us makes any attempt to move.

My heart has unfolded completely and it feels as open and as fragile as paper. It's as if a whole garden of brightly colored origami flowers has sprouted to life around it, and they're as brittle and flimsy and swaying in the breeze.

I love him. I always have and I always will. I am *in love* with him. And my dad is dying in the hospital and all the old shame and guilt that Van and I felt fifteen years ago is still there, wedged between us.

At the same time, we withdraw and stare into each other's eyes. Van caresses my cheek with his thumb and I do the same to him, and it's a tender gesture, full of love. I know then, without a shadow of a doubt, that he still loves me. He's *in love* with me.

And my dad is dying in the hospital and my dad is dying in the hospital and my dad is dying in the hospital and there's nothing we can do about it.

"I love you," I say in a desperately choked voice.

"I love you too," he replies.

He cups my face with his hands and my stomach lifts as

billions of butterflies take off, our lips coming together in the sweetest, most gentle kiss. Our mouths barely part, we hardly move, but seconds tick by. Then he rests his forehead against mine and we stay like that, tears streaming down both our faces as we're lost in the guilt and regrets of the past.

NICK IS SUPPOSED to be coming the next morning to take Van surfing, but Van cancels.

"I can't leave you," he says as he holds me in his arms in the kitchen.

I don't argue.

He drives us back to the hospital that morning and as I turn to face him, my insides are a whirling kaleidoscope of love mixed with the deepest sorrow.

Dad is asleep when we arrive. We sit on opposite sides of the bed, waiting for him to wake up, and once more our eyes are drawn back to each other. It's the strangest thing, being able to stare at another person, uninterrupted, as minutes tick by. I don't know how long we stay like that, but Dad's voice makes us jump.

"Nell . . ."

He instantly has my full attention. "Dad!" I stand up. "How are you feeling?"

He lifts his hand and I reach for it, but then I see his finger waggling between Van and me. "You . . ." he says, "two . . ."

A lump springs up in my throat.

No, please, Dad, don't say it . . . I can't bear it . . .

"I . . ." The strain shows on his face. Every word is exhausting him.

"It's OK, Dad." I'm desperate for him to *not* say the words.

If he asks us to stay away from each other—if he makes that his dying wish—it will *end* me.

He clutches my hand with even more strength than yesterday. Then he takes Van's hand too.

"I . . ." he says. "*Sssssssorry.*" He brings our hands together on his stomach, closing Van's hand over mine.

I sink down onto the chair.

"I'm *sssorry,*" Dad repeats. "You two . . . Together . . ."

He closes his eyes and his hands go limp, the effort too much for him.

I try to stifle my sobs, but can't. Through my blur of agony, I see Van's whole body shaking as he cries.

"We have to take him home." Van squeezes my hand so hard it hurts. "He would want to be at home."

I KNOW VAN is right and, days later, we bring Dad back to the cottage. He's overwhelmed to see that we've moved his bed to face the view.

He didn't want to be a burden, which is why he didn't ask for this himself, but of course he wants to spend his remaining time here, in the place where he grew up and never left.

The hospital team has arranged hospice care and a lovely woman called Kerrie helps us to get him settled, reassuring us about everything we need to do to keep him comfortable.

No one knows how long Dad has, but it may only be days. He's been sleeping a lot and he's drowsy when he's awake. His breathing is shallow and he's lost his appetite, refusing to eat or drink. Kerrie assures me that all of this is normal in a person's final days, and shows us how to keep his mouth moist with a sponge and how to massage his hands, which are cold from reduced circulation.

Luke keeps asking if he can see Grandad. Tomorrow is his fifth birthday.

"What do you think, Dad?" I ask when he's lucid.

I know he hated the idea of Luke coming to the hospital, but here at home, in his own bed, Dad could almost pass as normal.

"We'd keep the visit very brief. I thought we could sing him happy birthday and do his cake here, then Nick said he'll take him to Flambards for the rest of the day." That's the theme park not far from here.

Dad nods. "I would like that."

While Dad's asleep the next morning, Van and I quietly fix some balloons to the curtain rails in the annex. Dad wakes up while we're doing it.

"Bring paintings out too," he says.

"Mum's paintings?" Van asks.

Dad nods. "And yours. Brighten place up."

We dutifully carry the canvases out from the wardrobe and lean them against the walls, and I stick Van's sunset picture next to Luke's one from a few days ago. After calling my mother and filling her in, she sent the most enormous bunch of flowers yesterday so the room looks and smells lovely. She was actually very sad to hear what was happening—I'm not sure it fully sank in last time, but then, Dad pulled through, so maybe she didn't appreciate how hard it had been.

Dad's eyes rest on the sandcastle painting for a long time, before he nods off again.

When Nick and Luke arrive, our little boy is more restrained than usual. I don't know if Nick has warned him to be careful, but he's very gentle as he climbs up onto Dad's bed and kisses his cheek.

"Hello, Lukey," Dad says surprisingly cheerfully, grabbing his hand. "Happy birthday."

"I made you a card," Luke says, showing him the colorful painting on the front. "This is you and this is me."

As he talks Dad through his picture, Dad's eyes keep opening and closing slowly, but his smile remains in place.

"It's fantastic," Dad says warmly.

I leave them, going to the kitchen to fetch the cake, and taking a minute before returning with the candles alight. We sing happy birthday to Luke and then Dad falls asleep.

In the middle of the night, he wakes up. I'm sitting by his bed, keeping vigil, his hand in mine.

"Ruth," he says.

"No, it's Nell, Dad." My eyes fill with tears.

"Nelly," he says. "Where's Vian?"

"Van's asleep. I can go get him? He's on the floor in the living room," I feel compelled to add.

His face creases with pain. "Nelly, I'm sorry," he says. "You. Van. It's OK." Every word is labored.

"Please, Dad, don't worry," I beg.

"I love you, Nelly. So proud of you."

"I love you too, Dad. And I know you are."

He reaches down and pats the bed.

"What is it, Dad?" He's still patting the bed. I can barely speak for the lump in my throat.

"Scampi," he murmurs.

I turn my face away and cry my heart out, my whole body racking with silent sobs.

When I look back at him, he's slipped into unconsciousness.

He never wakes up, and the following day, we lose him completely.

IT SEEMS AS though everyone my father has ever known comes to his funeral. The church pews are packed with his old friends and colleagues from the National Trust properties where he used to work. Steven and Linzie, the farmers, and friends and acquaintances from up in the village come, plus Ellie's and my other mates' parents—even Ellie and Brooke make the long journeys home from Newcastle and London for it.

But the most surprising of all of those who come is my mum. She sits beside me on the front pew, with Van at my other side. Nick, Theresa, and Christopher are looking after Luke in the pew across from us so I don't have to worry about losing it in front of him.

I'm very tearful when Dad's former colleague gets up to talk about how loved and respected he was at the gardens, and how proud he was, not only of me, but also of Van, who was like a son to him.

Mum reaches across and takes my hand. Her fingers are cold and her grip unfamiliar. I long to hold Van's instead, but I don't. It's as if she needs me, her daughter, right now.

Her hand soon warms in mine.

The Castors hold the funeral reception at The Boatman and tell me not to worry about a thing. I'm incredibly grateful. I have no idea how people manage to stay on top of everything when they're drowning in grief.

I've cried so many tears that now I feel strangely numb.

People keep coming over to talk to me about Dad, but I wish I was at home, curled up on the couch with Van. Luke is a good distraction, as is Mum. Everyone keeps commenting on how alike we look—even those who said the same thing at my wedding a few years ago. We're both slim and about the same height, but she's wearing heels. It's strange to know that I must be marginally taller than her these days. She looks very attractive in a smart navy blue skirt suit, her still-golden blond hair styled up in an intricate topknot.

Luke is sad about his grandfather, but he doesn't really comprehend his loss yet, so he's quite perky. Theresa has been keeping him entertained for most of the afternoon and I keep catching Mum looking over at them.

"Do you want me to go and get him?" I ask when we have a moment alone. Van is currently talking to Nick and Ellie and I've been aching to go and join them. But Mum's car is coming soon to take her to the airport hotel—she's flying home first thing, so this is the last I'll see of her for a while.

She tears her eyes away from my mother-in-law and her grandson. "I don't think he really likes me."

"Of course he does, Mum," I reassure her. "He doesn't know you that well, but there's still time."

"Why don't you come and see us more?" She sounds accusatory, which winds me up.

"Why don't you come and see *us*?" I retort.

"I've never felt that welcome," she replies.

"*What?*"

"You and your dad. You're so close."

My nose prickles at her use of the present tense. I fumble in the pocket of my black shift dress for a tissue, while she stares at the floor, downcast.

"I'm sorry," she says flatly. "You and your dad were *always* so close. I've felt like a spare part over the years."

"You were never a spare part," I mumble, blowing my nose. "But yes, we were close."

"I'd like to see more of you—and Luke," she says.

"You'll always be welcome here with us, and we'll try to come and see you more. It's only the money. It's always been tight."

"I can help with that."

"We'll be OK. But thank you."

"It would be the least I could do," she persists.

"Thank you, Mum."

Her car arrives soon afterward, so I retrieve Luke and we both go outside to see her off.

"Give Grandma a hug," I prompt, leaning Luke toward her.

He wraps his arms around her neck and she smiles and closes her eyes.

"Did you say thank you to Grandma for the Playmobil fire engine she sent you?"

"Thank you," Luke replies dutifully.

"Thanks, Mum, you always get him great gifts," I add.

"I'll keep them coming," she promises with a smile, pinching my delighted son's nose.

"We'll try to see you soon," I vow.

"OK, dear." She gives me an awkward hug while I'm holding Luke and kisses me on my cheek, then she turns and climbs into the taxi. I wait and watch until the car disappears from view, feeling a pang when it does. I hope it's not too long before we see each other again—she's the only parent I have now.

Cuddling Luke close, I return inside and make a beeline for Van, Nick, and my friends.

"You OK?" Nick asks, putting his arm around me and pressing a kiss to my temple.

I feel Van's eyes on us as I nod. He's wearing a suit—one he had to go to Falmouth to buy. I've never seen him dressed so smartly and my eyes keep drifting back to him.

"How much longer are you here for?" I hear Brooke ask him.

"I'm not sure," Van replies. "I've already changed my ticket once, but I'll stick around for a bit longer."

My heart curls in at the edges. I know how desperately he's missing Libby. He must feel unbearably torn, because he wants to be here for me too, and I selfishly want him to stay for as long as possible.

Luke wriggles out of my arms and gets down, running over to Theresa.

On autopilot, I take two steps toward Van before coming to a sudden stop. I was about to put my arms around his waist—I wanted him to hold me, like he's been doing at home. I stare at him in a daze and his brow knots with confusion. Then I realize that all of my friends are looking at me and I spin on my heels and walk away.

I instantly regret it—I've just drawn even more attention to myself—but I panicked. One of Dad's former colleagues lifts his hand to get my attention, but I can't do it, I can't do any more small talk. Bolting up the stairs to Nick's apartment—which was also once mine—I let myself in with the key I still have.

Nick finds me there, in floods of tears, on his bed.

"Hey," he says gently, lying down beside me and gathering me in his arms. I'm crying so hard. My heart is *aching*. It *wants* Van. "What was that about?" Nick asks. "Why did you run away? You looked at Van and then took off."

Oh no, everyone noticed . . .

I cry even harder.

"Nell . . ." he murmurs, stroking his hand soothingly across my hair. "It's OK. It's going to be OK. I'm so sorry, baby, but it's going to be OK."

"I'm in love with Van."

The words are out of my mouth before I can stop them. I pull away from Nick and stare at him with disbelief.

He cocks his head to one side, his mind ticking over. "Do you mean . . ." His voice trails off, but he's still regarding me contemplatively. "You're in love with him," he states.

"Since I was fifteen," I whisper.

He breathes in sharply.

My eyes plead with him to understand.

"Does he know?" he asks carefully.

I tell him everything. I *purge* my soul. And he listens, taking it all in, not once giving me the impression that he's judging me. I couldn't stop talking, even if I felt like he was.

"It all makes sense now," he says eventually. "That's why you went off Drew."

His comment actually makes me laugh, but I'm far from entertained.

"Jeez, Nell," he mutters, dragging his hand across his face. He looks grave.

"Are you disgusted?"

He reels backward. "Come on," he scoffs. "You're not brother and sister, for pity's sake. You were *kids* when you lived together. I can't believe you've been carrying all this shit around for years."

"Dad—" I start to say, but he cuts me off.

"Your dad was doing what any father of any teenage girl would do—trying to prevent a guy from screwing his daughter!"

he erupts. "God rest his soul, but he should've told you sooner that he was OK with you being in love with each other."

"When Van was last here, I was with Joel," I try to explain, feeling defensive of my poor late father. "And when I went to Australia, I'd started seeing you and Van was with Sam."

Nick sighs heavily. "Yeah, sure, so maybe your dad didn't feel it was worth dredging up the past. Have you really never told anyone about it?" He glances at me sideways. "Not even Ellie?"

I shake my head.

"You should tell her," he says firmly. "She'll say the same thing as me. Get it out, Nell. Stop feeling guilty. You've had enough to deal with."

I need another cry after all of that.

By the time we make it back downstairs, most people have left. Ellie regards me with concern and holds out her hand to me.

"Are you OK, hon?" she asks.

I nod, my eyes flitting to Van's. His expression is unreadable. "I will be," I reply to Ellie. "When are you going back to Newcastle?"

"The day after tomorrow. Would you like me to come over for a cuppa in the morning?"

Nick slaps Van's chest before I can answer. "Tomorrow morning. Surfing. We're doing this, bro. Ellie is keeping Nell company."

I smile at Nick and then at Ellie. "Yes, that would be good."

Van nods too, agreeing to Nick's plan.

I REALLY WANT to take Luke home with us, but Nick dissuades me.

"You should talk to Van," he says in my ear as I hug him and our son goodbye.

Van drives us home, but neither of us says a word. Despair and nervousness are battling it out in my stomach as we take to the couch.

"You were upstairs with Nick for a long time."

What does he think we were doing?

"I told him everything," I whisper. "He understood."

Van looks shocked, and then he slowly hunches forward and buries his head in his hands, lost for words.

Dad made us feel so ashamed about our feelings for each other when we were teenagers that it's understandably hard to shake the guilt from our shoulders now, even after his apology at the hospital. We've bottled up our emotions for years, and although I feel better after confessing to Nick, Van hasn't had that same opportunity.

"Van." I place my hand on his back. "I need you."

"What do you want me to do?" he asks in a low, tormented voice.

"Can you hold me tonight?" I find the courage to ask.

He moves to embrace me, but I shake my head. "Not here. Upstairs."

He hesitates and then nods once.

When I come out of the bathroom, Van is nowhere to be seen. I head upstairs and get changed quickly into my vest and PJ shorts before climbing under the covers.

It's another ten minutes before I hear his footsteps on the stairs. I wasn't at all sure he was coming.

He appears in my doorway, seeming uncertain. Then he comes in and goes around to the other side of the bed, taking off his suit and tie and unbuttoning his shirt, laying each item of clothing on a chair. He does all of this with his back to me, and then he pulls a T-shirt on over his head and turns and climbs under the covers. Meeting my eyes momentarily, he holds his arm open to me. I snuggle in close and his arm comes around me to pull me into place. He's so warm and solid, an instant comfort. I breathe in deeply and feel him doing the same, his body gradually releasing tension beneath my palm. Sliding my hand up to his jaw, my thumb traces over his stubble, again and again, until I'm too tired to do it anymore. I fall asleep before he does.

IN THE EARLY hours of the morning, I come to. I'm still in Van's arms and, as I lie there, pondering the events of yesterday, everything feels oddly unreal. We buried Dad and his loss is incredibly raw, but right now, I don't feel like crying. I can't believe I told Nick everything, and he understood, he really did. I feel lighter.

Van's fingers move on my arm and as I shift back to look at him, he turns on his side toward me. He's asleep, but his hand comes forward, almost as though it's seeking out mine. I take hold of it and he stills. A moment later, his eyes open. He blinks, his gaze coming into focus as we stare at each other.

I don't know how many seconds pass—twenty, thirty, forty—but we reach for each other at the same time. Our mouths come together and our legs entwine, our arms slipping around each other's waists and pulling us closer. Our kiss, at first gentle, becomes more passionate. I'm *hungry* for him.

He flips me onto my back and pins my wrists to the mattress above my head. But my legs are free and they hook around his waist, pulling him against me.

He wants this as much as I do . . .

We gasp into each other's mouths as he rocks against me. Then he releases my wrists and my hands fly to his T-shirt, bringing it up and over his head. He makes short work of my vest top in turn and then my thumbs hook under the waistband of his boxers.

"I don't have anything," he pants, pressing his forehead hard against mine. "I can't have two children on opposite sides of the world."

It's a sharp, painful reminder that he will be leaving soon. It's already going to hurt so much and this will undoubtedly make the pain more acute. But how can we stop this now? We've been hurtling toward this point for half of our lives.

"I'm on the pill," I whisper.

His lips return to mine.

When we're both naked, he laces our fingers together. I didn't close the curtains last night and downriver the sun is rising. In the gray morning light seeping in through the windowpane, night-sky eyes lock with mine. And then we connect, our two bodies finally—*finally*—coming together as one.

It's so beautiful, I see fireworks.

VAN HAS ALREADY left with Nick by the time Ellie arrives. Everything still feels surreal—losing Dad, last night with Van, the fact that I've resolved to tell my oldest friend the secret that I've carried with me for so long. I can hear myself babbling, asking her about work and her love life and what she's been up to. I think she's a little freaked out, probably worrying that I'm in denial because I'm certainly not the lost, vacant girl I was at the pub yesterday.

"Are you OK?" Ellie asks eventually.

I try to take a deep breath, but my lungs won't inflate. "I have to tell you something."

Her expression is a mix of anticipation and alarm. She's waiting.

I swallow, my face prickling uncomfortably. "Van," I say. "Van and I. We're in love."

When I've finished telling her everything, she sighs. "I can't say I'm surprised." Her statement makes my face burn. "I don't mean I'd guessed," she hastily puts me straight. "I can't believe how well you hid it. I meant I'm not surprised because he's super-hot. I fancied him too. I would've told you if Brooke hadn't been so flipping vocal about stating her claim. Sorry," she says penitently, even as I laugh. "I don't know why I admitted to that. Oh, Nell!" she exclaims abruptly. "You have nothing to be ashamed of. *Nothing*. I don't think your dad was ever *disgusted* at the two of you. He felt betrayed, that's all. He thought you were close, yet you went behind his back and kept a huge secret from him. I've always thought of Van as your best friend—much more so than your brother. To be honest, I used to get a bit jealous about the connection you guys had. You should be straight about it from here on in. Tell people that this is how it is. Don't feel embarrassed. You're a couple of adults who lived in the same house for a bit as children. You're not doing anything wrong. And from the sounds of it, your dad *wanted* you to be happy with Van."

"What about when he goes home?" I ask, reaching for a tissue.

Her features grow serious. "I don't know. But you'll find a way to make it work."

How?

ELLIE HAS LEFT by the time Nick and Van return. Nick doesn't come in and I'm glad—I'll see him later when I collect Luke. I'm bringing him home for the rest of the week.

I wait in the hall, fidgeting as I listen to Nick and Van saying goodbye and the sound of the gate closing. Van opens the door with his key and comes into the hall, halting in his tracks at the sight of me.

His pupils dilate as he comes toward me, but I stay where I am, reaching up to push my fingers through his dark hair. It's damp and cold and he smells of the ocean. He lifts me in his strong arms and carries me upstairs to my bedroom. We've got some major catching up to do.

DAYS LATER, WE go to Kynance to watch Van's final sunset. I've returned Luke to Nick as I'm driving Van to the airport first thing. He's taking his mother's artwork home with him, but he swears he'll be back.

We don't know when that will be, or whether I'll be the one to go and visit him next time. We each only just about make do when it comes to finances, but somehow we'll find a way to see each other, and we've promised to speak as much as we can. Thank goodness for the invention of Skype—at least we'll be able to look at each other's faces. But we're not kidding ourselves—we know it's going to be hard.

Van has missed Libby dreadfully, made even more intense by having Luke with us over the last few days. Our time together has also been incredibly poignant because Dad's loss is still so raw, but we've somehow managed to experience moments of pure joy.

Parking up on the cliff, we walk down the steep dirt track to the beach, stepping aside regularly for people coming back up. The tide is on its way in and everyone is going home. We'll have to be quick if we don't want to get cut off ourselves.

There are worse things than being stuck on a deserted beach for hours, but I'm not so selfish as to make Van miss his flight, although the idea is tempting. We have half an hour at most, so I suggest he sets a timer on his watch in case we lose track of time, which is perfectly likely.

There are still a few stragglers when we reach the cove, but we do our best to ignore them, climbing up onto the rock where we shared our first kiss. Van smiles down at me, his expression bittersweet.

I tell him what I first noticed about his eyes, all those years ago, about how the green and gold splinters in the navy-blue background remind me of a still-life painting of a firework, suspended in a night sky.

He's amused, but grows serious. "I've always loved the way you see things. You were born to write."

I avert my gaze, my insides twisting with regret.

"It's not too late," he implores. "I know you feel that London and a magazine career is lost to you, but your children's stories are *crying* out to be written."

I give him a pointed look.

"Yes, I'll do the illustrations," he agrees wearily, grinning when I clap my hands with delight. "I can't say whether they'll be good enough and you have to promise me—*promise* me, Nell—that you won't feel obliged to use them if they're not, but I'm taking my paint set home with me and I'll see what I can do."

I stand on my tiptoes and loop my arms around his neck, pressing my lips to his. He pulls away.

"The Boatman . . ."

I sigh, my giddiness dispelling. "It's easy." I mean the work, the hours, the childcare situation, *everything*.

He shakes his head. "That's not a good enough reason. It doesn't inspire you. You should look for a publishing job in Cornwall—there must be some down here too."

"Come on, Van!" I snap, feeling annoyed as I take a step away from him. He's on another planet. "How am I going to do that? I'm thirty and I don't have any experience. Can you imagine how tough it would be to land a job here? How few and far between those sorts of jobs would be? Can you imagine how competitive the market is? It's not like I can work my way up from the bottom or start out doing work experience. I need the money! I can't work for free, and even if I *could* supplement my earnings with shifts at The Boatman, where would that leave me with Luke? I'm his mother and that comes before anything else. It's not going to happen," I state adamantly.

He sighs heavily. But then a thought seems to come to him. "What about a bookshop?" he asks, perking up. "That one in Falmouth yesterday had a sign up saying they needed help. You'd be working surrounded by books every day and feeling inspired. It would be a step in the right direction, surely? And you never know, if—sorry, *when*—your Fudge and Smudge stories are written, you might have a few contacts, a chance to get the books out on the shelves. It's only an idea, but worth considering?"

I cock my head to one side, before nodding and smiling at him. "OK. I'll pop into the bookshop in the next few days."

"Tomorrow," he commands.

"I'm taking you to the airport!"

"On your way home."

I shake my head, my nose prickling. "I'll be distraught."

"Oh, Nell," he murmurs. "That's exactly why you *should* go. It'll take your mind off things. Promise me," he urges.

I try to kiss him but he holds me back.

"Promise."

I nod, tearfully. "I promise."

As our lips meet, his watch timer goes off. A sob catches in my throat as we break away from each other.

Up on the cliffs, we settle down to watch the sunset. It's one of the most breathtaking I've ever seen and I know that I'll remember it forever. We stay there on the damp grass until the sky turns gray and then black, and then we go back to the cottage to make love to each other for the last time.

I haven't been able to bring myself to think about the logistics, other than the fact that we will speak on the phone as much as we can, but in the silence of the night, I feel cold with fear. How can we make this work? Van can't live without Libby and I can't live without Luke. I'd never take my son away from his father—I couldn't move to *London*, let alone Australia—and there's *no way* Sam will ever let Libby emigrate with Van. Van wouldn't want to take Libby from her mother, even if he could. He didn't have a relationship with his own father until he was ten years old, and look at how that came about. He'll do everything he can to spare Libby that sort of pain.

I am in love with someone who is rooted to his daughter and a country on the other side of the world and there is no getting away from that fact.

I can feel our happy ending slipping away.

It's devastating.

THIRTY-FIVE

S TOP RIGHT THERE."

"You scared the life out of me!" I exclaim as Ed Allister, my boss, pulls me to one side on the pavement,
making room for others to pass. "What's wrong?"

He grins, his brown eyes merry. "Nothing's wrong. I just
had to be here to see it."

"See what?"

He nods ahead at Dragonheart—the bookshop that he
owns and that has been my primary place of work for the past
five years. My brow furrows quizzically at him and then my
eyes widen with delight and anticipation.

"Have they arrived?" I gasp, rushing ahead before he can
answer. I clap my hands over my mouth and stare in at the
window display that Ed must've come in early to set up. He
already has his phone out and is clicking off pictures of my
face. I burst out laughing, beside myself.

I can't believe it. There they are—in the window—a whole
stack of them. Several books face outward: small hardbacks
with rich cream covers and Fudge and Smudge sitting on the
crab-apple tree, their tan faces looking exceptionally mischievous and their pointy ears almost as high as their hats. I do a

little jig on the spot and then turn and throw my arms around my boss.

"I'm so proud of you," he mutters in my ear before pulling away.

"Thank you," I whisper, overcome with emotion. "I wish Van were here to see it."

"He'll be here soon enough," he replies gruffly, patting my back as we head into the building.

I work in the very same children's bookshop in Falmouth that Van encouraged me to visit to inquire about a job. The weird thing is—and I think this is *properly* weird—I'd met Ed, my boss, before.

I'd been into this shop several times, browsing with Luke, so that's why I thought he seemed familiar when I came in to ask about a job. But the more we spoke to each other, the more perplexed he became.

"I feel like I've met you before," he said, scratching his head and making his milk-chocolate hair look even scruffier than it already did.

"Me too!" I exclaimed, glad it wasn't just me. "I work at The Boatman. Have you been in there?"

"Is that a pub?" he asked.

"Yes, in Helford, right on the river."

He looked thoughtful. "I know the pub you're talking about, but I haven't been there in years. I only moved from London a few months ago."

"Really? Where in London did you live?"

"Chiswick."

"No way! That's where I grew up! Well, until I was seven. I came to live with my dad when my mum moved abroad. What made you decide to relocate?"

I remember feeling very at ease, talking to him. It didn't feel like I was being interviewed for a job; it felt like I was chatting to an old friend.

"I used to come as a child," he revealed. "Had a couple more holidays here during my twenties and caught the bug. I needed a change of scene so I decided to buy this place." He looked around whimsically.

"Bastian," I whispered, as it hit me. "The boy from *The NeverEnding Story* . . ."

He gave me a funny look.

"You're Edward!" I cried. "I'm Nell! Don't you remember? Your mum and dad stayed in a cottage up in Mawgan. You came to my house after we'd caught a duckling!"

The look on his face—it was *brilliant*. He completely lit up, a dimple springing into place on his cheek and making him look super sweet, even at his age, which I seemed to recall was more or less the same as mine. "Of course I remember!" he exclaimed. "I can't believe this. Nell! I thought about you for years!" His face fell as a memory came back to him. "Your mum . . ."

I shook my head. "She wasn't my mum. She was my dad's girlfriend. But, yeah." I nodded, looking down. "It was tragic."

He offered me the job that same day.

"I HOPE YOU'RE celebrating tonight," Ed says at the end of our shift.

"I wish. No, Nick's taken Luke camping so it'll be me, myself, and I." I can't even speak to Van as it's the middle of the night in Australia.

"Why don't we go for dinner?" Ed asks.

"Really?"

"Sure. Come on, it's Saturday. We'll raise a toast."

"OK." I grin at him. Doesn't take much to persuade me.

He lives in Falmouth, but suggests going somewhere local to me so that I can drop my car home first—he'll drive so I can drink. We park in Helford and catch the small ferryboat across to the pub on the other side. It's a lovely summer's evening and the lower deck is drenched in sunshine. Ed goes inside to get our drinks, returning with a glass of Prosecco for me and a beer for himself.

"To Fudge and Smudge," he says, and even though his eyes are hidden behind dark sunglasses, I know they're smiling. "And you and Van, obviously," he adds with a grin. "Here's to the first of many more books to come. Cheers."

"Thank you," I say with heartfelt gratitude as he chinks my glass. "If it hadn't been for you . . ."

He waves me away and sips his beer. "You guys would've done it no matter what."

Ed's father and his younger brother—the brother his mother was pregnant with when we first met—own and run a small publishing company in London. Through them, Ed has contacts in the industry, and he helped Van and me submit our stories to publishers. We had interest from three, but decided to go with Ed's family business. His dad, Simon, and brother, Jamie, were as enthusiastic about the books as Ed was, so it felt right.

I couldn't believe it when we were offered those book deals nine months ago. I can picture Van's face clearly when I told him on FaceTime—he was gobsmacked. He kissed the screen! What I wouldn't have given to be able to tell him in person, but it was the best we could do.

The last five years have been hard—tougher at some points

than at others. It was very difficult at first. I'd lost Dad and then Van too. We spoke every day that he wasn't out at sea—sometimes twice a day—and that helped, but all I wanted was to be held by him and it was a long time before we could make that happen. I managed to go to Australia about eight months after Dad passed away, and Van and I had three weeks together. I was nervous about meeting Libby—what if she didn't like me? But she was such a little cutie and we had loads of laughs together.

How I pined for Luke during that time, though. I couldn't afford his flight as well as my own so he stayed behind. A year later, Van came to Cornwall to visit me, but once more, he had to come without Libby. It wasn't only the money; Sam didn't want her daughter disappearing abroad for weeks and she point-blank refused to let her go.

Since then, Van and I have seen each other about once a year, but it's not enough—it's nowhere *near* enough. It's been almost twelve months since we were last together, but he's coming over in a few days—and Libby, finally too. Sam has relented and I still can't believe it. Libby is taking a whole month off school! It's the British summer holidays and we're going to have the best time. I can hardly contain my excitement.

"WHAT ARE YOU up to tomorrow?" I ask Ed, dusting sand off the wooden table surface. The beach is literally across the road, five meters away. I love it here because I can chill out in the sunshine and Luke can play by the water, skimming stones and messing around with his pals.

"I'm going to take the boat out." The shop is closed on Sundays.

Ed bought a small sailing boat a few months ago, but I still haven't been out on it.

"Why don't you come?" he asks. "Or have you got other plans?"

"I'm afraid so," I reply ruefully. "I have to put up a bunk bed."

"A bunk bed?"

"For Libby and Luke. They're sleeping in the bedroom that Van and I used to share. I stupidly swapped our bunk for a single bed when I was a teenager."

I'm very open now about my relationship with Van. I took Ellie's advice five years ago and have told it to people straight ever since. If anything, people have found the idea of me falling in love with my best friend kind of romantic.

Mum was the only person to raise her eyebrows, but that's mainly because she's a snob and thinks I can do better. She made her feelings clear about Nick in that respect too.

We're on pretty good terms at the moment, probably the best we've ever been. We speak on the phone every few weeks, and Luke enjoys his chats with Grandma.

"You going to be all right building a bunk bed on your own?" Ed asks with concern.

I shrug. "Should be. I might have to beg poor Nick for help, otherwise, and he's got more than enough on his plate this week."

Nick and Stefanie, his girlfriend of three years, are tying the knot on Friday. I like her a lot and Luke adores her. As for Nick, he's absolutely besotted—I've witnessed *no signs* of him straying. I'm glad to see him so settled.

Nick wanted some one-on-one time with Luke before he and Stefanie set off on their honeymoon, hence the camping trip. Last time Van was over, Nick took Luke to Italy with him and Stefanie for two weeks, which worked well for everyone. But this time, Van and I are finally going to be able to spend time together as a foursome with Luke and Libby.

"Don't trouble him," Ed says with a frown. "I can give you a hand if you need it."

"No!" I wave him away. "You don't want to be coming all this way again."

"Let's do it tonight, then. After dinner."

"Really?" I ask dubiously.

"Why not?"

"I'd better stop drinking, then."

Ed and I hit it off straight away and I would definitely class us more as friends than colleagues, but it's only been in the last six months or so that we've started seeing each other socially. The main reason for this is that Ed's wife was a bitch. I say "was," but I mean "is," as in, she *is* a bitch, but *was* his wife. They broke up late last year after he walked in on her in bed with another man. I think he'd suspected her of straying—she had at least once before, in London—but it was still a shock to catch her in the act.

Tasha hadn't wanted to leave London—she'd complained to me on several occasions about how bored she was here. I used to find it hard to believe that such a nice guy could've married such a miserable, moany woman, but Ed claims that she wasn't always like that.

I only found out later that she'd agreed to their fresh start under duress. She'd confessed to an affair with her married boss after his wife had found out, thinking she'd get ahead of the game by telling Ed. Ed agreed to give her a second chance and they relocated to Cornwall, but I know the last few years have been a struggle for them. He opened up to me back in December after breaking down in the stockroom. I'd always liked working for him, but that day we became firm friends.

I adore Ed. He's such a lovely, kind man, and the thought of Tasha cheating on him makes me furious. He'll have no trouble replacing her when he's ready.

"I hope this weather holds out." I tilt my face up to the sun.

I hear a rustle of paper and glance at Ed to see that he's picked up the menu. "Five-day forecast is looking good," he murmurs.

"What does the monthly one say?" I ask with a grin.

He eyes me over the top of his sunglasses. "Wish I could tell you." He pushes the glasses back onto the bridge of his nose and scrutinizes the food options. I don't need to look—I already know what I'm having.

Ed scratches his arm. He's so tanned at the moment from all of the sailing he's been doing, and the light-brown hairs on his lean forearms are tinged blond. It's the best he's looked since I've known him. He lost weight after the split—not that he was overweight before—but now he looks fit and healthy and . . . yep, the waitress has noticed.

Ed thanks her distractedly as she collects empties left over from the last people who were sitting here. "Are you OK to order at the bar?" she asks him with a flirty smile.

"Sure," he replies, glancing at me once she's gone. "Do you know what you're having?"

"When do you reckon you'll be up for dating again?" I lean in closer to ask, giggling at the immediate comical expression on his face.

"Talk about an out-of-the-blue question."

"I'm just thinking you look kind of hot right now. You could totally pull if you wanted to."

"Gee, thanks," he replies sardonically.

I smile. "So? When are you planning to put yourself back out there?"

"It's not a question of *when*. *If* the right girl . . ." His voice trails off and he frowns. "Anyway, I'm not even divorced yet."

"Neither is Tasha, but that hasn't stopped her."

He snorts wryly under his breath. "Yeah, well, that's Tasha for you."

She's been wandering around Falmouth with a new man on her arm—not even the guy she cheated on Ed with.

I wish she'd move back to London. She complained about it for long enough, but she's still here, rubbing salt in Ed's wounds. She was flabbergasted when he filed for divorce—I think she thought she had him wrapped around her little finger and that he'd give her yet another chance.

"The waitress keeps looking at you," I whisper, leaning in closer again.

Ed tenses, his shoulders going rigid. "Really?" he whispers in return.

"Yeah." I grin at him. "She's pretty."

"I hadn't noticed."

"So start paying attention!"

"Are you all right out here or shall we move inside to eat?"

I laugh. "Nice change of subject. Let's stay out here for a bit longer."

"Do you know what you're having?" he asks again.

"Fish and chips. I'll go." I bend down to grab my bag from under the table.

"No, this is my treat," Ed says firmly, already on his feet. "We're celebrating."

"You got the drinks."

"Shh. Another Prosecco?"

I know when I'm beaten. "Yes, please." I beam at him and he looks amused as he turns away.

Plonking my handbag on the table in front of me, I pull out my copy of *Fudge and Smudge, the River Piskies*. It feels totally surreal—I can't believe that I wrote this and that Van illustrated it. It's been five years in the making, but we did it—we actually did it—and there are more in the pipeline. We signed a three-book deal and delivered them all straight up, and now we're working on another three. Hopefully there will be a market for them, but we're not in it for the money, anyway. It's just as well—the advance was minimal.

I open the book to the dedication:

For our cheeky little piskies, Luke and Libby

When they're older, they're probably going to hate that we referred to them as piskies. The thought makes me smile.

The kids have been amazing. I used to write the stories and read them to Luke, and when I'd addressed any suggestions he had, I'd pass them to Van to read to Libby.

Luke's captivation massively spurred me on. But my favorite moment was seeing his face when I showed him Van's very first picture. It was of Fudge and Smudge, huddled together on a branch of the crab-apple tree, with the river sparkling in the background. It's the same image we've used for the front cover of the first book.

Van had worked on that piece for months—a mixture of

pencil drawing and watercolor. He wouldn't let me see it as a work in progress, nor any of the drafts that he discarded. He wasn't at all confident that he could pull it off, but I was blown away when he showed me his work on FaceTime. He was so nervous, waiting for my reaction. The original piece is a lot larger, but I was able to get a true sense of how it would work as a book illustration when he sent me a smaller still by e-mail.

Luke thought it was magical, seeing the characters being brought to life.

Ed returns, removing his sunglasses and putting them down in front of him on the table. The sun has disappeared behind the buildings so now we're in the shade, unfortunately. Maybe we will move inside after all.

I slip my book away and return my bag to the sandy ground, smiling across at Ed.

"Cheers," he says, chinking my fresh glass.

"Thank you," I say again, and I mean it from the bottom of my heart. Ed didn't just put me in touch with the right people, he read the stories and helped get them ready for submission to publishers. When I commented on what a good editor he was, he revealed that he had worked with his dad and brother on and off over the years. He could've continued to be involved with the family business, but it sounds like it was a case of too many cooks. He didn't want relationships to be strained—especially between him and his younger brother—so he went out on his own.

"You're welcome," he replies, not making light of the sincerity in my eyes. He shakes his head. "It still blows my mind that you told me about Fudge and Smudge all those years ago."

He remembered this soon after I'd started working at Dragonheart, when I'd admitted to writing children's stories in my spare time. Under duress, I shyly told him what the stories were about and his face lit up with recognition. He reminded me of how we'd sat on the lawn outside the cottage while Van was in the studio, painting, and I laughed, recalling that Van had been in a mood that day. I've suspected ever since that Ed's hearing the stories as a child is probably why he's invested in them now.

"Twenty-five years ago," I say. "Took us long enough."

"Better late than never."

The waitress comes over again to clear the table. I give Ed a meaningful look as she takes his beer glass.

He thanks her, then narrows his eyes at me. "What?" he asks as she walks away again.

"You didn't even look at her!"

"I'm not interested," he brushes me off.

A thought strikes me from out of nowhere. "I know!" I say. "My friend Brooke! You *have* to meet her! She's recently moved back to Cornwall!"

Ed shakes his head.

"Seriously!" I exclaim. "She's single! She split up with her boyfriend a few months ago."

"Nell, please." He frowns and takes a sip of his beer.

"Oh, come on, Ed," I berate him. "She's stunning. Honestly, I really think you could get on. Maybe we could have a barbecue when Van arrives."

He puts his glass down with a forceful clunk.

"Fine, then, forget it."

He sighs. "If you invite me to a barbecue, of course I'll come. But please don't try to match-make me, OK?"

"OK." I shrug.

I won't need to, if Brooke's around.

"**STILL UP FOR** a bit of bunk-building?" Ed asks, pulling up behind my car on the drive.

"Are you sure?" I check apprehensively. "You've spent all day with me. You really want to do some DIY too? You know that's how people fall out?"

He smirks and unclicks his seatbelt in response.

"**I SHOULD'VE BROUGHT** my electric screwdriver," Ed muses later.

Last night I disassembled the single bed and moved it and all of the furniture out of Luke's bedroom. Now we've unpacked the bunk and there are planks of wood of varying sizes laid out on the floor and propped up against the walls.

He swoops down and picks up the instructions. "So we need that bit with this bit."

I'm reaching for my glass of Prosecco so I miss where he's pointing. "Sorry, which bits?"

"This would be more fun with a beer," he states as I take a sip of my drink.

"Why don't you stay in the annex tonight? It's all made up. Go on," I urge when he doesn't immediately say no. "I've got a spare toothbrush—I'll get it for you."

I jump to my feet, half-expecting him to call after me. I'm pleased when he doesn't.

I hand him a beer on my return. "Keys and toothbrush are on the windowsill in the hall, so you have an escape route for when it all becomes too much."

"Are you sure?" Ed tentatively accepts the bottle.

"Sure, I'm sure. Why not?"

"Thanks."

"No, thank *you*." I pull a face. "You're helping me out big time."

"Let's see about that later. Cheers."

"I CAN'T BELIEVE I'm trying to make a children's bed when I am completely and utterly wasted."

Ed chuckles. "We're almost done."

"Is this massively irresponsible?"

He opens his mouth to speak.

"Don't answer that question," I cut him off.

"I think we've followed the instructions correctly." He grabs the bunk rail and gives it a firm shake. "Feels solid."

"Maybe I should sleep up there tonight to test it," I say.

"At least you'd fit." He's smiling.

"Yeah, I know, I'm a short-ass."

He's just shy of six foot himself.

"I'm going up there," I claim with determination, hauling myself up the ladder.

"Careful."

"Ooh, I like it!" I flop onto my tummy. "I could *totally* do this. Come up!"

He shakes his head.

"Go on." I grab his arm and am faintly surprised by the feeling of his muscled bicep under my fingers.

"That would definitely exceed the weight limit." Ed steps out of my grasp.

I roll onto my side and prop my head up on my palm, grinning at him.

"Thanks, Ed." My voice is full of warmth.

"You're welcome." He looks and sounds earnest.

He has wood dust on his nose. "Here, you've got some . . ." I beckon him forward and his eyebrows pull together as I clean him off.

"You've got some too," he murmurs, brushing his thumb across my cheek. We meet each other's eyes and a nervy feeling starts up in my stomach. I jolt as my phone vibrates on the windowsill.

"Can you chuck me my phone?" I ask shakily.

"Van." He reads the display as he hands it over.

"Hello!" I exclaim as I answer.

"Hey!" Van says amiably, his face filling the screen.

"Wait!" I call after Ed, who was about to leave the room. "Van, say hi to Ed." I turn the screen around. Ed waves bashfully.

"Ed's been helping me *erect the bunk*," I say in a jolly voice. "Look." I show Van what I'm sitting on while Ed hovers in the doorway.

"Nice work," he says.

I return the screen to my face and giggle.

"Are you drunk?" he asks and rightfully so.

"Yep. We were celebrating. Oh! Where's my bag?" I look around, but my bag is nowhere to be seen.

"It's downstairs. I'll get it," Ed offers, leaving the room.

"Thank you!" I call after him, shifting to sit with my back against the wall.

Van is waiting. "Celebrating what?"

"You'll see," I reply mysteriously.

Van has short hair and a beard now—not a huge bushy one or anything, but it's definitely several millimeters more than stubble.

He also has a scar cutting through his left eyebrow. For a

while I couldn't look at it without feeling physical pain myself. He did it while surfing the Yanerbie Bombie in Streaky Bay, an absolutely enormous, *horrifically* powerful wave. He wiped out on the reef and got pretty badly bashed about—he was lucky he didn't break bones.

It kills me that I wasn't the first person he called—but how could I be? I can't be his emergency contact when I'm so far away. I'm thankful he has friends like Dave who he can depend on when things go wrong.

He promised me he wouldn't go surfing there again. The accident scared him too.

"Shall I call you back?" Van asks.

"No, hang on a minute."

Ed returns and hands me my bag. "Thank you. You don't have to go," I say quickly when he heads out the door again.

"I'll grab another drink," he replies.

I stare after his departing back and then return my eyes to the screen.

"He's there late," Van notes with a slight frown.

"He's staying in the annex tonight." I think I carry off non-chalance, but I feel slightly on edge. "We went out for dinner and then he came back to help me. We thought DIY would be more fun with alcohol."

No comment from Van.

"Anyway, as I said, we were celebrating!" I inject enthusiasm into my voice as I pull out my copy of *Fudge and Smudge*. "Ta-da!"

"You've got finished copies at last!" His demeanor completely transforms.

"Yes!" I tuck the tiny hardback under my chin and smile at him.

"Ah, man." He shakes his head, blown away.

"I wish you could have been there today to see them in the shop window. Ed came in early to put them out."

"I'll see them on the weekend. Are we still going in?"

"Yes."

We're doing a signing at the shop—Ed has had posters made up and everything. It has been the weirdest thing, serving customers while my face—and Van's—stares out from behind me on the wall.

"I don't know how I'm going to get through the next few days," I say with a sigh. The last two months have *dragged* by. "If I could fall asleep now and wake up on Thursday, I would."

He smiles. His eyes are even darker on the screen than in person—midnight blue, I've taken to calling them in my head. "You should get back to Ed. Can you say thanks to him from me? I feel bad that he's had to help you with that."

"He didn't mind. He's a nice guy."

"Yeah." He inhales sharply. "Love you."

"I love you too."

We sign off and I sit there for a minute, feeling slightly dazed. Then I crawl to the end of the bed and gingerly navigate the ladder.

"Ed?" I call on my way downstairs.

"In the kitchen. I opted for coffee," he says with a smile when I appear. "Want one?"

He's managed to find what he needs.

"Nah, think I'll stick to water. Van said to tell you thanks."

"It's no trouble. It's been fun."

"Yeah. It has." We smile at each other, but look away at the same time.

"I don't think I'm going to be long out of bed," I say with a yawn.

"Me neither," he replies. "I'll get this down me first." He takes a sip of his coffee.

I linger for a moment longer, making him promise not to rush off in the morning.

"I owe you a fry-up!" I call cheerfully before ducking into the bathroom.

"I'll hold you to that," he calls back.

I didn't hug or kiss him on the cheek, which would've been normal and appropriate behavior for us. It's just that . . . *That moment . . . upstairs . . .* It wasn't the first time it's happened.

LAST MONTH, I went to a birthday dinner for Ed at his apartment. His brother and a few close friends came down from London. I'd met them before at his housewarming party, and they've all been rallying round since the split. It was a brilliantly fun night and, afterward, I stayed back to help Ed clear up. He and I reached for an empty bottle of wine and our fingers brushed. When we met each other's eyes, I got the same edgy feeling in the pit of my stomach.

It freaked me out for a while afterward, but I reasoned that I was feeling lonely and neglected after a year without Van, and it was understandable that my body responded to a bit of human contact. I try to tell myself the same thing now and resolve to put it out of my mind.

ED KNOCKS ON the cottage door as I'm preparing to make breakfast. He chuckles when he sees the dark glasses I'm wearing.

"Oh dear. That bad, hey?"

"How are you?" I ask, returning to the kitchen.

He shrugs. "I'm all right. I didn't drink that much." He surveys the contents on the counter: eggs, bacon, sausages, a tin of baked beans, bread . . . "What can I do?"

"Nothing. I promised."

"Don't be silly," he mutters, grabbing a knife and slitting the bacon package open. "Are you really going to be able to stomach all of this?"

"It's for you," I reply.

"I'd be just as happy with a bacon butty."

Ooh. Maybe I *do* want food . . .

We end up out on the patio at the bench table, sitting side by side so we're both facing the view. It's a gorgeous, bright morning and the tide is in, the river surface as still as glass. The mature oaks on the right-hand side of the river are clumped so close together from high up on the steep banks to right down by the water's edge that their green treetops look like one big spongy mass. Birds in flight swoop under and around each other, like jet planes in a Red Arrows display, and a heron takes off from the branch of a dead tree trunk, defying gravity as its enormous wings shine white against the blue sky.

"What a place to grow up," Ed murmurs appreciatively.

"It was pretty special."

For the most part, I add silently to myself, thinking of the painful years after Ruth's death, when Van had left too.

"How did you cope with Luke and the water when he was little?"

"We were *very* careful," I say. "But yeah, we should've put a fence up. I thought I'd sort it out for next time, but there never was a next time."

"You're only thirty-five," he says.

"Yeah, but it's not going to happen now."

"Why not?"

"With Van on the other side of the world?" I cast him a look. "It's always been one of his greatest fears that I'll fall pregnant. He didn't even meet his dad until he was seven and that's no way to live. It would kill him to leave Libby and Sam would never let him take her with him—at least, not permanently. He'd have to split himself in two."

I always thought I'd have at least two children close together in age. I would've loved a boy followed by a girl and when Luke was born, it seemed that might become a reality. But the older Luke grew, the further away my dream drifted. Now he's had almost ten years of being an only child.

Maybe Nick and Stefanie will make a big brother of him, but I can't see how I ever will. Van is rooted to Australia until Libby turns eighteen—that is the earliest he'll consider leaving her. I can't imagine *ever* leaving Luke and relocating to the other side of the world—not even when he's an adult. I know Van is burying his head in the sand about it because the move will devastate him, but the alternative to both of us is incomprehensible.

"Do you want kids?" I ask Ed.

"Yeah, I always thought I'd have a couple."

"You and Tasha never . . ."

"We talked about it. It was supposed to be part of the plan for moving from London, but it was never the right time. I'm so glad now we didn't bring children into that mess."

"At least there's no rush for you. You're a guy."

"Thank you for that observation." He casts me a wry grin and polishes off the last of his breakfast.

FOUR DAYS LATER, I make my favorite journey in the world—driving to the airport. At least, it's my favorite journey until it becomes my *least* favorite journey when I'm dropping Van and Libby off again, but I'm trying very hard not to think about that.

Luke is in the front seat beside me and we've got the music turned right up. I'm singing "Don't Stop Believing" by the *Glee* cast at the top of my voice and Luke is indulging me. I'm probably far too old to be obsessed by this television series, but it makes me feel young. It's the sort of thing Ellie and I would've watched religiously as teenagers—she's hooked on it now too.

I still miss my old friend, who's firmly rooted in Newcastle with her husband, Liam, and their two children, Thomas, who's almost two, and Ciara, who's four months. They're coming to Cornwall next week for a family holiday so we'll catch up then. I've managed to tie it in with a date for our barbecue next Sunday. Brooke and Ed will both be there, although I've promised the latter that I won't interfere from here on in.

The song comes to an end and Luke turns down the volume.

"You all right?" I ask.

"Can't she sleep in with her dad?"

I sigh heavily. "Come on, Luke, don't start that again. It'll be fun sharing with Libby. Anyway, Van will be in my room, not the annex." *We've talked about that too . . .*

He huffs and stares out of the window. "Fine. But I'm having the top bunk."

"I thought we'd decided to discuss that when we got home," I say carefully. We were supposed to be keeping an open mind—I don't know how Libby will feel about taking the bottom bunk. "Please be nice," I beg, patting his leg. "You know how much I've been looking forward to them coming."

He turns the music back on.

AN HOUR LATER, we're standing in the Arrivals hall and I'm trying to steady the bouncing ball of nervous anticipation ricocheting off the walls of my stomach. Luke is kicking his foot against the railing, fidgety with boredom.

"Stop that," I berate him, ruffling his blond curls.

"How much longer?" he moans.

"Any minute now."

He rolls his honey-colored eyes.

When I next look back at the door, I'm staring straight at Van.

"There they are!" I cry, fighting the urge to run to him. We've already agreed that we'll keep our enthusiasm contained so we don't freak the kids out, but by God, it's hard. I'm giddy with joy.

He's heartbreakingly handsome: tall and tanned, his broad chest filling out his faded orange T-shirt and a dark-gray hoodie tied casually around his waist. His blue eyes sparkle as he approaches. I can barely drag my gaze away to smile at Libby, but then I do and, *gosh*, she's so pretty. Her daddy's eyes stare out at me from behind a wispy fringe—her hair is auburn-colored and comes to her shoulder blades, and she's so tall! Even taller than Luke. She's wearing hot pink leggings with white trainers and a light-gray hoodie covered with silver stars. She's smiling as I step forward to hug her.

"Hey, Luke!" I hear Van say in a warm, deep voice as I prattle on to Libby about how good it is to see her. Van shakes Luke's shoulder affectionately—they don't hug. We meet each other's eyes with a smile and then he steps forward and clasps my face in his hands, planting a chaste kiss on my lips.

Nope, no way.

I hook my arms around his waist and squeeze him hard, feeling my heart slamming into his. *He feels amazing* . . . It aches to let him go, but we do so with a meaningful stare. We'll say a proper hello later.

"Luke, you know Libby."

They've only met on FaceTime.

"Hi," he says shyly, hanging slightly back.

Her corresponding hello is much more confident.

"I can't believe how much you've shot up!" I say to her. "You must be the tallest girl in your year?"

She shrugs. "There are two others taller than me."

"Must be all that Aussie sunshine."

"It was bucketing down when we left," Van says. "Wasn't it, Libs?"

"Yep. Is it summer here?" She seems unconvinced, like she's been told this fact, but will believe it when she sees it.

"Supposedly," I reply with a grin.

"It'll be warmer than back home," Van promises.

I wrinkle my nose at him. *That's not necessarily true* . . .

He grins at me and my heart does another somersault.

"Come on, then, you cheeky little piskies," I say with a smile. "Let's get you home."

Libby and Luke glance at each other and pull faces. Judging by their expressions, I won't be able to get away with using that term of affection for much longer. I'd better make the most of it.

Libby is a chatterbox. She talks and asks questions for most of the journey home. I keep glancing across at Van, trying to contain my laughter.

"She doesn't take after you," I tease when his daughter is too busy talking about Pokémon with Luke to pay us any attention. Luke is also being surprisingly animated. We don't know where he got his usual "car journey quiet" from—not Nick or me, that's for sure. Must be my dad.

We come to a stop at some traffic lights and I reach across and rub my knuckles along Van's jaw. His beard is surprisingly soft. I've been dying to stroke it for months.

"What is your mum doing to my dad's face?" I hear Libby ask circumspectly.

I snatch my hand away and Van shakes his head, staring at the roof of the car as I crack up laughing.

I have a feeling that this trip is going to be quite a bit different to the last time when it was almost entirely just the two of us.

"CAN I SLEEP in the top bunk?" Libby asks as soon as she sees Luke's bedroom.

"Um . . ." My son glances at me uncertainly.

"Libs, if that's where Luke sleeps . . ." Van starts to say.

"No, it's OK," Luke interrupts awkwardly. "She can if she wants."

"Yay!" She proceeds to climb straight up there.

Luke glances at me again and I give him a questioning look. *Are you sure?*

He shrugs at me.

"Come up!" Libby urges him.

"Er, OK." Luke walks hesitantly over to the ladder.

"Come downstairs when you're ready," I say to them both, but mainly addressing Libby. "Your dad and I will be in the kitchen."

"Can we go out on the rowboat?" Libby calls after us.

"Maybe later, Libs," Van replies. "Let's chill out here for a bit first, eh?"

She's already chattering away to Luke by the time we reach the stairs. I cast a smile over my shoulder at Van, but manage to wait until we're in the relative privacy of the kitchen before throwing my arms around him. He holds me so tight that I can barely breathe, but I'm quite happy to make do without oxygen. We move to kiss each other at the same time and our lips stay locked as he walks me backward to the kitchen counter. He lifts me up and I wrap my legs around his waist, shivers rocketing up and down my spine as we kiss each other sense-less. Neither of us hears Libby and Luke appear until the for-mer speaks.

"Urgh. Grown-ups are gross."

We break apart, instantly. I blush madly and Van drags his hand across his face with embarrassment.

"Sorry, kids," I apologize, mortified. "Who wants a cookie?"

"Me!" they both cry simultaneously.

I've turned into my dad . . .

"Can we go on the rowboat now?" Libby asks as I crack open a whole packet of chocolate chip.

"*Libs,*" Van groans.

I giggle. Like I say, I think this trip is going to be a bit dif-ferent to last time . . .

LIBBY CONKS OUT at six forty-five, having gone thirty-eight hours with only four hours' sleep, but it's another hour and a quarter before Luke takes to his bed with a book.

Poor Van had even less sleep than his daughter, but he's determined to stay awake until we can safely retreat to my room. We sit in the kitchen and talk while his eyes grow heavy-lidded with exhaustion.

I reach across and trace my fingertip across the scar on his eyebrow, my insides contracting.

He swipes my hand and kisses the tips of my fingers. He doesn't want to dwell on his surfing accident. We've been over and over it on the phone.

"Sorry you have to wait so long to take me to bed," I say.

"You're worth waiting for," he replies.

"*Ohhh*, so *corny*!" I crack up laughing. "You should be the writer, not me."

"How's the next story going?" he asks with a grin.

"Slowly. I've been too excited about you coming to write."

"Has Ed seen any of it?"

"Before you?" I frown. "No."

He regards me thoughtfully and I experience a small, strange stab of guilt.

"Did you bring your art gear?" I ask.

He nods. "I brought a couple of recent illustrations too. I wondered if Luke might like them for his room."

"That's a great idea! We'll get them framed."

He smiles and leans forward in his seat, taking my other hand too. We stare at each other for a long moment.

"Come here," he says eventually, pulling me toward him. I straddle his lap and he cups my face in his hands, kissing me.

"To hell with this, let's go to the annex," I mutter. "I'll turn the old baby monitor on so we'll hear Luke if he comes downstairs."

We hurry outside, not bothering with shoes, and as soon as the door's unlocked, I'm up against the wall.

"What is *that*?" He slides his mouth away from mine.

"A surfboard."

"Yeah, I can see it's a surfboard, Nell."

"Nick left it for you to borrow while he's abroad."

"I love your husband."

"*Ex*-husband," I correct as Van picks me up and carries me to the bed.

The shock of our bare skin colliding reverberates throughout every inch of my body. It feels achingly good to be close to him again and we don't waste time with foreplay—the last twelve months have been more than enough.

Van conks out straight afterward and I kiss his forehead and let him be, pulling on my clothes and returning to my room so I'll be nearby if and when the kids wake up. But in the middle of the night he climbs into bed with me. I wake up in his arms.

ON FRIDAY, IT'S Nick and Stefanie's wedding. Luke is the ring bearer and I'm bursting with pride at the sight of him standing beside his dad at the register office. He looks so grown up.

Nick and Stefanie are heading off on their honeymoon tomorrow for two weeks, leaving the pub in the hands of Drew, who's returned home from Buckinghamshire with his wife and two children for the summer. Drew is a sports therapist now, and it's good to catch up with him and his family.

The next day is Saturday and time for our one and only book signing. The kids are excited, but Van and I are nervous. We have no idea if anyone will turn up at the shop, but Ed has asked us to sign the stock in any case, so it won't be a wasted journey.

Ed looks up from the till and smiles as we walk through the door, his eyes moving from me to Van. He comes out from behind the counter to shake his hand.

"It's great to see you again," Ed says.

"It's been a while," Van replies.

"Twenty-five years," I point out. "This is Libby." I shepherd her in front of me. "And obviously you know Luke." I glance around for my son, but he's already found his way to the toy section—we sell some to supplement book sales. Libby joins him.

"A few people have been in to ask about the signing," Ed tells us. "I reckon we'll have a decent turnout."

I hear a voice behind me. "Is that *Nell Forrester*? The *author*?"

I spin on my heels and crack up laughing at the sight of Ellie standing in the doorway, clutching her young son's hand. Her baby daughter is safely tucked into the carrier she's wearing.

I run and throw my arms around her, straddling her feet awkwardly due to the bundle strapped to her front. "What are you doing here?" I cry. "I thought you weren't coming until next week!"

"And miss your signing? Nah." She shakes her head. "Was never gonna happen." Shooting a look across the shop, she claps her hands comically to her face. "Oh my goodness, it's Van Stirling, the illustrator!"

He sniggers as they exchange another clumsy baby-bundle hug.

Van only really goes by Stirling now. Stanley Stirling is a bit of a mouthful, so Stanley has become more of a middle name.

"Hello again!" Ellie goes over to say a warm hi to Ed. "How are you? It's been ages since I saw you at Easter."

Van crouches down to speak to Ellie's son. My friend notices and introduces them.

"This is Thomas," she says.

"Hi, Thomas," Van responds.

"Have you been busy today?" I ask Ed with a smile while this is going on.

"Not too bad."

"You're not missing me, then?"

"You were only here two days ago." His warm brown eyes are amused. "Ask me next week."

Van stands back up as another customer comes through the door—*Brooke!*

"Hey!" she cries as I hurry to embrace her. She's brought her brother Brad's seven-year-old daughter, Megan.

"Thank you so much for coming!"

"I wouldn't have missed it for the world."

I turn and widen my eyes at Ed. "This is *Brooke*," I say significantly.

"Hello," she chirps, giving him a wave.

"Nice to meet you," he replies.

"Brad's parking the car," Brooke tells me as Ed starts tidying up behind the till. "He's come with Lisa and Emily." Lisa is Brad's wife and Emily is their younger daughter—she's four. "We passed Christopher and Theresa on their way here too."

I'm blown away by all the support. Even some of Dad's old friends come, including Steven and Linzie from the farm.

"Your father would have been so proud of you," Linzie says to me, before pressing Van's hand and adding, "*both*."

That makes us a little emotional.

Mostly, though, it feels as though we're having a party. The bookshop is crowded and the atmosphere is buzzing. A few locals come in to get their books signed, some of whom had bought them earlier in the week and were waiting for Van. I'm so proud to see him signing his name, and the day is right up there with some of the happiest of my life. I only wish Dad were here.

Afterward, we decide to head across the road to the pub for a celebratory drink.

"Come," I urge Ed.

He shakes his head. "I've got to shut up shop."

"Can't Kiran do it?" She's his Saturday staff—I cover for her occasionally when she can't come in, and she's covering for me while Van and Libby are here. She's a primary school teacher, so she was happy to pull in some extra cash over the holidays.

"I'll see you next Sunday, OK?" he replies with a small smile.

I try not to appear too disheartened, but I can't help it. "If you change your mind . . ."

"I know where you are," he finishes my sentence.

"Ed not coming?" Van asks as we leave.

"No, he can't."

He slips his arm around my waist as we cross the road, but I cast a disappointed look back over my shoulder at the shop. It won't be the same without Ed.

OUR FIRST FEW days together pass by in a blur. Van and Libby take a while to get over their jet-lag—Libby fares better than her father—but by Wednesday, we're in the swing of things.

Libby comes into the bathroom in the morning while I'm doing my hair. We're off to the Minack Theatre shortly for a children's storytelling session.

"Can I brush your hair for you?" she asks.

"You can if I can do yours?" I reply with a smile.

We go through to the kitchen and I pull up a chair at the table, sitting down and handing her a brush. She tentatively drags it through my shoulder-length locks, gradually getting more confident with her strokes.

"I can't do this with Mum's hair," she confides.

"Does she still have dreadlocks?" I ask.

"Yeah." She keeps brushing. "I'm going to be a hairdresser when I grow up."

"Cool."

Sitting there, staring out of the window at the retreating tide, I experience a feeling of déjà vu. When I was a child, Ruth used to brush my hair for me while I sat in this very same chair. It was one of the times I felt closest to her.

Ruth is still in my thoughts when Libby and I come to swap places. Libby is abnormally quiet and I think she likes me playing with her hair. I style it in a fishtail plait for her, feeling a swell of love for this little girl who isn't mine. When I'm done, I press a kiss to the top of her head and she looks up and smiles at me. I've always wanted a daughter. I try not to dwell on the sadness I feel, knowing that I'll never have one of my own. I only see Libby for a few short weeks a year, if I'm lucky—how could she ever be a substitute for the real thing?

THE MINACK THEATRE is built from stone on the edge of a high cliff, its stepped seats climbing backward from the stage below. Behind the stage is the most breathtaking backdrop you could imagine: to put it simply, sea and sky. It's a slightly overcast day, but the sun is trying its hardest to burn through the clouds and blast the gray from the normally deep-blue ocean. Fishing boats and naval ships pass by on the horizon, and colorful wildflowers and unusual-looking succulents burst out from the cracks and crevices. The sound of jaunty music coming from big speakers mingles with the babble of excited children and the cry of swooping seagulls.

Amazingly, the storytelling session is about the different types of fairy, and Libby and Luke keep glancing at us with incredulity as the exuberant performer introduces puppet versions of Spriggens, Knockers, Brownies, and Hedgerow Fairies, not to mention Piskies. All five fairy types have featured in our books.

I watch Libby laughing her head off, and feel wave upon wave of love.

When Van told me that Sam was pregnant, I died a little, knowing that he was about to become a father to someone else's child. At that moment, on the plane, I thought he was lost to me forever. I felt numb the entire time I was in Adelaide and Port Lincoln. On my return home, I found solace in Nick, but when I discovered that I was pregnant, my heart broke all over again.

I wanted Van to be the father.

And I wished that I were the mother of his child, not Sam.

Our lives would be far easier now if our children belonged to us and only us. That much is obvious.

But then Libby wouldn't be Libby.

And Luke wouldn't be Luke.

They are who they are—a combination of Van and Sam, and Nick and me—and when I think about the times I wished that Sam and Nick weren't a part of their makeup, I feel cold all over.

It has also occurred to me, in my bleakest moments, that without Sam on the scene, Van would be free to take Libby from Australia. But the very fact that I could even imagine a child losing her mother, or having to leave behind her two half-siblings, fills me with the deepest sense of shame.

I will always wish that Van and I could spend more time together, but not at the expense of our children or their other parents.

I don't think I'll ever be able to understand Ruth's death or Dad's cancer, but when it comes to Van and me, and Libby and Luke, I'm at peace with the paths we've walked.

I put my arms around our children and hug them close.

IT ABSOLUTELY POURS on Thursday and Friday, and Saturday morning is windy and overcast, but as the day progresses, the wind dies down, and I am thrilled when we wake up on Sunday to blue skies. It's perfect barbecue weather.

Van helps prepare the salads and marinades while the kids play together. He's a great cook, a skill he developed during the years he worked on a tuna boat with little else to entertain him on the long, slow journeys back from the open ocean with a cage full of fish. He works on a tugboat now, which suits his current lifestyle better. He's climbed up the ranks from deckhand to tugboat apprentice mate, and is well on his way to becoming captain one day. I'm so proud of him.

Ellie and Liam arrive first, with Thomas and Ciara. I wrestle four-month-old Ciara away from her mother and we head outside to the patio. Van puts up the umbrella so Ciara is under the shade, and then we watch as a panicked Liam runs after two-year-old Thomas down the steep hill.

"This is how it's going to be for the whole day, isn't it?" Ellie says resignedly as Van turns around to bang on the annex window.

"Libby!" he calls. She and Luke have turned the space into a playroom and it's currently full of Legos.

"Yeah?" she calls back.

"Can you come and babysit for a bit?"

I expect to hear grumbling, as I'm sure I'd get from Luke, but she pops her head around the side of the building a moment later, a cheeky grin on her face. "How much will you pay me?"

"Does your mother pay you?" he asks drily.

"No." She shrugs and grins.

"You said you're missing Jake so go and play with Thomas."

Aside from Libby's half-sister, Brittney, who's now seven, Sam also has a son from a third relationship, Jake, age two. She's still with Jake's father and Van says he wouldn't be surprised if there were more children on the horizon. Apparently, Libby is a brilliant older sibling.

She yells over her shoulder at Luke, "Let's roll down the hill!"

I shake my head with despair as my son tears out of the building.

"Come on, Thomas, you want to roll down the hill with us?" Libby asks, bouncing on her feet.

"At least the tide's out," Van comments.

"Do you remember trying to wash off that mud?" I ask,

prompting him to flash me a rueful smile. I go back to something he said a moment ago. "Did Libby tell you she's missing Jake?"

"Yeah, a bit. Although I imagine Sam is missing Libby more. Libby plays with Jake all the time—Sam says she's a godsend."

I don't like to think of Libby pining for her siblings back home—I know she's very close to Brittney too.

I'd hoped for siblings for Luke, not just for now, but for when he's older, with children of his own. I never had aunts and uncles—both my parents were only children—and my grandparents on either side died young. I'm glad I can consider Nick's parents a part of my own extended family, because the only blood relative I have now, aside from Luke, is my mother.

"You OK?" Ellie asks me when Van and Liam retire to the bottom of the hill to catch the kids.

"Lost in my thoughts," I murmur, stroking my fingers across her daughter's super-fine, light-brown hair. I bend down and inhale. "Mmm."

Ellie smiles and glances downhill at Van, her expression becoming pensive. A car crunches onto the gravel driveway, diverting me. I go to see who it is.

"Hello!" I cry, opening the gate and greeting Ed as he climbs out of his car. "It's so good to see you." It really is. I've missed him this week—I didn't even know how much until now.

"Hey, you too," he replies with a smile as we kiss each other's cheeks. He's wearing shorts and a yellow polo shirt that really brings out the color on his arms.

"Who's this?" he asks, bending down to peer at the baby I'm still holding.

"Ciara."

"Ellie's daughter," he realizes. "I couldn't see her properly last weekend when she was in the carrier."

"I know, I snaffled her today before Ellie could lock her up again."

"She's gorgeous." He nods at my hair. "Very Princess Leia."

I laugh. "Libby's work. She's taken to styling it every morning. I can't say no."

I currently have two blond buns fixed to either side of my head.

"Suits you," he says with a grin, moving past me to the boot of his car. He brings out a six-pack of beer and a bottle of Prosecco.

"Ooh," I joke warily, taking the bottle from him. "This could be dangerous."

He grins and I'm disturbed to acknowledge that the edgy feeling has started back up.

It's the dimple, I tell myself, remembering my teenage crush on Drew. *I always was a sucker for one.*

"How's work been this week?" I ask.

"Fine," he replies, slamming the trunk.

"Missing me yet?" I josh, jigging Ciara in my arms as she starts making chatty baby noises.

"I'm just about coping," he replies drily.

I laugh and turn toward the gate, but the hairs on the back of my neck stand up at the sight of Van on the patio, staring at us with an odd look on his face. He smiles and comes forward to shake Ed's hand, and they exchange perfectly pleasant greetings.

"I'll stick these in the kitchen," Van says, taking possession of the six-pack. "There are some more on ice—want one?" he calls over his shoulder at Ed.

"Sure, thanks."

Ed goes over to say hi to Luke and the others, but something makes me tag after Van.

"You OK?" I ask once we're alone. Ciara doesn't count, although she's still making noises and I'm not entirely convinced they're happy ones.

"Yeah, I'm fine," he replies, not meeting my eyes as he takes the Prosecco from me.

"Are you sure?" I force out the question.

It's a while before he looks at me, but when he does, the tension I'm already feeling racks up a notch. His expression is impenetrable. What is he thinking? I'm not sure I want to know. If Van becomes possessive around Ed, it'll make things incredibly difficult.

"I'm fine," he repeats quietly.

"*Van . . .*" I murmur, jigging Ciara a bit more purposefully. "Please don't worry. We're only friends." As soon as the statement is out of my mouth, I regret it. I can't believe I've now put it out there like it's an issue. But how can I not address his fears when he's looking at me like this? It's not anger, or jealousy, it's something else.

"I know you are," he says, shaking his head and glancing at Ciara, who definitely needs her mummy now. "Sorry, I just felt a bit strange, seeing you guys coming in through the gate."

"Strange how?"

He shrugs and looks away.

I touch his arm. "Please try to explain."

"I don't know. Like someone had walked over my grave."

I stare at him with dismay and then Ciara starts to cry in earnest.

"I'm all right. Really," he says firmly, kissing my temple. "Take her back to Ellie. I'll be out in a sec."

I don't want to leave him, but I do.

Brooke arrives soon afterward, so I'm distracted with welcoming her, but I'm attuned to where Van is at all times. He actually seems OK, and when he fires up the barbecue and starts grilling the meat, Ed and Liam hang with him, drinking beers and chatting. The kids have taken Thomas into the annex and we can keep an eye on them through the window, and Ciara has fallen asleep in her pram, so my friends and I are able to sit in the sunshine and catch up on each other's news. I have to bite my tongue to stop myself from asking Brooke what she thinks of Ed. They said polite "hello agains," but are yet to have a proper conversation.

Van laughs at something Ed says, drawing my attention back to him.

He seems laid-back and happy, which in turn relaxes me.

It's strange—the boy I grew up with was often jealous and possessive, but the man before me is more mellow. When did he change? Somehow I've missed seeing that happen. I've missed so much.

It occurs to me, in a surreal way, that I might not know Van very well. When I calculate the time I've actually spent in his presence since those years we lived together as children, I'm shocked to discover that it amounts to less than eight months.

I wonder if Van and I would've changed if we'd had more time together, if we'd been able to live like a normal couple. Would we have grown into different people than we are now? Or are we who we were always meant to be?

In my efforts to get Brooke and Ed talking, I end up sitting between Van and Ed, with Brooke opposite Ed. Thomas is secured to a chair with a booster seat at the end between Van and Ellie, and Libby and Luke are on a picnic rug, but it's still a squeeze around the bench table with six adults.

"What do you do, Brooke?" Ed asks conversationally.

"I'm an interior designer," she replies.

"Do you run your own business or ?"

"That's the plan," she says. "I've got to start from scratch now that I've moved back, so if you know of anyone . . ."

"I'll keep you in mind," he says. "Have you got a business card?"

"Yes, in my purse. I'll get one for you later." She smiles and I knock Ed's knee under the table.

Nice one, pal.

He knocks mine in return.

Back off, buster.

I try to keep a straight face.

"So you own that sweet bookshop we went to last weekend?" Brooke continues with their chat.

"Yep." Ed nods.

"What's it like being Nell's boss?" she asks with a grin, forking a tiny mound of couscous into her mouth.

Ed chuckles. "Sometimes it feels like it's the other way around."

"What's that supposed to mean?" I demand to know. "Are you saying I'm bossy?"

Everyone laughs, except for Ed.

"No, I'm saying you're good at what you do. It's a compliment," he adds, giving me a sideways smile before returning his attention to Brooke. "Did you know that we met as kids?" He waggles his thumb at Van and me.

"No?" Brooke cocks an eyebrow, intrigued.

"My parents and I stayed at a cottage up in the village. The day we came to collect the keys, Nell and Van had caught a duckling."

Libby's ears prick up from over on the picnic rug. "Really, Dad?"

"Yep." Van nods at her.

"Van heard her cheeping and ran inside to tell me," I say. "Our dog, Scampi, was going absolutely crazy." I smile at Van. "Your mum was working so we didn't want to disturb her. We took the rowboat out by ourselves—we were only ten." I turn back to the rest of the table.

"Can we take the rowboat out on our own?" Libby interrupts excitedly.

"No." Van's reply is abrupt and final.

She and Luke grumble to each other as I carry on. "We had this race against time to catch the little thing before the tide went out again and we got banked. We were half successful. We caught the duckling, but had to climb out and walk home, leaving *Platypus*—our boat—tied to a tree. Van's mum was so cross. Poor Ed was standing up here with his parents when we emerged, looking like mud monsters. You weren't too freaked out though, were you?" I grin at Ed.

"Not at all," he replies with a smile. "I wanted to be part of your gang."

This makes me elbow Van in the ribs, remembering how unwelcoming he was that day.

"Yeah, all right," he mutters under his breath.

"I remember telling Van that you reminded me of the boy from *The NeverEnding Story*."

"Which one?" Brooke asks.

"Bastian, the one who reads the book. Van used to remind me of Atreyu. We'd been to watch the movie only weeks before."

Van shakes his head with amusement and Ed laughs.

"So you pegged me as a book geek, even then," Ed says.

"You're hardly a geek," Brooke chips in, causing me to knock Ed's knee again. He doesn't knock mine back this time.

"Nell said you have a sailing boat?" Brooke prompts him.

Ed shrugs. "A small one."

"We should all go out in it sometime."

He grins and shakes his head. "It really is a small one—two-person."

"Oh." She giggles.

I wait for him to invite her out—just her—but he doesn't.

How could they not fancy each other? Brooke is stunning and Ed is . . . Well, he's just . . . *lovely.*

At that moment, Ciara wakes up. "I'll get her." I climb out awkwardly from between the two men.

Ellie opens her arms, but I nod at her plate. "You finish up, I'm happy."

She pulls a worried face. "Are you sure?"

"Absolutely." I stay on my feet, patting Ciara's back and shushing her.

"Aw, are you getting broody again?" Brooke teases me knowingly.

I feel a pang, but force a smile. "It's hard not to with this one."

"I would take her for a bit, but I'm not very good with babies," Brooke says.

"You're great with your brother's kids!" I protest.

"Only now they're older. Babies scare me. I'm not sure how I'd ever manage one full-time."

"It's different when they're your own," I reply, kissing Ciara's temple.

THE NEXT DAY, we all get up and out of the house early to take the kids to Hollywell Bay Beach, which is about an hour away on the north coast. It isn't far from Newquay and can get busy in the summer, but we're taking a picnic and plan to spend the whole day there.

A freshwater stream spills out to sea from the rural inland and we walk beside it until Libby and Luke can resist no longer, taking off their shoes and wading through the water. The stream hugs grassy slopes on one side and on the other is the beach itself. A couple of children are already building sandcastles on the riverbanks while their parents hammer brightly striped wind shelters into the sand.

The main beach is deceptively big—almost a mile of golden sand—but it's hidden from view behind high sand dunes. We dump our gear and climb up to check out the view, weaving our way between huge tufts of marram grass. Van has brought the kids' boogie boards—I reminded him what we used to do at this beach as children. When we reach the top of a steep, sandy incline, Van hands Luke his board and, without delay, launches himself from the top on Libby's. Luke swiftly follows suit with a yell, and I watch and laugh as they belly-slide on their boards the whole way down. Libby laughs too, but she's also jumping up and down with annoyance at her father's impertinence.

"Sorry, Libs," Van says on his return, sheepishly handing over her board. She promptly snatches it and takes off, squealing.

I'm so happy to see Van in this lighter mood. He was quiet last night, going to bed early with what he claimed was an alcohol-induced headache.

"They're going to be worn out tonight," I comment as we perch at the top of the dune and watch as the kids make a full descent.

He doesn't answer, his eyes on Luke and Libby as they turn around and start the long trek back up again.

"Are you feeling all right? Not hungover, are you?"

"No, I'm fine," he replies, scratching his beard. "Beers in the daytime always knock me out."

"You had fun, though, right?"

"Yeah."

But he hesitated before answering.

"Are you OK?"

He sighs, his lips turning down at the corners. "You don't have to keep asking."

"I'm worried about you."

"All right, kids?" he shouts. "Gonna go again?"

Luke and Libby are huffing and puffing as they slip and slide over the sand, but they laugh and nod.

We wait until they've reached the top and shot off down the dune again before continuing with our conversation.

"Yesterday was great," Van surprises me by saying. "Everyone enjoyed themselves and I really like your friends."

"I'm so relieved to hear you say that." It's not an understatement. "Libby was fantastic with Thomas, wasn't she? I think Ellie and Liam were blown away by her."

"Yeah, she's a good girl," he replies fondly. "And Thomas is a cute kid."

He seems to be making an effort to chat, which is probably why I start rambling.

"Brooke was funny, refusing to hold Ciara, but I was pleased when she remembered to give Ed her card. Hopefully, something will come out of that connection."

"Mmm, it must be hard to start from scratch with a new business," he muses.

"I thought Ed and Brooke got on well, though, don't you? It's amazing that she's moved back here and they're both single."

It's a moment before he speaks, and when he does, he sounds cynical. "You can give up on that one."

"Well, maybe it won't work out for them straight away," I continue as he lifts his hand to wave at the kids. "I mean, Ed's not even divorced yet, but he will be soon. If they see each other a few times—"

"It's not going to happen, Nell," he cuts me off gruffly.

I shoot him a look. "What makes you say that?"

He pauses. "Because Ed is in love with you."

The color drains from my cheeks. He's still staring at the kids and they're almost upon us now.

"Go on, off you go again," he urges them, and there's no trace of anger or anguish in his voice. They set off again, laughing.

Van turns to look at me. I push my flyaway hair off my face and realize my hands are shaking. I feel like I could throw up.

"It's all right," he murmurs and his voice is gentle.

Now *I* can't meet *his* eyes.

"How can you say that?" I can barely get the words out past the lump in my throat.

"Because it's true," he replies softly.

I shake my head, but I can't deny it, not the way I adamantly want to. Deep down, I think I've known that Ed has feelings for me. But I haven't been able to bear facing up to the fact that there may be consequences.

I force myself to look at Van. "What do you want me to do? Do you want me to leave my job?"

"Of course not!" he scoffs.

I shake my head, my eyes stinging with tears. "You're so different to how you used to be."

He leans back on his elbows. "You mean I'm no longer a jealous prick?"

I can't even find the will to laugh at that comment.

"I've grown up, Nell," he mutters. "Things aren't so black and white anymore, not like they were when we were kids." He reaches across and rubs my back. I'm still sitting rigidly upright. "It's all right," he says. "I didn't mean to upset you or make you feel uncomfortable. But it's hard for me to not say anything, OK? It's given me pause for thought."

"What does *that* mean?"

"I don't know," he replies simply, his brow knotted together as we stare at each other. "But it's going to be OK."

My eyes fill with tears.

"Hey." He leans forward and cups the back of my head, drawing me in for a kiss.

My head is all over the place as our lips meet.

We break apart as the kids return.

"One last time and then we'll take those to the water," Van tells Luke and Libby, getting to his feet. "Come on." He pulls me up, but doesn't let go of my hand, and it's impossible not to laugh as we run down the sand dune together.

VAN DISCOURAGES ME from talking about Ed again that week and as I don't want to spoil the short time we have together, I'm content to obey his request. But on Friday night, Kiran, the person who's covering for me at Dragonheart, calls me at home.

"I'm so sorry to bother you," she says in a wretched voice. "But Ed was off work today with the flu and now I've come down with a vomiting bug. He says he'll go in tomorrow, but he sounds awful. He didn't want me to trouble you, but it seems crazy, him working if he's still ill. There's no chance you could cover for us, is there?"

"Of course I can," I reply without hesitation. It's Saturday, our busiest day. The shop is just about manageable with one person, but one person ill would be a living nightmare for them. "I'll let Ed know," I tell Kiran. "You go and rest up, OK? I hope you don't suffer too badly."

"Thank you, I really appreciate this."

Van supports my decision. "We'll have a local day. The kids could probably do with a chilled one."

"The traffic is rubbish on Saturdays anyway," I point out as I pick up my mobile, preparing to text Ed the plan.

I'M ACTUALLY LOOKING forward to a day at work after two weeks off. Usually, Ed is there in the mornings and I'm not comfortable acknowledging how much I miss seeing his friendly face as I unlock the door and enter the dark, empty shop. But my heart feels fuller as I breathe in the familiar smell and set about opening up, stocking the shelves with fresh new books and replenishing the till.

We have a few busy periods throughout the day, but all in all it's nothing I can't handle.

At three thirty, Ed calls.

"Hey, how are you feeling?"

"A lot better," he replies.

He doesn't sound it.

"I hope you're in bed."

"Sort of. I'll come in shortly to relieve you so you can head off early."

"No way," I snap. "Stay where you are. Do you need anything? I could pick you up some soup or bread or whatever on my way back to the car?"

"No, you've already done enough. You sure you don't mind staying until closing time?"

"Of course not. A couple more hours isn't going to make a difference."

There's silence at the other end of the line. "Thanks, Nell," he says eventually. "I'll see you in a couple of weeks."

That suddenly feels like a very long time away.

On impulse, I text Van to ask what he thinks about me dropping some supplies to Ed's on my way home. I immediately regret putting that on him, and the regret strengthens during the next twenty minutes that he doesn't reply. But then my phone buzzes and I snatch it up: Go for it. All good here x

I DON'T TELL Ed that I'm coming until I'm almost on his doorstep.

He opens the door, looking slightly bewildered. His milk-chocolate hair is flat on one side and sticking up on the other and his tanned jaw is tinged even darker in color with two-day-old stubble. He's wearing a crumpled, soft-looking light-gray T-shirt. My heart goes out to him.

"Hey." My tone is full of sympathy. "How are you feeling?"

He rubs the back of his neck and nods. "Yeah. OK."

"Can I come in?"

He opens the door wider for me to pass. He's turned his battered brown leather couch into a makeshift bed, dragging his pillows and duvet out from his bedroom. *Aw, Ed* . . . I hate to think of him having no one to look after him while he's ill.

The modern kitchen is open-plan, separated from the living room by an island unit. I walk over and put the shopping bags down.

"Have you eaten anything?"

"Toast."

"How about some chicken noodle soup?" I offer with a smile, pulling out a sachet.

"I'll do it, you get home."

"Sit down," I say firmly. "It's nice to have a break from the mayhem."

He pulls up a stool at his island unit while I fill the kettle and switch it on, looking under the counter for a saucepan.

"How's your week been?" he asks.

"Nice. *Busy*," I add emphatically. "Lots of beach action."

"Do the kids surf?" he asks.

"Luke does a little—Nick takes him out occasionally. Van's been teaching Libby. The beaches here are a bit more forgiving than some of the reef breaks he surfs back home. I've been mostly chilling out on the beach with my book."

I never did persevere with learning to surf after doing that course with Joel.

Measuring out boiling water and tipping it into the pan, I pour in the soup mixture and give it a stir. When I glance at Ed on the other side of the island unit, he's staring at the island top, downcast.

"You should stay warm." I nod at his makeshift bed. "I'll bring this over."

A look of distress passes over his features, prompting me to freeze. But then he slides down from his stool and relocates to the couch, making me wonder what I saw. I try to ignore the niggling feeling in the pit of my stomach as I serve up his soup and carry it over.

"This is really kind of you," he murmurs, accepting the bowl and spoon.

I take to his armchair. "I'm sure you'd do the same for me. Well, maybe you wouldn't," I correct myself. "I live a forty-minute drive away, whereas you're five minutes from work. It's not exactly a hardship."

"I'd do the same for you," he agrees in a low voice, his eyes meeting mine momentarily as he blows on the hot soup lapping against the edges of his spoon.

"Have you called Brooke, yet?"

I don't know why I ask such a stupid question—especially not after the conversation I had earlier in the week with Van. Maybe I'm trying to make light of the situation. Maybe I'm trying to pretend that Ed and I have the easy, platonic friendship I've always fooled myself into believing we have. But it's still a stupid question because I already know his answer.

"No."

I nod, not bothering to act surprised.

"She reminded me a bit of Tasha," he divulges.

"No!" *Now* I'm surprised. "In what way?"

"Some of her mannerisms . . . Her long blond hair . . ."

"*I* have blond hair."

He lets out a small snort of amusement. "That would be about all you have in common."

"So, it's a 'no' for poor Brooke, then?"

"I don't think she'll be single for long," he says drily.

"No, you're right about that."

Ed nods at some papers on the coffee table in front of me.

"What's this?" I ask, picking them up.

"Settlement papers," he replies. "Tasha wants half of the business."

"What? But she's never done a day's work in it! Or *for* it. It's nothing to do with her!" I'm outraged.

"Doesn't matter," he replies darkly. "What's mine is hers, apparently." He pauses. "What she's really after is the house."

"Is she even planning on staying in Cornwall?"

"I doubt it. She'll sell up as soon as all of this is settled, but that's not the way she'll play it if we go to court." He sighs. "I really don't want to go to court."

"What will you do?" I ask worriedly.

"I think I'll give her my share of the house."

"And keep the bookshop?"

He nods.

"Surely the house is worth more," I say with a frown. "I hope you've got a good lawyer."

He stares at me directly. "I just want to be rid of her, Nell, so I can start again."

The look in his eyes makes that funny feeling kick in again. It's disconcerting.

He sighs and puts his bowl back on the coffee table, then nods toward the door. "You should get home to Van."

"He'll be all right with the kids for a bit longer." I'm fighting an overwhelming urge to get up and give him a hug.

What is this?

I've always had a protective personality. I mothered Van when we were younger and I feel very protective of Ed too.

I know in my heart that what Van said is true; Ed has feelings for me that go beyond friendship. I think I've known it for a while.

So what am I doing here?

Encouraging him?

Because that would be cruel, and I've never considered myself to be cruel.

The truth is I wanted to come. I wanted to care for him.

I wanted to see him.

Ed interrupts my thoughts. "Are you OK?"

But my thoughts continue to assault me.

Van must've known that. Why didn't he stop me?

An uneasy feeling settles over me.

"I think I'd better go," I mumble, to his surprise. I'd only just said I'd stay. "No, I'll see myself out." I stop him in his tracks as he makes a move to get up.

"Nell?"

"I'm fine. Give me a call if you need me on Monday, OK?"

He nods. His confused expression is the last thing I see before I walk out.

THE KIDS ARE already in bed by the time I get back to the cottage, although I very much doubt they're sleeping. We don't mind them whispering to each other for a bit, as long as they don't squabble. On the whole, they get on well, but by the end of each day, Van and I are keen for some peace and quiet.

I find Van in the kitchen with a beer, sitting and staring out of the window at the darkening night.

"Hey," he says when he notices me.

"Hi."

He pushes his chair out from the table, not quite managing the knack of silence as he gets up. I flinch and slip my arms around his waist, resting my cheek against his broad chest. He holds me as I try to swallow the lump in my throat.

Our love-making that night is bittersweet, and I'm teetering on the brink of tears the whole time. We've now passed the halfway point of our time together and every day is bringing us closer to him going home.

Libby is also quieter than her usual self that week. On Thursday morning, I come out of the bathroom to see Van hugging her in the hallway. Luke, I gather, is over in the annex, waiting for her to go and play.

"Everything OK?" I ask with concern.

"Missing her mum," Van replies in a husky voice, as Libby lets out an anguished sob. "It's the longest she's been away from home."

"I'm sorry, darling," I say softly, rubbing her back. Van's blue eyes are pained as they lock with mine.

Aside from the text I sent Ed on Monday, asking if he was back at work, and the reply I received saying that he was, we haven't had any contact with each other, so I'm tense when we go to the pub across the river for Sunday lunch and Ed pulls up outside with his sailing boat on a trailer.

"There's Ed!" Luke cries out.

Van gets up from the bench table where we're sitting and crosses the road to where Ed is climbing out of his car.

"All right, mate," I hear him say, shaking Ed's hand. "You need some help with this?"

Ed glances across the road at me and lifts his hand. I wave back and force a smile, hearing him ask Van if he's finished eating before accepting his offer.

"Mum, can I go out on the boat with Ed?" Luke asks me animatedly.

"Wait and see," I reply.

"Can I get down from the table?"

"Have you finished?" I nod at his almost empty plate.

"Yeah, I'm full."

"OK. Careful crossing the road!" I caution as Libby also jumps to her feet, clambering her knife and fork together on her plate.

"I'm full too," she says.

They've been dying to go back to the beach ever since their food arrived.

I'm not sure why *I'm* still sitting here, frankly. We've already paid for our meals at the bar and everyone else has left, but I'm rooted to the spot, watching as Ed and Van work together to get the boat to the water. Luke bounces up and down on the pebbled sand near the shore and lifts his hands over his head in a victory cheer at something Ed says, before they both glance my way.

Ed points at Luke, followed by his boat, then holds his hands palms-up in a question.

I nod, flashing him the OK sign.

Libby bounces on her feet. The waitress comes to clear the

table and I drag myself to a standing position, knowing that if I remain here now, it's going to seem odd. I cross the road and jump down onto the beach. The sun comes out from behind the clouds and strikes the water right in front of me, making it sparkle brilliant white, like cut glass under a strobe light. Shielding my eyes, I arrive in time to see Ed returning from the direction of the boat-hire place with two borrowed children's life jackets.

"Hi." I smile at him.

"Hey." He smiles in return, handing Van one of the life jackets for Libby.

"Are you sure you don't mind?" I ask as Luke slips on the other.

"Not at all." He bends down to adjust Luke's straps, making sure it's a snug fit.

"Only for a little while, OK, kids?" Van orders firmly when they're ready. "Make sure you both do *exactly* what Ed says or you'll end up in the water. By that, I mean I'll dunk you in myself if you annoy him."

Luke nods solemnly, while Libby giggles, not taking the threat at all seriously.

Van and I stand on the jetty and watch as they set off, the small white boat tilting to the side in the wind, its white sails billowing out as it glides across the water. The children's laughter carries toward us.

"I don't understand," I say in not much more than a whisper.

Van's attention is fixed on our children, but emotion has gathered in his eyes.

If he believes that Ed is in love with me, if there's even a tiny chance that he thinks those feelings might be in *any* way reciprocated, why is he being so amiable, so helpful, so *nice*?

"He's a good guy," he replies in a low voice.

"So?" I can't keep the angst from mine.

He glances at me and there's a world of regret, love, tenderness and acceptance. "This is no life, Nell."

I let out a sob.

"Shh." He takes me in his arms. "Stop. We'll talk about it later."

I don't want to talk about it later. I don't want to talk about it at all. In fact, I point-blank refuse that night when the kids are in bed, making frantic, heartfelt love to him in an attempt to bring us closer, to help us reconnect. But it's there, between us, this subject, and although he's not pushing me to talk about it, I know that he will. It's only a matter of time. Time that is swiftly running out.

IT HAPPENS AT Glendurgan on the last day of their holiday. The kids are tearing around the maze, their heads bobbing up and down above the low cherry laurel hedge as they squeal with laughter. I'm remembering Van and me as children, when Dad used to work here, and I know that Van is lost in the past too.

He reaches across, takes my hand, and tells me that he loves me.

"Don't say it," I beg.

"We gave it a good go."

"Please."

"Don't cry," he implores.

"How can you ask me not to cry?" I gasp.

"Hold it together for them."

His words help quell the onslaught of my emotions, but I resent him for saying it.

"Hear me out," he asks as I bite my lip. "We've done five years of this, and we've got at *least* another eight more on the cards. I can't leave Libby before she's eighteen."

"I know that," I interrupt. "I understand. I wouldn't leave Luke, either."

"What we have is a lonely existence, Nell. Not just for you."

I'm shocked. "You want to date other women?"

He doesn't answer.

"Is there anyone else?" I ask.

"Of course there isn't," he snaps.

"But there could be," I realize, dully.

"We're thirty-five," he says. "I know you want more children."

My heart contracts.

"I can't give them to you."

"I'll make do," I tell him desperately.

"I don't want you to have to make do!" Van raises his voice, prompting a couple nearby to glance over at us. "I want to give you everything, but I can't."

He takes me by my arm and guides me away so we have more privacy. I stare down at the giant gunnera plants nearby and wish that I could hide under them, pretending to play with the fairies, as we did as children. But this is no fairy tale.

"I love you," he says, his expression fierce. "I've loved you as my sister, I've loved you as my friend, and God knows I love you as my lover. But . . ." He looks toward the maze, where Libby is squealing with laughter. "*I love her more.*" His voice chokes up and tears fill his eyes, something I see a second before my own vision turns blurry.

"You know I wouldn't have it any other way." I sniff as I delve into my bag and pull out tissues for both of us. We turn away from the maze to dry our eyes and it hurts to witness his pain, as it always has.

"You deserve more," he says, taking a ragged breath. "You deserve so much more. Ed could give that to you."

"But I love *you*! I've always loved you! I *will* always love you."

"I will always love you too. That doesn't mean there's not room in our hearts to love someone else, to start something new, something that will last. It's too hard, this *living in limbo* that we're doing. I know we could carry on like this, but I don't want you to give up some of the best years of your life when I know how much you're missing out on. Your dad never gave anyone else a chance, and he was lonely, Nell. Maybe you couldn't see it because you didn't want to see it, but you weren't enough for him, however hard you tried to be. You were the best daughter he could've hoped for, but he needed more. I don't want you to end up like that." He takes a deep breath. "Sometimes two people are meant to be together. Sometimes they're not."

"Well, in this case, we *are*," I state passionately.

He stares at me for a long moment and I feel like I'm sinking, drowning.

"Five years from now . . ."

"Don't," I cut him off. "Don't say those words to me."

"I'm letting you go, Nell," he whispers.

"You can't," I reply. "I'm yours."

FORTY

A COMMOTION IN THE DOORWAY MAKES ME JOLT upright, and I glance over my shoulder as one of the friendlier nurses bustles in with a foldaway bed.

"His daddy called," she tells me with a smile. "He asked if it might be possible to arrange a bed for you."

I'm so grateful, I could weep. "Thank you so much," I say in a whisper, trying not to wake Luke.

I don't correct her mistake. Luke's "daddy" is in Amsterdam right now, celebrating five years of marriage with his wife and their toddler, Zach.

"No, no, you sit down," she commands when I try to give her a hand. She's quick to finish up, leaving me to it.

I kick off my shoes and throw back the covers, gingerly climbing into bed and trying to get comfortable. Glancing at Luke, I start at the sight of him gazing back at me.

"Sorry, darling," I whisper. "I hoped you'd sleep through all that."

"You didn't have to stay," he replies.

"I didn't want to leave you here alone."

"I'll be fine, Mum. You should go home and get some rest."

"I can get plenty here. Do you need anything?" I ask.

"No, I'm fine. Go to sleep," he urges.

"OK. You too. Night night."

"Night."

"I love you," I say.

"I love you more," he replies.

He closes his eyes, a smile playing about the corners of his lips.

He honestly has no idea.

THREE YEARS LATER

ERE I AM AGAIN . . .
 I stand and stare at the doors, my pulse jumping every time they open and fail to deliver. Luke sighs and folds his arms across his chest, glancing around the Arrivals hall with a bored look on his face. I had to persuade him to come with me. He wanted to go surfing, but I needed the distraction.

"They'll be here soon," I murmur.

He sighs again and rakes his hand through his light-blond curls. He looks so much like his father did at his age. He's not short of female attention, either, but has so far avoided picking up Nick's former reputation. My son is more responsible with the hearts girls have tried to bestow on him.

"Pretty nuts that you're going to be going to university together," I say casually, trying to make conversation.

"Mm."

I don't know if that's a good "mm" or a bad "mm," and chances are he's not sure himself. I don't blame him for being apprehensive. University is supposed to be a fresh start, but that's not so easy when someone you know is tagging along with you.

Of course, if he really wanted a fresh start, Luke would have opted to study farther afield than Falmouth.

There are two main reasons he chose to stay close to home. One is the money—the cost these days is much more taxing on students than it used to be, so he can save by commuting. The second is the same reason Libby opted to study at Falmouth: its access to Cornwall's beaches. Libby is even more of a surf addict than Luke. She wanted to study abroad and it was her junior surf champion status that helped her to win a scholarship.

"Maybe you can take Libby surfing this afternoon, if she's not too tired?" I suggest, glancing up at him. He towers over me now.

"Maybe."

Hold back on the enthusiasm, son . . .

I think he finds the prospect of surfing with her daunting.

He goes rigid, his eyes growing wide. With my heart in my throat, I turn to see what—or indeed, whom—has caught his attention. My eyes make it no further than Van's.

My head spins as he comes toward us, knocking me sideways with his agonizing familiarity. He still has a beard, but he's grown into it more, and his face has weathered, with creases at the corners of his eyes and a hint of gray around his temples. He reminds me of a photograph I once saw of his father.

I force myself to turn my attention to the eighteen-year-old girl at his side and do a double take.

Libby is *stunning*. Tall and strong and beautiful, with long auburn hair cascading down her back in soft waves, her blue eyes peeking out from behind a thick, choppy fringe. She looks so much like her father.

"Hi!" she exclaims, dropping her rucksack to the floor and opening her arms.

"I can't believe how much you've grown!" I cry, stepping forward to engulf her in a hug.

Really, she's the one engulfing me—she must be Luke's height.

I'm aware of Van greeting Luke in a similar manner, his deep Australian voice hitting me squarely in my solar plexus.

He turns to me and butterflies crowd my stomach as I lift my gaze to meet his. His eyes are full of a sentiment I can't bear to try to decipher.

He's here . . . After all these years, he's here . . .

He takes my hands and steps closer, very gently resting his forehead against mine. My eyes fall shut as the years fold back on themselves. I've imagined this moment so many times.

Emotion wells up from deep inside me, but then he lifts his head and steps away, letting me go.

I inhale sharply and turn to the kids.

Only to stop short. They're staring at each other like they've never seen each other before. A shiver goes down my spine as I glimpse the future—a future where my son wants to move to the other side of the world for the love of a girl. I shake my head to rid myself of my imaginings and Luke and Libby simultaneously break eye contact, looking anywhere but at each other as we set off toward the car park.

Libby is going to be studying fashion design at Falmouth, while Luke has chosen a career in architecture. It was a decision he came to during the summer he turned fifteen and was holed up on the couch with his broken ankle. Bored of watching television and playing video games, he started to read the books I'd been bringing home for him. He had never been much of a reader and if it weren't for his accident, I doubt he ever would have picked up the novel that inspired him. I said at the time that it might take five years for him to make sense of what had happened—in reality, it took a lot less than that.

"Are you looking forward to visiting your campus, Libby?" I smile at her in the rearview mirror, doing my best to fill the awkward silence that has descended upon the car.

"Yeah, I can't wait," she replies.

"You're at Penryn Campus, right?" Luke asks.

"Yep. Are you at Falmouth?"

"Yeah. It's about a twenty-minute bus ride away from you."

"But you're not living at uni, are you?"

"No. I'm staying at home. It's not that far."

"Luke has the annex, which is separate to the cottage, so he has his own space," I chip in, glad to see them warming up.

"I remember the annex!" Libby cries, thawing fully. "We played Legos in it, didn't we?"

"Yeah." I can hear the smile in Luke's voice.

"Do you have a car?" Libby asks him.

"Yeah, my dad got me one for my eighteenth birthday. It's not until next week, but he gave it to me early."

We're having a big party at The Boatman to celebrate. Even Grandma and Robert are coming over for it.

"He'll be able to bring you back for Sunday lunches, sometimes," I say. "I might even do your washing for you too."

"Result!" she cries, punching the air.

Van chuckles and looks out of the window, his fingers tapping against his thigh.

I resist the urge to reach over and squeeze his hand.

Eventually, I give up on the small talk and Libby takes the baton, engaging Luke in discussions about surfing and what he gets up to with his friends. Van and I sit in silence and the atmosphere is loaded between us.

Finally, we arrive at the whitewashed cottage that he once called home. Luke and Libby clamber out, the latter talking excitedly about how the cottage looks exactly the same as she remembered it. But I know Van has spotted the addition that has been made to the property since he was last here. It glints in the sunshine, silver against the shades of green: green grass, green river, green trees.

My heart is in shreds.

"You have to be really careful with the road," we hear Luke warning Libby as we climb out of the car. He pulls the gate closed after her, even though we're only a few paces behind. I'm going to drive Van and Libby up to the village to the holiday home they're renting, but it's not ready yet so we've got time to kill.

The front door opens and Danny tears out, crashing into Luke, who laughs and promptly scoops him up into a bear hug.

Beside me, Van's breath catches.

Danny spies me over his big brother's shoulder, his huge brown eyes widening further and his arms stretching in my direction. Luke passes him over and, as his small body aligns with mine, the tatters currently blowing wild against the walls of my chest slowly begin to lace back together again.

"This is Van," I say to my son, swiveling so they're facing each other. "And this is Daniel."

"Hello, buddy," Van replies in a sweet voice. "Nice to meet you in person at last."

If he's been feeling as anxious as I have, he's doing a good job of hiding it. But then he tenses, staring past my shoulder, and I turn to see Ed emerging from the cottage with our sleepy almost-three-year-old in his arms.

Ivy Ruth Allister.

I asked Van for his blessing before we christened our daughter with his mother's name. Daniel has my father's as a middle name: Geoffrey.

"Hey!" Ed calls as Ivy makes predictable noises of dissent. She gets so jealous of Danny, but her brother, at four and a half, would give her the world if he could. Right now, he's content simply to give her me, so he wriggles to get down so I can take her. Ed and Van greet each other warmly and then Van returns to say a proper hello to the little girl he has, until now, only met on FaceTime.

"Hello, cutie," he says, as Ivy clutches my shoulders with her tiny hands, clinging on to me like a baby koala.

"Can you say hello to Van?" I prompt, pressing a kiss to her squashy cheek.

"Hello," she obeys with a toothy grin.

"She looks like you," he comments, straightening up and meeting my eyes.

"That's what they say," I reply nervily, pushing Ivy's fine blond hair away from her face. Danny has Ed's coloring.

Voices come from inside the annex—Luke is giving Libby a tour, from the sounds of it.

Van walks over and runs his hand along the top of the wire fence—it reaches his waist. "This makes life easier, I bet."

"Yeah, even if it does spoil the view a bit," Ed replies with a grin, succumbing to his young son's request to pick him up. "We still manage a fair bit of hill rolling, though, don't we, Danny?"

Danny nods eagerly.

I hold Ivy close as we go inside. She's like a shield, protecting my fragile heart.

"Mind if I use the bathroom?" Van asks.

"Go for it. You know where it is," Ed calls over his shoulder.

Ed turns to me once we're in the kitchen, his expression full of compassion as he opens his arm wide. I step into his embrace. Danny is still in his other arm and I, in turn, have Ivy balanced on my hip. He kisses my forehead and tears prick my eyes as I bury my face against his warm neck and breathe him in. Our two children start giggling and I lift my head to see them sticking their tongues out at each other.

My heart expands with love and the same emotion is reflected in my husband's eyes as we smile at each other.

All of those moments . . . Our children's first laughs, their first steps, birthdays, Christmases, anniversaries . . . So many happy moments that we've shared.

I stand on my tiptoes and kiss Ed's lips, the storm inside me settling to a beautiful calm as he tenderly returns the gesture.

How can I regret this?

I can't.

I *don't*.

WHEN VAN WENT home eight years ago after his last visit to Cornwall, I was a mess. Ed didn't seem to know what to do with me. In later years, he confessed how much it had hurt, seeing me so broken, but even if I had known the pain I was causing, I would have been useless to stop it.

At first, I resisted all of Van's efforts to end things between us. I thought we could go on like that forever if we had to and I tried to convince him of the same. After a few months, he appeared to be willing to indulge me. I didn't know that he had resolved to let me go gently.

Meanwhile, Ed's divorce came through and, as predicted, Tasha put the house on the market and moved back to London without delay, leaving estate agents to deal with the sale. A few days before Christmas, almost a year to the day that I'd found Ed in the stockroom in pieces, he admitted that he was also thinking about selling up and moving away.

I was floored.

After Van left, I'd distanced myself from Ed, not wanting Van to have any more ammunition to end things between us. But somehow, along the way, I'd also lost Ed as a friend. He had stopped confiding in me.

I convinced him to go for a drink with me after work to talk about it. I still remember walking through the streets of Falmouth, beneath Christmas lights sparkling prettily in the dark night, to find a cozy pub with a crackling fire burning in the hearth. But I felt so cold—chilled to my bones at the thought of him leaving.

"I thought you loved it here in Cornwall," I said.

"I did," he replied. "But it's been tough lately. I think I might need a fresh start."

"Wasn't *this* your fresh start?"

"It was supposed to be." He sighed.

We were feet away from each other, but he felt distant. We'd lost the easy companionship that we'd had only months before. At work, it wasn't as noticeable—we were professional.

"I know everything fell apart with you and Tasha, but you seemed to be coping OK with the split."

"I am."

"Ed, please talk to me," I urged, and an old familiar instinct kicked in, making me reach across to cover his hand with mine. He withdrew it like I'd given him an electric shock.

I stared at him, but he seemed agitated, dragging his fingers through his hair and making it stick up every which way. He wouldn't look at me as he drank from his pint glass, but I remained patient and eventually he met my eyes again.

An edgy feeling started up in my stomach as we looked at each other and the thought that came to me was, *maybe there is room in my heart for someone else . . .*

"I don't want you to leave."

"Why?" he asked.

I shook my head, trying to put up temporary shutters around Van so I could focus. "Not because I want to keep my job."

His mouth curved into a small, lovely smile, and I had an urge to lean in and kiss him.

"I care about you," I said. "A lot."

He nodded and reached for his pint.

"And not just as a friend."

The glass froze in the air, inches from his lips. He placed it back down on the table and turned to look at me properly. "What are you saying?" he asked, his eyebrows pulling together.

"I care about you. I have for a long time. But Van . . ."

My voice trailed off and he reached for his pint again, taking several gulps.

"Van wanted to break up with me in the summer." I finished my sentence.

Stunned by the revelation, he restored his glass firmly to the sticky tabletop.

"I never told you," I continued. "I was devastated, but I'm coming around to accepting his decision now. The last five years have been hard. He doesn't think we can do eight more."

My vision clouded at that point, blissfully obscuring the look of pity in his eyes. I shook my head and swiped at my tears, knowing I had to make him understand. "But that's not why he wanted to end it." I swallowed, steeling myself. "He suspected that there was something going on between you and me. *Not physically*," I added quickly at his look of horror. "*Emotionally*. And he was right," I added. "At least on my part. Do you care about me, Ed? As more than a friend?"

He stared at me for a moment before giving me a single nod. "But I never thought you'd be able to see past Van," he said quietly.

"Neither did I. But I think I might've been wrong." I swallowed. "I need to speak to him. Will you give me some time? Can we talk again when you get back after Christmas?"

He was going to visit his family in London, shutting up the shop for the week between Christmas and New Year.

He nodded.

We hugged each other goodbye, the first time we had touched properly in over six months. He made a move to withdraw after a brief embrace, but I held on and after a moment he gathered me even closer, allowing us to reconnect on a different level.

And I felt it, my heart unfolding and unfurling toward him, opening itself up to a new love, a new beginning.

I called Van that night.

"What you said to me in the summer, the day before you left, about you wanting me to find room in my heart for someone else. Do you still mean it?"

A strange sort of acceptance seemed to come over him. "Ed?" he asked.

I nodded, tears streaming down my cheeks like a tidal river going out to sea.

"Yes," he replied gently. "I still mean it."

ED BREAKS APART from me at the sound of the bathroom door unlocking. It's been eight years since Van and I were last together, and Ed and I have been married for five and a half of them, but he will always be respectful of the history Van and I share.

"Where are Libby and Luke?" Van asks, walking into the kitchen.

"Still in the annex, getting better acquainted," I reply casually.

He shoots me a sharp look and I laugh. "Don't worry, Dad, Luke is a good boy."

"He might be good, but he's still a boy," he replies drily, stalking out of the kitchen.

Ed flashes me a grin as I trail after Van.

"You know, you're not going to be around to keep an eye on them for long," I whisper as Van comes to a halt, staring with alarm at the now-closed door of the annex.

He walks over to the window and peers inside, jerking away and cursing under his breath in his hurry to get to the door. I glance through the glass to see Luke leaning with his back against the wall and Libby sitting cross-legged farther down his bed, Luke's bare foot resting in her lap. They both shoot their heads toward the door as it flies open.

"What's going on?" Van asks.

"I'm checking out Luke's war wounds," Libby replies insouciantly as I follow him inside. "That must've hurt," she continues addressing Luke. "How long were you out of the water?"

"A few months, but it took a year to heal properly."

"His broken ankle," I say to Van, trying to hide my amusement at the stumped look on his face.

"I dislocated my shoulder once," Libby says nonchalantly. "At Blacks—Blackfellows—in Elliston."

"I think I've heard of it," Luke says with surprise.

"Yeah, it's kinda famous. I surf there a lot. The reef is full of holes and once I wiped out and got swept into a cave. Man, I was seeing stars, and then my arm got stuck between a couple of rocks and I couldn't break free. I thought I was a goner, but I managed to get out."

"Oh my God!" I exclaim. "You could've drowned!

Libby shrugs and laughs. "You gotta pay to play."

I catch sight of Luke's expression and am glad Van is preoccupied. I haven't seen that look on my son's face since he fell head over heels in love with Angela Rakesmith, his first serious girlfriend. He and Angie got together soon after he broke his ankle. She was a great diversion once the baby came along. Two children under the age of two kept me busy, to say the least. I'd been eight months pregnant with Ivy when Luke was in the hospital. I still remember how grateful I was when Ed arranged that cot bed. He had to stay at home to look after Danny.

I walk over to Van, who's staring at the paintings on the wall.

"I can't believe they haven't been replaced with posters of cars and girls by now," he murmurs with amazement.

"All your old pebbles are on Ivy and Danny's windowsill now too."

"What are you saying?" Luke is sidetracked by our conversation.

"Van is surprised that you've still got his original Fudge and Smudge illustrations up," I reveal.

"Oh. Yeah." He shrugs, self-consciously.

"That's so cool," Libby says, hopping down from the bed and coming over to take a closer look. "Why haven't I got any of these?" she asks her father.

"I didn't think you wanted them," he replies.

"*Yeah*, I want them," she states irately, frowning at the wall. "They're awesome."

"Libby, I *specifically* asked you about five years ago if you'd like me to frame any of these for your room at my house, and you said no," Van states pedantically.

"I was *thirteen*, Dad," Libby replies pointedly. "I was a little bitch at that age."

I can't help laughing.

"Have you got any more?" she asks.

"Your dad has plenty," I answer on her father's behalf. He's too consumed with rolling his eyes and tutting to speak. "In fact, there are some already framed on the walls at the bookshop. You can take them on Saturday, if you like, and I'll sort out some more for the shop."

"Awesome!" Libby replies, gratified. "I'll stick 'em up on my wall at uni."

We're doing our first signing in eight years at Dragonheart. It's kicking off a whole tour, although we're focusing primarily on Cornwall and its neighboring counties, where the series has been most popular—I didn't want to be far from Ivy and Danny at their age.

Our cheeky little piskies are going from strength to strength: we now have twelve books and we won't stop there. We're still not exactly raking it in, but we adore doing what we do, creating something we believe in and working together. Van and I may not be lovers anymore, but we will always be friends. Our books are our babies, the only children we will ever have together.

Van is here in the UK to help Libby get herself set up and to do the tour, but soon he'll be going home again. Home to his job as a tug captain, home to his elderly father, home to his girlfriend (probably), just . . . *home* . . . He loves living in Australia and Libby doesn't want him cramping his style, anyway.

The irony is bittersweet.

Through the window, I notice Ed putting a tray down on the bench table.

"Afternoon tea's ready," I say.

"Aw, man," Libby groans, her eyes wide at the sight of a cake stand piled high with scones. I baked them yesterday, and Ed has bought in plenty of clotted cream and strawberry jam from the village shop.

We all crowd around the table, Libby chattering excitedly, Ivy clambering onto her daddy's lap, Luke spinning a squealing Danny round in a circle on the patio, and me, standing and pouring the tea, enjoying the ambience.

I once asked Van, in a moment of weakness, before Ed and I got married, "Do you regret setting me on the path that led me to him?"

It was Van, after all, who had suggested I go for the job at Dragonheart.

He shook his head, emotion lurking in the depths of his night-sky eyes.

"I'll never regret seeing you happy, Nell. It's all I ever wanted."

As I settle beside him at the table, I think back on another memory, to when he and I had finally called it quits. I'd called Ellie in bits and she was trying to console me.

"What's that saying?" she asked. "If you love someone, set them free. If they come back, they're yours. If they don't, they never were."

I don't need hindsight or five years to look back on this moment and know that I am exactly where I'm meant to be. I smile at my husband across the table, glad that he knows he can trust me, even as Van and I set off alone on this tour together. Ed knows I will never hurt him the way that his ex-wife did. He knows that I love him and that I love our children and that there is no way I will ever do anything to jeopardize the life that we have together. I *am* happy. *So very happy.*

But Ellie was wrong.

I was always Van's. I'll always *be* Van's—at least, a part of me will.

Under the table, he hooks my little finger with his.

And he knows it.

ACKNOWLEDGMENTS

I don't think I will ever start an acknowledgments page without first thanking you, my readers. I truly believe I have some of the loveliest, most passionate readers in the world, and I can't wait to hear what you think of this story. Now for the other thanks, of which there are many . . .

Thank you to my wonderful editor, Suzanne Baboneau, and the entire team at Simon & Schuster for the fantastic job that they do, not least Bec Farrell, Jess Barratt, Pip Watkins, Sara-Jade Virtue, Dawn Burnett, Laura Hough, Gill Richardson, Richard Vlietstra, Joe Roche, Dominic Brendon, Poppy Jennings, Emma Capron, and Jo Dickinson. Big thanks also to my copyeditor, Anne O'Brien, and Maisie Lawrence, for everything she did for me while at S&S.

About a year and a half ago, I received a letter from my cousin, Dave Beaty, in South Australia, updating me on news about his twentysomething sons, Tom and Morgan. Dave's descriptions of Tom and Morgan's fishing jobs—which included Tom hand-feeding killer whales—sent shivers down my spine. I *had* to have a character who did these things! It has been a huge pleasure to get to know my cousins better (or "cousins, once removed," if we're being technical about it) and I can't thank

Tom and Morgan enough for sharing the stories that inspired so much of this book. I have dedicated *Five Years from Now* to their mother, Pascale, who very sadly passed away in September 2015.

My family holidays are often dictated by where my next book will be set, and in this case it was Cornwall in the summer of 2017. We stayed in a cottage on the Helford River and the setting was *so* perfect that I've hardly changed a thing about it. Thank you to Linda Dandy for making our stay at Rock Cottage so pleasant (rockcottagecornwall.com, if you'd like to check it out yourself).

Huge thanks to Dan Joel of www.danjoelsurf.com, who not only taught our ten-year-old son to surf, but who was so generous with his time when I later contacted him to ask for help with my research. The way he described some of the wave action made me wonder why he wasn't a writer himself!

Thank you to Ruth Glover for sharing her knowledge of Cornish beaches with me, the lovely gardener at Trelissick who gave me a behind-the-scenes tour, and Dr. Lewis Barnes for helping me with my medical research.

Thanks to Kate White for sharing her memories of working at Uluru, and thanks also to my parents, Vern and Jen Schuppan, and my brother Kerrin and his family, for the holiday to the rock that inspired parts of this story. Special thanks to my dad, who spoke those "five years from now" words to me as a teenager—the advice has proved apt over the years.

Huge thanks to the lovely friends who read early drafts of this book and gave me valuable feedback: Jane Hampton, Katherine Reid, Dani Atkins, and Kimberly Atkins.

Thanks also to the bloggers and my fellow authors for the brilliant online community that you provide—especially

Giovanna Fletcher and Lindsey Kelk, who have been fantastically supportive this last year.

Finally, thank you to my awesome husband, Greg Toon, and our children, Indy and Idha, who not only make me laugh every day, but who inspire me in so many ways. I'm glad that I messed up my A levels, took a year out, and ended up going to a different university, because if I hadn't, I wouldn't have met your dad—and you wouldn't exist. I love you all very much.

FIVE YEARS FROM NOW

Paige Toon

A Conversation with Paige Toon

Discussion Guide

BOOK
ENDS

PUTNAM
— EST. 1838 —

A CONVERSATION
WITH PAIGE TOON

What inspired you to write *Five Years from Now*?

The phrase "Five years from now, you'll look back and understand why this happened" was something my own father said to me when I was going through a rough patch as a teenager. His words stuck with me, and many years later, I did indeed look back at that troubled time with a different perspective. I realized that, if my head had been in a better place and I hadn't messed up the school exams that I had been so stressed about at the time, I never would have taken a gap year or gone to a different university from the one I had initially hoped to attend. And I never would have met my future husband there, so my two children would not exist. Those words formed the basis of the idea: a love story told in five-year stages. Every stage shows us how the characters have grown and moved forward and how they dealt with whatever had happened to them five years previously.

Are any of the characters in *Five Years from Now* based on real people? How did you come to Nell's and Van's complex characters?

I very rarely base my characters on real people as that would feel too restrictive to me—I'd worry that I'd never be able to do them justice. But Van's profession and his hometown in Australia were inspired by a letter my cousin wrote to me about his two sons, and a lot of the detail that features in the book is based on real-life events—more on that below . . .

While *Five Years from Now* is a heartbreaking love story, it's also a tale of the important bonds of family and friendship. Which was your favorite dynamic to write other than Nell and Van's relationship, and why?

I did love Nell's relationship with her father, and it certainly made me feel very emotional at times and highly connected to the story, but romantic love will always appeal to me the most. I adored writing about Nell's relationships with both Nick and Ed and seeing how they developed over time and with their changing circumstances.

What do you think lies at the core of Nell and Van's relationship? Why is it so special?

I think it's special because they've loved each other in so many different ways, across so many decades. They go from childhood almost-step-siblings to teenagers trying to come to terms with new feelings toward each other, from estranged lovers to lovers and friends. They go through so much—both together and apart—and their bond feels truly unbreakable. I wrote the story to a time line of my own life, so I felt especially connected to it, writing in cultural references that meant something to me and drawing from my own feelings of nostalgia.

What was your favorite age of Nell's and Van's lives to write, and why?

It wasn't five or ten, as I most enjoyed being inside Nell's head and those two sections are written in the third person, rather than the first—mainly because I felt that telling the story from the perspective of a small child might be a bit restrictive and it would be harder to set the scene. I adored stepping into Nell's shoes at the age of fifteen, and I don't think it's a coincidence that that section is the longest. First love is so powerful to write about. But I also enjoyed writing certain key scenes from each of the other sections, most of which involve either sexy, heated moments between Nell and Van or heartbreaking ones. I love experiencing the highest highs and the lowest lows along with my characters. It's strangely cathartic.

Although not the focus of the novel, you insert such detail into specific hobbies and careers in these characters' lives—from surfing to prawn fishing, and even gardening. Did you conduct any research to create these nuanced backstories? Are any of these based on your own experience?

They're not based on my own experiences, but on the experiences of some family members. My cousin, who is older than I am by almost twenty years and lives in a remote seaside town in South Australia, sent me a letter detailing the lives of his twenty-something sons. I remember thinking, I have *got* to have a character who does some of these things! Both sons are surfers and have had run-ins with great white sharks, and they also have experience working as fishermen. One is a tuna fisherman who is often out at sea for two months, bringing the fish back in from the open ocean. He has to scuba dive down into the giant nets and help trapped sharks navigate their way out so they don't harm the tuna, and one of his colleagues hand-fed a dead fish to a killer whale once! And the other used to be a prawn fisherman and he has some incredible stories, although he now works on a tugboat. It was lovely reconnecting with them when I was doing my research. We chatted on FaceTime and over Facebook, and they gave me so many of the details that feature in the book. Recently I caught up with one of them in Port Lincoln for the first time in years (the other was out at sea on a tuna boat!), and it was so heartwarming to see him and visit some of the places that had inspired Van's life there. I also spoke to a big wave surfer who lives in Cornwall, who should be a writer himself given his way with words—he really brought surfing to life for me. And I did a lot of research while I was in Cornwall, visiting Glendurgan Garden, where Nell's dad works, and speaking to gardeners from the National Trust. Nell's childhood home is very much based on the river cottage we stayed in—it's called Rock Cottage and it sits above the Mawgan Creek of the Helford River, if you want to look it up. There are lots of pictures of the places in my *Five Years from Now* highlights folder on my Instagram page.

There is a terrific sense of place in *Five Years from Now*. How did you choose the settings for the novel?

I had set my previous novel, *The Last Piece of My Heart*, in Cornwall and I loved the setting so much—I was nowhere near done with it. I'm still not—the book I'm writing now, *Seven Summers*, will also be set there! As for Australia, it's where I grew up, and my family, going back generations, still lives there. For years I felt torn between Australia and the UK, and this is a theme that sometimes repeats in my books.

But I've never written such a permanent reason for why two characters find themselves rooted to different countries on opposite sides of the world. I'm always looking for ways to keep my characters apart—unrequited love stories are my absolute favorites—but usually my characters find a way out of their dilemma. This is probably the trickiest situation any of them have ever found themselves in.

The responsibilities of parenthood and difficult decisions parents make in the service of their children are running themes throughout the novel. What do you think is the most important quality of a good parent?

I do believe that, ultimately, a parent should put their children first, but I also feel that there are times when you should put your partner first, or even yourself—if your home isn't a happy one, then it will have a knock-on effect on the children anyway, so putting them first at all costs is not necessarily the right thing to do.

What do you want readers to take away from *Five Years from Now*?

That's a hard one to answer because this book devastates me, to be honest! This is a very emotional book with difficult circumstances at its core. I hope that readers will enjoy getting lost in the story, experiencing love in many different forms, and that the characters will stay with them for a long time.

Without giving anything away, did you always know how the story would end?

When I was thinking about this story in the months leading up to writing it, I was trying to think of a realistic ending that would tie everything up perfectly—but I couldn't. While I would say that I do write happy endings, sometimes they are bittersweet. In a way, that means my novels are not too predictable.

DISCUSSION GUIDE

1. Nell and Van's love story spans decades from childhood through adulthood. Which was your favorite age of their relationship, and why? Which age do you think was the most pivotal in their relationship?

2. Why do you think Nell and Van are drawn to each other time and time again throughout their lives? What is special about their relationship? Do you think Nell and Van are meant to be together?

3. How do the bonds of family and friends positively and negatively impact Nell and Van's trajectories in life? Without these forces, do you think their stories would have ended differently?

4. What was your reaction after reading the discovery that occurred when Nell and Van were fifteen? If that event hadn't have happened, how do you think this would have altered Nell and Van's love story?

5. What was your favorite scene in the novel, and why?

6. Do you think Nell's father did the right thing by Nell and Van throughout their lives? Why or why not? If you were him, how would you have handled their situation?

7. Which romantic relationship in Nell's life do you think was the best for her? What about the worst?

8. Throughout the novel multiple characters say, "Maybe five years from now, you'll look back and understand why this happened." Do you agree with this statement in your own life? Why or why not? Do you think Nell or Van would agree or disagree?

9. Do you believe in fate? Do you think Nell and Van were fated to meet? How do you think they changed each other's lives?

10. What were your thoughts on the ending?

ABOUT THE AUTHOR

Paige Toon grew up between England, Australia, and America and has been writing emotional love stories since 2007. She has published sixteen novels, a three-part spin-off series for young adults, and a collection of short stories. Her books have sold nearly 2 million copies worldwide. She lives in Cambridge-shire, England, with her husband and their two children.